SAMUEL JOHNSON was born on September 18, 1709, at Lichfield, England. The son of a bookseller, Johnson attended Pembroke College, Oxford, from 1728 to December, 1729, and intermittently thereafter, receiving an M.A. from Oxford in 1755. On July 9, 1735, he married the recently widowed Mrs. Henry Porter, a woman twenty years his senior, whom he remained devoted to until her death in 1752. Beginning in 1738, he became a regular contributor to *Gentleman's Magazine,* and in May, 1738, *London,* his imitation of Juvenal, was published. This was followed by *The Life of Savage* (February, 1744), *The Vanity of Human Wishes* (January, 1749), and the production of his tragedy, *Irene* (February, 1749). In April, 1755, Johnson's two-volume *Dictionary* was published, a massive undertaking that was the first English dictionary in the modern sense of the word. Johnson created almost every edition of *The Rambler* (1750-1752), as well as nearly all numbers of *The Idler* (1758-1760). *Rasselas* was written during the evenings of one week in 1759, and Johnson's eight-volume edition of Shakespeare was completed in 1765, while his critical and biographical *Lives of the Poets* appeared in ten volumes between 1779 and 1781. During his last years, Dr. Johnson devoted himself to society and conversation, and his sayings and doings were carefully reported by James Boswell and Mrs. Thrale. He died in London on December 13, 1784.

THE SELECTED WRITINGS OF
Samuel Johnson

Edited and with an Introduction by
KATHARINE ROGERS

A SIGNET CLASSIC
NEW AMERICAN LIBRARY
TIMES MIRROR
NEW YORK AND SCARBOROUGH, ONTARIO
THE NEW ENGLISH LIBRARY LIMITED, LONDON

NAL BOOKS ARE AVAILABLE AT QUANTITY DISCOUNTS
WHEN USED TO PROMOTE PRODUCTS OR SERVICES. FOR
INFORMATION PLEASE WRITE TO PREMIUM MARKETING
DIVISION, THE NEW AMERICAN LIBRARY, INC., 1633
BROADWAY, NEW YORK, NEW YORK 10019.

Library of Congress Catalog Card Number: 80-84910

SIGNET, SIGNET CLASSICS, MENTOR, PLUME, MERIDIAN
and NAL BOOKS are published *in the United States* by The New
American Library, Inc., 1633 Broadway, New York, New York
10019, *in Canada* by The New American Library of Canada
Limited, 81 Mack Avenue, Scarborough, Ontario M1L 1M8,
in the United Kingdom by The New English Library Limited,
Barnard's Inn, Holborn, London EC1N 2JR, England

First Printing, March, 1981

1 2 3 4 5 6 7 8 9

PRINTED IN THE UNITED STATES OF AMERICA

Contents

General Introduction

Samuel Johnson's first prose work (1735) was a translation of a *Voyage to Abyssinia* by the Portuguese Jesuit Jerome Lobo. The Preface he composed for it shows that at twenty-four his characteristic style and attitudes were already taking shape.

> [Lobo] appears, by his modest and unaffected narration, to have described things as he saw them, to have copied nature from the life, and to have consulted his senses, not his imagination. He meets with no basilisks that destroy with their eyes, his crocodiles devour their prey without tears, and his cataracts fall from the rocks without deafening the neighboring inhabitants.
>
> The reader will here find no regions cursed with irremediable barrenness, or blessed with spontaneous fecundity; no perpetual gloom, or unceasing sunshine; nor are the nations here described either devoid of all sense of humanity, or consummate in all private or social virtues. Here are no Hottentots without religious polity or articulate language; no Chinese perfectly polite, and completely skilled in all sciences; he will discover, what will always be discovered by a diligent and impartial enquirer, that wherever human nature is to be found, there is a mixture of vice and virtue, a contest of passion and reason; and that the Creator doth not appear partial in his distributions, but has balanced, in most countries, their particular inconveniences by particular favors.

Already we see Johnson's characteristic heavily enforced parallel structure—

1

The reader will here find

$$
\begin{cases}
\text{no regions} \begin{cases} \text{cursed with irremediable barrenness,} \\ \qquad\qquad\text{or} \\ \text{blessed with spontaneous fecundity;} \end{cases} \\
\\
\text{no} \begin{cases} \text{perpetual gloom} \\ \qquad\text{or} \\ \text{unceasing sunshine;} \end{cases}
\end{cases}
$$

nor are the nations here described

$$
\begin{cases}
\text{either devoid of all sense of humanity} \\
\text{or consummate in all private or social virtues.}
\end{cases}
$$

—as well as his preference for Latinate, generalizing diction. Already the techniques were formed for a style which would become increasingly meaningful as it became weighted with Johnson's deep experience of life.

What is more fundamentally significant, Johnson singled out for praise Lobo's honesty: foregoing the temptation to embellish his narrative with exotic attractions, Lobo represented plain human nature, which, Johnson believed, was essentially the same everywhere. Johnson was always to distrust the imagination for its tendency to make life appear more grand or exciting than it really is, and he constantly brought romantic flights down to sober fact.

He insisted upon rigorous honesty in conversation and demonstrated it in his writing. Few critics inspire such confidence that they are reporting their responses as they feel them, unaffected by preconceived theories, deference to fashion, or intellectual pretentiousness. Johnson shows William Shakespeare's faults "in the proportion in which they appear to me, without envious malignity or superstitious veneration"; and he acknowledges that, great as *Paradise Lost* undoubtedly is, "None ever wished it longer." He cannot comment on James Thomson's tedious poem *Liberty* in his life of the poet, for, though he tried to read it when it first appeared, he "soon desisted" and "never tried again." Unembarrassed to respond with his emotions as well as his intellect, he confides in his concluding note on *All's Well That Ends Well*, "I cannot reconcile my heart to Bertram," the worthless hero.

Genuine himself, Johnson unerringly recognized cant in

others, whether it was Alexander Pope's pretense that he was superior to personal attacks (as Johnson actually was) or John Milton's conviction that his motives were invariably idealistic. On Milton's renouncing affiliation with the Presbyterians, Johnson remarked: "He that changes his party by his humor is not more virtuous than he that changes it by his interest; he loves himself rather than truth." Johnson further pointed out that Milton's claim for liberty did not extend to everyone, for he was "severe and arbitrary" to the women in his home. Johnson was one of the first to notice that "there appears in his books something like a Turkish contempt of females, as subordinate and inferior beings. . . . He thought woman made only for obedience, and man only for rebellion." Nevertheless, Johnson fully acknowledged not only the two men's greatness as poets, but Pope's filial devotion and Milton's nobility of mind. Johnson's comment on Milton's system for continuing his studies after he became blind, by forcing his daughters to read to him in languages they did not understand, finely combines humane balance with clear penetrating judgment: ". . . it is hard to determine whether the daughters or the father are most to be lamented. . . . If few men would have resolution to write books with such embarrassments, few likewise would have wanted ability to find some better expedient." How precisely Johnson marked both Milton's heroic intellectualism and his selfish ineptitude in private life.

Johnson, who did not present himself as a champion of liberty, was much more fair to women. In his life he appreciated intelligent women and generously helped female authors; in his writings, he rejected the narrow ideals conventional in his day—the "good sort of woman" whose merit consists of freedom from faults, or the model housewife whose highest concern is "preserving the whiteness of pickled mushrooms." He made a point of including the Princess Nekayah among the intellectual pilgrims of *Rasselas*, who seeks knowledge and experience precisely as her brother does, and equally disdains trivial employments and petty rivalries.

Johnson never indulged in the dishonesty of glib generalization: he examined general statements for himself and made sure that they matched the facts as he knew them. Like all neoclassicists, he believed that particulars derive their significance from the general truth they illustrate. But his generalizations never evade experience as do the *a priori* abstractions of lesser thinkers; rather, they summarize the concrete particulars he has learned. His sentences sweep together and condense a wide range of details into the balance of parallel or antithetical constructions.

Johnson scornfully dismissed "the cant of those who judge by principles rather than perception." Theory can so easily distort or narrow our authentic responses. By imposing preconceptions on poetry, for example, we can blind ourselves to the obvious fact that Pope was a great poet. Instead of simply accepting a critical rule, Johnson applied his reason to it, in order to distinguish between "the accidental prescriptions of authority, when time has procured them veneration" and the genuine laws of reason, "invincibly supported by their conformity to the order of nature and operations of the intellect." Thus he found no intrinsic reason why a play must not mix tragedy and comedy—though, his honesty compelled him to add, Shakespeare's indubitable success in tragicomedy does not necessarily prove that it is a good form. On the other hand, a unified action is required by reason once one understands the nature of a play. Despite his conservatism, Johnson clearly distinguished "that which is established because it is right, from that which is right only because it is established." He rationally explained his reliance on tradition on the grounds that "what has been longest known has been most considered" and therefore "is best understood."

Johnson cut through all undue reverence for critical rules by observing that "there is always an appeal open from criticism to nature." Assuming, as did all critics of his time, that art should represent life, he evaluated literary works by comparing them directly to life as he experienced it. Shakespeare's Menenius, the clownish senator in *Coriolanus*, violates the neoclassical rules because he does not conform to one's abstract ideal of Roman senatorial dignity; but Shakespeare's characterization is justified because it has been drawn from life, the proper source of literature. Johnson's down-to-earth emphasis on practical effects and usefulness helped him get to the essentials of theoretical issues. How simply he demolished the vain speculations of Soame Jenyns by questioning why he published them: it is hard to defend vanity publishing when we consider that "The only end of writing is to enable the readers better to enjoy life, or better to endure it."

Contemporary neoclassical theorists argued, with seeming plausibility, that the action of a play must be limited to one day and a single place, since the audience knows that it has been sitting in one place for only a few hours. By examining how we actually respond to a play, Johnson saw that this limitation is irrelevant, since we are all the time aware that we are watching actors in a theater rather than Antony and Cleopatra in ancient Alexandria. Since we do not literally mistake the representation for reality, we can just as easily imagine ourselves transported from Alexandria to Rome as we can imagine ourselves in Alexandria in the first place. How, then, can a drama move us if we do not suppose it to be real? It moves because it "is credited with all the credit due to a drama . . . as a just picture of a real original," which brings "realities to mind." Instead of accepting deductive theories because they seem logical, Johnson sensibly asks himself how literature affects us and how it helps us to enjoy or endure life.

Indeed, Johnson's criticism, as well as his thinking on most issues, could be described as common sense raised to an extraordinarily high power. Johnson brought his vast learning, wide experience, and comprehensive understanding to support such reactions as most people feel, thus endowing common sense with unexampled authority. Typically, his opinions are those we ourselves would form if only we had his confident knowledge and his superb power of articulation.

Johnson used his great abilities not to separate himself from ordinary people, but to express their thoughts better than they could themselves. Though he arrived at his conclusions independently of the modish or traditional response, he valued them the more because they were confirmed by general experience. He rejoiced to concur with the common reader's admiration of Thomas Gray's "Elegy Written in a Country Churchyard," "for by the common sense of readers uncorrupted with literary prejudices . . . the refinements of subtilty and the dogmatism of learning, must be finally decided all claim to poetical honors." Having the authority of outstanding competence in criticism and scholarship, he can afford to put them both aside. When Johnson praised the "Elegy" for abounding "with images which find a mirror in every mind, and with sentiments to which every bosom returns an echo," he was commending qualities which he sought and achieved in his own writings. As his close friend Hester Thrale said,

"His soul was not different than that of another person, but ... greater."[1]

Johnson's generalizing intellect was anchored to everyday life by wide experience. His acquaintance ranged from prostitutes and disreputable hack writers to the most elegant intellectuals in England. His early practice as a miscellaneous journalist gave him competent knowledge of medicine, science, politics, agriculture, and trade, in addition to the literature and classical scholarship which were his primary interests. And he made the most of his experience, retaining virtually everything he read and judiciously observing the varied situations in which he found himself. His picture of the compulsive housewife Lady Bustle is supported by plenty of convincing detail. However, his most valuable observation appears in penetrating remarks on human psychology, based on rigorous examination of motives, starting with his own. Thus he could pinpoint the fallacy in the natural assumption that an author is the best judge of his own works: "On that which has cost him much labor he sets a high value, because he is unwilling to think that he has been diligent in vain; what has been produced without toilsome efforts is considered with delight as a proof of vigorous faculties and fertile invention." Whichever the case, and regardless of the actual objective achievement, the human ego manages to find a basis for self-congratulation.

But Johnson not only analyzed his experience intellectually; he truly felt it. Even the vicarious experience of literature moved him extraordinarily. As a child, he was so frightened by the ghost scenes in *Hamlet* that he ran to the street door so he could have people around him, and as a man he could not bear to reread the final scenes of *King Lear* until he had to in order to edit the play. The struggle and suffering he actually experienced remained vividly in his mind to deepen and widen his sympathy for other human beings. After an unhappy, misunderstood childhood, and after being disfigured by scrofula, which also impaired his vision and hearing, he was forced by poverty, to leave Oxford University after only a year. He then went through a depression, which left him

---

[1] Quoted by Walter Jackson Bate, *Samuel Johnson* (New York: Harcourt, Brace, Jovanovich, 1975), p. 4. All unidentified quotations in the introduction come from Johnson's writings included in this anthology.

haunted by fear of madness all his life, and developed the tics and compulsive movements which made strangers suspect he was mentally deficient. Unable to pursue a profession because he lacked a degree, Johnson served ineffectually in his father's bookshop, failed as a schoolteacher, and finally went to London to be a writer. There he struggled for recognition until he published his *Dictionary* in 1755. (It was the first English dictionary in the modern sense and remained standard for over a century; he compiled it single-handedly, aside from clerical assistance.) He did not win financial security until he received a government pension in 1762. Even after that, the struggle with pathological depression continued. Indeed, the wonderfully balanced and authoritative Preface to his edition of Shakespeare (1765) was composed on the verge of a mental breakdown. The weight of such suffering, and the strength which rose above it, is clearly felt behind Johnson's moral generalizations.

Johnson successfully contended with the afflictions of human life, but he refused to palliate them. Unlike his Deist and Stoic sages in *Rasselas*, he knew that no theory could remove the pain of poverty, illness, or bereavement. He loathed the glib optimistic theories of people like the prosperous dilettante Soame Jenyns—partly because they were not drawn from actual experience, but primarily because they glossed over real suffering. Perhaps such theorists "never saw the miseries which they imagine thus easy to be borne," and so they can airily describe poverty as "want of riches," and go on to argue that the poor should be kept ignorant lest education make them dissatisfied with their lot. Johnson, who never forgot what it was to be poor, pointed out that at best poverty is the want "of all that can soften the miseries of life . . . or delight imagination"; at worst, "want of necessaries." It may be a necessary evil, but at least we should not encourage it by denying poor people the chance of escaping it through education. For his part, Johnson was "always afraid of determining on the side of envy or cruelty."

Johnson was sensitive to the sufferings of many groups who were casually oppressed by his conventional contemporaries —enslaved blacks, domestic servants, children of tyrannical parents, and animals subjected to vivisection (Cartesian philosophers of the time maintained that the lower animals are incapable of feeling pain). He pointed out that tyranny is especially hard to bear when it is sanctioned by law and custom. He insisted that theories of cultural superiority, class privilege, legal authority, or scientific progress had to be repudiated once they were shown to cause individual suffering. He would not sanction a specious principle which in fact served more to curtail the pleasures of others than to uphold morality, especially when it might be expressing "envy or cruelty" toward the poor. When someone objected to giving money to beggars because they would only spend it on gin or tobacco, Johnson asked, "And why should they be denied such sweeteners of their existence? . . . Life is a pill which none of us can bear to swallow without gilding."[2]

Johnson's assumption that human existence requires sweeteners is as characteristic as his insistence that the poor should have them as well as the rich. Honestly recognizing the inherent limitations of human life and human nature, he repudiated the illusions, nourished by our pride and complacency, that the first can be made consistently happy and the second consistently rational and virtuous. Human life everywhere must be accepted as "a state in which much is to be endured, and little to be enjoyed." It cannot be radically improved by social institutions, because these are necessarily imperfect. Governments may be relatively enlightened, but no form "has been yet discovered by which cruelty can be wholly prevented." For government cannot exist without subordination, which "supposes power on one part and subjection on the other; and if power be in the hands of men it will sometimes be abused." Moreover, the most conscientious supreme magistrate "can never know all the crimes that are committed, and can seldom punish all that he knows." No society can be totally free of envy, for, though material goods might be equally shared, love and esteem cannot be.

These problems are inevitable because they are rooted in human nature. Expectations based on belief in man's absolute rationality or virtue are bound to be disappointed. "Inconsistencies cannot both be right, but, imputed to man, they may both be true." Human beings are likely to abuse power,

---

[2] Hester Lynch Piozzi, *Anecdotes of the Late Samuel Johnson, Johnsonian Miscellanies*, ed. George Birkbeck Hill (New York: Barnes and Noble, 1966), I, 204–5.

because "he who is in no danger of hearing remonstrances but from his own conscience, will seldom be long without the art of controlling his convictions, and modifying justice by his own will." Consistent harmony is not possible in marriage, because no two human beings have the reason and goodness to get along with each other all the time. And yet no one can bear "to live without feeling or exciting sympathy." Thus one cannot ensure happiness in marriage or outside it: "Marriage has many pains, but celibacy has no pleasures."

The fundamental cause of human unhappiness is what Johnson called the "hunger of imagination," our ability and constant tendency to imagine something more satisfying than reality can offer. We repine because we cannot rise to those better or more important selves we imagine ourselves to be. We dream impossible dreams, such as governing the perfect state or living the pure intellectual life, and are dissatisfied because we cannot put them into effect. We struggle to achieve the goal that will give us permanent fulfillment, only to find that no such goal exists. Johnson found his perfect symbol in the Great Pyramid of Egypt, the ultimate achievement of a Pharaoh with unlimited wealth and power at his command, and a monument of human ingenuity and effort. But considered in terms of its usefulness in increasing human happiness, it is a mere heap of stone, "a monument of the insufficiency of human enjoyments."

Johnson's rejection of the comforting illusions that we can realize our imagined ideals in ourselves, our lives, or our institutions, his insistence that people are governed by selfish motives and that any course of life is beset with problems, are not, however, so bleak as they initially appear. Johnson managed to be soberly realistic without cynicism, critical without destructiveness. For one thing, his pessimism was lightened by an enormous capacity for enjoying life—eating, reading, conversation, parties. Though a confirmed city-dweller, he thoroughly enjoyed a rigorous tour through the primitive Hebrides when he was sixty-four, and as an aged man he looked "upon every day to be lost, in which I do not make a new acquaintance."[3] In the same way, Rasselas and his companions enjoy their investigations into the choice

---

[3] James Boswell, *Life of Johnson* (London: Oxford University Press, 1953), p. 1358.

of life, even though they must conclude that choice to be meaningless. Happiness is unattainable, but life still offers many pleasures.

Nor should human nature be despised because it is manifestly imperfect. Already in his Preface to Lobo's *Voyage*, Johnson had recognized and accepted the fact that human nature everywhere shows "a mixture of vice and virtue . . . passion and reason." Though clear-sighted in exposing failings, Johnson was charitable in explaining them. After relentlessly listing the foolish arts used to win popularity, going down the scale from retailing gossip to imitating cats or dogs, Johnson reminds us that we "should not rigorously blame" those who practice them; "for it is always necessary to be loved, but not always necessary to be reverenced." After exposing the ways people dishonestly idealize the self they present in letters to their friends, Johnson warns us that to brand these falsifications hypocrisy "would show more severity than knowledge"; for the writers have in fact deluded themselves. Often his satiric butt turns out to be a representative of universal human frailty. After exposing the folly of the risen tradesman who retires to the country only to count the coaches that pass his window, Johnson points out that more sophisticated people are equally self-deluded in their pleasures. How many fashionable ladies at a concert are there because they genuinely enjoy music? Moreover, we should not deride any of the pleasures, however imaginary, which make life easier to bear.

In the same way, no occupation is to be despised. "Whoever steadily perseveres in the exertion of all his faculties, does what is great with respect to himself; and what will not be despised by Him, who has given to all created beings their different abilities. . . . He that despises for its littleness anything really useful" is too narrow-minded to see "that by pursuing the same principles everything limited will appear contemptible." Johnson rises above the sophistication which can see the limits of small people's pursuits to the wisdom which can put them in proportion with the limits of all human endeavor.

The inevitable limitations of human nature do not deprive it of grandeur. The fact that no great man is a hero to his valet is the result of life's conditions, not of any sham in the greatness; for "We are all naked till we are dressed, and hungry till we are fed." Great men are necessarily, like ourselves, "delighted with slight amusements, busied with trifling employments, and disturbed by little vexations." Yet, at the same time that they share the weaknesses common to humanity, they retain the merit of their greatness—a greatness which furthermore serves to affirm the human potentiality we all share.

Johnson offers wit, humor, ingenious reasoning, broad knowledge, and superb style—but above all, he offers the wisdom which enables us "better to endure" life. He points to the general view, the universal qualities and wide implications; but at the same time we feel confident that he has reached his generalizations through personal observation and honest evaluation of felt experience. He offers us concrete particulars we can grasp, but also shows how they fit into the general order of human values and experience. Though he relates particulars to principles, he is never doctrinaire in enforcing them. Though he manifestly thinks and feels for himself, he respects tradition and looks for the common denominator; thus he speaks for humanity as well as himself. His conclusions take on universal importance and are confirmed by our own recognition of their truth. Moreover, because Johnson has thought out his conclusions, we respect them even when we do not agree with them. Even when his arguments do not convince us, they force us to examine our own assumptions.

Johnson's refusal to palliate or glamorize further confirms our confidence in his honesty, as he confronts the limits, the pains, the discontent inherent in human life. And he can help us to deal with them because he has felt them himself. He never minimizes suffering and evil or tries to explain them away by a theory. Rather, he presents them as they are and shows how we can overcome them. "The Vanity of Human Wishes" (1749) demonstrates that this life does not offer any road to happiness, but concludes that the human mind can make "the happiness she does not find." Consistently in Johnson's writing we feel the strength gained from rising above trials and controlling violent emotions. Johnson felt the weaknesses he criticized, faced them for what they were, struggled against them, and transmitted his insight and resolution to his readers. Therefore his grimmest criticisms and exhortations are constructive. He accepts that we can do no more than nurture our good motives and restrain our bad, make the best use of the talents we have been given, and take advantage of what comforts and pleasures life affords. Our pursuits may be empty, to the eye of abstract reason; but they must not be condemned, because we need them. Johnson's teachings carry conviction because he has recognized the difficulties of living and personally demonstrated how they can be overcome.

Poems

Prologue Spoken at the Opening of
the Theater in Drury Lane, 1747

[This poem, written for the reopening of Drury Lane under
the management of Johnson's friend David Garrick, traces
the development of English drama from the Renaissance
(lines 1–2). After William Shakespeare came the more correct but less moving Ben Jonson. Drama of the Restoration
(1660–1700), written by "the wits of Charles," was notably
obscene; Aphra Behn and Tom D'Urfey (line 42) were
minor playwrights of that period. Eighteenth-century tragedy,
such as Joseph Addison's much-admired *Cato* (1713), was
correct and moral, but failed to engage the passions. By
1747, farces such as *Harlequin Doctor Faustus* (1723), which
featured spectacle and pantomime rather than wit, characterization, and thought, dominated the theater (lines 36–38, 44).]

When Learning's triumph o'er her barbarous foes
First reared the stage, immortal Shakespeare rose;
Each change of many-colored life he drew,
Exhausted worlds, and then imagined new:
Existence saw him spurn her bounded reign,
And panting Time toiled after him in vain:
His powerful strokes presiding truth impressed,
And unresisted Passion stormed the breast.
   Then Jonson came, instructed from the school,
To please in method, and invent by rule;
His studious patience, and laborious art,
By regular approach essayed the heart;
Cold Approbation gave the lingering bays,[1]
For those who durst not censure, scarce could praise.
A mortal born he met the general doom,
But left, like Egypt's kings, a lasting tomb.

[1] *bays:* the laurel wreath of the poet. Ben Jonson was the Poet
Laureate.

The wits of Charles found easier ways to fame,
Nor wished for Jonson's art, or Shakespeare's flame;
Themselves they studied, as they felt, they writ,
Intrigue was plot, obscenity was wit.
Vice always found a sympathetic friend;
They pleased their age, and did not aim to mend.
Yet bards like these aspired to lasting praise,
And proudly hoped to pimp in future days.
Their cause was general, their supports were strong,
Their slaves were willing, and their reign was long;
Till Shame regained the post that Sense betrayed,
And Virtue called Oblivion to her aid.

Then crushed by rules, and weakened as refined,
For years the power of Tragedy declined;
From bard to bard, the frigid caution crept,
Till Declamation roared, while Passion slept.
Yet still did Virtue deign the stage to tread,
Philosophy remained, though Nature fled.
But forced at length her ancient reign to quit,
She saw great *Faustus* lay the ghost of wit:
Exulting Folly hailed the joyful day,
And pantomime and song confirmed her sway.
But who the coming changes can presage,
And mark the future periods of the stage?—
Perhaps if skill could distant times explore,
New Behns, new D'Urfeys, yet remain in store.
Perhaps, where Lear has raved, and Hamlet died,
On flying cars new sorcerers may ride.
Perhaps, for who can guess th' effects of chance?
Here Hunt may box, or Mahomet may dance.[2]

Hard is his lot that here by fortune placed
Must watch the wild vicissitudes of taste;
With every meteor of caprice must play,
And chase the new-blown bubbles of the day.
Ah! let not censure term our fate our choice,
The stage but echoes back the public voice.
The drama's laws the drama's patrons give,
For we that live to please, must please to live.

Then prompt no more the follies you decry,
As tyrants doom their tools of guilt to die,
'Tis yours this night to bid the reign commence

---

[2] Edward Hunt was a boxer and Mahomet a rope dancer.

Of rescued Nature and reviving Sense;
To chase the charms of sound, the pomp of show,
For useful mirth, and salutary woe;
Bid scenic Virtue[3] form the rising age,
And Truth diffuse her radiance from the stage.

The Vanity of Human Wishes

[Johnson imitated—that is, re-created—the Tenth Satire of
the Roman Juvenal (60?–130? A.D.) in terms of his own
time. He followed Juvenal's structure, only substituting scholarship for eloquence in the original. He supplemented or
replaced Juvenal's classical examples with modern ones. And,
most significantly, he turned Juvenal's Stoical conclusion into
a Christian one. This was the first of Johnson's works to be
printed with his name.]

Let observation with extensive view,
Survey mankind, from China to Peru;
Remark each anxious toil, each eager strife,
And watch the busy scenes of crowded life;
Then say how hope and fear, desire and hate,
O'erspread with snares the clouded maze of fate,
Where wavering man, betrayed by venturous pride,
To tread the dreary paths without a guide,
As treacherous phantoms in the mist delude,
Shuns fancied ills, or chases airy good;
How rarely reason guides the stubborn choice,
Rules the bold hand, or prompts the suppliant voice;
How nations sink, by darling schemes oppressed,
When vengeance listens to the fool's request.[1]
Fate wings with every wish th' afflictive dart,
Each gift of nature, and each grace of art,
With fatal heat impetuous courage glows,
With fatal sweetness elocution flows,
Impeachment stops the speaker's powerful breath,
And restless fire precipitates on death.
    But scarce observed, the knowing and the bold

---

[3] Virtue represented on the stage.
[1] I.e., the fulfillment of foolish wishes brings destruction.

Fall in the general massacre of gold;
Wide-wasting pest! that rages unconfined,
And crowds with crimes the records of mankind;
For gold his sword the hireling ruffian draws,
For gold the hireling judge distorts the laws;
Wealth heaped on wealth, nor truth nor safety buys,
The dangers gather as the treasures rise.
  Let history tell where rival kings command,
And dubious title shakes the madded land,
When statutes glean the refuse of the sword,[2]
How much more safe the vassal than the lord;
Low skulks the hind beneath the rage of power,
And leaves the wealthy traitor in the Tower,[3]
Untouched his cottage, and his slumbers sound,
Though confiscation's vultures hover round.
  The needy traveler, serene and gay,
Walks the wild heath, and sings his toil away.
Does envy seize thee? crush th' upbraiding joy,
Increase his riches and his peace destroy;
Now fears in dire vicissitude[4] invade.
The rustling brake alarms, and quivering shade.
Nor light nor darkness bring his pain relief,
One shows the plunder, and one hides the thief.
  Yet still one general cry the skies assails,
And gain and grandeur load the tainted gales;
Few know the toiling statesman's fear or care,
Th' insidious rival and the gaping heir.
  Once more, Democritus,[5] arise on earth,
With cheerful wisdom and instructive mirth,
See motley life in modern trappings dressed,
And feed with varied fools th' eternal jest:
Thou who couldst laugh where want enchained caprice,
Toil crushed conceit, and man was of a piece;
Where wealth unloved without a mourner died,
And scarce a sycophant was fed by pride;
Where ne'er was known the form of mock debate,

---

[2] I.e., when the law seizes what war has left.
[3] Prominent people accused of treason were usually imprisoned in the Tower of London.
[4] I.e., a succession of various fears.
[5] Greek philosopher (fifth century B.C.), sometimes known as the "laughing philosopher."

Or seen a new-made mayor's unwieldy state;
Where change of favorites made no change of laws,
And senates heard before they judged a cause;
How wouldst thou shake at Britain's modish tribe,
Dart the quick taunt, and edge the piercing gibe!
Attentive truth and nature to descry,
And pierce each scene with philosophic eye.
To thee were solemn toys or empty show,
The robes of pleasure and the veils of woe:
All aid the farce, and all thy mirth maintain,
Whose joys are causeless, or whose griefs are vain.

Such was the scorn that filled the sage's mind,
Renewed at every glance on humankind;
How just that scorn ere yet thy voice declare,[6]
Search every state, and canvass every prayer.

Unnumbered suppliants crowd preferment's gate,
Athirst for wealth, and burning to be great;
Delusive fortune hears th' incessant call,
They mount, they shine, evaporate, and fall.
On every stage the foes of peace attend,
Hate dogs their flight, and insult mocks their end.
Love ends with hope, the sinking statesman's door
Pours in the morning worshipper no more;
For growing names the weekly scribbler lies,
To growing wealth the dedicator flies,[7]
From every room descends the painted face,
That hung the bright palladium[8] of the place,
And smoked in kitchens, or in auctions sold,
To better features yields the frame of gold;
For now no more we trace in every line
Heroic worth, benevolence divine:
The form distorted justifies the fall,
And detestation rids th' indignant wall.

But will not Britain hear the last appeal,
Sign her foes' doom, or guard her favorites' zeal?
Through freedom's sons no more remonstrance rings,
Degrading nobles and controlling kings;

---

[6] I.e., before you pronounce whether his scorn was justified.
[7] I.e., the hack journalist writes in favor of and the author dedicates his works to rising politicians.
[8] Sacred guardian image (from the Palladium, the statue of Pallas Athene that safeguarded Troy).

Our supple tribes repress their patriot throats,
And ask no questions but the price of votes;
With weekly libels and septennial ale,[9]
Their wish is full to riot and to rail.

In full-blown dignity, see Wolsey[10] stand,
Law in his voice, and fortune in his hand:
To him the church, the realm, their powers consign,
Through him the rays of regal bounty shine,
Turned by his nod the stream of honor flows,
His smile alone security bestows:
Still to new heights his restless wishes tower,
Claim leads to claim, and power advances power;
Till conquest unresisted ceased to please,
And rights submitted, left him none to seize.
At length his sovereign frowns—the train of state
Mark the keen glance, and watch the sign to hate.
Where'er he turns he meets a stranger's eye,
His suppliants scorn him, and his followers fly;
At once is lost the pride of aweful state,
The golden canopy, the glittering plate,
The regal palace, the luxurious board,
The liveried army, and the menial lord.
With age, with cares, with maladies oppressed,
He seeks the refuge of monastic rest.
Grief aids disease, remembered folly stings,
And his last sighs reproach the faith of kings.

Speak thou, whose thoughts at humble peace repine,
Shall Wolsey's wealth, with Wolsey's end be thine?
Or liv'st thou now, with safer pride content,
The wisest justice on the banks of Trent?[11]
For why did Wolsey near the steeps of fate,
On weak foundations raise th' enormous weight?
Why but to sink beneath misfortune's blow,
With louder ruin to the gulfs below?

What gave great Villiers to th' assassin's knife,
And fixed disease on Harley's closing life?

[9] A Parliamentary election had to be held at least every seven years.
Voters were commonly bribed with drink, as well as money.
[10] Cardinal Thomas Wolsey rose from humble beginnings to the highest
power as Henry VIII's chief minister; he was disgraced in 1529. Line
120 alludes to Shakespeare's *Henry VIII*, III, ii, 456–58.
[11] Justice of the Peace by the Trent River, in provincial England (near
Lichfield, Johnson's birthplace).

What murdered Wentworth, and what exiled Hyde,
By kings protected, and to kings allied?[12]
What but their wish indulged in courts to shine,
And power too great to keep, or to resign?
   When first the college rolls receive his name,
The young enthusiast quits his ease for fame;
Through all his veins the fever of renown
Burns from the strong contagion of the gown;
O'er Bodley's dome his future labors spread,
And Bacon's mansion trembles o'er his head.[13]
Are these thy views? proceed, illustrious youth,
And virtue guard thee to the throne of Truth!
Yet should thy soul indulge the generous heat,
Till captive Science[14] yields her last retreat;
Should Reason guide thee with her brightest ray,
And pour on misty Doubt resistless day;
Should no false Kindness lure to loose delight,
Nor Praise relax, nor Difficulty fright;
Should tempting Novelty thy cell refrain,
And Sloth effuse her opiate fumes in vain;
Should Beauty blunt on fops her fatal dart,
Nor claim the triumph of a lettered heart;
Should no disease thy torpid veins invade,
Nor Melancholy's phantoms haunt thy shade;[15]
Yet hope not life from grief or danger free,
Nor think the doom of man reversed for thee:
Deign on the passing world to turn thine eyes,
And pause awhile from letters, to be wise;
There mark what ills the scholar's life assail,

---

[12] George Villiers, Duke of Buckingham and favorite of James I, was assassinated; Robert Harley, Earl of Oxford and first minister to Queen Anne, lost his health (Johnson believed) as a result of two years' imprisonment in the Tower; Thomas Wentworth, Earl of Strafford and chief adviser to Charles I, was condemned to death by a Puritan Parliament; and Edward Hyde, Earl of Clarendon, close adviser to Charles II and father-in-law of the future James II, was disgraced and fled to France.

[13] The Bodleian, the main library of Oxford; and the study of Roger Bacon, a medieval scientist. Johnson noted: "There is a tradition that the study of Friar Bacon, built on an arch over the bridge, will fall, when a man greater than Bacon shall pass under it." Johnson was doubtless thinking of himself in this description of the scholar, for years later he burst into tears on reading the passage.

[14] *Science:* knowledge.

[15] *shade:* obscure retirement.

Toil, envy, want, the patron, and the jail.[16]
See nations slowly wise, and meanly just,
To buried merit raise the tardy bust.[17]
If dreams yet flatter, once again attend,
Hear Lydiat's life, and Galileo's end.[18]

Nor deem, when learning her last prize bestows,
The glittering eminence exempt from foes;
See when the vulgar 'scape, despised or awed,
Rebellion's vengeful talons seize on Laud.[19]
From meaner minds, through smaller fines content,
The plundered palace or sequestered rent;
Marked out by dangerous parts[20] he meets the shock,
And fatal Learning leads him to the block:
Around his tomb let Art and Genius weep,
But hear his death, ye blockheads, hear and sleep.

The festal blazes, the triumphal show,
The ravished standard, and the captive foe,
The senate's thanks, the gazette's pompous tale,
With force resistless o'er the brave prevail.
Such bribes the rapid Greek[21] o'er Asia whirled,
For such the steady Romans shook the world;
For such in distant lands the Britons shine,
And stain with blood the Danube or the Rhine;
This power has praise, that virtue scarce can warm,
Till fame supplies the universal charm.
Yet reason frowns on war's unequal game,
Where wasted nations raise a single name,
And mortgaged states their grandsires' wreaths regret,
From age to age in everlasting debt;
Wreaths which at last the dear-bought right convey

---

[16] Johnson replaced his original "garret" with "patron" in 1755, through indignation over Lord Chesterfield's neglect when he was struggling to complete the *Dictionary*.

[17] I.e., recognize great writers belatedly, as Milton's bust was placed in Westminster Abbey in 1737, over sixty years after his death.

[18] Thomas Lydiat, a distinguished mathematician, lived and died poor; the eminence of Galileo Galilei drew the attention of the Inquisition, which persecuted him in 1633.

[19] The learned William Laud rose to be Archbishop of Canterbury; when he used his leadership of the Church of England to oppress the Puritans, they insisted on his impeachment and execution (1645).

[20] *parts:* intellectual ability.

[21] Alexander the Great.

To rust on medals, or on stones decay.
    On what foundation stands the warrior's pride,
How just his hopes let Swedish Charles[22] decide;
A frame of adamant, a soul of fire,
No dangers fright him, and no labors tire;
O'er love, o'er fear, extends his wide domain,
Unconquered lord of pleasure and of pain;
No joys to him pacific scepters yield,
War sounds the trump, he rushes to the field;
Behold surrounding kings their power combine,
And one capitulate, and one resign;
Peace courts his hand, but spreads her charms in vain;
"Think nothing gained," he cries, "till nought remain,
"On Moscow's walls till Gothic standards fly,
"And all be mine beneath the polar sky."
The march begins in military state,
And nations on his eye suspended wait;
Stern Famine guards the solitary coast,
And Winter barricades the realms of Frost;
He comes, not want and cold his course delay;—
Hide, blushing Glory, hide Pultowa's day:
The vanquished hero leaves his broken bands,
And shows his miseries in distant lands;
Condemned a needy supplicant to wait,
While ladies interpose, and slaves debate.
But did not Chance at length her error mend?
Did no subverted empire mark his end?
Did rival monarchs give the fatal wound?
Or hostile millions press him to the ground?
His fall was destined to a barren strand,
A petty fortress, and a dubious hand;
He left the name, at which the world grew pale,
To point a moral, or adorn a tale.
    All times their scenes of pompous woes afford,

[22] Charles XII of Sweden, the greatest warrior of Johnson's day, known as "the Alexander of the North." Voltaire's *History of Charles XII* (1731) had made his story well known. He forced the King of Denmark to surrender on terms and deposed the King of Poland (line 200), but after a bitter struggle was defeated by Czar Peter I of Russia at Pultowa (Poltava, 1709). "Gothic" (line 203) means Swedish. Charles spent several years in exile and was finally, it was believed, assassinated by one of his own soldiers.

From Persia's tyrant to Bavaria's lord.
In gay hostility, and barbarous pride,
With half mankind embattled at his side,
Great Xerxes comes to seize the certain prey,
And starves exhausted regions in his way;
Attendant Flattery counts his myriads o'er,
Till counted myriads soothe his pride no more;
Fresh praise is tried till madness fires his mind,
The waves he lashes, and enchains the wind;
New powers are claimed, new powers are still bestowed,
Till rude resistance lops the spreading god;
The daring Greeks deride the martial show,
And heap their valleys with the gaudy foe;
Th' insulted sea with humbler thoughts he gains,
A single skiff to speed his flight remains;
Th' incumbered oar scarce leaves the dreaded coast
Through purple billows and a floating host.[23]
　　The bold Bavarian in a luckless hour,
Tries the dread summits of Caesarean power,
With unexpected legions bursts away,
And sees defenseless realms receive his sway;
Short sway! fair Austria spreads her mournful charms,
The queen, the beauty, sets the world in arms;
From hill to hill the beacon's rousing blaze
Spreads wide the hope of plunder and of praise;
The fierce Croatian, and the wild Hussar,
And all the sons of ravage crowd the war;
The baffled prince in honor's flattering bloom
Of hasty greatness finds the fatal doom,
His foes' derision, and his subjects' blame,
And steals to death from anguish and from shame.[24]
　　Enlarge my life with multitude of days,
In health, in sickness, thus the suppliant prays;
Hides from himself his state, and shuns to know,

---

[23] Xerxes, King of Persia, thought he could easily conquer Greece, but was decisively defeated; according to legend, he was so arrogant that he tried to punish the sea and the winds when they did not cooperate with his plans (line 232). He got away from Greece with only one ship, which had to push through a sea of corpses.
[24] Charles Albert, Elector of Bavaria, invaded Austria and got himself elected Holy Roman Emperor (1742, line 242), but Empress Maria Theresa of Austria roused her subjects against him; he was defeated and lost his own territory of Bavaria.

That life protracted is protracted woe.
Time hovers o'er, impatient to destroy,
And shuts up all the passages of joy:
In vain their gifts the bounteous seasons pour,
The fruit autumnal, and the vernal flower,
With listless eyes the dotard views the store,
He views, and wonders that they please no more;
Now pall the tasteless meats and joyless wines,
And luxury with sighs her slave resigns.
Approach, ye minstrels, try the soothing strain,
Diffuse the tuneful lenitives of pain:
No sounds, alas, would touch th' impervious ear,
Though dancing mountains witnessed Orpheus near;[25]
Nor lute nor lyre his feeble powers attend,[26]
Nor sweeter music of a virtuous friend,
But everlasting dictates crowd his tongue,
Perversely grave, or positively wrong.
The still returning tale, and lingering jest,
Perplex the fawning niece and pampered guest,
While growing hopes scarce awe the gathering sneer,
And scarce a legacy can bribe to hear;
The watchful guests still hint the last[27] offense,
The daughter's petulance, the son's expense,
Improve his heady rage with treacherous skill,
And mold his passions till they make his will.

Unnumbered maladies his joints invade,
Lay siege to life and press the dire blockade;
But unextinguished avarice still remains,
And dreaded losses aggravate his pains;
He turns, with anxious heart and crippled hands,
His bonds of debt, and mortgages of lands;
Or views his coffers with suspicious eyes,
Unlocks his gold, and counts it till he dies.

But grant the virtues of a temperate prime,[28]
Bless with an age exempt from scorn or crime;
An age that melts with unperceived decay,
And glides in modest innocence away;
Whose peaceful day Benevolence endears,

[25] According to myth, Orpheus' music was so powerful it moved inanimate things.
[26] *attend:* pay attention to.
[27] *last:* latest.
[28] *prime:* prime of life.

Whose night congratulating Conscience cheers;
The general favorite as the general friend;
Such age there is, and who shall wish its end?

Yet even on this her load Misfortune flings,
To press the weary minutes' flagging wings:
New sorrow rises as the day returns,
A sister sickens, or a daughter mourns.
Now kindred Merit fills the sable bier,
Now lacerated Friendship claims a tear.
Year chases year, decay pursues decay,
Still drops some joy from withering life away;
New forms arise, and different views engage,
Superfluous lags the veteran on the stage,
Till pitying Nature signs the last release,
And bids afflicted worth retire to peace.

But few there are whom hours like these await,
Who set unclouded in the gulfs of fate.
From Lydia's monarch should the search descend,
By Solon cautioned to regard his end,[29]
In life's last scene what prodigies surprise,
Fears of the brave, and follies of the wise?
From Marlborough's eyes the streams of dotage flow,
And Swift expires a driveler and a show.[30]

The teeming mother, anxious for her race,
Begs for each birth the fortune of a face:
Yet Vane could tell what ills from beauty spring;
And Sedley cursed the form that pleased a king.[31]
Ye nymphs of rosy lips and radiant eyes,
Whom pleasure keeps too busy to be wise,
Whom joys with soft varieties invite,
By day the frolic, and the dance by night,
Who frown with vanity, who smile with art,
And ask the latest fashion of the heart,

[29] Croesus, the fabulously wealthy King of Lydia, was warned by Solon that no one should count his life happy until it was over; in the end, Croesus was captured and is said to have committed suicide.
[30] John Churchill, Duke of Marlborough (1650–1722), one of England's greatest generals, failed mentally and physically during his last years; Jonathan Swift (1667–1745) also sank into senility, and it is said that his servants showed him to tourists for a fee.
[31] Anne Vane (1705–36) was mistress to Frederick, Prince of Wales; Catharine Sedley (1657–1717) to James, Duke of York (later James II).

What care, what rules your heedless charms shall save,
Each nymph your rival, and each youth your slave?
Against your fame with fondness hate combines,
The rival batters, and the lover mines.
With distant voice neglected Virtue calls,
Less heard and less, the faint remonstrance falls;
Tired with contempt, she quits the slippery reign,
And Pride and Prudence take her seat in vain.
In crowd at once, where none the pass defend,
The harmless Freedom, and the private Friend.
The guardians yield, by force superior plied;
By Interest,[32] Prudence; and by Flattery, Pride.
Now beauty falls betrayed, despised, distressed,
And hissing Infamy proclaims the rest.

    Where then shall hope and fear their objects find?
Must dull suspense corrupt the stagnant mind?
Must helpless man, in ignorance sedate,[33]
Roll darkling[34] down the torrent of his fate?
Must no dislike alarm, no wishes rise,
No cries attempt the mercies of the skies?
Inquirer, cease, petitions yet remain,
Which heaven may hear, nor deem religion vain.
Still raise for good the supplicating voice,
But leave to heaven the measure and the choice,
Safe in His power, whose eyes discern afar
The secret ambush of a specious prayer.
Implore His aid, in His decisions rest,
Secure whate'er He gives, He gives the best.
Yet when the sense of sacred presence fires,
And strong devotion to the skies aspires,
Pour forth thy fervors for a healthful mind,
Obedient passions, and a will resigned;
For love, which scarce collective man can fill;[35]
For patience sovereign o'er transmuted ill;[36]
For faith, that panting for a happier seat,
Counts death kind Nature's signal of retreat:

---

[32] *Interest:* self-interest.
[33] *sedate:* calm, apathetic.
[34] *darkling:* in the dark.
[35] True Christian love, unlimited and therefore embracing all mankind (?).
[36] Patience so great it can transmute an evil into a good (?).

These goods for man the laws of heaven ordain,
These goods He grants, who grants the power to gain;
With these celestial wisdom calms the mind,
And makes the happiness she does not find.

A Short Song of Congratulation

[Johnson sent this poem to his friend Hester Thrale on the occasion of Sir John Lade's twenty-first birthday. Lade, Henry Thrale's nephew, came into a large inheritance, which he was soon to squander. On one occasion he asked Johnson whether he should marry, and Johnson replied, "I would advise no man to marry, Sir, who is not likely to propagate understanding."]

Long-expected one and twenty
    Lingering year at last is flown,
Pomp and pleasure, pride and plenty,
    Great Sir John, are all your own.

Loosened from the minor's tether,
    Free to mortgage or to sell,
Wild as wind, and light as feather,
    Bid the slaves of thrift farewell.

Call the Bettys, Kates, and Jennys,
    Every name that laughs at care,
Lavish of your grandsire's guineas,
    Show the spirit of an heir.

All that prey on vice and folly
    Joy to see their quarry fly,
Here the gamester light and jolly,
    There the lender grave and sly.

Wealth, Sir John, was made to wander,
    Let it wander as it will;
See the jockey, see the pander,
    Bid them come, and take their fill.

When the bonny blade carouses,
   Pockets full, and spirits high,
What are acres? What are houses?
   Only dirt, or wet or dry.

If the guardian or the mother
   Tell the woes of willful waste,
Scorn their counsel and their pother,
   You can hang or drown at last.

On the Death of Dr. Robert Levett

[Levett, a good but unprepossessing man who served as a
doctor to the poor, became a member of Johnson's household
in 1763; he died in 1782, at the age of seventy-six.]

Condemned to hope's delusive mine,
   As on we toil from day to day,
By sudden blasts, or slow decline,
   Our social comforts drop away.

Well tried through many a varying year,
   See Levett to the grave descend;
Officious,[1] innocent, sincere,
   Of every friendless name the friend.

Yet still he fills affection's eye,
   Obscurely[2] wise, and coarsely kind;
Nor, lettered[3] arrogance, deny
   Thy praise to merit unrefined.

When fainting nature called for aid,
   And hovering death prepared the blow,
His vigorous remedy displayed
   The power of art without the show.

[1] *officious:* eager to help.
[2] *obscurely:* without notice.
[3] *lettered:* educated.

In misery's darkest caverns known,
  His useful care was ever nigh,
Where hopeless anguish poured his groan,
  And lonely want retired to die.

No summons mocked by chill delay,
  No petty gain disdained by pride,
The modest wants of every day
  The toil of every day supplied.

His virtues walked their narrow round,
  Nor made a pause, nor left a void;
And sure th' Eternal Master found
  The single talent well employed.[4]

The busy day, the peaceful night,
  Unfelt, uncounted, glided by;
His frame was firm, his powers were bright,
  Though now his eightieth year was nigh.

Then with no throbbing fiery pain,
  No cold gradations of decay,
Death broke at once the vital chain,
  And freed his soul the nearest way.

---

[4] Christ's parable of the talents (Matthew 25:14–30) teaches that everyone should make the most of the talents God has given him.

Periodical Essays

[For many years, Johnson supported himself by writing for periodicals. He brought out *The Rambler* (1750–52) as separate papers twice weekly while he was working on his *Dictionary*. He contributed twenty-nine papers to *The Adventurer* (1753–54), a periodical conducted by his friend John Hawkesworth. *The Idler* (1758–60) was a series of lead essays in *The Universal Chronicle*. His demolition of Soame Jenyns's *Free Enquiry into the Nature and Origin of Evil*, in *The Literary Magazine* (1757), is the finest of his many book reviews.]

Selections from *The Rambler*

No. 4. Saturday, 31 March 1750.

[Modern Fiction]

The works of fiction, with which the present generation seems more particularly delighted, are such as exhibit life in its true state, diversified only by accidents that daily happen in the world, and influenced by passions and qualities which are really to be found in conversing with mankind.

This kind of writing may be termed not improperly the comedy of romance, and is to be conducted nearly by the rules of comic poetry. Its province is to bring about natural events by easy means, and to keep up curiosity without the help of wonder: it is therefore precluded from the machines[1] and expedients of the heroic romance, and can neither employ giants to snatch away a lady from the nuptial rites, nor knights to bring her back from captivity; it can neither bewilder its personages in desarts, nor lodge them in imaginary castles.

I remember a remark made by Scaliger upon Pontanus, that all his writings are filled with the same images; and that if you take from him his lillies and his roses, his satyrs and his dryads, he will have nothing left that can be called poetry. In like manner, almost all the fictions of the last age will vanish, if you deprive them of a hermit and a wood, a battle and a shipwreck.

Why this wild strain of imagination found reception so long, in polite[2] and learned ages, it is not easy to conceive; but we cannot wonder that, while readers could be procured,

[1] *machines:* supernatural contrivances.
[2] *polite:* civilized.

the authors were willing to continue it: for when a man had by practice gained some fluency of language, he had no further care than to retire to his closet,[3] let loose his invention, and heat his mind with incredibilities; a book was thus produced without fear of criticism, without the toil of study, without knowledge of nature, or acquaintance with life.

The task of our present writers is very different; it requires, together with that learning which is to be gained from books, that experience which can never be attained by solitary diligence, but must arise from general converse, and accurate observation of the living world. Their performances have, as Horace expresses it, *plus oneris quantum veniae minus*, little indulgence, and therefore more difficulty. They are engaged in portraits of which every one knows the original, and can detect any deviation from exactness of resemblance. Other writings are safe, except from the malice of learning, but these are in danger from every common reader; as the slipper ill executed was censured by a shoemaker who happened to stop in his way at the Venus of Apelles.[4]

But the fear of not being approved as just copyers of human manners,[5] is not the most important concern that an author of this sort ought to have before him. These books are written chiefly to the young, the ignorant, and the idle, to whom they serve as lectures of conduct, and introductions into life. They are the entertainment of minds unfurnished with ideas, and therefore easily susceptible of impressions; not fixed by principles, and therefore easily following the current of fancy; not informed by experience, and consequently open to every false suggestion and partial account.

That the highest degree of reverence should be paid to youth, and that nothing indecent should be suffered to approach their eyes or ears; are precepts extorted by sense and virtue from an ancient writer, by no means eminent for chastity of thought.[6] The same kind, tho' not the same degree of caution, is required in every thing which is laid before them,

---

[3] *closet:* small private room; here, study.
[4] A shoemaker pointed out that in drawing a subject's sandals, Apelles had represented them with one loop too few (Pliny, *Natural History*, XXXV, xxxvi).
[5] *manners:* customary behavior, ways of acting.
[6] Juvenal, Satire XIV, lines 1–58.

to secure them from unjust prejudices, perverse opinions, and incongruous combinations of images.

In the romances formerly written, every transaction and sentiment was so remote from all that passes among men, that the reader was in very little danger of making any applications to himself; the virtues and crimes were equally beyond his sphere of activity; and he amused himself with heroes and with traitors, deliverers and persecutors, as with beings of another species, whose actions were regulated upon motives of their own, and who had neither faults nor excellencies in common with himself.

But when an adventurer is levelled with the rest of the world, and acts in such scenes of the universal drama, as may be the lot of any other man; young spectators fix their eyes upon him with closer attention, and hope by observing his behaviour and success to regulate their own practices, when they shall be engaged in the like part.

For this reason these familiar histories may perhaps be made of greater use than the solemnities of professed morality, and convey the knowledge of vice and virtue with more efficacy than axioms and definitions. But if the power of example is so great, as to take possession of the memory by a kind of violence, and produce effects almost without the intervention of the will, care ought to be taken that, when the choice is unrestrained, the best examples only should be exhibited; and that which is likely to operate so strongly, should not be mischievous or uncertain in its effects.

The chief advantage which these fictions have over real life is, that their authors are at liberty, tho' not to invent, yet to select objects, and to cull from the mass of mankind, those individuals upon which the attention ought most to be employ'd; as a diamond, though it cannot be made, may be polished by art, and placed in such a situation, as to display that lustre which before was buried among common stones.

It is justly considered as the greatest excellency of art, to imitate nature; but it is necessary to distinguish those parts of nature, which are most proper for imitation: greater care is still required in representing life, which is so often discoloured by passion, or deformed by wickedness. If the world be promiscuously⁷ described, I cannot see of what use it can be to

---

⁷ *promiscuously:* indiscriminately.

read the account; or why it may not be as safe to turn the eye immediately upon mankind, as upon a mirror which shows all that presents itself without discrimination.

It is therefore not a sufficient vindication of a character, that it is drawn as it appears, for many characters ought never to be drawn; nor of a narrative, that the train of events is agreeable to observation and experience, for that observation which is called knowledge of the world, will be found much more frequently to make men cunning than good. The purpose of these writings is surely not only to show mankind, but to provide that they may be seen hereafter with less hazard; to teach the means of avoiding the snares which are laid by Treachery for Innocence, without infusing any wish for that superiority with which the betrayer flatters his vanity; to give the power of counteracting fraud, without the temptation to practise it; to initiate youth by mock encounters in the art of necessary defence, and to increase prudence without impairing virtue.

Many writers, for the sake of following nature, so mingle good and bad qualities in their principal personages, that they are both equally conspicuous; and as we accompany them through their adventures with delight, and are led by degrees to interest ourselves in their favour, we lose the abhorrence of their faults, because they do not hinder our pleasure, or, perhaps, regard them with some kindness for being united with so much merit.

There have been men indeed splendidly wicked, whose endowments threw a brightness on their crimes, and whom scarce any villainy made perfectly detestable, because they never could be wholly divested of their excellencies; but such have been in all ages the great corrupters of the world, and their resemblance ought no more to be preserved, than the art of murdering without pain.

Some have advanced, without due attention to the consequences of this notion, that certain virtues have their correspondent faults, and therefore that to exhibit either apart is to deviate from probability. Thus men are observed by Swift to be "grateful in the same degree as they are resentful." This principle, with others of the same kind, supposes man to act from a brute impulse, and persue a certain degree of inclination, without any choice of the object; for, otherwise, though it should be allowed that gratitude and resentment arise from the same constitution of the passions, it follows not that they will be equally indulged when reason is consulted; yet unless that consequence be admitted, this sagacious maxim becomes an empty sound, without any relation to practice or to life.

Nor is it evident, that even the first motions[8] to these effects are always in the same proportion. For pride, which produces quickness of resentment, will obstruct gratitude, by unwillingness to admit that inferiority which obligation implies; and it is very unlikely, that he who cannot think he receives a favour will acknowledge or repay it.

It is of the utmost importance to mankind, that positions of this tendency should be laid open and confuted; for while men consider good and evil as springing from the same root, they will spare the one for the sake of the other, and in judging, if not of others at least of themselves, will be apt to estimate their virtues by their vices. To this fatal error all those will contribute, who confound the colours of right and wrong, and instead of helping to settle their boundaries, mix them with so much art, that no common mind is able to disunite them.

In narratives, where historical veracity has no place, I cannot discover why there should not be exhibited the most perfect idea of virtue; of virtue not angelical, nor above probability, for what we cannot credit we shall never imitate, but the highest and purest that humanity can reach, which, exercised in such trials as the various revolutions of things shall bring upon it, may, by conquering some calamities, and enduring others, teach us what we may hope, and what we can perform. Vice, for vice is necessary to be shewn, should always disgust; nor should the graces of gaiety, or the dignity of courage, be so united with it, as to reconcile it to the mind. Wherever it appears, it should raise hatred by the malignity of its practices, and contempt by the meanness of its stratagems; for while it is supported by either parts[9] or spirit, it will be seldom heartily abhorred. The Roman tyrant[10] was content to be hated, if he was but feared; and there are thousands of the readers of romances willing to be thought wicked, if they may be allowed to be wits. It is therefore to be steadily in-

---

[8] *motions:* impulses.
[9] *parts:* intellectual ability.
[10] Caligula, as told in Suetonius' *Lives of the Caesars.*

culcated, that virtue is the highest proof of understanding, and the only solid basis of greatness; and that vice is the natural consequence of narrow thoughts, that it begins in mistake, and ends in ignominy.

No. 12. Saturday, 28 April 1750.

[Hardships of Domestic Service]

TO THE RAMBLER.

SIR,

As you seem to have devoted your labours to virtue, I cannot forbear to inform you of one species of cruelty, with which the life of a man of letters perhaps does not often make him acquainted; and which, as it seems to produce no other advantage to those that practise it than a short gratification of thoughtless vanity, may become less common when it has been once exposed in its various forms, and its full magnitude.

I am the daughter of a country gentleman, whose family is numerous, and whose estate, not at first sufficient to supply us with affluence, has been lately so much impaired by an unsuccessful lawsuit, that all the younger children are obliged to try such means as their education affords them, for procuring the necessaries of life. Distress and curiosity concurred to bring me to London, where I was received by a relation with the coldness which misfortune generally finds. A week, a long week, I lived with my cousin, before the most vigilant enquiry could procure us the least hopes of a place, in which time I was much better qualified to bear all the vexations of servitude. The first two days she was content to pity me, and only wish'd I had not been quite so well bred, but people must comply with their circumstances. This lenity, however, was soon at an end; and, for the remaining part of the week, I heard every hour of the pride of my family, the obstinacy of my father, and of people better born than myself that were common servants.

At last, on Saturday noon, she told me, with very visible satisfaction, that Mrs. Bombasine, the great silk-mercer's[11]

11 *silk-mercer*: dealer in silk and velvet; bombasine, or bombazine, was a material for dresses.

lady, wanted a maid, and a fine place it would be, for there would be nothing to do but to clean my mistress's room, get up her linen, dress the young ladies, wait at tea in the morning, take care of a little miss just come from nurse, and then sit down to my needle. But madam was a woman of great spirit, and would not be contradicted, and therefore I should take care, for good places were not easily to be got.

With these cautions, I waited on madam Bombasine, of whom the first sight gave me no ravishing ideas. She was two yards round the waist, her voice was at once loud and squeaking, and her face brought to my mind the picture of the full-moon. Are you the young woman, says she, that are come to offer yourself? It is strange when people of substance want a servant, how soon it is the town-talk. But they know they shall have a belly-full that live with me. Not like people at the other end of the town, we dine at one o'clock. But I never take any body without a character; what friends[12] do you come of? I then told her that my father was a gentleman, and that we had been unfortunate.——A great misfortune, indeed, to come to me and have three meals a-day!——So your father was a gentleman, and you are a gentlewoman I suppose—such gentlewomen! Madam, I did not mean to claim any exemptions, I only answered your enquiry——Such gentlewomen! people should set their children to good trades, and keep them off the parish. Pray go to the other end of the town, there are gentlewomen, if they would pay their debts: I am sure we have lost enough by gentlewomen. Upon this, her broad face grew broader with triumph, and I was afraid she would have taken me for the pleasure of continuing her insult; but happily the next word was, Pray, Mrs. gentlewoman, troop down stairs. You may believe I obeyed her.

I returned and met with a better reception from my cousin than I expected; for while I was out, she had heard that Mrs. Standish,[13] whose husband had lately been raised from a clerk in an office, to be commissioner of the excise, had taken a fine house, and wanted a maid.

To Mrs. Standish I went, and, after having waited six hours, was at last admitted to the top of the stairs, when she came out of her room, with two of her company. There was a smell of punch. So young woman, you want a place, whence

---

[12] *friends:* family.
[13] *standish:* inkstand.

do you come?—From the country, madam.——Yes, they all
come out of the country. And what brought you to town, a
bastard? Where do you lodge? At the Seven-Dials?[14] What,
you never heard of the foundling house?[15] Upon this, they all
laughed so obstreperously, that I took the opportunity of
sneaking off in the tumult.

I then heard of a place at an elderly lady's. She was at
cards; but in two hours, I was told, she would speak to me. She
asked me if I could keep an account, and ordered me to write.
I wrote two lines out of some book that lay by her. She wonder'd what people meant, to breed up poor girls to write at
that rate. I suppose, Mrs. Flirt, if I was to see your work,[16] it
would be fine stuff!—You may walk. I will not have love-
letters written from my house to every young fellow in the
street.

Two days after, I went on the same persuit to Lady Lofty,
dressed, as I was directed, in what little ornaments I had,
because she had lately got a place at court. Upon the first
sight of me, she turns to the woman that showed me in, Is
this the lady that wants a place? Pray what place wou'd you
have, miss? a maid of honour's place? Servants now a-days!
——Madam, I heard you wanted——Wanted what? Somebody finer than myself! A pretty servant indeed—I should be
afraid to speak to her—I suppose, Mrs. Minx, these fine
hands cannot bear wetting—A servant indeed! Pray move
off—I am resolved to be the head person in this house—You
are ready dressed, the taverns will be open.[17]

I went to enquire for the next place in a clean linen gown,
and heard the servant tell his lady, there was a young woman,
but he saw she would not do. I was brought up however. Are
you the trollop that has the impudence to come for my place?
What, you have hired that nasty gown, and are come to steal
a better.—Madam, I have another, but being obliged to walk
—Then these are your manners, with your blushes and your
courtesies, to come to me in your worst gown. Madam, give
me leave to wait upon you in my other. Wait on me, you saucy
slut! Then you are sure of coming—I could not let such a drab

[14] *Seven-Dials:* a low district of London.
[15] *foundling house:* hospital for unwanted (usually illegitimate) infants.
[16] *work:* sewing.
[17] Prostitutes picked up customers at taverns.

come near me—Here, you girl that came up with her, have
you touch'd her? If you have, wash your hands before you
dress me.——Such trollops! Get you down. What, whimper-
ing? Pray walk.

I went away with tears; for my cousin had lost all patience.
However she told me, that having a respect for my relations,
she was willing to keep me out of the street, and would let
me have another week.

The first day of this week I saw two places. At one I was
asked where I had lived? And upon my answer, was told by
the lady, that people should qualify themselves in ordinary
places, for she should never have done if she was to follow
girls about. At the other house, I was a smirking hussy, and
that sweet face I might make money of——For her part, it was
a rule with her, never to take any creature that thought
herself handsome.

The three next days were spent in Lady Bluff's entry, where
I waited six hours every day for the pleasure of seeing the
servants peep at me, and go away laughing——Madam will
stretch her small shanks in the entry; she will know the house
again——At sun-set the two first days I was told, that my
lady would see me to-morrow; and on the third, that her
woman[18] staid.

My week was now near its end, and I had no hopes of a
place. My relation, who always laid upon me the blame of
every miscarriage, told me that I must learn to humble myself, and that all great ladies had particular ways; that if I
went on in that manner, she could not tell who would keep
me; she had known many that had refused places, sell their
cloaths, and beg in the streets.

It was to no purpose that the refusal was declared by me to
be never on my side; I was reasoning against interest,[19] and
against stupidity; and therefore I comforted myself with the
hope of succeeding better in my next attempt, and went to
Mrs. Courtly, a very fine lady, who had routs[20] at her house,
and saw the best company in town.

I had not waited two hours before I was called up, and
found Mr. Courtly and his lady at piquet, in the height of

---

[18] *woman:* personal maid.
[19] *interest:* self-interest.
[20] *routs:* large fashionable parties.

good humour. This I looked on as a favourable sign, and stood at the lower end of the room in expectation of the common questions. At last Mr. Courtly call'd out, after a whisper, Stand facing the light, that one may see you. I chang'd my place and blush'd. They frequently turn'd their eyes upon me, and seem'd to discover many subjects of merriment; for at every look they whisper'd, and laugh'd with the most violent agitations of delight. At last Mr. Courtly cried out, Is that colour your own, child? Yes, says the lady, if she has not robb'd the kitchen hearth. This was so happy a conceit, that it renew'd the storm of laughter, and they threw down their cards in hopes of better sport. The lady then called me to her, and began with an affected gravity to enquire what I could do? But first turn about, and let us see your fine shape; Well, what are you fit for, Mrs. Mum? You would find your tongue, I suppose, in the kitchen. No, no, says Mr. Courtly, the girl's a good girl yet, but I am afraid a brisk young fellow, with fine tags on his shoulder——— Come, child, hold up your head; what? you have stole nothing———Not yet, says the lady, but she hopes to steal your heart quickly.———Here was a laugh of happiness and triumph, prolonged by the confusion which I could no longer repress. At last the lady recollected herself: Stole? no——but if I had her, I should watch her; for that downcast eye—— Why cannot you look people in the face? Steal? says her husband, she would steal nothing but, perhaps, a few ribbands before they were left off by her lady. Sir, answer'd I, why should you, by supposing me a thief, insult one from whom you had received no injury? Insult, says the lady; are you come here to be a servant, you saucy baggage, and talk of insulting? What will this world come to, if a gentleman may not jest with a servant? Well, such servants! pray be gone, and see when you will have the honour to be so insulted again. Servants insulted—a fine time.——Insulted! Get down stairs, you slut, or the footman shall insult you.

The last day of the last week was now coming, and my kind cousin talked of sending me down in the waggon to preserve me from bad courses. But in the morning she came and told me that she had one trial more for me; Euphemia wanted a maid, and perhaps I might do for her; for, like me, she must fall her crest, being forced to lay down her chariot upon the loss of half her fortune by bad securities, and with her way of giving her money to every body that pretended to want it, she could have little beforehand; therefore I might serve her; for, with all her fine sense, she must not pretend to be nice.

I went immediately, and met at the door a young gentle-woman, who told me she had herself been hired that morning, but that she was order'd to bring any that offered up stairs. I was accordingly introduced to Euphemia, who, when I came in, laid down her book, and told me, that she sent for me not to gratify an idle curiosity, but lest my disappointment might be made still more grating by incivility; that she was in pain to deny any thing, much more what was no favour; that she saw nothing in my appearance which did not make her wish for my company; but that another, whose claims might perhaps be equal, had come before me. The thought of being so near to such a place, and missing it, brought tears into my eyes, and my sobs hinder'd me from returning my acknowledgments. She rose up confused, and supposing by my concern that I was distressed, placed me by her, and made me tell her my story: which when she had heard, she put two guineas in my hand, ordering me to lodge near her, and make use of her table till she could provide for me. I am now under her protection, and know not how to show my gratitude better than by giving this account to the Rambler.

ZOSIMA

No. 18. Saturday, 19 May 1750.

[Unhappiness in Marriage]

There is no observation more frequently made by such as employ themselves in surveying the conduct of mankind, than that marriage, though the dictate of nature, and the institution of providence, is yet very often the cause of misery, and that those who enter into that state can seldom forbear to express their repentance, and their envy of those whom either chance or caution has withheld from it.

This general unhappiness has given occasion to many sage maxims among the serious, and smart remarks among the gay; the moralist and the writer of epigrams have equally shown their abilities upon it; some have lamented, and some have ridiculed it; but as the faculty of writing has been chiefly a masculine endowment, the reproach of making the world miserable has been always thrown upon the women, and the grave and the merry have equally thought themselves at liberty to conclude either with declamatory complaints, or satirical censures, of female folly or fickleness, ambition or cruelty, extravagance or lust.

Led by such a number of examples, and incited by my share in the common interest, I sometimes venture to consider this universal grievance, having endeavoured to divest my heart of all partiality, and place myself as a kind of neutral being between the sexes, whose clamours, being equally vented on both sides with all the vehemence of distress, all the apparent confidence of justice, and all the indignation of injured virtue, seem entitled to equal regard. The men have, indeed, by their superiority of writing, been able to collect the evidence of many ages, and raise prejudices in their favour by the venerable testimonies of philosophers, historians and poets; but the pleas of the ladies appeal to passions of more forcible operation than the reverence of antiquity. If they have not so great names on their side, they have stronger arguments; it is to little purpose that Socrates, or Euripides, are produced against the sighs of softness, and the tears of beauty. The most frigid and inexorable judge would, at least, stand suspended between equal powers, as Lucan was perplexed in the determination of the cause, where the deities were on one side, and Cato on the other.[21]

But I, who have long studied the severest and most abstracted philosophy, have now, in the cool maturity of life, arrived to such command over my passions, that I can hear the vociferations of either sex without catching any of the fire from those that utter them. For I have found, by long experience, that a man will sometimes rage at his wife, when in reality his mistress has offended him; and a lady complain of the cruelty of her husband, when she has no other enemy than bad cards. I do not suffer myself to be any longer imposed upon by oaths on one side, or fits on the other; nor when the husband hastens to the tavern, and the lady retires to her

<hr />

[21] Lucan, *Pharsalia*, I, lines 127–8. Cato was noted for extreme virtue.

closet, am I always confident that they are driven by their miseries; since I have sometimes reason to believe, that they purpose not so much to sooth their sorrows, as to animate their fury. But how little credit soever may be given to particular accusations, the general accumulation of the charge shows, with too much evidence, that married persons are not very often advanced in felicity; and, therefore, it may be proper to examine at what avenues so many evils have made their way into the world. With this purpose, I have reviewed the lives of my friends, who have been least successful in connubial contracts, and attentively considered by what motives they were incited to marry, and by what principles they regulated their choice.

One of the first of my acquaintances that resolved to quit the unsettled thoughtless condition of a batchelor, was Prudentius, a man of slow parts, but not without knowledge or judgment in things which he had leisure to consider gradually before he determined them. Whenever we met at a tavern, it was his province to settle the scheme of our entertainment, contract with the cook, and inform us when we had called for wine to the sum originally proposed. This grave considerer found by deep meditation that a man was no loser by marrying early, even though he contented himself with a less fortune; for estimating the exact worth of annuities, he found that, considering the constant diminution of the value of life, with the probable fall of the interest of money, it was not worse to have ten thousand pounds at the age of two and twenty years, than a much larger fortune at thirty; for many opportunities, says he, occur of improving money, which if a man misses, he may not afterwards recover.

Full of these reflections, he threw his eyes about him, not in search of beauty, or elegance, dignity, or understanding, but of a woman with ten thousand pounds. Such a woman, in a wealthy part of the kingdom, it was not very difficult to find; and by artful management with her father, whose ambition was to make his daughter a gentlewoman, my friend got her, as he boasted to us in confidence two days after his marriage, for a settlement[22] of seventy-three pounds a year less

---

[22] *settlement:* money settled on a woman by her husband at marriage, to be used for the benefit of herself and her children, in exchange for the fortune which she brought him.

than her fortune might have claimed, and less than he would himself have given, if the fools had been but wise enough to delay the bargain.

Thus, at once delighted with the superiority of his parts, and the augmentation of his fortune, he carried Furia to his own house, in which he never afterwards enjoyed one hour of happiness. For Furia was a wretch of mean intellects, violent passions, a strong voice, and low education, without any sense of happiness but that which consisted in eating, and counting money. Furia was a scold. They agreed in the desire of wealth, but with this difference, that Prudentius was for growing rich by gain, Furia by parsimony. Prudentius would venture his money with chances very much in his favour; but Furia very wisely observing that what they had was, while they had it, *their own*, thought all traffick too great a hazard, and was for putting it out at low interest, upon good security. Prudentius ventured, however, to insure a ship, at a very unreasonable price, but happening to lose his money, was so tormented with the clamours of his wife, that he never durst try a second experiment. He has now grovelled seven and forty years under Furia's direction, who never once mentioned him, since his bad luck, by any other name than that of "the insurer."

The next that married from our society was Florentius. He happened to see Zephyretta in a chariot at a horse-race, danced with her at night, was confirmed in his first ardour, waited on her next morning, and declared himself her lover. Florentius had not knowledge enough of the world, to distinguish between the flutter of coquetry, and the sprightliness of wit, or between the smile of allurement, and that of chearfulness. He was soon waked from his rapture by conviction that his pleasure was but the pleasure of a day. Zephyretta had in four and twenty hours spent her stock of repartee, gone round the circle of her airs, and had nothing remaining for him but childish insipidity, or for herself, but the practice of the same artifices upon new men.

Melissus was a man of parts, capable of enjoying, and of improving life. He had passed through the various scenes of gayety with that indifference and possession of himself, natural to men who have something higher and nobler in their prospect. Retiring to spend the summer in a village little frequented, he happened to lodge in the same house with Ianthe, and was unavoidably drawn to some acquaintance, which her wit and politeness soon invited him to improve. Having no opportunity of any other company, they were always together; and, as they owed their pleasures to each other, they began to forget that any pleasure was enjoyed before their meeting. Melissus, from being delighted with her company, quickly began to be uneasy in her absence, and being sufficiently convinced of the force of her understanding, and finding, as he imagined, such a conformity of temper as declared them formed for each other, addressed her as a lover, after no very long courtship obtained her for his wife, and brought her next winter to town in triumph.

Now began their infelicity. Melissus had only seen her in one scene, where there was no variety of objects, to produce the proper excitements to contrary desires. They had both loved solitude and reflection, where there was nothing but solitude and reflection to be loved; but when they came into publick life, Ianthe discovered[23] those passions which accident rather than hypocrisy had hitherto concealed. She was, indeed, not without the power of thinking, but was wholly without the exertion of that power, when either gayety, or splendour, played on her imagination. She was expensive in her diversions, vehement in her passions, insatiate of pleasure however dangerous to her reputation, and eager of applause by whomsoever it might be given. This was the wife which Melissus the philosopher found in his retirement, and from whom he expected an associate in his studies, and an assistant to his virtues.

Prosapius, upon the death of his younger brother, that the family might not be extinct, married his housekeeper, and has ever since been complaining to his friends that mean notions are instilled into his children, that he is ashamed to sit at his own table, and that his house is uneasy for want of suitable companions.

Avaro, master of a very large estate, took a woman of bad reputation, recommended to him by a rich uncle, who made that marriage the condition on which he should be his heir. Avaro now wonders to perceive his own fortune, his wife's, and his uncle's, insufficient to give him that happiness which is to be found only with a woman of virtue.

I intend to treat in more papers on this important article of life, and shall, therefore, make no reflexion upon these his-

[23] *discovered:* revealed.

tories, except that all whom I have mentioned failed to obtain happiness, for want of considering that marriage is the strictest tye of perpetual friendship; that there can be no friendship without confidence, and no confidence without integrity; and that he must expect to be wretched, who pays to beauty, riches, or politeness, that regard which only virtue and piety can claim.

No. 45. Tuesday, 21 August 1750.

[Unhappiness in Marriage]

TO THE RAMBLER.

SIR,

Though, in the dissertations which you have given us on marriage, very just cautions are laid down against the common causes of infelicity, and the necessity of having, in that important choice, the first regard to virtue is carefully inculcated; yet I cannot think the subject so much exhausted, but that a little reflection would present to the mind many questions in the discussion of which great numbers are interested, and many precepts which deserve to be more particularly and forcibly impressed.

You seem, like most of the writers that have gone before you, to have allowed, as an uncontested principle, that "Marriage is generally unhappy": but I know not whether a man who professes to think for himself, and concludes from his own observations, does not depart from his character when he follows the crowd thus implicitly, and receives maxims without recalling them to a new examination, especially when they comprise so wide a circuit of life, and include such variety of circumstances. As I have an equal right with others to give my opinion of the objects about me, and a better title to determine concerning that state which I have tried, than many who talk of it without experience, I am unwilling to be restrained by mere authority from advancing what, I believe, an accurate view of the world will confirm, that marriage is not commonly unhappy, otherwise than as life is unhappy; and that most of those who complain of connubial miseries, have as much satisfaction as their nature would have admitted, or their conduct procured in any other condition.

It is, indeed, common to hear both sexes repine at their change, relate the happiness of their earlier years, blame the folly and rashness of their own choice, and warn those whom they see coming into the world against the same precipitance and infatuation. But it is to be remembred, that the days which they so much wish to call back, are the days not only of celibacy but of youth, the days of novelty and improvement, of ardour and of hope, of health and vigour of body, of gayety and lightness of heart. It is not easy to surround life with any circumstances in which youth will not be delightful; and I am afraid that whether married or unmarried, we shall find the vesture of terrestrial existence more heavy and cumbrous, the longer it is worn.

That they censure themselves for the indiscretion of their choice, is not a sufficient proof that they have chosen ill, since we see the same discontent at every other part of life which we cannot change. Converse with almost any man, grown old in a profession, and you will find him regretting that he did not enter into some different course, to which he too late finds his genius better adapted, or in which he discovers that wealth and honour are more easily attained. "The merchant," says Horace, "envies the soldier, and the soldier recounts the felicity of the merchant; the lawyer when his clients harrass him, calls out for the quiet of the countryman; and the countryman, when business calls him to town, proclaims that there is no happiness but amidst opulence and crowds." Every man recounts the inconveniencies of his own station, and thinks those of any other less, because he has not felt them. Thus the married praise the ease and freedom of a single state, and the single fly to marriage from the weariness of solitude. From all our observations we may collect with certainty, that misery is the lot of man, but cannot discover in what particular condition it will find most alleviations; or whether all external appendages are not, as we use them, the causes either of good or ill.

Whoever feels great pain naturally hopes for ease from change of posture; he changes it, and finds himself equally tormented: and of the same kind are the expedients by which we endeavour to obviate or elude those uneasinesses, to which mortality will always be subject. It is not likely that the married state is eminently miserable, since we see such numbers, whom the death of their partners has set free from it, entering it again.

Wives and husbands are, indeed, incessantly complaining of each other; and there would be reason for imagining that almost every house was infested with perverseness or oppression beyond human sufferance, did we not know upon how small occasions some minds burst out into lamentations and reproaches, and how naturally every animal revenges his pain upon those who happen to be near, without any nice[24] examination of its causes. We are always willing to fancy ourselves within a little of happiness, and when, with repeated efforts, we cannot reach it, persuade ourselves that it is intercepted by an ill-paired mate, since, if we could find any other obstacle, it would be our own fault that it was not removed.

Anatomists have often remarked, that though our diseases are sufficiently numerous and severe, yet when we enquire into the structure of the body, the tenderness of some parts, the minuteness of others, and the immense multiplicity of animal functions that must concur to the healthful and vigorous exercise of all our powers, there appears reason to wonder rather that we are preserved so long, than that we perish so soon, and that our frame subsists for a single day, or hour, without disorder, rather than that it should be broken or obstructed by violence of accidents, or length of time.

The same reflection arises in my mind, upon observation of the manner in which marriage is frequently contracted. When I see the avaricious and crafty taking companions to their tables, and their beds, without any enquiry, but after farms and money; or the giddy and thoughtless uniting themselves for life to those whom they have only seen by the light of tapers at a ball; when parents make articles[25] for their children, without enquiring after their consent; when some marry for heirs to disappoint their brothers, and others throw themselves into the arms of those whom they do not love, because they have found themselves rejected where they were more solicitous to please; when some marry because their servants cheat them, some because they squander their own

---

[24] *nice:* here, careful; five paragraphs below, fastidious.
[25] *articles:* stipulations of a marriage contract.

money, some because their houses are pestered with company, some because they will live like other people, and some only because they are sick of themselves, I am not so much inclined to wonder that marriage is sometimes unhappy, as that it appears so little loaded with calamity; and cannot but conclude that society has something in itself eminently agreeable to human nature, when I find its pleasures so great that even the ill choice of a companion can hardly over-balance them.

By the ancient custom of the Muscovites the men and women never saw each other till they were joined beyond the power of parting. It may be suspected that by this method many unsuitable matches were produced, and many tempers associated that were not qualified to give pleasure to each other. Yet, perhaps, among a people so little delicate, where the paucity of gratifications, and the uniformity of life gave no opportunity for imagination to interpose its objections, there was not much danger of capricious dislike, and while they felt neither cold nor hunger they might live quietly together, without any thought of the defects of one another.

Amongst us, whom knowledge has made nice, and affluence wanton, there are, indeed, more cautions requisite to secure tranquillity; and yet if we observe the manner in which those converse, who have singled out each other for marriage, we shall, perhaps, not think that the Russians lost much by their restraint. For the whole endeavour of both parties, during the time of courtship, is to hinder themselves from being known, and to disguise their natural temper, and real desires, in hypocritical imitation, studied compliance, and continued affectation. From the time that their love is avowed, neither sees the other but in a mask, and the cheat is managed often on both sides with so much art, and discovered afterwards with so much abruptness, that each has reason to suspect that some transformation has happened on the wedding-night, and that by a strange imposture one has been courted, and another married.

I desire you, therefore, Mr. Rambler, to question all who shall hereafter come to you with matrimonial complaints, concerning their behaviour in the time of courtship, and inform them that they are neither to wonder nor repine, when a contract begun with fraud has ended in disappointment.

I am, &c.

No. 51. Tuesday, 10 September 1750.

[A Compulsive Housewife]

TO THE RAMBLER.

SIR,

As you have allowed a place in your paper to Euphelia's letters from the country, and appear to think no form of human life unworthy of your attention, I have resolved, after many struggles with idleness and diffidence, to give you some account of my entertainment in this sober season of universal retreat,[26] and to describe to you the employments of those who look with contempt on the pleasures and diversions of polite life, and employ all their powers of censure and invective upon the uselessness, vanity, and folly of dress, visits, and conversation.

When a tiresome and vexatious journey of four days had brought me to the house, where an invitation, regularly sent for seven years together, had at last induced me to pass the summer, I was surprised, after the civilities of my first reception, to find, instead of the leisure and tranquillity, which a rural life always promises, and, if well conducted, might always afford, a confused wildness of care, and a tumultuous hurry of diligence, by which every face was clouded, and every motion agitated. The old lady, who is my father's relation, was, indeed, very full of the happiness which she received from my visit, and, according to the forms of obsolete breeding, insisted that I should recompense the long delay of my company with a promise not to leave her till winter. But, amidst all her kindness and caresses, she very frequently turned her head aside, and whispered, with anxious earnestness, some order to her daughters, which never failed to send them out with unpolite precipitation. Sometimes her impatience would not suffer her to stay behind; she begged my pardon, she must leave me for a moment; she went, and returned and sat down again, but was again disturbed by some new care, dismissed her daughters with the same trepidation,

[26] Fashionable people usually retired from London to the country during the summer.

and followed them with the same countenance of business and solicitude.

However I was alarmed at this show of eagerness and disturbance, and however my curiosity was excited by such busy preparations as naturally promised some great event, I was yet too much a stranger to gratify myself with enquiries; but finding none of the family in mourning, I pleased myself with imagining that I should rather see a wedding than a funeral.

At last we sat down to supper, when I was informed that one of the young ladies, after whom I thought myself obliged to enquire, was under a necessity of attending some affair that could not be neglected: Soon afterward my relation began to talk of the regularity of her family, and the inconvenience of London hours; and at last let me know that they had purposed that night to go to bed sooner than was usual, because they were to rise early in the morning to make cheesecakes. This hint sent me to my chamber, to which I was accompanied by all the ladies, who begged me to excuse some large sieves of leaves and flowers that covered two thirds of the floor, for they intended to distil them when they were dry, and they had no other room that so conveniently received the rising sun.

The scent of the plants hindered me from rest, and therefore I rose early in the morning with a resolution to explore my new habitation. I stole unperceived by my busy cousins into the garden, where I found nothing either more great or elegant, than in the same number of acres cultivated for the market. Of the gardener I soon learned that his lady was the greatest manager in that part of the country, and that I was come hither at the time in which I might learn to make more pickles and conserves, than could be seen at any other house a hundred miles round.

It was not long before her ladyship gave me sufficient opportunities of knowing her character, for she was too much pleased with her own accomplishments to conceal them, and took occasion, from some sweetmeats which she set next day upon the table, to discourse for two long hours upon robs[27] and gellies; laid down the best methods of conserving, reserving, and preserving all sorts of fruit; told us with great

---

[27] *robs:* syrups.

contempt of the London lady in the neighbourhood, by whom these terms were very often confounded; and hinted how much she should be ashamed to set before company, at her own house, sweetmeats of so dark a colour as she had often seen at Mistress Sprightly's.

It is, indeed, the great business of her life, to watch the skillet on the fire, to see it simmer with the due degree of heat, and to snatch it off at the moment of projection;[28] and the employments to which she has bred her daughters, are to turn rose-leaves in the shade, to pick out the seeds of currants with a quill, to gather fruit without bruising it, and to extract bean-flower water for the skin. Such are the tasks with which every day, since I came hither, has begun and ended, to which the early hours of life are sacrificed, and in which that time is passing away which never shall return.

But to reason or expostulate are hopeless attempts. The lady has settled her opinions, and maintains the dignity of her own performances with all the firmness of stupidity accustomed to be flattered. Her daughters having never seen any house but their own, believe their mother's excellence on her own word. Her husband is a mere sportsman, who is pleased to see his table well furnished, and thinks the day sufficiently successful, in which he brings home a leash[29] of hares to be potted by his wife.

After a few days I pretended to want books, but my lady soon told me that none of her books would suit my taste; for her part she never loved to see young women give their minds to such follies, by which they would only learn to use hard words; she bred up her daughters to understand a house, and whoever should marry them, if they knew any thing of good cookery, would never repent it.

There are, however, some things in the culinary science too sublime for youthful intellects, mysteries into which they must not be initiated till the years of serious maturity, and which are referred to the day of marriage, as the supreme qualification for connubial life. She makes an orange pudding, which is the envy of all the neighbourhood, and which she

---

[28] *projection*: the casting of some ingredient into a crucible; in alchemy (the source of Cornelia's facetious comparison), casting the powder of philosophers' stone into molten metal to turn it into gold.
[29] *leash*: set of three.

has hitherto found means of mixing and baking with such secrecy, that the ingredient to which it owes its flavour has never been discovered. She, indeed, conducts this great affair with all the caution that human policy can suggest. It is never known beforehand when this pudding will be produced; she takes the ingredients privately into her own closet, employs her maids and daughters in different parts of the house, orders the oven to be heated for a pye, and places the pudding in it with her own hands, the mouth of the oven is then stopped, and all enquiries are vain.

The composition of the pudding she has, however, promised Clarinda, that if she pleases her in marriage, she shall be told without reserve. But the art of making English capers she has not yet persuaded herself to discover, but seems resolved that the secret shall perish with her, as some alchymists have obstinately suppressed the art of transmuting metals.

I once ventured to lay my fingers on her book of receipts, which she left upon the table, having intelligence that a vessel of gooseberry wine had burst the hoops. But though the importance of the event sufficiently engrossed her care, to prevent any recollection of the danger to which her secrets were exposed, I was not able to make use of the golden moments; for this treasure of hereditary knowledge was so well concealed by the manner of spelling used by her grandmother, her mother, and herself, that I was totally unable to understand it, and lost the opportunity of consulting the oracle, for want of knowing the language in which its answers were returned.

It is, indeed, necessary, if I have any regard to her ladyship's esteem, that I should apply myself to some of these oeconomical accomplishments; for I overheard her, two days ago, warning her daughters, by my mournful example, against negligence of pastry, and ignorance in carving: for you saw, said she, that, with all her pretensions to knowledge, she turned the partridge the wrong way when she attempted to cut it, and, I believe, scarcely knows the difference between paste raised, and paste in a dish.[30]

The reason, Mr. Rambler, why I have laid Lady Bustle's character before you, is a desire to be informed whether, in your opinion, it is worthy of imitation, and whether I shall

---

[30] I.e., pastry rising either by itself or with the support of a dish.

throw away the books which I have hitherto thought it my duty to read, for the *Lady's closet opened*, the *Compleat servant-maid*, and the *Court cook*, and resign all curiosity after right and wrong, for the art of scalding damascenes[31] without bursting them, and preserving the whiteness of pickled mushrooms.

Lady Bustle has, indeed, by this incessant application to fruits and flowers, contracted her cares into a narrow space, and set herself free from many perplexities with which other minds are disturbed. She has no curiosity after the events of a war, or the fate of heroes in distress; she can hear, without the least emotion, the ravage of a fire, or devastations of a storm; her neighbours grow rich or poor, come into the world or go out of it, without regard, while she is pressing the gelly-bag, or airing the store-room; but I cannot perceive that she is more free from disquiets than those whose understandings take a wider range. Her marigolds when they are almost cured, are often scattered by the wind, the rain sometimes falls upon fruit when it ought to be gathered dry. While her artificial wines are fermenting, her whole life is restlessness and anxiety. Her sweetmeats are not always bright, and the maid sometimes forgets the just proportions of salt and pepper, when venison is to be baked. Her conserves mould, her wines sour, and pickles mother; and, like all the rest of mankind, she is every day mortified with the defeat of her schemes, and the disappointment of her hopes.

With regard to vice and virtue she seems a kind of neutral being. She has no crime but luxury,[32] nor any virtue but chastity; she has no desire to be praised but for her cookery, nor wishes any ill to the rest of mankind, but that whenever they aspire to a feast, their custards may be wheyish, and their pye-crusts tough.

I am now very impatient to know whether I am to look on these ladies as the great patterns of our sex, and to consider conserves and pickles as the business of my life; whether the censures which I now suffer be just, and whether the brewers of wines, and the distillers of washes, have a right to look with insolence on the weakness of

CORNELIA.

---

[31] *damascenes:* a type of plums.
[32] *luxury:* overindulgence in elaborate food, etc.

No. 59. Tuesday, 9 October 1750.

[Suspirius, the Screech-Owl]

It is common to distinguish men by the names of animals which they are supposed to resemble. Thus a hero is frequently termed a lion, and a statesman a fox, an extortioner gains the appellation of vulture, and a fop the title of monkey. There is also among the various anomalies of character, which a survey of the world exhibits, a species of beings in human form, which may be properly marked out as the screech-owls of mankind.

These screech-owls seem to be settled in an opinion that the great business of life is to complain, and that they were born for no other purpose than to disturb the happiness of others, to lessen the little comforts, and shorten the short pleasures of our condition, by painful remembrances of the past, or melancholy prognosticks of the future; their only care is to crush the rising hope, to damp the kindling transport, and allay the golden hours of gaiety with the hateful dross of grief and suspicion.

To those, whose weakness of spirits, or timidity of temper, subjects them to impressions from others, and who are apt to suffer by fascination, and catch the contagion of misery, it is extremely unhappy to live within the compass of a screech-owl's voice; for it will often fill their ears in the hour of dejection, terrify them with apprehensions, which their own thoughts would never have produced, and sadden, by intruded sorrows, the day which might have been passed in amusements or in business; it will burthen the heart with unnecessary discontents, and weaken for a time that love of life, which is necessary to the vigorous prosecution of any undertaking.

Though I have, like the rest of mankind, many failings and weaknesses, I have not yet, by either friends or enemies, been charged with superstition; I never count the company which I enter, and I look at the new moon indifferently over either shoulder. I have, like most other philosophers, often heard the cuckoo without money in my pocket, and have been sometimes reproached as fool-hardy for not turning down my eyes when a raven flew over my head. I never go home abruptly because a snake crosses my way, nor have any particular dread of a climacterical year; yet I confess that, with all my scorn of old women, and their tales, I consider it as an unhappy day when I happen to be greeted, in the morning, by Suspirius the screech-owl.

I have now known Suspirius fifty-eight years and four months, and have never yet passed an hour with him in which he has not made some attack upon my quiet. When we were first acquainted, his great topick was the misery of youth without riches, and whenever we walked out together he solaced me with a long enumeration of pleasures, which, as they were beyond the reach of my fortune, were without the verge of my desires, and which I should never have considered as the objects of a wish, had not his unseasonable representations placed them in my sight.

Another of his topicks is the neglect of merit, with which he never fails to amuse every man whom he sees not eminently fortunate. If he meets with a young officer, he always informs him of gentlemen whose personal courage is unquestioned, and whose military skill qualifies them to command armies, that have, notwithstanding all their merit, grown old with subaltern commissions. For a genius in the church, he is always provided with a curacy for life. The lawyer he informs of many men of great parts and deep study, who have never had an opportunity to speak in the courts: And meeting Serenus the physician, "Ah doctor," says he, "what a-foot still, when so many blockheads are rattling their chariots? I told you seven years ago that you would never meet with encouragement, and I hope you will now take more notice, when I tell you, that your Greek, and your diligence, and your honesty, will never enable you to live like yonder apothecary, who prescribes to his own shop, and laughs at the physician."

Suspirius has, in his time, intercepted fifteen authors in their way to the stage; persuaded nine and thirty merchants to retire from a prosperous trade for fear of bankrupcy, broke off an hundred and thirteen matches by prognostications of unhappiness, and enabled the small-pox to kill nineteen ladies, by perpetual alarms of the loss of beauty.

Whenever my evil stars bring us together, he never fails to represent to me the folly of my persuits, and informs me that we are much older than when we began our acquaintance, that the infirmities of decrepitude are coming fast upon me, that whatever I now get I shall enjoy but a little time, that fame is to a man tottering on the edge of the grave of very little importance, and that the time is at hand when I ought to look for no other pleasures than a good dinner and an easy chair.

Thus he goes on in his unharmonious strain, displaying present miseries, and foreboding more, νυκτικόραξ ᾄδει θανατηφόρον, [night-raven always death-bringing] every syllable is loaded with misfortune, and death is always brought nearer to the view.[33] Yet, what always raises my resentment and indignation, I do not perceive that his mournful meditations have much effect upon himself. He talks, and has long talked of calamities, without discovering, otherwise than by the tone of his voice, that he feels any of the evils which he bewails or threatens, but has the same habit of uttering lamentations, as others of telling stories, and falls into expressions of condolence for past, or apprehension of future mischiefs, as all men studious of their ease have recourse to those subjects upon which they can most fluently or copiously discourse.

It is reported of the Sybarites, that they destroyed all their cocks, that they might dream out their morning dreams without disturbance. Though I would not so far promote effeminacy as to propose the Sybarites for an example, yet since there is no man so corrupt or foolish, but something useful may be learned from him, I could wish that, in imitation of a people not often to be copied, some regulations might be made to exclude screech-owls from all company, as the enemies of mankind, and confine them to some proper receptacle, where they may mingle sighs at leisure, and thicken the gloom of one another.

"Thou prophet of evil," says Homer's Agamemnon, "thou never foretellest me good, but the joy of thy heart is to predict misfortunes." Whoever is of the same temper might there find the means of indulging his thoughts, and improving his vein of denunciation, and the flock of screech-owls might hoot together without injury to the rest of the world.

Yet, though I have so little kindness for this dark generation, I am very far from intending to debar the soft and

[33] Quotation from *The Greek Anthology*, XI, 186.

tender mind from the privilege of complaining, when the sigh rises from the desire not of giving pain, but of gaining ease. To hear complaints with patience, even when complaints are vain, is one of the duties of friendship; and though it must be allowed that he suffers most like a hero that hides his grief in silence,

> *Spem vultu simulat, premit altum corde dolorem,*
> *Aeneid,* 1.209.

His outward smiles conceal'd his inward smart.

> Dryden.

yet, it cannot be denied that he who complains acts like a man, like a social being who looks for help from his fellow-creatures. Pity is to many of the unhappy a source of comfort in hopeless distresses, as it contributes to recommend them to themselves, by proving that they have not lost the regard of others; and heaven seems to indicate the duty even of barren compassion, by inclining us to weep for evils which we cannot remedy.

No. 60. Saturday, 13 October 1750.

[Biography]

All joy or sorrow for the happiness or calamities of others is produced by an act of the imagination, that realises the event however fictitious, or approximates it however remote, by placing us, for a time, in the condition of him whose fortune we contemplate; so that we feel, while the deception lasts, whatever motions would be excited by the same good or evil happening to ourselves.

Our passions are therefore more strongly moved, in proportion as we can more readily adopt the pains or pleasures proposed to our minds, by recognising them as once our own, or considering them as naturally incident to our state of life. It is not easy for the most artful writer to give us an interest in happiness or misery, which we think ourselves never likely to feel, and with which we have never yet been made acquainted. Histories of the downfal of kingdoms, and revolutions of empires, are read with great tranquillity; the imperial tragedy pleases common auditors only by its pomp of ornament, and grandeur of ideas; and the man whose faculties have been engrossed by business, and whose heart never fluttered but at the rise or fall of stocks, wonders how the attention can be seized, or the affections agitated by a tale of love.

Those parallel circumstances, and kindred images, to which we readily conform our minds, are, above all other writings, to be found in narratives of the lives of particular persons; and therefore no species of writing seems more worthy of cultivation than biography, since none can be more delightful or more useful, none can more certainly enchain the heart by irresistible interest, or more widely diffuse instruction to every diversity of condition.

The general and rapid narratives of history, which involve a thousand fortunes in the business of a day, and complicate innumerable incidents in one great transaction, afford few lessons applicable to private life, which derives its comforts and its wretchedness from the right or wrong management of things which nothing but their frequency makes considerable, *Parva, si non fiant quotidie* ["Small things, if they did not occur every day"], says Pliny,[34] and which can have no place in those relations which never descend below the consultation of senates, the motions of armies, and the schemes of conspirators.

I have often thought that there has rarely passed a life of which a judicious and faithful narrative would not be useful. For, not only every man has, in the mighty mass of the world, great numbers in the same condition with himself, to whom his mistakes and miscarriages, escapes and expedients, would be of immediate and apparent use; but there is such an uniformity in the state of man, considered apart from adventitious and separable decorations and disguises, that there is scarce any possibility of good or ill, but is common to human kind. A great part of the time of those who are placed at the

---

[34] *Epistles*, III, 1.

greatest distance by fortune, or by temper, must unavoidably pass in the same manner; and though, when the claims of nature are satisfied, caprice, and vanity, and accident, begin to produce discriminations and peculiarities, yet the eye is not very heedful, or quick, which cannot discover the same causes still terminating their influence in the same effects, though sometimes accelerated, sometimes retarded, or perplexed by multiplied combinations. We are all prompted by the same motives, all deceived by the same fallacies, all animated by hope, obstructed by danger, entangled by desire, and seduced by pleasure.

It is frequently objected to relations of particular lives, that they are not distinguished by any striking or wonderful vicissitudes. The scholar who passed his life among his books, the merchant who conducted only his own affairs, the priest, whose sphere of action was not extended beyond that of his duty, are considered as no proper objects of publick regard, however they might have excelled in their several stations, whatever might have been their learning, integrity, and piety. But this notion arises from false measures of excellence and dignity, and must be eradicated by considering, that, in the esteem of uncorrupted reason, what is of most use is of most value.

It is, indeed, not improper to take honest advantages of prejudice, and to gain attention by a celebrated name; but the business of the biographer is often to pass slightly over those performances and incidents, which produce vulgar greatness, to lead the thoughts into domestick privacies, and display the minute details of daily life, where exterior appendages are cast aside, and men excel each other only by prudence and by virtue. The account of Thuanus[35] is, with great propriety, said by its author to have been written, that it might lay open to posterity the private and familiar character of that man, *cujus ingenium et candorem ex ipsius scriptis sunt olim semper miraturi*, whose candour[36] and genius will to the end of time be by his writings preserved in admiration.

---

[35] Nicolas Rigault's account of the French historian Jacques-Auguste de Thou.
[36] *candour*: kindness.

There are many invisible circumstances which, whether we read as enquirers after natural or moral knowledge, whether we intend to enlarge our science,[37] or increase our virtue, are more important than publick occurrences. Thus Sallust, the great master of nature, has not forgot, in his account of Catiline, to remark that "his walk was now quick, and again slow," as an indication of a mind revolving something with violent commotion.[38] Thus the story of Melanchthon affords a striking lecture on the value of time, by informing us, that when he made an appointment, he expected not only the hour, but the minute to be fixed, that the day might not run out in the idleness of suspense; and all the plans and enterprizes of De Wit are now of less importance to the world, than that part of his personal character which represents him as "careful of his health, and negligent of his life."[39]

But biography has often been allotted to writers who seem very little acquainted with the nature of their task, or very negligent about the performance. They rarely afford any other account than might be collected from publick papers, but imagine themselves writing a life when they exhibit a chronological series of actions or preferments; and so little regard the manners or behaviour of their heroes, that more knowledge may be gained of a man's real character, by a short conversation with one of his servants, than from a formal and studied narrative, begun with his pedigree, and ended with his funeral.

If now and then they condescend to inform the world of particular facts, they are not always so happy as to select the most important. I know not well what advantage posterity can receive from the only circumstance by which Tickell has distinguished Addison from the rest of mankind, "the irregularity of his pulse"[40]: nor can I think myself overpaid for the time spent in reading the life of Malherb, by being enabled to relate, after the learned biographer, that Malherb

---

[37] *science:* knowledge.
[38] Catiline conspired against the Roman Republic (63 B.C.); Sallust (86 B.C.–c. 34 B.C.) was a Roman historian.
[39] Philip Melanchthon was a noted theologian of the Reformation; Jan de Witt, a Dutch statesman, was murdered by a mob (1672).
[40] In Thomas Tickell's Preface to Joseph Addison's *Works* (1721); Tickell, Addison's friend, must have known more significant details.

had two predominant opinions; one, that the looseness of a single woman might destroy all the boast of ancient descent; the other, that the French beggars made use very improperly and barbarously of the phrase "noble Gentleman," because either word included the sense of both.[41]

There are, indeed, some natural reasons why these narratives are often written by such as were not likely to give much instruction or delight, and why most accounts of particular persons are barren and useless. If a life be delayed till interest and envy are at an end, we may hope for impartiality, but must expect little intelligence; for the incidents which give excellence to biography are of a volatile and evanescent kind, such as soon escape the memory, and are rarely transmitted by tradition. We know how few can portray a living acquaintance, except by his most prominent and observable particularities, and the grosser features of his mind; and it may be easily imagined how much of this little knowledge may be lost in imparting it, and how soon a succession of copies will lose all resemblance of the original.

If the biographer writes from personal knowledge, and makes haste to gratify the publick curiosity, there is danger lest his interest, his fear, his gratitude, or his tenderness, overpower his fidelity, and tempt him to conceal, if not to invent. There are many who think it an act of piety to hide the faults or failings of their friends, even when they can no longer suffer by their detection; we therefore see whole ranks of characters adorned with uniform panegyrick, and not to be known from one another, but by extrinsick and casual circumstances. "Let me remember," says Hale, "when I find myself inclined to pity a criminal, that there is likewise a pity due to the country."[42] If we owe regard to the memory of the dead, there is yet more respect to be paid to knowledge, to virtue, and to truth.

[41] From the *Memoirs* of François de Malherbe, by his friend the Marquis de Racan.
[42] Lord Chief Justice Sir Matthew Hale, from Gilbert Burnet's biography of him (1682).

No. 79. Tuesday, 18 December 1750.

[Suspicion]

Suspicion, however necessary it may be to our safe passage through ways beset on all sides by fraud and malice, has been always considered, when it exceeds the common measures, as a token of depravity and corruption; and a Greek writer of sentences[43] has laid down as a standing maxim, that "he who believes not another on his oath, knows himself to be perjured."

We can form our opinions of that which we know not, only by placing it in comparison with something that we know: whoever therefore is over-run with suspicion, and detects artifice and stratagem in every proposal, must either have learned by experience or observation the wickedness of mankind, and been taught to avoid fraud by having often suffered or seen treachery, or he must derive his judgment from the consciousness of his own disposition, and impute to others the same inclinations which he feels predominant in himself.

To learn caution by turning our eyes upon life, and observing the arts by which negligence is surprised, timidity overborne, and credulity amused, requires either great latitude of converse and long acquaintance with business, or uncommon activity of vigilance, and acuteness of penetration. When therefore a young man, not distinguished by vigour of intellect, comes into the world full of scruples and diffidence; makes a bargain with many provisional limitations; hesitates in his answer to a common question, lest more should be intended than he can immediately discover; has a long reach in detecting the projects of his acquaintance; considers every caress as an act of hypocrisy, and feels neither gratitude nor affection from the tenderness of his friends, because he believes no one to have any real tenderness but for himself; whatever expectations this early sagacity may raise of his future eminence or riches, I can seldom forbear to consider him as a wretch incapable of generosity or benevolence, as a villain early completed beyond the need of common opportunities and gradual temptations.

[43] *sentences:* aphorisms.

Upon men of this class instruction and admonition are generally thrown away, because they consider artifice and deceit as proofs of understanding; they are misled at the same time by the two great seducers of the world, vanity and interest, and not only look upon those who act with openness and confidence, as condemned by their principles to obscurity and want, but as contemptible for narrowness of comprehension, shortness of views, and slowness of contrivance.

The world has been long amused with the mention of policy in publick transactions, and of art in private affairs; they have been considered as the effects of great qualities, and as unattainable by men of the common level: yet I have not found many performances either of art, or policy, that required such stupendous efforts of intellect, or might not have been effected by falshood and impudence, without the assistance of any other powers. To profess what he does not mean, to promise what he cannot perform, to flatter ambition with prospects of promotion, and misery with hopes of relief, to sooth pride with appearances of submission, and appease enmity by blandishments and bribes, can surely imply nothing more or greater than a mind devoted wholly to its own purposes, a face that cannot blush, and a heart that cannot feel.

These practices are so mean and base, that he who finds in himself no tendency to use them, cannot easily believe that they are considered by others with less detestation; he therefore suffers himself to slumber in false security, and becomes a prey to those who applaud their own subtilty, because they know how to steal upon his sleep, and exult in the success which they could never have obtained, had they not attempted a man better than themselves, who was hindered from obviating their stratagems, not by folly, but by innocence.

Suspicion is, indeed, a temper so uneasy and restless, that it is very justly appointed the concomitant of guilt. It is said, that no torture is equal to the inhibition of sleep long continued; a pain, to which the state of that man bears a very exact analogy, who dares never give rest to his vigilance and circumspection, but considers himself as surrounded by secret foes, and fears to entrust his children, or his friend, with the secret that throbs in his breast, and the anxieties that break into his face. To avoid, at this expence, those evils to which easiness and friendship might have exposed him, is surely to buy safety at too dear a rate, and, in the language of the Roman satirist, to save life by losing all for which a wise man would live.[44]

When in the diet of the German empire, as Camerarius relates, the princes were once displaying their felicity, and each boasting the advantages of his own dominions, one who possessed a country not remarkable for the grandeur of its cities, or the fertility of its soil, rose to speak, and the rest listened between pity and contempt, till he declared, in honour of his territories, that he could travel through them without a guard, and if he was weary, sleep in safety upon the lap of the first man whom he should meet; a commendation which would have been ill exchanged for the boast of palaces, pastures, or streams.

Suspicion is not less an enemy to virtue than to happiness: he that is already corrupt is naturally suspicious, and he that becomes suspicious will quickly be corrupt. It is too common for us to learn the frauds by which ourselves have suffered; men who are once persuaded that deceit will be employed against them, sometimes think the same arts justified by the necessity of defence. Even they whose virtue is too well established to give way to example, or be shaken by sophistry, must yet feel their love of mankind diminished with their esteem, and grow less zealous for the happiness of those by whom they imagine their own happiness endangered.

Thus we find old age, upon which suspicion has been strongly impressed by long intercourse with the world, inflexible and severe, not easily softened by submission, melted by complaint, or subdued by supplication. Frequent experience of counterfeited miseries, and dissembled virtue, in time overcomes that disposition to tenderness and sympathy, which is so powerful in our younger years, and they that happen to petition the old for compassion or assistance, are doomed to languish without regard, and suffer for the crimes of men who have formerly been found undeserving or ungrateful.

Historians are certainly chargeable with the depravation of mankind, when they relate without censure those stratagems of war by which the virtues of an enemy are engaged to his destruction. A ship comes before a port, weather-beaten and shattered, and the crew implore the liberty of repairing their

[44] Juvenal, Satire VIII, l. 84.

breaches, supplying themselves with necessaries, or burying their dead. The humanity of the inhabitants inclines them to consent, the strangers enter the town with weapons concealed, fall suddenly upon their benefactors, destroy those that make resistance, and become masters of the place; they return home rich with plunder, and their success is recorded to encourage imitation.

But surely war has its laws, and ought to be conducted with some regard to the universal interest of man. Those may justly be pursued as enemies to the community of nature, who suffer hostility to vacate the unalterable laws of right, and pursue their private advantage by means, which, if once established, must destroy kindness, cut off from every man all hopes of assistance from another, and fill the world with perpetual suspicion and implacable malevolence. Whatever is thus gained ought to be restored, and those who have conquered by such treachery may be justly denied the protection of their native country.

Whoever commits a fraud is guilty not only of the particular injury to him whom he deceives, but of the diminution of that confidence which constitutes not only the ease but the existence of society. He that suffers by imposture has too often his virtue more impaired than his fortune. But as it is necessary not to invite robbery by supineness, so it is our duty not to suppress tenderness by suspicion; it is better to suffer wrong than to do it, and happier to be sometimes cheated than not to trust.

No. 130. Saturday, 15 June 1751.

[History of a Beauty]

TO THE RAMBLER.

SIR,

You have very lately observed that in the numerous subdivisions of the world, every class and order of mankind have joys and sorrows of their own; we all feel hourly pain and pleasure from events which pass unheeded before other eyes, but can scarcely communicate our perceptions to minds preoccupied by different objects, any more than the delight of well disposed colours or harmonious sounds can be imparted to such as want the senses of hearing or of sight.

I am so strongly convinced of the justness of this remark, and have on so many occasions discovered with how little attention pride looks upon calamity of which she thinks herself not in danger, and indolence listens to complaint when it is not echoed by her own remembrance, that though I am about to lay the occurrences of my life before you, I question whether you will condescend to peruse my narrative, or without the help of some female speculatist be able to understand it.

I was born a beauty. From the dawn of reason I had my regard turned wholly upon myself, nor can recollect any thing earlier than praise and admiration. My mother, whose face had luckily advanced her to a condition above her birth, thought no evil so great as deformity. She had not the power of imagining any other defect than a cloudy complexion, or disproportionate features; and therefore contemplated me as an assemblage of all that could raise envy or desire, and predicted with triumphant fondness the extent of my conquests, and the number of my slaves.

She never mentioned any of my young acquaintance before me, but to remark how much they fell below my perfection; how one would have had a fine face but that her eyes were without lustre; how another struck the sight at a distance, but wanted my hair and teeth at a nearer view; another disgraced an elegant shape with a brown skin; some had short fingers, and others had dimples in a wrong place.

As she expected no happiness nor advantage but from beauty, she thought nothing but beauty worthy of her care; and her maternal kindness was chiefly exercised in contrivances to protect me from any accident that might deface me with a scar, or stain me with a freckle: she never thought me sufficiently shaded from the sun, or screened from the fire. She was severe or indulgent with no other intention than the preservation of my form; she excused me from work, lest I should learn to hang down my head, or harden my finger with a needle; she snatched away my book, because a young lady in the neighbourhood had made her eyes red with reading by a candle; but she would scarcely suffer me to eat, lest I should spoil my shape, nor to walk lest I should swell my ancle with a sprain. At night I was accurately surveyed from head to foot, lest I should have suffered any diminution of my charms in the adventures of the day; and was never permitted to sleep, till I had passed through the cosmetick discipline, part of which was a regular lustration performed with bean-flower water and may-dews; my hair was perfumed with variety of unguents, by some of which it was to be thickened, and by others to be curled. The softness of my hands was secured by medicated gloves, and my bosom rubbed with a pomade prepared by my mother, of virtue to discuss[45] pimples, and clear discolorations.

I was always called up early, because the morning air gives a freshness to the cheeks; but I was placed behind a curtain in my mother's chamber, because the neck is easily tanned by the rising sun. I was then dressed with a thousand precautions, and again heard my own praises, and triumphed in the compliments and prognostications of all that approached me.

My mother was not so much prepossessed with an opinion of my natural excellencies as not to think some cultivation necessary to their completion. She took care that I should want none of the accomplishments included in female education, or considered as necessary in fashionable life. I was looked upon in my ninth year as the chief ornament of the dancing-master's ball, and Mr. Ariet used to reproach his other scholars with my performances on the harpsichord. At twelve I was remarkable for playing my cards with great elegance of manner, and accuracy of judgment.

At last the time came when my mother thought me perfect in my exercises, and qualified to display in the open world those accomplishments which had yet only been discovered in select parties, or domestic assemblies. Preparations were therefore made for my appearance on a publick night, which she considered as the most important and critical moment of my life. She cannot be charged with neglecting any means of recommendation, or leaving any thing to chance which prudence could ascertain. Every ornament was tried in every position, every friend was consulted about the colour of my dress, and the manteaumakers[46] were harrassed with directions and alterations.

---

[45] *discuss:* drive away.
[46] *manteaumakers:* dressmakers.

At last the night arrived from which my future life was to be reckoned. I was dressed and sent out to conquer, with a heart beating like that of an old knight-errant at his first sally. Scholars have told me of a Spartan matron, who, when she armed her son for battle, bade him bring back his shield or be brought upon it.[47] My venerable parent dismissed me to a field, in her opinion of equal glory, with a command to show that I was her daughter, and not to return without a lover.

I went, and was received like other pleasing novelties with a tumult of applause. Every man who valued himself upon the graces of his person, or the elegance of his address, crouded about me, and wit and splendor contended for my notice. I was delightfully fatigued with incessant civilities, which were made more pleasing by the apparent envy of those whom my presence exposed to neglect, and returned with an attendant equal in rank and wealth to my utmost wishes, and from this time stood in the first rank of beauty, was followed by gazers in the mall,[48] celebrated in the papers of the day, imitated by all who endeavoured to rise into fashion, and censured by those whom age or disappointment forced to retire.

My mother, who pleased herself with the hopes of seeing my exaltation, dressed me with all the exuberance of finery; and when I represented to her that a fortune might be expected proportionate to my appearance, told me that she should scorn the reptile who could enquire after the fortune of a girl like me. She advised me to prosecute my victories, and time would certainly bring me a captive who might deserve the honour of being enchained for ever.

My lovers were indeed so numerous, that I had no other care than that of determining to whom I should seem to give the preference. But having been steadily and industriously instructed to preserve my heart from any impressions which might hinder me from consulting my interest, I acted with less embarrassment, because my choice was regulated by principles more clear and certain than the caprice of approbation. When I had singled out one from the rest as more worthy of encouragement, I proceeded in my measures by the

---

[47] I.e., he was to come back victorious (with his shield) or dead (upon it).
[48] *the Mall:* a fashionable promenade in St. James's Park, London.

rules of art; and yet when the ardour of the first visits was spent, generally found a sudden declension of my influence; I felt in myself the want of some power to diversify amusement, and enliven conversation, and could not but suspect that my mind failed in performing the promises of my face. This opinion was soon confirmed by one of my lovers, who married Lavinia with less beauty and fortune than mine, because he thought a wife ought to have qualities which might make her amiable when her bloom was past.

The vanity of my mother would not suffer her to discover any defect in one that had been formed by her instructions, and had all the excellence which she herself could boast. She told me that nothing so much hindered the advancement of women as literature and wit, which generally frightened away those that could make the best settlements, and drew about them a needy tribe of poets and philosophers, that filled their heads with wild notions of content, and contemplation, and virtuous obscurity. She therefore enjoined me to improve my minuet step with a new French dancing-master, and wait the event of the next birth-night.[49]

I had now almost completed my nineteenth year: if my charms had lost any of their softness, it was more than compensated by additional dignity; and if the attractions of innocence were impaired, their place was supplied by the arts of allurement. I was therefore preparing for a new attack, without any abatement of my confidence, when in the midst of my hopes and schemes, I was seized by that dreadful malady which has so often put a sudden end to the tyranny of beauty.[50] I recovered my health after a long confinement; but when I looked again on that face which had been often flushed with transport at its own reflexion, and saw all that I had learned to value, all that I had endeavoured to improve, all that had procured me honours or praises, irrecoverably destroyed, I sunk at once into melancholy and despondence. My pain was not much consoled or alleviated by my mother, who grieved that I had not lost my life together with my beauty, and declared, that she thought a young woman divested of her charms had nothing for which those who loved her could desire to save her from the grave.

[49] Fashionable people dressed with particular splendor for the court festival held on the evening of a royal birthday.
[50] I.e., smallpox.

Having thus continued my relation to the period from which my life took a new course, I shall conclude it in another letter, if by publishing this you show any regard for the correspondence of,

Sir, &c.
VICTORIA.

No. 144. Saturday, 3 August 1751.

[Methods of Detraction]

It is impossible to mingle in conversation without observing the difficulty with which a new name makes its way into the world. The first appearance of excellence unites multitudes against it; unexpected opposition rises up on every side; the celebrated and the obscure join in the confederacy; subtilty furnishes arms to impudence, and invention leads on credulity.

The strength and unanimity of this alliance is not easily conceived. It might be expected that no man should suffer his heart to be inflamed with malice, but by injuries; that none should busy himself in contesting the pretensions of another, but when some right of his own was involved in the question; that at least hostilities commenced without cause, should quickly cease; that the armies of malignity should soon disperse, when no common interest could be found to hold them together; and that the attack upon a rising character should be left to those who had something to hope or fear from the event.

The hazards of those that aspire to eminence would be much diminished if they had none but acknowledged rivals to encounter. Their enemies would then be few, and what is of yet greater importance, would be known. But what caution is sufficient to ward off the blows of invisible assailants, or what force can stand against unintermitted attacks, and a continual succession of enemies? Yet such is the state of the world, that no sooner can any man emerge from the crowd, and fix the eyes of the publick upon him, than he stands as a mark to the arrows of lurking calumny, and receives, in the tumult of hostility, from distant and from nameless hands, wounds not always easy to be cured.

It is probable that the onset against the candidates for renown, is originally incited by those who imagine themselves in danger of suffering by their success; but when war is once declared, volunteers flock to the standard, multitudes follow the camp only for want of employment, and flying squadrons are dispersed to every part, so pleased with an opportunity of mischief that they toil without prospect of praise, and pillage without hope of profit.

When any man has endeavoured to deserve distinction, he will be surprised to hear himself censured where he could not expect to have been named; he will find the utmost acrimony of malice among those whom he never could have offended.

As there are to be found in the service of envy men of every diversity of temper and degree of understanding, calumny is diffused by all arts and methods of propagation. Nothing is too gross or too refined, too cruel or too trifling to be practised; very little regard is had to the rules of honourable hostility, but every weapon is accounted lawful; and those that cannot make a thrust at life are content to keep themselves in play with petty malevolence, to teaze with feeble blows and impotent disturbance.

But as the industry of observation has divided the most miscellaneous and confused assemblages into proper classes, and ranged the insects of the summer, that torment us with their drones or stings, by their several tribes; the persecutors of merit, notwithstanding their numbers, may be likewise commodiously distinguished into Roarers, Whisperers, and Moderators.

The Roarer is an enemy rather terrible than dangerous. He has no other qualifications for a champion of controversy than a hardened front and strong voice. Having seldom so much desire to confute as to silence, he depends rather upon vociferation than argument, and has very little care to adjust one part of his accusation to another, to preserve decency[51] in his language, or probability in his narratives. He has always a store of reproachful epithets and contemptuous appellations, ready to be produced as occasion may require, which by constant use he pours out with resistless volubility. If the wealth of a trader is mentioned, he without hesitation devotes him to bankruptcy; if the beauty and elegance of a lady be com-

---

[51] *decency*: appropriateness.

mended, he wonders how the town can fall in love with rustic deformity; if a new performance of genius happens to be celebrated, he pronounces the writer a hopeless ideot, without knowledge of books or life, and without the understanding by which it must be acquired. His exaggerations are generally without effect upon those whom he compels to hear them; and though it will sometimes happen that the timorous are awed by his violence, and the credulous mistake his confidence for knowledge, yet the opinions which he endeavours to suppress soon recover their former strength, as the trees that bend to the tempest erect themselves again when its force is past.

The Whisperer is more dangerous. He easily gains attention by a soft address, and excites curiosity by an air of importance. As secrets are not to be made cheap by promiscuous publication, he calls a select audience about him, and gratifies their vanity with an appearance of trust by communicating his intelligence in a low voice. Of the trader he can tell that though he seems to manage an extensive commerce, and talks in high terms of the funds, yet his wealth is not equal to his reputation; he has lately suffered much by an expensive project, and had a greater share than is acknowledged in the rich ship that perished by the storm. Of the beauty he has little to say, but that they who see her in a morning do not discover all those graces which are admired in the park. Of the writer he affirms with great certainty, that though the excellence of the work be incontestable, he can claim but a small part of the reputation; that he owed most of the images and sentiments to a secret friend; and that the accuracy and equality of the stile was produced by the successive correction of the chief criticks of the age.

As every one is pleased with imagining that he knows something not yet commonly divulged, secret history easily gains credit; but it is for the most part believed only while it circulates in whispers, and when once it is openly told, is openly confuted.

The most pernicious enemy is the man of Moderation. Without interest in the question, or any motive but honest curiosity, this impartial and zealous enquirer after truth, is ready to hear either side, and always disposed to kind interpretations and favourable opinions. He has heard the trader's affairs reported with great variation, and after a diligent com-

parison of the evidence, concludes it probable that the splendid superstructure of business being originally built upon a
narrow basis, has lately been found to totter; but between
dilatory payment and bankruptcy there is a great distance;
many merchants have supported themselves by expedients for
a time, without any final injury to their creditors; and what
is lost by one adventure may be recovered by another. He believes that a young lady pleased with admiration, and desirous
to make perfect what is already excellent, may heighten her
charms by artificial improvements, but surely most of her
beauties must be genuine, and who can say that he is wholly
what he endeavours to appear? The author he knows to be a
man of diligence, who perhaps does not sparkle with the fire
of Homer, but has the judgment to discover his own deficiencies, and to supply them by the help of others; and in his
opinion modesty is a quality so amiable and rare, that it
ought to find a patron wherever it appears, and may justly be
preferred by the publick suffrage to petulant wit and ostentatious literature.

He who thus discovers failings with unwillingness, and ex-
tenuates the faults which cannot be denied, puts an end at
once to doubt or vindication; his hearers repose upon his
candour and veracity, and admit the charge without allowing
the excuse.

Such are the arts by which the envious, the idle, the peevish,
and the thoughtless, obstruct that worth which they cannot
equal, and by artifices thus easy, sordid, and detestable, is
industry defeated, beauty blasted, and genius depressed.

No. 148. Saturday, 17 August 1751.

[Parental Tyranny]

Politicians remark that no oppression is so heavy or lasting
as that which is inflicted by the perversion and exorbitance of
legal authority. The robber may be seized, and the invader
repelled whenever they are found; they who pretend no right
but that of force, may by force be punished or suppressed.
But when plunder bears the name of impost, and murder is

perpetrated by a judicial sentence, fortitude is intimidated and wisdom confounded; resistance shrinks from an alliance with rebellion, and the villain remains secure in the robes of the magistrate.

Equally dangerous and equally detestable are the cruelties often exercised in private families, under the venerable sanction of parental authority; the power which we are taught to honour from the first moments of reason; which is guarded from insult and violation by all that can impress awe upon the mind of man; and which therefore may wanton in cruelty without controul, and trample the bounds of right with innumerable transgressions, before duty and piety will dare to seek redress, or think themselves at liberty to recur to any other means of deliverance than supplications by which insolence is elated, and tears by which cruelty is gratified.

It was for a long time imagined by the Romans, that no son could be the murderer of his father, and they had therefore no punishment appropriated to parricide. They seem likewise to have believed with equal confidence that no father could be cruel to his child, and therefore they allowed every man the supreme judicature in his own house, and put the lives of his offspring into his hands. But experience informed them by degrees, that they had determined too hastily in favour of human nature; they found that instinct and habit were not able to contend with avarice or malice; that the nearest relation might be violated; and that power, to whomsoever entrusted, might be ill employed. They were therefore obliged to supply and to change their institutions; to deter the parricide by a new law, and to transfer capital punishments from the parent to the magistrate.

There are indeed many houses which it is impossible to enter familiarly, without discovering that parents are by no means exempt from the intoxications of dominion; and that he who is in no danger of hearing remonstrances but from his own conscience, will seldom be long without the art of controlling his convictions, and modifying justice by his own will.

If in any situation the heart were inaccessible to malignity, it might be supposed to be sufficiently secured by parental relation. To have voluntarily become to any being the occasion of its existence, produces an obligation to make that existence happy. To see helpless infancy stretching out her hands and pouring out her cries in testimony of dependance, without any powers to alarm jealousy, or any guilt to alienate affection, must surely awaken tenderness in every human mind; and tenderness once excited will be hourly encreased by the natural contagion of felicity, by the repercussion of communicated pleasure, and the consciousness of the dignity of benefaction. I believe no generous or benevolent man can see the vilest animal courting his regard, and shrinking at his anger, playing his gambols of delight before him, calling on him in distress, and flying to him in danger, without more kindness than he can persuade himself to feel for the wild and unsocial inhabitants of the air and water. We naturally endear to ourselves those to whom we impart any kind of pleasure, because we imagine their affection and esteem secured to us by the benefits which they receive.

There is indeed another method by which the pride of superiority may be likewise gratified. He that has extinguished all the sensations of humanity, and has no longer any satisfaction in the reflection that he is loved as the distributor of happiness, may please himself with exciting terror as the inflicter of pain; he may delight his solitude with contemplating the extent of his power and the force of his commands, in imagining the desires that flutter on the tongue which is forbidden to utter them, or the discontent which preys on the heart in which fear confines it; he may amuse himself with new contrivances of detection, multiplications of prohibition, and varieties of punishment; and swell with exultation when he considers how little of the homage that he receives he owes to choice.

That princes of this character have been known, the history of all absolute kingdoms will inform us; and since, as Aristotle observes, ἡ οἰκονομικὴ μοναρχία, "the government of a family is naturally monarchical," it is like other monarchies too often arbitrarily administered. The regal and parental tyrant differ only in the extent of their dominions, and the number of their slaves. The same passions cause the same miseries; except that seldom any prince, however despotick, has so far shaken off all awe of the publick eye as to venture upon those freaks of injustice, which are sometimes indulged under the secrecy of a private dwelling. Capricious injunctions, partial decisions, unequal allotments, distributions of reward not by merit but by fancy, and punishments regulated not by the degree of the offence, but by the humour of the judge, are too frequent where no power is known but that of a father.

That he delights in the misery of others no man will confess, and yet what other motive can make a father cruel? The king may be instigated by one man to the destruction of another; he may sometimes think himself endangered by the virtues of a subject; he may dread the successful general or the popular orator; his avarice may point out golden confiscations; and his guilt may whisper that he can only be secure, by cutting off all power of revenge.

But what can a parent hope from the oppression of those who were born to his protection, of those who can disturb him with no competition, who can enrich him with no spoils? Why cowards are cruel may be easily discovered; but for what reason not more infamous than cowardice can that man delight in oppression who has nothing to fear?

The unjustifiable severity of a parent is loaded with this aggravation, that those whom he injures are always in his sight. The injustice of a prince is often exercised upon those of whom he never had any personal or particular knowledge; and the sentence which he pronounces, whether of banishment, imprisonment, or death, removes from his view the man whom he condemns. But the domestick oppressor dooms himself to gaze upon those faces which he clouds with terror and with sorrow; and beholds every moment the effects of his own barbarities. He that can bear to give continual pain to those who surround him, and can walk with satisfaction in the gloom of his own presence; he that can see submissive misery without relenting, and meet without emotion the eye that implores mercy, or demands justice, will scarcely be amended by remonstrance or admonition; he has found means of stopping the avenues of tenderness, and arming his heart against the force of reason.

Even though no consideration should be paid to the great law of social beings, by which every individual is commanded to consult the happiness of others, yet the harsh parent is less to be vindicated than any other criminal, because he less provides for the happiness of himself. Every man, however little he loves others, would willingly be loved; every man

hopes to live long, and therefore hopes for that time at which
he shall sink back to imbecillity,[52] and must depend for ease
and chearfulnes upon the officiousness[53] of others. But how
has he obviated the inconveniences of old age, who alienates
from him the assistance of his children, and whose bed must
be surrounded in his last hours, in the hours of languor and
dejection, of impatience and of pain, by strangers to whom
his life is indifferent, or by enemies to whom his death is
desirable?

Piety will indeed in good minds overcome provocation,
and those who have been harrassed by brutality will forget
the injuries which they have suffered so far as to perform the
last duties with alacrity and zeal. But surely no resentment
can be equally painful with kindness thus undeserved, nor can
severer punishment be imprecated upon a man not wholly
lost in meanness and stupidity, than through the tediousness
of decrepitude, to be reproached by the kindness of his own
children, to receive not the tribute but the alms of attendance,
and to owe every relief of his miseries not to gratitude but to
mercy.

No. 156. Saturday, 14 September 1751.

[Rules of Criticism]

Every government, say the politicians, is perpetually degenerating towards corruption, from which it must be rescued at
certain periods by the resuscitation of its first principles, and
the re-establishment of its original constitution. Every animal
body, according to the methodick physicians, is, by the predominance of some exuberant quality, continually declining
towards disease and death, which must be obviated by a seasonable reduction of the peccant humour to the just equipoise
which health requires.[54]

In the same manner the studies of mankind, all at least

---

[52] *imbecillity:* weakness.
[53] *officiousness:* ready helpfulness.
[54] According to traditional medicine, health depended upon a proper
balance of the four humors of the body.

which, not being subject to rigorous demonstration, admit the influence of fancy and caprice, are perpetually tending to error and confusion. Of the great principles of truth which the first speculatists discovered, the simplicity is embarrassed by ambitious additions, or the evidence obscured by inaccurate argumentation; and as they descend from one succession of writers to another, like light transmitted from room to room, they lose their strength and splendour, and fade at last in total evanescence.

The systems of learning therefore must be sometimes reviewed, complications analised into principles, and knowledge disentangled from opinion. It is not always possible, without a close inspection, to separate the genuine shoots of consequential reasoning, which grow out of some radical[55] postulate, from the branches which art has engrafted on it. The accidental prescriptions of authority, when time has procured them veneration, are often confounded with the laws of nature, and those rules are supposed coeval with reason, of which the first rise cannot be discovered.

Criticism has sometimes permitted fancy to dictate the laws by which fancy ought to be restrained, and fallacy to perplex the principles by which fallacy is to be detected; her superintendance of others has betrayed her to negligence of herself; and, like the ancient Scythians, by extending her conquests over distant regions, she has left her throne vacant to her slaves.

Among the laws of which the desire of extending authority, or ardour of promoting knowledge has prompted the prescription, all which writers have received, had not the same original right to our regard. Some are to be considered as fundamental and indispensable, others only as useful and convenient; some as dictated by reason and necessity, others as enacted by despotick antiquity; some as invincibly supported by their conformity to the order of nature and operations of the intellect; others as formed by accident, or instituted by example, and therefore always liable to dispute and alteration.

That many rules have been advanced without consulting nature or reason, we cannot but suspect, when we find it peremptorily decreed by the ancient masters, that "only three

[55] *radical:* fundamental.

speaking personages should appear at once upon the stage";[56] a law which, as the variety and intricacy of modern plays has made it impossible to be observed, we now violate without scruple, and, as experience proves, without inconvenience.

The original of this precept was merely accidental. Tragedy was a monody or solitary song in honour of Bacchus, improved afterwards into a dialogue by the addition of another speaker; but the ancients, remembering that the tragedy was at first pronounced only by one, durst not for some time venture beyond two; at last when custom and impunity had made them daring, they extended their liberty to the admission of three, but restrained themselves by a critical edict from further exorbitance.

By what accident the number of acts was limited to five, I know not that any author has informed us; but certainly it is not determined by any necessity arising either from the nature of action or propriety of exhibition. An act is only the representation of such a part of the business of the play as proceeds in an unbroken tenor, or without any intermediate pause. Nothing is more evident than that of every real, and by consequence of every dramatick action, the intervals may be more or fewer than five; and indeed the rule is upon the English stage every day broken in effect, without any other mischief than that which arises from an absurd endeavour to observe it in appearance. Whenever the scene is shifted the act ceases, since some time is necessarily supposed to elapse while the personages of the drama change their place.

With no greater right to our obedience have the criticks confined the dramatic action to a certain number of hours. Probability requires that the time of action should approach somewhat nearly to that of exhibition, and those plays will always be thought most happily conducted which croud the greatest variety into the least space. But since it will frequently happen that some delusion must be admitted, I know not where the limits of imagination can be fixed. It is rarely observed that minds not prepossessed by mechanical criticism feel any offence from the extension of the intervals between the acts; nor can I conceive it absurd or impossible, that he who can multiply three hours into twelve or twenty-four, might image with equal ease a greater number.

---

[56] Horace, *Art of Poetry*, l. 192; he also declared that a play must have no more and no less than five acts (l. 189).

I know not whether he that professes to regard no other laws than those of nature, will not be inclined to receive tragi-comedy to his protection, whom, however generally condemned, her own laurels have hitherto shaded from the fulminations of criticism. For what is there in the mingled drama which impartial reason can condemn? The connexion of important with trivial incidents, since it is not only common but perpetual in the world, may surely be allowed upon the stage, which pretends only to be the mirrour of life. The impropriety of suppressing passions before we have raised them to the intended agitation, and of diverting the expectation from an event which we keep suspended only to raise it, may be speciously urged. But will not experience show this objection to be rather subtle than just? is it not certain that the tragic and comic affections have been moved alternately with equal force, and that no plays have oftner filled the eye with tears, and the breast with palpitation, than those which are variegated with interludes of mirth?

I do not however think it safe to judge of works of genius merely by the event. These resistless vicissitudes[57] of the heart, this alternate prevalence of merriment and solemnity, may sometimes be more properly ascribed to the vigour of the writer than the justness of the design: and instead of vindicating tragi-comedy by the success of Shakespeare, we ought perhaps to pay new honours to that transcendent and unbounded genius that could preside over the passions in sport; who, to actuate the affections, needed not the slow gradation of common means, but could fill the heart with instantaneous jollity or sorrow, and vary our disposition as he changed his scenes. Perhaps the effects even of Shakespeare's poetry might have been yet greater, had he not counter-acted himself; and we might have been more interested in the distresses of his heroes had we not been so frequently diverted by the jokes of his buffoons.

There are other rules more fixed and obligatory. It is necessary that of every play the chief action should be single; for since a play represents some transaction, through its regular maturation to its final event, two actions equally important must evidently constitute two plays.

As the design of tragedy is to instruct by moving the passions, it must always have a hero, a personage apparently and

[57] *vicissitudes:* changes.

incontestably superior to the rest, upon whom the attention may be fixed, and the anxiety suspended. For though of two persons opposing each other with equal abilities and equal virtue, the auditor will inevitably in time choose his favourite, yet as that choice must be without any cogency of conviction, the hopes or fears which it raises will be faint and languid. Of two heroes acting in confederacy against a common enemy, the virtues or dangers will give little emotion, because each claims our concern with the same right, and the heart lies at rest between equal motives.

It ought to be the first endeavour of a writer to distinguish nature from custom, or that which is established because it is right, from that which is right only because it is established; that he may neither violate essential principles by a desire of novelty, nor debar himself from the attainment of beauties within his view by a needless fear of breaking rules which no literary dictator had authority to enact.

No. 168. Saturday, 26 October 1751.

[Appropriate Diction]

It has been observed by Boileau, that "a mean or common thought expressed in pompous diction, generally pleases more than a new or noble sentiment delivered in low and vulgar language; because the number is greater of those whom custom has enabled to judge of words, than whom study has qualified to examine things."

This solution might satisfy, if such only were offended with meanness of expression as are unable to distinguish propriety of thought, and to separate propositions or images from the vehicles by which they are conveyed to the understanding. But this kind of disgust is by no means confined to the ignorant or superficial; it operates uniformly and universally upon readers of all classes; every man, however profound or abstracted, perceives himself irresistibly alienated by low terms; they who profess the most zealous adherence to truth are forced to admit that she owes part of her charms to her ornaments, and loses much of her power over the soul, when she appears disgraced by a dress uncouth or ill-adjusted.

We are all offended by low terms, but are not disgusted alike by the same compositions, because we do not all agree to censure the same terms as low. No word is naturally or intrinsically meaner than another; our opinion therefore of words, as of other things arbitrarily and capriciously established, depends wholly upon accident and custom. The cottager thinks those apartments splendid and spacious, which an inhabitant of palaces will despise for their inelegance; and to him who has passed most of his hours with the delicate and polite, many expressions will seem sordid, which another, equally acute, may hear without offence; but a mean term never fails to displease him to whom it appears mean, as poverty is certainly and invariably despised, though he who is poor in the eyes of some, may by others be envied for his wealth.

Words become low by the occasions to which they are applied, or the general character of them who use them; and the disgust which they produce, arises from the revival of those images with which they are commonly united. Thus if, in the most solemn discourse, a phrase happens to occur which has been successfully employed in some ludicrous narrative, the gravest auditor finds it difficult to refrain from laughter, when they who are not prepossessed by the same accidental association, are utterly unable to guess the reason of his merriment. Words which convey ideas of dignity in one age, are banished from elegant writing or conversation in another, because they are in time debased by vulgar mouths, and can be no longer heard without the involuntary recollection of unpleasing images.

When Mackbeth is confirming himself in the horrid purpose of stabbing his king, he breaks out amidst his emotions into a wish natural to a murderer,

———— ———— Come, thick night!
And pall thee in the dunnest smoke of hell,
That my keen knife see not the wound it makes;
Nor heaven peep through the blanket of the dark,
To cry, hold, hold! ———— ————[58]

[58] *Macbeth*, I, v, 50–54. Actually, the speech is Lady Macbeth's. This is an example of the minor errors which resulted from Johnson's habitually quoting from memory.

In this passage is exerted all the force of poetry, that force which calls new powers into being, which embodies sentiment, and animates matter; yet perhaps scarce any man now peruses it without some disturbance of his attention from the counteraction of the words to the ideas. What can be more dreadful than to implore the presence of night, invested not in common obscurity, but in the smoke of hell? Yet the efficacy of this invocation is destroyed by the insertion of an epithet now seldom heard but in the stable, and *dun*[59] night may come or go without any other notice than contempt.

If we start into raptures when some hero of the Iliad tells us that δόρυ μάινεται, his lance rages with eagerness to destroy; if we are alarmed at the terror of the soldiers commanded by Caesar to hew down the sacred grove, who dreaded, says Lucan, lest the axe aimed at the oak should fly back upon the striker,

> —————— *Si robora sacra ferirent,*
> *In sua credebant redituras membra secures,*
>
> *Pharsalia*, III.430–31.

> None dares with impious steel the grove to rend,
> Lest on himself the destin'd stroke descend.

we cannot surely but sympathise with the horrors of a wretch about to murder his master, his friend, his benefactor, who suspects that the weapon will refuse its office,[60] and start back from the breast which he is preparing to violate. Yet this sentiment is weakened by the name of an instrument used by butchers and cooks in the meanest employments; we do not immediately conceive that any crime of importance is to be committed with a *knife*; or who does not, at last, from the long habit of connecting a knife with sordid offices, feel aversion rather than terror?

Mackbeth proceeds to wish, in the madness of guilt, that the inspection of heaven may be intercepted, and that he may in the involutions[61] of infernal darkness escape the eye of

---

[59] *dun*: dingy brown, or murky (Shakespeare's meaning); it could also mean a dun horse and was proverbially used as a quasi-proper name for any horse.
[60] *office*: function.
[61] *involutions*: wrappings.

providence. This is the utmost extravagance of determined wickedness; yet this is so debased by two unfortunate words, that while I endeavour to impress on my reader the energy of the sentiment, I can scarce check my risibility, when the expression forces itself upon my mind; for who, without some relaxation of his gravity, can hear of the avengers of guilt "peeping through a blanket"?

These imperfections of diction are less obvious to the reader, as he is less acquainted with common usages; they are therefore wholly imperceptible to a foreigner, who learns our language from books, and will strike a solitary academick less forcibly than a modish lady.

Among the numerous requisites that must concur to complete an author, few are of more importance than an early entrance into the living world. The seeds of knowledge may be planted in solitude, but must be cultivated in public. Argumentation may be taught in colleges, and theories formed in retirement, but the artifice of embellishment, and the powers of attraction, can be gained only by general converse.

An acquaintance with prevailing customs and fashionable elegance is necessary likewise for other purposes. The injury that grand imagery suffers from unsuitable language, personal merit may fear from rudeness and indelicacy. When the success of Æneas depended on the favour of the queen upon whose coasts he was driven, his celestial protectress thought him not sufficiently secured against rejection by his piety or bravery, but decorated him for the interview with preternatural beauty.[62] Whoever desires, for his writings or himself, what none can reasonably contemn, the favour of mankind, must add grace to strength, and make his thoughts agreeable as well as useful. Many complain of neglect who never tried to attract regard. It cannot be expected that the patrons of science or virtue should be solicitous to discover excellencies which they who possess them shade and disguise. Few have abilities so much needed by the rest of the world as to be caressed on their own terms; and he that will not condescend to recommend himself by external embellishments, must submit to the fate of just sentiments meanly expressed, and be ridiculed and forgotten before he is understood.

---

[62] Venus, the mother of Aeneas, enhanced his appearance so that Queen Dido would fall in love with and help him (*Aeneid*, I, ll. 586–93).

No. 188. Saturday, 4 January 1752.

[Social Success]

None of the desires dictated by vanity is more general, or less blameable, than that of being distinguished for the arts of conversation. Other accomplishments may be possessed without opportunity of exerting them, or wanted without danger that the defect can often be remarked; but as no man can live otherwise than in an hermitage, without hourly pleasure or vexation, from the fondness or neglect of those about him, the faculty of giving pleasure is of continual use. Few are more frequently envied than those who have the power of forcing attention wherever they come, whose entrance is considered as a promise of felicity, and whose departure is lamented, like the recess of the sun from northern climates, as a privation of all that enlivens fancy, or inspirits gaiety.

It is apparent, that to excellence in this valuable art, some peculiar qualifications are necessary; for every one's experience will inform him, that the pleasure which men are able to give in conversation, holds no stated proportion to their knowledge or their virtue. Many find their way to the tables and the parties of those who never consider them as of the least importance in any other place; we have all, at one time or other, been content to love those whom we could not esteem, and been persuaded to try the dangerous experiment of admitting him for a companion whom we knew to be too ignorant for a counsellor, and too treacherous for a friend.

I question whether some abatement of character is not necessary to general acceptance. Few spend their time with much satisfaction under the eye of uncontestable superiority; and therefore, among those whose presence is courted at assemblies of jollity, there are seldom found men eminently distinguished for powers or acquisitions. The wit whose vivacity condemns slower tongues to silence, the scholar whose knowledge allows no man to fancy that he instructs him, the critick who suffers no fallacy to pass undetected, and the reasoner who condemns the idle to thought, and the negligent to attention, are generally praised and feared, reverenced and avoided.

He that would please must rarely aim at such excellence as depresses his hearers in their own opinion, or debars them from the hope of contributing reciprocally to the entertainment of the company. Merriment, extorted by sallies of imagination, sprightliness of remark, or quickness of reply, is too often what the Latins call, the "Sardinian Laughter," a distortion of the face without gladness of heart.

For this reason, no stile of conversation is more extensively acceptable than the narrative. He who has stored his memory with slight anecdotes, private incidents, and personal particularities, seldom fails to find his audience favourable. Almost every man listens with eagerness to contemporary history; for almost every man has some real or imaginary connection with a celebrated character, some desire to advance, or oppose a rising name. Vanity often co-operates with curiosity. He that is a hearer in one place qualifies himself to become a speaker in another; for though he cannot comprehend a series of argument, or transport the volatile spirit of wit without evaporation, he yet thinks himself able to treasure up the various incidents of a story, and pleases his hopes with the information which he shall give to some inferior society.

Narratives are for the most part heard without envy, because they are not supposed to imply any intellectual qualities above the common rate. To be acquainted with facts not yet echoed by plebeian mouths, may happen to one man as well as to another, and to relate them when they are known, has in appearance so little difficulty, that every one concludes himself equal to the task.

But it is not easy, and in some situations of life not possible, to accumulate such a stock of materials as may support the expence of continual narration; and it frequently happens, that they who attempt this method of ingratiating themselves, please only at the first interview; and, for want of new supplies of intelligence, wear out their stories by continual repetition.

There would be, therefore, little hope of obtaining the praise of a good companion, were it not to be gained by more compendious methods; but such is the kindness of mankind to all, except those who aspire to real merit and rational dignity, that every understanding may find some way to excite benevolence; and whoever is not envied, may learn the art of procuring love. We are willing to be pleased, but are not willing to admire; we favour the mirth or officiousness that solicits our regard, but oppose the worth or spirit that enforces it.

The first place among those that please, because they desire only to please, is due to the "merry fellow," whose laugh is loud, and whose voice is strong; who is ready to echo every jest with obstreperous approbation, and countenance every frolick with vociferations of applause. It is not necessary to a merry fellow to have in himself any fund of jocularity, or force of conception; it is sufficient that he always appears in the highest exaltation of gladness, for the greater part of mankind are gay or serious by infection, and follow without resistance the attraction of example.

Next to the merry fellow is the "good-natured man," a being generally without benevolence, or any other virtue, than such as indolence and insensibility confer. The characteristick of a good-natured man is to bear a joke; to sit unmoved and unaffected amidst noise and turbulence, profaneness and obscenity; to hear every tale without contradiction; to endure insult without reply; and to follow the stream of folly, whatever course it shall happen to take. The good-natured man is commonly the darling of the petty wits, with whom they exercise themselves in the rudiments of raillery; for he never takes advantage of failings, nor disconcerts a puny satirist with unexpected sarcasms; but while the glass continues to circulate, contentedly bears the expence of uninterrupted laughter, and retires rejoicing at his own importance.

The "modest man" is a companion of a yet lower rank, whose only power of giving pleasure is not to interrupt it. The modest man satisfies himself with peaceful silence, which all his companions are candid[63] enough to consider as proceeding not from inability to speak, but willingness to hear.

Many, without being able to attain any general character of excellence, have some single art of entertainment which serves them as a passport through the world. One I have known for fifteen years the darling of a weekly club, because every night, precisely at eleven, he begins his favourite song, and during the vocal performance by correspondent motions of his hand, chalks out a giant upon the wall. Another has endeared himself to a long succession of acquaintances by

---

[63] *candid:* favorably disposed, willing to think the best.

sitting among them with his wig reversed; another by contriving to smut the nose of any stranger who was to be initiated in the club; another by purring like a cat, and then pretending to be frighted; and another by yelping like a hound, and calling to the drawers[64] to drive out the dog.

Such are the arts by which cheerfulness is promoted, and sometimes friendship established; arts, which those who despise them should not rigorously blame, except when they are practised at the expence of innocence; for it is always necessary to be loved, but not always necessary to be reverenced.

No. 200. Saturday, 15 February 1752.

[Prospero, the Nouveau-Riche]

TO THE RAMBLER.

MR. RAMBLER,

Such is the tenderness or infirmity of many minds, that when any affliction oppresses them, they have immediate recourse to lamentation and complaint, which, though it can only be allowed reasonable when evils admit of remedy, and then only when addressed to those from whom the remedy is expected, yet seems even in hopeless and incurable distresses to be natural, since those by whom it is not indulged, imagine that they give a proof of extraordinary fortitude by suppressing it.

I am one of those who, with the Sancho of Cervantes, leave to higher characters the merit of suffering in silence, and give vent without scruple to any sorrow that swells in my heart.[65] It is therefore to me a severe aggravation of a calamity, when it is such as in the common opinion will not justify the acerbity of exclamation, or support the solemnity of vocal grief. Yet many pains are incident to a man of delicacy, which the unfeeling world cannot be persuaded to pity, and which, when they are separated from their peculiar and personal circum-

---

[64] *drawers:* waiters in a tavern.
[65] *Don Quixote,* I, ch. 8.

stances, will never be considered as important enough to claim attention, or deserve redress.

Of this kind will appear to gross and vulgar apprehensions, the miseries which I endured in a morning visit to Prospero, a man lately raised to wealth by a lucky project, and too much intoxicated by sudden elevation, or too little polished by thought and conversation, to enjoy his present fortune with elegance and decency.[66]

We set out in the world together; and for a long time mutually assisted each other in our exigencies, as either happened to have money or influence beyond his immediate necessities. You know that nothing generally endears men so much as participation of dangers and misfortunes; I therefore always considered Prospero as united with me in the strongest league of kindness, and imagined that our friendship was only to be broken by the hand of death. I felt at his sudden shoot of success an honest and disinterested joy; but as I want no part of his superfluities, am not willing to descend from that equality in which we hitherto have lived.

Our intimacy was regarded by me as a dispensation from ceremonial visits; and it was so long before I saw him at his new house, that he gently complained of my neglect, and obliged me to come on a day appointed. I kept my promise, but found that the impatience of my friend arose not from any desire to communicate his happiness, but to enjoy his superiority.

When I told my name at the door, the footman went to see if his master was at home, and, by the tardiness of his return, gave me reason to suspect that time was taken to deliberate. He then informed me, that Prospero desired my company, and showed the staircase carefully secured by mats from the pollution of my feet. The best apartments[67] were ostentatiously set open, that I might have a distant view of the magnificence which I was not permitted to approach; and my old friend receiving me with all the insolence of condescension at the top of the stairs, conducted me to a back room, where he told me he always breakfasted when he had not great company.

---

[66] According to Boswell, Prospero was drawn from Johnson's friend the great actor David Garrick, who never entirely forgave the satire (*Life of Johnson*, Oxford Standard Authors, p. 155). Prospero is the great magician in Shakespeare's *Tempest*, and Asper means "harsh."
[67] *apartments:* rooms.

On the floor where we sat, lay a carpet covered with a cloth, of which Prospero ordered his servant to lift up a corner, that I might contemplate the brightness of the colours, and the elegance of the texture, and asked me whether I had ever seen any thing so fine before? I did not gratify his folly with any outcries of admiration, but coldly bad the footman let down the cloth.

We then sat down, and I began to hope that pride was glutted with persecution, when Prospero desired that I would give the servant leave to adjust the cover of my chair, which was slipt a little aside to show the damask; he informed me that he had bespoke ordinary chairs for common use, but had been disappointed by his tradesman. I put the chair aside with my foot, and drew another so hastily, that I was entreated not to rumple the carpet.

Breakfast was at last set, and as I was not willing to indulge the peevishness that began to seize me, I commended the tea; Prospero then told me, that another time I should taste his finest sort, but that he had only a very small quantity remaining, and reserved it for those whom he thought himself obliged to treat with particular respect.

While we were conversing upon such subjects as imagination happened to suggest, he frequently digressed into directions to the servant that waited, or made a slight[68] enquiry after the jeweller or silversmith; and once as I was pursuing an argument with some degree of earnestness, he started from his posture of attention, and ordered, that if Lord Lofty called on him that morning, he should be shewn into the best parlour.

My patience was not yet wholly subdued. I was willing to promote his satisfaction, and therefore observed, that the figures on the china were eminently pretty. Prospero had now an opportunity of calling for his Dresden china, which, says he, I always associate with my chased tea-kettle. The cups were brought; I once resolved not to have looked upon them, but my curiosity prevailed. When I had examined them a little, Prospero desired me to set them down, for they who were accustomed only to common dishes, seldom handled china with much care. You will, I hope, commend my philosophy, when I tell you that I did not dash his baubles to the ground.

---

[68] *slight:* trifling.

He was now so much elevated with his own greatness, that he thought some humility necessary to avert the glance of envy, and therefore told me with an air of soft composure, that I was not to estimate life by external appearance, that all these shining acquisitions had added little to his happiness, that he still remembered with pleasure the days in which he and I were upon the level, and had often, in the moment of reflection, been doubtful, whether he should lose much by changing his condition for mine.

I began now to be afraid lest his pride should, by silence and submission, be emboldened to insults that could not easily be borne, and, therefore, cooly considered, how I should repress it without such bitterness of reproof as I was yet unwilling to use. But he interrupted my meditation, by asking leave to be dressed, and told me, that he had promised to attend some ladies in the park, and, if I was going the same way, would take me in his chariot. I had no inclination to any other favours, and, therefore, left him without any intention of seeing him again, unless some misfortune should restore his understanding.

I am, &c.
ASPER.

Though I am not wholly insensible of the provocations which my correspondent has received, I cannot altogether commend the keenness of his resentment, nor encourage him to persist in his resolution of breaking off all commerce with his old acquaintance. One of the golden precepts of Pythagoras directs that "a friend should not be hated for little faults"; and surely, he, upon whom nothing worse can be charged, than that he mats his stairs, and covers his carpet, and sets out his finery to show before those whom he does not admit to use it, has yet committed nothing that should exclude him from common degrees of kindness. Such improprieties often proceed rather from stupidity than malice. Those who thus shine only to dazzle, are influenced merely by custom and example, and neither examine, nor are qualified to examine, the motives of their own practice, or to state the nice limits between elegance and ostentation. They are often innocent of the pain which their vanity produces, and insult others when they have no worse purpose than to please themselves.

He that too much refines his delicacy will always endanger his quiet. Of those with whom nature and virtue oblige us to converse, some are ignorant of the arts of pleasing, and offend when they design to caress; some are negligent, and gratify themselves without regard to the quiet of another; some perhaps, are malicious, and feel no greater satisfaction in prosperity, than that of raising envy and trampling inferiority. But whatever be the motive of insult, it is always best to overlook it, for folly scarcely can deserve resentment, and malice is punished by neglect.

Selections from *The Adventurer*

No. 84. Saturday, 25 August 1753.

[Journey in a Stagecoach]

TO THE ADVENTURER.

SIR,

It has been observed, I think, by Sir William Temple, and after him by almost every other writer, that England affords a greater variety of characters, than the rest of the world. This is ascribed to the liberty prevailing amongst us, which gives every man the privilege of being wise or foolish his own way, and preserves him from the necessity of hypocrisy, or the servility of imitation.

That the position itself is true, I am not completely satisfied. To be nearly acquainted with the people of different countries can happen to very few; and in life, as in every thing else beheld at a distance, there appears an even uniformity; the petty discriminations which diversify the natural character, are not discoverable but by a close inspection; we therefore find them most at home, because there we have most opportunities of remarking them. Much less am I convinced, that this particular diversification, if it be real, is the consequence of peculiar liberty: for where is the government to be found, that superintends individuals with so much vigilance, as not to leave their private conduct without restraint? Can it enter into a reasonable mind to imagine, that men of every other nation are not equally masters of their own time or houses with ourselves, and equally at liberty to be parsimonious or profuse, frolic or sullen, abstinent or luxurious? Liberty is certainly necessary to the full play of predominant humours; but such liberty is to be found alike under the government of the many or the few; in monarchies or in commonwealths.

How readily the predominant passion snatches an interval of liberty, and how fast it expands itself when the weight of restraint is taken away, I had lately an opportunity to discover, as I took a journey into the country in a stage coach; which, as every journey is a kind of adventure, may be very properly related to you, though I can display no such extraordinary assembly as Cervantes has collected at Don Quixote's inn.[1]

In a stage coach the passengers are for the most part wholly unknown to one another, and without expectation of ever meeting again when their journey is at an end; one should therefore imagine, that it was of little importance to any of them, what conjectures the rest should form concerning him. Yet so it is, that as all think themselves secure from detection, all assume that character of which they are most desirous, and on no occasion is the general ambition of superiority more apparently indulged.

On the day of our departure, in the twilight of the morning, I ascended the vehicle, with three men and two women my fellow travellers. It was easy to observe the affected elevation of mien with which every one entered, and the supercilious civility with which they paid their compliments to each other. When the first ceremony was dispatched, we sat silent for a long time, all employed in collecting importance into our faces, and endeavouring to strike reverence and submission into our companions.

It is always observable that silence propagates itself, and that the longer talk has been suspended, the more difficult it is to find any thing to say. We began now to wish for conversation; but no one seemed inclined to descend from his dignity, or first to propose a topic of discourse. At last a corpulent gentleman, who had equipped himself for this expedition with a scarlet surtout, and a large hat with a broad lace,[2] drew out his watch, looked on it in silence, and then held it dangling at his finger. This was, I suppose, understood by all the company as an invitation to ask the time of the day; but no body appeared to heed his overture: and his desire to be talking so far overcame his resentment, that he let us know of his own accord that it was past five, and that in two hours we should be at breakfast.

---

[1] *Don Quixote*, I, chs. 32–47.
[2] *surtout:* overcoat; *lace:* braid.

His condescension was thrown away; we continued all obdurate: the ladies held up their heads: I amused myself with watching their behaviour; and of the other two, one seemed to employ himself in counting the trees as we drove by them, the other drew his hat over his eyes, and counterfeited a slumber. The man of benevolence, to shew that he was not depressed by our neglect, hummed a tune and beat time upon his snuff-box.

Thus universally displeased with one another, and not much delighted with ourselves, we came at last to the little inn appointed for our repast, and all began at once to recompence themselves for the constraint of silence by innumerable questions and orders to the people that attended us. At last, what every one had called for was got, or declared impossible to be got at that time, and we were persuaded to sit round the same table; when the gentleman in the red surtout looked again upon his watch, told us that we had half an hour to spare, but he was sorry to see so little merriment among us; that all fellow travellers were for the time upon the level, and that it was always his way to make himself one of the company. "I remember," says he, "it was on just such a morning as this that I and my lord Mumble and the duke of Tenterden were out upon a ramble; we called at a little house as it might be this; and my landlady, I warrant you, not suspecting to whom she was talking, was so jocular and facetious, and made so many merry answers to our questions, that we were all ready to burst with laughter. At last the good woman happening to overhear me whisper the duke and call him by his title, was so surprised and confounded that we could scarcely get a word from her: and the duke never met me from that day to this, but he talks of the little house, and quarrels with me for terrifying the landlady."

He had scarcely had time to congratulate himself on the veneration which this narrative must have procured him from the company, when one of the ladies having reached out for a plate on a distant part of the table, began to remark "the inconveniences of travelling, and the difficulty which they who never sat at home without a great number of attendants found in performing for themselves such offices as the road required; but that people of quality often travelled in disguise, and might be generally known from the vulgar by their condescension to poor inn-keepers, and the allowance which they made for any defect in their entertainment: that for her part, while people were civil and meant well, it was never her custom to find fault; for one was not to expect upon a journey all that one enjoyed at one's own house."

A general emulation seemed now to be excited. One of the men, who had hitherto said nothing, called for the last news paper; and having perused it a while with deep pensiveness, "It is impossible," says he, "for any man to guess how to act with regard to the stocks; last week it was the general opinion that they would fall; and I sold out twenty thousand pounds in order to a purchase: they have now risen unexpectedly; and I make no doubt but at my return to London I shall risk thirty thousand pounds amongst them again."

A young man, who had hitherto distinguished himself only by the vivacity of his look, and a frequent diversion of his eyes from one object to another, upon this closed his snuff-box, and told us that "he had a hundred times talked with the chancellor and the judges on the subject of the stocks; that for his part he did not pretend to be well acquainted with the principles on which they were established, but had always heard them reckoned pernicious to trade, uncertain in their produce, and unsolid in their foundation; and that he had been advised by three judges, his most intimate friends, never to venture his money in the funds, but to put it out upon land security, till he could light upon an estate in his own country."

It might be expected that, upon these glimpses of latent dignity, we should all have began to look around us with veneration, and have behaved like the princes of romance, when the enchantment that disguises them is dissolved, and they discover the dignity of each other: yet it happened, that none of these hints made much impression on the company; every one was apparently suspected of endeavouring to impose false appearances upon the rest; all continued their haughtiness, in hopes to enforce their claims; and all grew every hour more sullen, because they found their representations of themselves without effect.

Thus we travelled on four days with malevolence perpetually increasing, and without any endeavour but to outvie each other in superciliousness and neglect; and when any two of us could separate ourselves for a moment, we vented our indignation at the sauciness of the rest.

At length the journey was at an end, and time and chance, that strip off all disguises, have discovered that the intimate of lords and dukes is a nobleman's butler, who has furnished a shop with the money he has saved; the man who deals so largely in the funds, is the clerk of a broker in Change-alley; the lady who so carefully concealed her quality, keeps a cook-shop behind the Exchange; and the young man who is so happy in the friendship of the judges, engrosses and tran-scribes for bread in a garret of the Temple.[3] Of one of the women only I could make no disadvantageous detection, be-cause she had assumed no character, but accommodated her-self to the scene before her, without any struggle for distinc-tion or superiority.

I could not forbear to reflect on the folly of practising a fraud, which, as the event shewed, had been already practised too often to succeed, and by the success of which no advantage could have been obtained; of assuming a character, which was to end with the day; and of claiming upon false pretences hon-ours which must perish with the breath that paid them.

But Mr. Adventurer, let not those who laugh at me and my companions, think this folly confined to a stage coach. Every man in the journey of life takes the same advantage of the ig-norance of his fellow travellers, disguises himself in counter-feited merit, and hears those praises with complacency which his conscience reproaches him for accepting. Every man de-ceives himself while he thinks he is deceiving others; and for-gets that the time is at hand when every illusion shall cease; when fictitious excellence shall be torn away; and All must be shown to All in their real state.

I am, Sir,

Your humble Servant,
VIATOR.

No. 128. Saturday, 26 January 1754.

[Smallness of Human Pursuits]

It is common among all the classes of mankind, to charge each other with trifling away life: every man looks on the oc-cupation or amusement of his neighbour, as something below the dignity of our nature, and unworthy of the attention of a rational being.

---

[3] *the Temple:* district in London occupied by lawyers.

A man who considers the paucity of the wants of nature, and who, being acquainted with the various means by which all manual occupations are now facilitated, observes what numbers are supported by the labour of a few, would, indeed, be inclined to wonder, how the multitudes who are exempted from the necessity of working either for themselves or others, find business to fill up the vacuities of life. The greater part of mankind neither card the fleece, dig the mine, fell the wood, nor gather in the harvest; they neither tend herds, nor build houses; in what then are they employed?

This is certainly a question, which a distant prospect of the world will not enable us to answer. We find all ranks and ages mingled together in a tumultuous confusion, with haste in their motions and eagerness in their looks; but what they have to persue or avoid, a more minute observation must inform us.

When we analize the croud into individuals, it soon appears that the passions and imaginations of men will not easily suffer them to be idle; we see things coveted merely because they are rare, and persued because they are fugitive; we see men conspire to fix an arbitrary value on that which is worthless in itself, and then contend for the possession. One is a collector of fossils,[4] of which he knows no other use than to shew them; and when he has stocked his own repository, grieves that the stones which he has left behind him should be picked up by another. The florist nurses a tulip, and repines that his rival's beds enjoy the same showers and sunshine with his own. This man is hurrying to a concert, only lest others should have heard the new musician before him; another bursts from his company to the play, because he fancies himself the patron of an actress: some spend the morning in consultations with their taylor, and some in directions to their cook; some are forming parties for cards, and some laying wagers at a horse race.

It cannot, I think, be denied, that some of these lives are passed in trifles, in occupations by which the busy neither benefit themselves nor others, and by which no man could be long engaged, who seriously considered what he was doing, or had knowledge enough to compare what he is with what he might be made. However, as people who have the same inclination generally flock together, every trifler is kept in countenance by the sight of others as unprofitably active as himself; by kindling the heat of competition, he in time thinks himself im-

---

[4] *fossils:* any minerals dug from the earth.

portant, and by having his mind intensely engaged he is secured from weariness of himself.

Some degree of self approbation is always the reward of diligence; and I cannot, therefore, but consider the laborious cultivation of petty pleasures, as a more happy and more virtuous disposition, than that universal contempt and haughty negligence, which is sometimes associated with powerful faculties, but is often assumed by indolence when it disowns its name, and aspires to the appellation of greatness of mind.

It has been long observed, that drollery and ridicule is the most easy kind of wit; let it be added, that contempt and arrogance is the easiest philosophy. To find some objection to every thing, and to dissolve in perpetual laziness under pretence that occasions are wanting to call forth activity, to laugh at those who are ridiculously busy without setting an example of more rational industry, is no less in the power of the meanest than of the highest intellects.

Our present state has placed us at once in such different relations, that every human employment, which is not a visible and immediate act of goodness, will be in some respect or other subject to contempt: but it is true, likewise, that almost every act, which is not directly vicious, is in some respect beneficial and laudable. "I often," says Bruyere, "observe from my window, two beings of erect form and amiable countenance, endowed with the powers of reason, able to clothe their thoughts in language, and convey their notions to each other. They rise early in the morning, and are every day employed till sun-set in rubbing two smooth stones together, or in other terms in polishing marble."[5]

"If lions could paint," says the fable, "in the room of those pictures which exhibit men vanquishing lions, we should see lions feeding upon men." If the stone cutter could have written like Bruyere, what would he have replied?

"I look up," says he, "every day from my shop, upon a man whom the idlers, who stand still to gaze upon my work, often celebrate as a wit and a philosopher. I often perceive his face clouded with care, and am told that his taper is sometimes burning at midnight. The sight of a man who works so much

[5] Loosely paraphrased from Jean de la Bruyère, *Characters*, XII.102. Actually, the context of this quotation makes the same point Johnson will do.

harder than myself, excited my curiosity. I heard no sound of tools in his apartment, and, therefore, could not imagine what he was doing; but was told at last, that he was writing descriptions of mankind, who when he had described them would live just as they had lived before; that he sate up whole nights to change a sentence, because the sound of a letter was too often repeated; that he was often disquieted with doubts, about the propriety of a word which every body understood; that he would hesitate between two expressions equally proper, till he could not fix his choice but by consulting his friends; that he will run from one end of Paris to the other, for an opportunity of reading a period to a nice[6] ear; that if a single line is heard with coldness and inattention, he returns home dejected and disconsolate; and that by all this care and labour, he hopes only to make a little book, which at last will teach no useful art, and which none who has it not will perceive himself to want. I have often wondered for what end such a being as this was sent into the world; and should be glad to see those, who live thus foolishly, seized by an order of the government, and obliged to labour at some useful occupation."

Thus, by a partial and imperfect representation, may every thing be made equally ridiculous. He that gazed with contempt on human beings rubbing stones together, might have prolonged the same amusement by walking through the city, and seeing others with looks of importance heaping one brick upon another; or by rambling into the country, where he might observe other creatures of the same kind driving a piece of sharp iron into the clay, or, in the language of men less enlightened, ploughing the field.

As it is thus easy by a detail of minute circumstances to make every thing little, so it is not difficult by an aggregation of effects to make every thing great. The polisher of marble may be forming ornaments for the palaces of virtue and the schools of science; or providing tables, on which the actions of heroes and the discoveries of sages shall be recorded, for the incitement and instruction of future generations. The mason is exercising one of the principal arts by which reasoning beings are distinguished from the brute, the art to which life owes much of its safety and all its convenience, by which we are secured from the inclemency of the seasons, and forti-

---

[6] *nice:* fastidious.

fied against the ravages of hostility; and the ploughman is changing the face of nature, diffusing plenty and happiness over kingdoms, and compelling the earth to give food to her inhabitants.

Greatness and littleness are terms merely comparative; and we err in our estimation of things, because we measure them by some wrong standard. The trifler proposes to himself only to equal or excel some other trifler, and is happy or miserable as he succeeds or miscarries: the man of sedentary desire and unactive ambition, sits comparing his power with his wishes; and makes his inability to perform things impossible, an excuse to himself for performing nothing. Man can only form a just estimate of his own actions, by making his power the test of his performance, by comparing what he does with what he can do. Whoever steadily perseveres in the exertion of all his faculties, does what is great with respect to himself; and what will not be despised by Him, who has given to all created beings their different abilities: he faithfully performs the task of life, within whatever limits his labours may be confined, or how soon soever they may be forgotten.

We can conceive so much more than we can accomplish, that whoever tries his own actions by his imagination, may appear despicable in his own eyes. He that despises for its littleness any thing really useful, has no pretensions to applaud the grandeur of his conceptions; since nothing but narrowness of mind hinders him from seeing, that by persuing the same principles every thing limited will appear contemptible.

He that neglects the care of his family, while his benevolence expands itself in scheming the happiness of imaginary kingdoms, might with equal reason sit on a throne dreaming of universal empire, and of the diffusion of blessings over all the globe: yet even this globe is little, compared with the system of matter within our view; and that system barely something more than non-entity, compared with the boundless regions of space, to which neither eye nor imagination can extend.

From conceptions, therefore, of what we might have been, and from wishes to be what we are not, conceptions that we know to be foolish, and wishes which we feel to be vain, we must necessarily descend to the consideration of what we are. We have powers very scanty in their utmost extent, but which in different men are differently proportioned. Suitably to these powers we have duties prescribed, which we must neither decline for the sake of delighting ourselves with easier amusements, nor overlook in idle contemplation of greater excellence or more extensive comprehension.

In order to the right conduct of our lives, we must always remember, that we are not born to please ourselves. He that studies simply his own satisfaction, will always find the proper business of his station too hard or too easy for him. But if we bear continually in mind, our relation to the Father of Being, by whom we are placed in the world, and who has allotted us the part which we are to bear in the general system of life, we shall be easily persuaded to resign our own inclinations to Unerring Wisdom, and do the work decreed for us with chearfulness and diligence.

Selections from *The Idler*

No. 16. Saturday, 29 July 1758.

[Drugget, the Retired Tradesman]

I paid a visit yesterday to my old friend Ned Drugget, at his country lodgings. Ned began trade with a very small fortune; he took a small house in an obscure street, and for some years dealt only in remnants. Knowing that "light gains make a heavy purse,"[1] he was content with moderate profit; having observed or heard the effects of civility, he bowed down to the counter edge at the entrance and departure of every customer, listened, without impatience, to the objections of the ignorant, and refused, without resentment, the offers of the penurious. His only recreation was to stand at his own door and look into the street. His dinner was sent him from a neighbouring alehouse, and he opened and shut the shop at a certain hour with his own hands.

His reputation soon extended from one end of the street to the other, and Mr. Drugget's exemplary conduct was recommended by every master to his apprentice, and by every father to his son. Ned was not only considered as a thriving trader, but as a man of elegance and politeness, for he was remarkably neat in his dress, and would wear his coat threadbare without spotting it; his hat was always brushed, his shoes glossy, his wig nicely curled, and his stockings without a wrinkle. With such qualifications it was not very difficult for him to gain the heart of Miss Comfit, the only daughter of Mr. Comfit the confectioner.

Ned is one of those whose happiness marriage has encreased. His wife had the same disposition with himself, and his method of life was very little changed, except that he dis-

[1] Francis Bacon, essay "Of Ceremonies and Respects."

missed the lodgers from the first floor and took the whole house into his own hands.

He had already, by his parsimony, accumulated a considerable sum, to which the fortune of his wife was now added. From this time he began to grasp at greater acquisitions, and was always ready, with money in his hand, to pick up the refuse of a sale, or to buy the stock of a trader who retired from business. He soon added his parlour to his shop, and was obliged, a few months afterwards, to hire a warehouse.

He had now a shop splendidly and copiously furnished with every thing that time had injured, or fashion had degraded, with fragments of tissues, odd yards of brocade, vast bales of faded silk, and innumerable boxes of antiquated ribbons. His shop was soon celebrated through all quarters of the town, and frequented by every form of ostentatious poverty. Every maid, whose misfortune it was to be taller than her lady, matched her gown at Mr. Drugget's; and many a maiden who had passed a winter with her aunt in London, dazzled the rusticks, at her return, with cheap finery which Drugget had supplied. His shop was often visited in a morning by ladies, who left their coaches in the next street, and crept through the alley in linnen gowns. Drugget knows the rank of his customers by their bashfulness, and when he finds them unwilling to be seen, invites them up stairs, or retires with them to the back window.

I rejoiced at the encreasing prosperity of my friend, and imagined that as he grew rich, he was growing happy. His mind has partaken the enlargement of his fortune. When I stepped in for the first five years, I was welcomed only with a shake of the hand; in the next period of his life, he beckoned across the way for a pot of beer; but, for six years past, he invites me to dinner; and, if he bespeaks me the day before, never fails to regale me with a fillet of veal.

His riches neither made him uncivil nor negligent: he rose at the same hour, attended with the same assiduity, and bowed with the same gentleness. But for some years he has been much inclined to talk of the fatigues of business, and the confinement of a shop, and to wish that he had been so happy as to have renewed his uncle's lease of a farm, that he might have lived without noise and hurry, in a pure air, in the artless society of honest villagers, and the contemplation of the works of nature.

I soon discovered the cause of my friend's philosophy. He

thought himself grown rich enough to have a lodging in the country, like the mercers on Ludgate-hill, and was resolved to enjoy himself in the decline of life. This was a revolution not to be made suddenly. He talked three years of the pleasures of the country, but passed every night over his own shop. But at last he resolved to be happy, and hired a lodging in the country, that he may steal some hours in the week from business; for, says he, "when a man advances in life he loves to entertain himself sometimes with his own thoughts."

I was invited to this seat of quiet and contemplation among those whom Mr. Drugget considers as his most reputable friends, and desires to make the first witnesses of his elevation to the highest dignities of a shopkeeper. I found him at Islington, in a room which overlooked the high road, amusing himself with looking through the window, which the clouds of dust would not suffer him to open. He embraced me, told me I was welcome into the country; and asked me, if I did not feel myself refreshed. He then desired that dinner might be hastened, for fresh air always sharpened his appetite, and ordered me a toast and a glass of wine after my walk. He told me much of the pleasure he found in retirement, and wondered what had kept him so long out of the country. After dinner company came in, and Mr. Drugget again repeated the praises of the country, recommended the pleasures of meditation, and told them, that he had been all the morning at the window, counting the carriages as they passed before him.

No. 17. Saturday, 5 August 1758.

[Experimentation on Animals]

The rainy weather which has continued the last month, is said to have given great disturbance to the inspectors of barometers. The oraculous glasses have deceived their votaries; shower has succeeded shower, though they predicted sunshine and dry skies; and by fatal confidence in these fallacious promises, many coats have lost their gloss, and many curls been moistened to flaccidity.

This is one of the distresses to which mortals subject themselves by the pride of speculation. I had no part in this learned disappointment, who am content to credit my senses, and to believe that rain will fall when the air blackens, and that the weather will be dry when the sun is bright. My caution indeed does not always preserve me from a shower. To be wet may happen to the genuine Idler, but to be wet in opposition to theory, can befall only the Idler that pretends to be busy. Of those that spin out life in trifles, and die without a memorial, many flatter themselves with high opinions of their own importance, and imagine that they are every day adding some improvement to human life. To be idle and to be poor have always been reproaches, and therefore every man endeavours with his utmost care, to hide his poverty from others, and his idleness from himself.

Among those whom I never could persuade to rank themselves with Idlers, and who speak with indignation of my morning sleeps and nocturnal rambles; one passes the day in catching spiders that he may count their eyes with a microscope; another erects his head, and exhibits the dust of a marigold separated from the flower with dexterity worthy of Leeuwenhoeck himself. Some turn the wheel of electricity, some suspend rings to a loadstone, and find that what they did yesterday they can do again to-day. Some register the changes of the wind, and die fully convinced that the wind is changeable.

There are men yet more profound, who have heard that two colourless liquors may produce a colour by union, and that two cold bodies will grow hot if they are mingled: they mingle them, and produce the effect expected, say it is strange, and mingle them again.

The Idlers that sport only with inanimate nature may claim some indulgence; if they are useless they are still innocent: but there are others, whom I know not how to mention without more emotion than my love of quiet willingly admits. Among the inferiour professors of medical knowledge, is a race of wretches, whose lives are only varied by varieties of cruelty; whose favourite amusement is to nail dogs to tables and open them alive; to try how long life may be continued in various degrees of mutilation, or with the excision or laceration of the vital parts; to examine whether burning irons are felt more acutely by the bone or tendon; and whether the more lasting agonies are produced by poison forced into the mouth or injected into the veins.

It is not without reluctance that I offend the sensibility of the tender mind with images like these. If such cruelties were not practised it were to be desired that they should not be conceived, but since they are published every day with ostentation, let me be allowed once to mention them, since I mention them with abhorrence.

Mead has invidiously remarked of Woodward that he gathered shells and stones, and would pass for a philosopher.[2] With pretensions much less reasonable, the anatomical novice tears out the living bowels of an animal, and stiles himself physician, prepares himself by familiar cruelty for that profession which he is to exercise upon the tender and the helpless, upon feeble bodies and broken minds, and by which he has opportunities to extend his arts of torture, and continue those experiments upon infancy and age, which he has hitherto tried upon cats and dogs.

What is alleged in defence of these hateful practices, every one knows; but the truth is, that by knives, fire, and poison, knowledge is not always sought, and is very seldom attained. The experiments that have been tried, are tried again; he that burned an animal with irons yesterday, will be willing to amuse himself with burning another to-morrow. I know not, that by living dissections any discovery has been made by which a single malady is more easily cured. And if the knowledge of physiology has been somewhat encreased, he surely buys knowledge dear, who learns the use of the lacteals at the expence of his humanity. It is time that universal resentment should arise against these horrid operations, which tend to harden the heart, extinguish those sensations which give man confidence in man, and make the physician more dreadful than the gout or stone.

---

[2] *philosopher:* Richard Mead (1673–1754) was a distinguished physician and scholar; John Woodward (1665–1728), also a physician and scholar, was particularly interested in fossils.

No. 18. Saturday, 12 August 1758.

[Folly of Human Amusements]

TO THE IDLER.

SIR,

It commonly happens to him who endeavours to obtain distinction by ridicule, or censure, that he teaches others to practise his own arts against himself, and that, after a short enjoyment of the applause paid to his sagacity, or of the mirth excited by his wit, he is doomed to suffer the same severities of scrutiny, to hear inquiry detecting his faults, and exaggeration sporting with his failings.

The natural discontent of inferiority will seldom fail to operate in some degree of malice against him, who professes to superintend the conduct of others, especially if he seats himself uncalled in the chair of judicature, and exercises authority by his own commission.

You cannot, therefore, wonder that your observations on human folly, if they produce laughter at one time, awaken criticism at another; and that among the numbers whom you have taught to scoff at the retirement of Drugget,[8] there is one that offers his apology.

The mistake of your old friend is by no means peculiar. The public pleasures of far the greater part of mankind are counterfeit. Very few carry their philosophy to places of diversion, or are very careful to analyse their enjoyments. The general condition of life is so full of misery, that we are glad to catch delight without inquiring whence it comes, or by what power it is bestowed.

The mind is seldom quickened to very vigorous operations but by pain, or the dread of pain. We do not disturb ourselves with the detection of fallacies which do us no harm, nor willingly decline a pleasing effect to investigate its cause. He that is happy, by whatever means, desires nothing but the continuance of happiness, and is no more sollicitous to distribute his sensations into their proper species, than the common gazer on

[8] See *Idler* No. 16.

the beauties of the spring to separate light into its original rays.

Pleasure is therefore seldom such as it appears to others, nor often such as we represent it to ourselves. Of the ladies that sparkle at a musical performance, a very small number has any quick sensibility of harmonious sounds. But every one that goes has her pleasure. She has the pleasure of wearing fine cloaths, and of shewing them, of outshining those whom she suspects to envy her; she has the pleasure of appearing among other ladies in a place whither the race of meaner mortals seldom intrudes, and of reflecting that, in the conversations of the next morning, her name will be mentioned among those that sat in the first row; she has the pleasure of returning courtesies, or refusing to return them, of receiving compliments with civility, or rejecting them with disdain. She has the pleasure of meeting some of her acquaintance, of guessing why the rest are absent, and of telling them that she saw the opera, on pretence of inquiring why they would miss it. She has the pleasure of being supposed to be pleased with a refined amusement, and of hoping to be numbered among the votresses of harmony. She has the pleasure of escaping for two hours the superior of a sister, or the controul of a husband; and from all these pleasures she concludes that heavenly musick is the balm of life.

All assemblies of gaiety are brought together by motives of the same kind. The theatre is not filled with those, that know or regard the skill of the actor, nor the ballroom, by those who dance, or attend to the dancers. To all places of general resort, where the standard of pleasure is erected, we run with equal eagerness, or appearance of eagerness, for very different reasons. One goes that he may say he has been there, another because he never misses. This man goes to try what he can find, and that to discover what others find. Whatever diversion is costly will be frequented by those who desire to be thought rich: and whatever has, by any accident, become fashionable, easily continues its reputation, because every one is ashamed of not partaking it.

To every place of entertainment we go with expectation, and desire of being pleased; we meet others who are brought by the same motives; no one will be the first to own the disappointment; one face reflects the smile of another, till each believes the rest delighted, and endeavours to catch and transmit the circulating rapture. In time, all are deceived by the cheat to which all contribute. The fiction of happiness is propagated by every tongue, and confirmed by every look, till at last all profess the joy which they do not feel, consent to yield to the general delusion; and when the voluntary dream is at an end, lament that bliss is of so short a duration.

If Drugget pretended to pleasures, of which he had no perception, or boasted of one amusement where he was indulging another, what did he which is not done by all those who read his story? of whom some pretend delight in conversation, only because they dare not be alone; some praise the quiet of solitude, because they are envious of sense and impatient of folly; and some gratify their pride, by writing characters which expose the vanity of life.

I am, Sir,
Your humble servant.

No. 22. Saturday, 9 September 1758.[4]

[Vultures and Men]

Many naturalists are of opinion, that the animals which we commonly consider as mute, have the power of imparting their thoughts to one another. That they can express general sensations is very certain; every being that can utter sounds, has a different voice for pleasure and for pain. The hound informs his fellows when he scents his game; the hen calls her chickens to their food by her cluck, and drives them from danger by her scream.

Birds have the greatest variety of notes; they have indeed a variety, which seems almost sufficient to make a speech adequate to the purposes of a life, which is regulated by instinct, and can admit little change or improvement. To the cries of birds, curiosity or superstition has been always attentive, many have studied the language of the feathered tribes, and some have boasted that they understood it.

---

[4] This was the original *Idler* Number 22 published in *The Universal Chronicle*; Johnson suppressed it in the first collected edition of *The Idler*.

The most skilful or most confident interpreters of the silvan dialogues have been commonly found among the philosophers of the East, in a country where the calmness of the air, and the mildness of the seasons, allow the student to pass a great part of the year in groves and bowers. But what may be done in one place by peculiar opportunities, may be performed in another by peculiar diligence. A shepherd of Bohemia has, by long abode in the forests, enabled himself to understand the voice of birds, at least he relates with great confidence a story of which the credibility may be considered by the learned.

"As I was sitting, (said he) within a hollow rock, and watching my sheep that fed in the valley, I heard two vultures interchangeably crying on the summit of the cliff. Both voices were earnest and deliberate. My curiosity prevailed over my care of the flock; I climbed slowly and silently from crag to crag, concealed among the shrubs, till I found a cavity where I might sit and listen without suffering, or giving disturbance.

"I soon perceived, that my labour would be well repaid; for an old vulture was sitting on a naked prominence, with her young about her, whom she was instructing in the arts of a vulture's life, and preparing, by the last lecture, for their final dismission to the mountains and the skies.

" 'My children,' said the old vulture, 'you will the less want[5] my instructions because you have had my practice before your eyes; you have seen me snatch from the farm the household fowl, you have seen me seize the leveret in the bush, and the kid in the pasture, you know how to fix your talons, and how to balance your flight when you are laden with your prey. But you remember the taste of more delicious food; I have often regaled you with the flesh of man.' 'Tell us,' said the young vultures, 'where man may be found, and how he may be known; his flesh is surely the natural food of a vulture. Why have you never brought a man in your talons to the nest?' 'He is too bulky,' said the mother; 'when we find a man, we can only tear away his flesh and leave his bones upon the ground.' 'Since man is so big,' said the young ones, 'how do you kill him. You are afraid of the wolf and of the bear, by what power are vultures superior to man, is man more defenseless than a sheep?' 'We have not the strength of man,' returned the mother, 'and I am sometimes in doubt whether we have the subtilty; and the vultures would seldom feast upon his flesh,

[5] *want:* need.

had not nature, that devoted him to our uses, infused into him a strange ferocity, which I have never observed in any other being that feeds upon the earth. Two herds of men will often meet and shake the earth with noise, and fill the air with fire. When you hear noise and see fire which flashes along the ground, hasten to the place with your swiftest wing, for men are surely destroying one another; you will then find the ground smoking with blood and covered with carcasses, of which many are dismembered and mangled for the convenience of the vulture.' 'But when men have killed their prey,' said the pupil, 'why do they not eat it? When the wolf has killed a sheep he suffers not the vulture to touch it till he has satisfied himself. Is not man another kind of wolf?' 'Man,' said the mother, 'is the only beast who kills that which he does not devour, and this quality makes him so much a benefactor to our species.' 'If men kill our prey and lay it in our way,' said the young one, 'what need shall we have of labouring for ourselves.' 'Because man will, sometimes,' replied the mother, 'remain for a long time quiet in his den. The old vultures will tell you when you are to watch his motions. When you see men in great numbers moving close together, like a flight of storks, you may conclude that they are hunting, and that you will soon revel in human blood.' 'But still,' said the young one, 'I would gladly know the reason of this mutual slaughter. I could never kill what I could not eat.' 'My child,' said the mother, 'this is a question which I cannot answer, tho' I am reckoned the most subtile bird of the mountain. When I was young I used frequently to visit the ayry of an old vulture who dwelt upon the Carpathian rocks; he had made many observations; he knew the places that afforded prey round his habitation, as far in every direction as the strongest wing can fly between the rising and setting of the summer sun; he had fed year after year on the entrails of men. His opinion was, that men had only the appearance of animal life, being really vegetables with a power of motion; and that as the boughs of an oak are dashed together by the storm, that swine may fatten upon the falling acorns, so men are by some unaccountable power driven one against another, till they lose their motion, that vultures may be fed. Others think they have observed something of contrivance and policy among these mischievous beings, and those that hover more closely round them, pretend, that there is, in every herd, one that gives directions to the rest, and seems to be more eminently delighted with a wide carnage. What it is that intitles him to such pre-eminence we know not; he is seldom the biggest or the swiftest, but he shows by his eagerness and diligence that he is, more than any of the others, a friend to vultures.' "

No. 23. Saturday, 23 September 1758.

[Insecurity of Friendship]

Life has no pleasure higher or nobler than that of friendship. It is painful to consider, that this sublime enjoyment may be impaired or destroyed by innumerable causes, and that there is no human possession of which the duration is less certain.

Many have talked, in very exalted language, of the perpetuity of friendship, of invincible constancy, and unalienable kindness; and some examples have been seen of men who have continued faithful to their earliest choice, and whose affection has predominated over changes of fortune, and contrariety of opinion.

But these instances are memorable, because they are rare. The friendship which is to be practised or expected by common mortals, must take its rise from mutual pleasure, and must end when the power ceases of delighting each other.

Many accidents therefore may happen, by which the ardour of kindness will be abated, without criminal baseness or contemptible inconstancy on either part. To give pleasure is not always in our power; and little does he know himself, who believes that he can be always able to receive it.

Those who would gladly pass their days together may be separated by the different course of their affairs; and friendship, like love, is destroyed by long absence, though it may be encreased by short intermissions. What we have missed long enough to want it, we value more when it is regained; but that which has been lost till it is forgotten, will be found at last with little gladness, and with still less, if a substitute has supplied the place. A man deprived of the companion to whom he used to open his bosom, and with whom he shared the hours of leisure and merriment, feels the day at first hanging heavy on him; his difficulties oppress, and his doubts distract him; he sees time come and go without his wonted gratification, and all is sadness within the solitude about him. But this uneasiness never lasts long, necessity produces expedients, new amusements are discovered, and new conversation is admitted.

No expectation is more frequently disappointed, than that which naturally arises in the mind, from the prospect of meeting an old friend, after long separation. We expect the attraction to be revived, and the coalition to be renewed; no man considers how much alteration time has made in himself, and very few enquire what effect it has had upon others. The first hour convinces them, that the pleasure, which they have formerly enjoyed, is for ever at an end; different scenes have made different impressions, the opinions of both are changed, and that similitude of manners[6] and sentiment is lost, which confirmed them both in the approbation of themselves.

Friendship is often destroyed by opposition of interest, not only by the ponderous and visible interest, which the desire of wealth and greatness forms and maintains, but by a thousand secret and slight competitions, scarcely known to the mind upon which they operate. There is scarcely any man without some favourite trifle which he values above greater attainments, some desire of petty praise which he cannot patiently suffer to be frustrated. This minute ambition is sometimes crossed before it is known, and sometimes defeated by wanton petulance; but such attacks are seldom made without the loss of friendship; for whoever has once found the vulnerable part will always be feared, and the resentment will burn on in secret of which shame hinders the discovery.

This, however, is a slow malignity, which a wise man will obviate as inconsistent with quiet, and a good man will repress as contrary to virtue; but human happiness is sometimes violated by some more sudden strokes.

A dispute begun in jest, upon a subject which a moment before was on both parts regarded with careless indifference, is continued by the desire of conquest, till vanity kindles into rage, and opposition rankles into enmity. Against this hasty mischief I know not what security can be obtained; men will be sometimes surprized into quarrels, and though they might both hasten to reconciliation, as soon as their tumult has sub-

---

[6] *manners:* ways of acting.

sided, yet two minds will seldom be found together, which can at once subdue their discontent, or immediately enjoy the sweets of peace, without remembering the wounds of the conflict.

Friendship has other enemies. Suspicion is always hardening the cautious, and disgust repelling the delicate. Very slender differences will sometimes part those whom long reciprocation of civility or beneficence has united. Lonelove and Ranger retired into the country to enjoy the company of each other, and returned in six weeks cold and petulant; Ranger's pleasure was to walk in the fields, and Lonelove's to sit in a bower; each had complied with the other in his turn, and each was angry that compliance had been exacted.

The most fatal disease of friendship is gradual decay, or dislike hourly encreased by causes too slender for complaint, and too numerous for removal. Those who are angry may be reconciled; those who have been injured may receive a recompence; but when the desire of pleasing and willingness to be pleased is silently diminished, the renovation of friendship is hopeless; as, when the vital powers sink into languor, there is no longer any use of the physician.

No. 26. Saturday, 14 October 1758.[7]

[Betty Broom, the Maid]

MR. IDLER,

I never thought that I should write any thing to be printed; but having lately seen your first essay, which was sent down into the kitchen, with a great bundle of gazettes and useless papers, I find that you are willing to admit any correspondent, and therefore hope you will not reject me. If you publish my letter, it may encourage others, in the same condition with myself, to tell their stories, which may be perhaps as useful as those of great ladies.

I am a poor girl. I was bred in the country at a charity school, maintained by the contributions of wealthy neigh-

[7] According to Boswell, Betty Broom's story was based on that of an actual charity-school girl (*Life of Johnson*, Oxford Standard Authors, p. 1254).

bours. The ladies our patronesses visited us from time to time, examined how we were taught, and saw that our cloaths were clean. We lived happily enough, and were instructed to be thankful to those at whose cost we were educated. I was always the favourite of my mistress; she used to call me to read and shew my copybook to all strangers, who never dismissed me without commendation, and very seldom without a shilling.

At last the chief of our subscribers having passed a winter in London, came down full of an opinion new and strange to the whole country. She held it little less than criminal to teach poor girls to read and write. They who are born to poverty, she said, are born to ignorance, and will work the harder the less they know. She told her friends, that London was in confusion by the insolence of servants, that scarcely a wench was to be got "for all work," since education had made such numbers of fine ladies, that nobody would now accept a lower title than that of a waiting maid, or something that might qualify her to wear laced shoes and long ruffles, and to sit at work in the parlour window. But she was resolved, for her part, to spoil no more girls; those who were to live by their hands should neither read nor write out of her pocket; the world was bad enough already, and she would have no part in making it worse.

She was for a short time warmly opposed; but she persevered in her notions, and withdrew her subscription. Few listen without a desire of conviction to those who advise them to spare their money. Her example and her arguments gained ground daily, and in less than a year the whole parish was convinced, that the nation would be ruined if the children of the poor were taught to read and write.

Our school was now dissolved; my mistress kissed me when we parted, and told me, that, being old and helpless, she could not assist me, advised me to seek a service, and charged me not to forget what I had learned.

My reputation for scholarship, which had hitherto recommended me to favour, was, by the adherents to the new opinion, considered as a crime; and, when I offered myself to any mistress, I had no other answer, than, "Sure, child, you would not work; hard work is not fit for a penwoman; a scrubbing-brush would spoil your hand, child!"

I could not live at home; and while I was considering to what I should betake me, one of the girls, who had gone from our school to London, came down in a silk gown, and told her acquaintance how well she lived, what fine things she saw, and what great wages she received. I resolved to try my fortune, and took my passage in the next week's waggon to London. I had no snares laid for me at my arrival, but came safe to a sister of my mistress, who undertook to get me a place. She knew only the families of mean tradesmen; and I, having no high opinion of my own qualifications, was willing to accept the first offer.

My first mistress was wife of a working watchmaker, who earned more than was sufficient to keep his family in decency and plenty, but it was their constant practice to hire a chaise on Sunday, and spend half the wages of the week on Richmond-Hill; on Monday he commonly lay half in bed, and spent the other half in merriment; Tuesday and Wednesday consumed the rest of his money; and three days every week were passed in extremity of want by us who were left at home, while my master lived on trust at an alehouse. You may be sure that of the sufferers the maid suffered most, and I left them, after three months, rather than be starved.

I was then maid to a hatter's wife. There was no want to be dreaded, for they lived in perpetual luxury. My mistress was a diligent woman, and rose early in the morning to set the journeymen to work; my master was a man much beloved by his neighbours, and sat at one club or other every night. I was obliged to wait on my master at night, and on my mistress in the morning. He seldom came home before two, and she rose at five. I could no more live without sleep than without food, and therefore entreated them to look out for another servant.

My next removal was to a linen draper's, who had six children. My mistress, when I first entered the house, informed me, that I must never contradict the children, nor suffer them to cry. I had no desire to offend, and readily promised to do my best. But when I gave them their breakfast I could not help all first; when I was playing with one in my lap, I was forced to keep the rest in expectation. That which was not gratified always resented the injury with a loud outcry, which put my mistress in a fury at me, and procured sugar plums to the child. I could not keep six children quiet, who were bribed to be clamorous, and was therefore dismissed, as a girl honest, but not good-natured.

I then lived with a couple that kept a petty shop of remnants and cheap linen. I was qualified to make a bill, or keep a book, and being therefore often called, at a busy time, to serve the customers, expected that I should now be happy, in proportion as I was useful. But my mistress appropriated every day part of the profit to some private use, and, as she grew bolder in her theft, at last deducted such sums, that my master began to wonder how he sold so much, and gained so little. She pretended to assist his enquiries, and began, very gravely, to hope that "Betty was honest, and yet those sharp girls were apt to be light fingered." You will believe that I did not stay there much longer.

The rest of my story I will tell you in another letter, and only beg to be informed, in some paper, for which of my places, except perhaps the last, I was disqualified, by my skill in reading and writing.

I am, Sir,
Your very humble servant,
BETTY BROOM.

No. 31. Saturday, 18 November 1758.

[Sober, the Idler]

Many moralists have remarked, that pride has of all human vices the widest dominion, appears in the greatest multiplicity of forms, and lies hid under the greatest variety of disguises; of disguises, which, like the moon's "veil of brightness," are both its "lustre and its shade,"[8] and betray it to others, tho' they hide it from ourselves.

It is not my intention to degrade pride from this preeminence of mischief, yet I know not whether idleness may not maintain a very doubtful[9] and obstinate competition.

There are some that profess idleness in its full dignity, who call themselves the "Idle," as Busiris in the play "calls himself the Proud";[10] who boast that they do nothing, and thank their stars that they have nothing to do; who sleep every night till they can sleep no longer, and rise only that exercise may enable them to sleep again; who prolong the reign of darkness

---

[8] Samuel Butler, *Hudibras* (1664), II, i, 905–8.
[9] *doubtful:* i.e., making the outcome uncertain.
[10] In Edward Young's tragedy *Busiris* (1719).

by double curtains, and never see the sun but to "tell him how they hate his beams";[11] whose whole labour is to vary the postures of indulgence, and whose day differs from their night but as a couch or chair differs from a bed.

These are the true and open votaries of idleness, for whom she weaves the garlands of poppies, and into whose cup she pours the waters of oblivion; who exist in a state of unruffled stupidity,[12] forgetting and forgotten; who have long ceased to live, and at whose death the survivors can only say, that they have ceased to breathe.

But idleness predominates in many lives where it is not suspected, for being a vice which terminates in itself, it may be enjoyed without injury to others, and is therefore not watched like fraud, which endangers property, or like pride which naturally seeks its gratifications in another's inferiority. Idleness is a silent and peaceful quality, that neither raises envy by ostentation, nor hatred by opposition; and therefore no body is busy to censure or detect it.

As pride sometimes is hid under humility, idleness is often covered by turbulence and hurry. He that neglects his known duty and real employment, naturally endeavours to croud his mind with something that may bar out the remembrance of his own folly, and does any thing but what he ought to do with eager diligence, that he may keep himself in his own favour.

Some are always in a state of preparation, occupied in previous measures, forming plans, accumulating materials, and providing for the main affair. These are certainly under the secret power of idleness. Nothing is to be expected from the workman whose tools are for ever to be sought. I was once told by a great master, that no man ever excelled in painting, who was eminently curious[13] about pencils[14] and colours.

There are others to whom idleness dictates another expedient, by which life may be passed unprofitably away without the tediousness of many vacant hours. The art is, to fill the day with petty business, to have always something in hand which may raise curiosity, but not solicitude, and keep the mind in a state of action, but not of labour.

[11] John Milton, *Paradise Lost*, IV, 37.
[12] *stupidity:* apathy.
[13] *curious:* solicitous.
[14] *pencils:* brushes.

This art has for many years been practised by my old friend Sober, with wonderful success.[15] Sober is a man of strong desires and quick imagination, so exactly ballanced by the love of ease, that they can seldom stimulate him to any difficult undertaking; they have, however, so much power, that they will not suffer him to lie quite at rest, and though they do not make him sufficiently useful to others, they make him at least weary of himself.

Mr. Sober's chief pleasure is conversation; there is no end of his talk or his attention; to speak or to hear is equally pleasing; for he still fancies that he is teaching or learning something, and is free for the time from his own reproaches.

But there is one time at night when he must go home, that his friends may sleep; and another time in the morning, when all the world agrees to shut out interruption. These are the moments of which poor Sober trembles at the thought. But the misery of these tiresome intervals, he has many means of alleviating. He has persuaded himself that the manual arts are undeservedly overlooked; he has observed in many trades the effects of close thought, and just ratiocination. From speculation he proceeded to practice, and supplied himself with the tools of a carpenter, with which he mended his coal-box very successfully, and which he still continues to employ, as he finds occasion.

He has attempted at other times the crafts of the shoemaker, tinman, plumber, and potter; in all these arts he has failed, and resolves to qualify himself for them by better information. But his daily amusement is chemistry. He has a small furnace, which he employs in distillation, and which has long been the solace of his life. He draws oils and waters, and essences and spirits, which he knows to be of no use; sits and counts the drops as they come from his retort, and forgets that, while a drop is falling, a moment flies away.

Poor Sober! I have often teaz'd him with reproof, and he has often promised reformation; for no man is so much open to conviction as the idler, but there is none on whom it operates so little. What will be the effect of this paper I know not; perhaps he will read it and laugh, and light the fire in his furnace; but my hope is that he will quit his trifles, and betake himself to rational and useful diligence.

---

[15] Sober was modeled on Johnson himself.

No. 51. Saturday, 7 April 1759.

[No Man a Hero to His Valet]

It has been commonly remarked, that eminent men are least eminent at home, that bright characters lose much of their splendor at a nearer view, and many who fill the world with their fame, excite very little reverence among those that surround them in their domestick privacies.

To blame or to suspect is easy and natural. When the fact is evident, and the cause doubtful, some accusation is always engendered between idleness and malignity. This disparity of general and familiar esteem is therefore imputed to hidden vices, and to practices indulged in secret, but carefully covered from the publick eye.

Vice will indeed always produce contempt. The dignity of Alexander, tho' nations fell prostrate before him, was certainly held in little veneration by the partakers of his midnight revels, who had seen him, in the madness of wine, murder his friend, or set fire to the Persian palace at the instigation of a harlot;[16] and it is well remembered among us, that the avarice of Marlborough kept him in subjection to his wife,[17] while he was dreaded by France as her conqueror, and honoured by the emperor as his deliverer.

But though where there is vice there must be want of reverence, it is not reciprocally true, that when there is want of reverence there is always vice. That awe which great actions or abilities impress will be inevitably diminished by acquaintance, tho' nothing either mean or criminal should be found.

Of men, as of every thing else, we must judge according to our knowledge. When we see of a hero only his battles, or of a writer only his books, we have nothing to allay our ideas of their greatness. We consider the one only as the guardian of his country, and the other only as the instructor of mankind.

[16] Alexander the Great was supposed to have killed his friend Clitus when drunk and to have burned the palace of Persepolis to please the courtesan Thais.

[17] John Churchill, Duke of Marlborough, a great general, was noted for avarice; his wife, Sarah, the favorite of Queen Anne, held several lucrative appointments at Court.

We have neither opportunity nor motive to examine the minuter parts of their lives, or the less apparent peculiarities of their characters; we name them with habitual respect, and forget, what we still continue to know, that they are men like other mortals.

But such is the constitution of the world, that much of life must be spent in the same manner by the wise and the ignorant, the exalted and the low. Men, however distinguished by external accidents or intrinsick qualities, have all the same wants, the same pains, and, as far as the senses are consulted, the same pleasures. The petty cares and petty duties are the same in every station to every understanding, and every hour brings some occasion on which we all sink to the common level. We are all naked till we are dressed, and hungry till we are fed; and the general's triumph, and sage's disputation, end, like the humble labours of the smith or plowman, in a dinner or in sleep.

Those notions which are to be collected by reason in opposition to the senses, will seldom stand forward in the mind, but lie treasured in the remoter repositories of memory, to be found only when they are sought. Whatever any man may have written or done, his precepts or his valour will scarcely over-ballance the unimportant uniformity which runs thro' his time. We do not easily consider him as great, whom our own eyes shew us to be little; nor labour to keep present to our thoughts the latent excellencies of him who shares with us all our weaknesses and many of our follies; who like us is delighted with slight amusements, busied with trifling employments, and disturbed by little vexations.

Great powers cannot be exerted, but when great exigencies make them necessary. Great exigencies can happen but seldom, and therefore those qualities which have a claim to the veneration of mankind, lie hid, for the most part, like subterranean treasures, over which the foot passes as on common ground, till necessity breaks open the golden cavern.

In the ancient celebrations of victory, a slave was placed on the triumphal car, by the side of the general, who reminded him by a short sentence, that he was a man. Whatever danger there might be lest a leader, in his passage to the capitol, should forget the frailties of his nature, there was surely no need of such an admonition; the intoxication could not have continued long; he would have been at home but a few hours

before some of his dependents would have forgot his greatness, and shown him, that notwithstanding his laurels he was
yet a man.

There are some who try to escape this domestic degradation, by labouring to appear always wise or always great, but
he that strives against nature, will for ever strive in vain. To
be grave of mien and slow of utterance; to look with solicitude
and speak with hesitation, is attainable at will; but the shew
of wisdom is ridiculous when there is nothing to cause doubt,
as that of valour where there is nothing to be feared.

A man who has duly considered the condition of his being,
will contentedly yield to the course of things: he will not pant
for distinction where distinction would imply no merit, but
tho' on great occasions he may wish to be greater than others,
he will be satisfied in common occurrences not to be less.

No. 60. Saturday, 9 June 1759.

[Minim, the Critic]

Criticism is a study by which men grow important and
formidable at very small expence. The power of invention has
been conferred by nature upon few, and the labour of learning those sciences[18] which may, by mere labour, be obtained,
is too great to be willingly endured; but every man can exert
such judgment as he has upon the works of others; and he
whom nature has made weak, and idleness keeps ignorant,
may yet support his vanity by the name of a critick.

I hope it will give comfort to great numbers who are passing
thro' the world in obscurity, when I inform them how easily
distinction may be obtained. All the other powers of literature
are coy and haughty, they must be long courted, and at last are
not always gained; but criticism is a goddess easy of access and
forward of advance, who will meet the slow and encourage the
timorous; the want of meaning she supplies with words, and
the want of spirit she recompenses with malignity.

This profession has one recommendation peculiar to itself,
that it gives vent to malignity without real mischief. No gen-

---

[18] *sciences:* branches of knowledge.

ius was ever blasted by the breath of criticks. The poison
which, if confined, would have burst the heart, fumes away in
empty hisses, and malice is set at ease with very little danger
to merit. The critick is the only man whose triumph is without another's pain, and whose greatness does not rise upon
another's ruin.

To a study at once so easy and so reputable, so malicious
and so harmless, it cannot be necessary to invite my readers by
a long or laboured exhortation; it is sufficient, since all would
be criticks if they could, to shew by one eminent example that
all can be criticks if they will.

Dick Minim, after the common course of puerile studies, in
which he was no great proficient, was put apprentice to a
brewer, with whom he had lived two years, when his uncle
died in the city, and left him a large fortune in the stocks. Dick
had for six months before used[19] the company of the lower
players,[20] of whom he had learned to scorn a trade, and being
now at liberty to follow his genius, he resolved to be a man of
wit and humour. That he might be properly initiated in his
new character, he frequented the coffee-houses near the theatres, where he listened very diligently day, after day, to those
who talked of language and sentiments, and unities and catas-
trophes,[21] till by slow degrees he began to think that he understood something of the stage, and hoped in time to talk
himself.

But he did not trust so much to natural sagacity, as wholly
to neglect the help of books. When the theatres were shut, he
retired to Richmond with a few select writers, whose opinions
he impressed upon his memory by unwearied diligence; and
when he returned with other wits to the town, was able to tell,
in very proper phrases, that the chief business of art is to copy
nature; that a perfect writer is not to be expected, because
genius decays as judgment increases; that the great art is the
art of blotting, and that according to the rule of Horace
every piece should be kept nine years.[22]

---

[19] *used:* frequented.
[20] *players:* actors.
[21] The unities of time, place, and action were required by neoclassical
critics of drama; a catastrophe is the final event of a drama.
[22] All the opinions in this and the following paragraphs were well-worn
critical commonplaces, which had been expressed by Pope, Addison, and
Johnson himself.

Of the great authors he now began to display the characters, laying down as an universal position that all had beauties and defects. His opinion was, that Shakespeare, committing himself wholly to the impulse of nature, wanted that correctness which learning would have given him; and that Jonson, trusting to learning, did not sufficiently cast his eye on nature. He blamed the stanza of Spenser, and could not bear the hexameters of Sidney. Denham and Waller he held the first reformers of English numbers, and thought that if Waller could have obtained the strength of Denham, or Denham the sweetness of Waller, there had been nothing wanting to complete a poet. He often expressed his commiseration of Dryden's poverty, and his indignation at the age which suffered him to write for bread; he repeated with rapture the first lines of *All for Love*, but wondered at the corruption of taste which could bear any thing so unnatural as rhyming tragedies. In Otway he found uncommon powers of moving the passions, but was disgusted by his general negligence, and blamed him for making a conspirator his hero; and never concluded his disquisition, without remarking how happily the sound of the clock is made to alarm the audience. Southern would have been his favourite, but that he mixes comick with tragick scenes, intercepts the natural course of the passions, and fills the mind with a wild confusion of mirth and melancholy. The versification of Rowe he thought too melodious for the stage, and too little varied in different passions. He made it the great fault of Congreve, that all his persons were wits, and that he always wrote with more art than nature. He considered *Cato* rather as a poem than a play, and allowed Addison to be the complete master of allegory and grave humour, but paid no great deference to him as a critick. He thought the chief merit of Prior was in his easy tales and lighter poems, tho' he allowed that his *Solomon* had many noble sentiments elegantly expressed. In Swift he discovered an inimitable vein of irony, and an easiness which all would hope and few would attain. Pope he was inclined to degrade from a poet to a versifier, and thought his numbers rather luscious than sweet. He often lamented the neglect of *Phaedra and Hippolitus*, and wished to see the stage under better regulations.

These assertions passed commonly uncontradicted; and if now and then an opponent started up, he was quickly repressed by the suffrages of the company, and Minim went away from every dispute with elation of heart and increase of confidence.

He now grew conscious of his abilities, and began to talk of the present state of dramatick poetry; wondered what was become of the comick genius which supplied our ancestors with wit and pleasantry, and why no writer could be found that durst now venture beyond a farce. He saw no reason for thinking that the vein of humour was exhausted, since we live in a country where liberty suffers every character to spread itself to its utmost bulk, and which therefore produces more originals than all the rest of the world together. Of tragedy he concluded business[23] to be the soul, and yet often hinted that love predominates too much upon the modern stage.

He was now an acknowledged critick, and had his own seat in the coffee-house,[24] and headed a party in the pit.[25] Minim has more vanity than ill-nature, and seldom desires to do much mischief; he will perhaps murmur a little in the ear of him that sits next him, but endeavours to influence the audience to favour, by clapping when an actor exclaims "ye Gods," or laments the misery of his country.

By degrees he was admitted to rehearsals, and many of his friends are of opinion, that our present poets are indebted to him for their happiest thoughts; by his contrivance the bell was rung twice in *Barbarossa*, and by his persuasion the author of *Cleone* concluded his play without a couplet; for what çan be more absurd, said Minim, than that part of a play should be rhymed, and part written in blank verse? and by what acquisition of faculties is the speaker who never could find rhymes before, enabled to rhyme at the conclusion of an act!

He is the great investigator of hidden beauties, and is particularly delighted when he finds "the sound an echo to the sense."[26] He has read all our poets with particular attention to this delicacy of versification, and wonders at the supineness

---

[23] *business:* action.
[24] *coffee-house:* place where coffee and other drinks were sold and men gathered for literary or political conversation.
[25] *pit:* section of the theater frequented by fashionable young men and would-be critics.
[26] Alexander Pope, *An Essay on Criticism*, l. 365. Johnson questioned this doctrine.

with which their works have been hitherto perused, so that no man has found the sound of a drum in this distich,

> When pulpit, drum ecclesiastic,
> Was beat with fist instead of a stick;

and that the wonderful lines upon honour and a bubble have hitherto passed without notice.

> Honour is like the glassy bubble,
> Which costs philosophers such trouble,
> Which one part crack'd, the whole does fly,
> And wits are crack'd to find out why.[27]

In these verses, says Minim, we have two striking accommodations of the sound to the sense. It is impossible to utter the two lines emphatically without an act like that which they describe; "bubble" and "trouble" causing a momentary inflation of the cheeks by the retention of the breath, which is afterwards forcibly emitted, as in the practice of "blowing bubbles." But the greatest excellence is in the third line, which is "crack'd" in the middle to express a crack, and then shivers into monosyllables. Yet has this diamond lain neglected with common stones, and among the innumerable admirers of *Hudibras* the observation of this superlative passage has been reserved for the sagacity of Minim.

No. 77. Saturday, 6 October 1759.

[Easy Writing]

Easy poetry is universally admired, but I know not whether any rule has yet been fixed, by which it may be decided when poetry can be properly called easy; Horace has told us that it is such as "every reader hopes to equal, but after long labour finds unattainable." This is a very loose description, in which

[27] Butler, *Hudibras*, I, i, 11–12, II, ii, 385–88.

only the effect is noted; the qualities which produce this effect remain to be investigated.

Easy poetry is that in which natural thoughts are expressed without violence to the language. The discriminating character of ease consists principally in the diction, for all true poetry requires that the sentiments be natural. Language offers violence by harsh or by daring figures, by transposition, by unusual acceptations[28] of words, and by any licence, which would be avoided by a writer of prose. Where any artifice appears in the construction of the verse, that verse is no longer easy. Any epithet which can be ejected without diminution of the sense, any curious[29] iteration of the same word, and all unusual, tho' not ungrammatical structure of speech, destroy the grace of easy poetry.

The first lines of Pope's *Iliad* afford examples of many licences which an easy writer must decline.

> Achilles' *wrath*, to Greece the *direful spring*
> Of woes unnumber'd, *heav'nly* Goddess sing,
> The wrath which *hurl'd* to Pluto's *gloomy reign*
> The souls of *mighty* chiefs untimely slain.

In the first couplet the language is distorted by inversions, clogged with superfluities, and clouded by a harsh metaphor; and in the second there are two words used in an uncommon sense, and two epithets inserted only to lengthen the line; all these practices may in a long work easily be pardoned, but they always produce some degree of obscurity and ruggedness.

Easy poetry has been so long excluded by ambition of ornament, and luxuriance of imagery, that its nature seems now to be forgotten. Affectation, however opposite to ease, is sometimes mistaken for it, and those who aspire to gentle elegance, collect female phrases[30] and fashionable barbarisms, and imagine that style to be easy which custom has made familiar. Such was the idea of the poet who wrote the following verses to a "Countess Cutting Paper."[31]

---

[28] *acceptations:* meanings.
[29] *curious:* artful, carefully worked out.
[30] *female phrases:* expressions used by fashionable women, such as "vap'rish" (out of sorts).
[31] Pope's "On the Countess of Burlington Cutting Paper."

Pallas grew *vap'rish once and odd,*
  She would not *do the least right thing*
Either for Goddess or for God,
  Nor work, nor play, nor paint, nor sing.

Jove frown'd and "Use (he cry'd) those eyes
  So skillful, and those hands so taper;
Do something exquisite and wise"—
  She bow'd, obey'd him, and cut paper.

This vexing him who gave her birth,
  Thought by all heav'n a *burning shame,*
What does she next, but bids on earth
  Her Burlington do just the same?

Pallas, you give yourself *strange airs;*
  But sure you'll find it hard to spoil
The sense and taste, of one that bears
  The name of Savile and of Boyle.

Alas! one bad example shown,
  How quickly all the sex pursue!
See, madam! see, the arts o'erthrown
  Between John Overton and *you.*

It is the prerogative of easy poetry to be understood as long
as the language lasts; but modes of speech, which owe their
prevalence only to modish folly, or to the eminence of those
that use them, die away with their inventors, and their meaning, in a few years, is no longer known.

Easy poetry is commonly sought in petty compositions upon
minute subjects; but ease, tho' it excludes pomp, will admit
greatness. Many lines in Cato's soliloquy are at once easy and
sublime.

'Tis the Divinity that stirs within us;
'Tis heav'n itself that points out an hereafter,
And intimates eternity to man.
——— If there's a pow'r above us,
And that there is all nature cries aloud
Thro' all her works, he must delight in virtue,
And that which he delights in must be happy.

Cato, v.1.7–9, 15–18.

Nor is ease more contrary to wit than to sublimity; the celebrated stanza of Cowley,[32] on a lady elaborately dressed, loses
nothing of its freedom by the spirit of the sentiment.

> Th' adorning thee with so much art
>   Is but a barb'rous skill,
> 'Tis like the pois'ning of a dart
>   Too apt before to kill.
>
> "The Waiting-Maid," ll.13–16.

Cowley seems to have possessed the power of writing easily
beyond any other of our poets, yet his pursuit of remote
thoughts led him often into harshness of expression. Waller
often attempted, but seldom attained it; for he is too frequently driven into transpositions. The poets, from the time
of Dryden, have gradually advanced in embellishment, and
consequently departed from simplicity and ease.

To require from any author many pieces of easy poetry,
would be indeed to oppress him with too hard a task. It is
less difficult to write a volume of lines swelled with epithets,
brightened by figures, and stiffened by transpositions, than to
produce a few couplets graced only by naked elegance and
simple purity, which require so much care and skill, that I
doubt whether any of our authors has yet been able, for twenty
lines together, nicely[33] to observe the true definition of easy
poetry.

No. 88. Saturday, 22 December 1759.

[What Have Ye Done?]

When the philosophers of the last age were first congre-
gated into the Royal Society, great expectations were raised of
the sudden progress of useful arts; the time was supposed to
be near when engines should turn by a perpetual motion, and
health be secured by the universal medicine; when learning

[32] Abraham Cowley (1618–67), then highly celebrated as a metaphysical (therefore witty) poet.
[33] *nicely:* precisely.

should be facilitated by a real character, and commerce extended by ships which could reach their ports in defiance of the tempest.

But improvement is naturally slow. The society met and parted without any visible diminution of the miseries of life. The gout and stone were still painful, the ground that was not plowed brought no harvest, and neither oranges nor grapes would grow upon the hawthorn. At last, those who were disappointed began to be angry; those likewise who hated innovation were glad to gain an opportunity of ridiculing men who had depreciated, perhaps with too much arrogance, the knowledge of antiquity. And it appears from some of their earliest apologies, that the philosophers felt with great sensibility the unwelcome importunities of those who were daily asking, "What have ye done?"

The truth is, that little had been done compared with what fame had been suffered to promise; and the question could only be answered by general apologies and by new hopes, which, when they were frustrated, gave a new occasion to the same vexatious enquiry.

This fatal question has disturbed the quiet of many other minds. He that in the latter part of his life too strictly enquires what he has done, can very seldom receive from his own heart such an account as will give him satisfaction.

We do not indeed so often disappoint others as ourselves. We not only think more highly than others of our own abilities, but allow ourselves to form hopes which we never communicate, and please our thoughts with employments which none ever will allot us, and with elevations to which we are never expected to rise; and when our days and years have passed away in common business or common amusements, and we find at last that we have suffered our purposes to sleep till the time of action is past, we are reproached only by our own reflections; neither our friends nor our enemies wonder that we live and die like the rest of mankind, that we live without notice and die without memorial; they know not what task we had proposed, and therefore cannot discern whether it is finished.

He that compares what he has done with what he has left undone, will feel the effect which must always follow the comparison of imagination with reality; he will look with contempt on his own unimportance, and wonder to what purpose he came into the world; he will repine that he shall leave behind him no evidence of his having been, that he has added nothing to the system of life, but has glided from youth to age among the crowd, without any effort for distinction.

Man is seldom willing to let fall the opinion of his own dignity, or to believe that he does little only because every individual is a very little being. He is better content to want diligence than power, and sooner confesses the depravity of his will than the imbecillity of his nature.

From this mistaken notion of human greatness it proceeds, that many who pretend to have made great advances in wisdom so loudly declare that they despise themselves. If I had ever found any of the self-contemners much irritated or pained by the consciousness of their meanness, I should have given them consolation by observing, that a little more than nothing is as much as can be expected from a being who with respect to the multitudes about him is himself little more than nothing. Every man is obliged by the supreme master of the universe to improve all the opportunities of good which are afforded him, and to keep in continual activity such abilities as are bestowed upon him. But he has no reason to repine though his abilities are small and his opportunities few. He that has improved the virtue or advanced the happiness of one fellow-creature, he that has ascertained a single moral proposition, or added one useful experiment to natural knowledge, may be contented with his own performance, and, with respect to mortals like himself, may demand, like Augustus, to be dismissed at his departure with applause.[34]

No. 97. Saturday, 23 February 1760.

[Travel Books]

It may, I think, be justly observed, that few books disappoint their readers more than the narrations of travellers. One part of mankind is naturally curious to learn the sentiments,

[34] Suetonius, *Lives of the Caesars*, "Augustus," Sect. 99.

manners, and condition of the rest; and every mind that has leisure or power to extend its views, must be desirous of knowing in what proportion Providence has distributed the blessings of nature or the advantages of art, among the several nations of the earth.

This general desire easily procures readers to every book from which it can expect gratification. The adventurer upon unknown coasts, and the describer of distant regions, is always welcomed as a man who has laboured for the pleasure of others, and who is able to enlarge our knowledge and rectify our opinions; but when the volume is opened, nothing is found but such general accounts as leave no distinct idea behind them, or such minute enumerations as few can read with either profit or delight.

Every writer of travels should consider, that, like all other authors, he undertakes either to instruct or please, or to mingle pleasure with instruction. He that instructs must offer to the mind something to be imitated or something to be avoided; he that pleases must offer new images to his reader, and enable him to form a tacit comparison of his own state with that of others.

The greater part of travellers tell nothing, because their method of travelling supplies them with nothing to be told. He that enters a town at night and surveys it in the morning, and then hastens away to another place, and guesses at the manners of the inhabitants by the entertainment which his inn afforded him, may please himself for a time with a hasty change of scenes, and a confused remembrance of palaces and churches; he may gratify his eye with variety of landscapes; and regale his palate with a succession of vintages; but let him be contented to please himself without endeavour to disturb others. Why should he record excursions by which nothing could be learned, or wish to make a show of knowledge which, without some power of intuition unknown to other mortals, he never could attain.

Of those who crowd the world with their itineraries, some have no other purpose than to describe the face of the country; those who sit idle at home, and are curious to know what is done or suffered in distant countries, may be informed by one of these wanderers, that on a certain day he set out early with the caravan, and in the first hour's march saw, towards the outh, a hill covered with trees, then passed over a stream which ran northward with a swift course, but which is probably dry in the summer months; that an hour after he saw something to the right which looked at a distance like a castle with towers, but which he discovered afterwards to be a craggy rock; that he then entered a valley in which he saw several trees tall and flourishing, watered by a rivulet not marked in the maps, of which he was not able to learn the name; that the road afterward grew stony, and the country uneven, where he observed among the hills many hollows worn by torrents, and was told that the road was passable only part of the year: that going on they found the remains of a building, once perhaps a fortress to secure the pass, or to restrain the robbers, of which the present inhabitants can give no other account than that it is haunted by fairies; that they went to dine at the foot of a rock, and traveled the rest of the day along the banks of a river, from which the road turned aside towards evening, and brought them within sight of a village, which was once a considerable town, but which afforded them neither good victuals nor commodious lodging.

Thus he conducts his reader thro' wet and dry, over rough and smooth, without incidents, without reflection; and, if he obtains his company for another day, will dismiss him again at night equally fatigued with a like succession of rocks and streams, mountains and ruins.

This is the common style of those sons of enterprize, who visit savage countries, and range through solitude and desolation; who pass a desart, and tell that it is sandy; who cross a valley, and find that it is green. There are others of more delicate sensibility, that visit only the realms of elegance and softness; that wander through Italian palaces, and amuse the gentle reader with catalogues of pictures; that hear masses in magnificent churches, and recount the number of the pillars or variegations of the pavement. And there are yet others, who, in disdain of trifles, copy inscriptions elegant and rude, ancient and modern; and transcribe into their book the walls of every edifice, sacred or civil. He that reads these books must consider his labour as its own reward; for he will find nothing on which attention can fix, or which memory can retain.

He that would travel for the entertainment of others, should remember that the great object of remark is human life. Every nation has something peculiar in its manufacturers, its works of genius, its medicines, its agriculture, its customs, and its policy.[35] He only is a useful traveller who brings home something by which his country may be benefited; who procures some supply of want or some mitigation of evil, which may enable his readers to compare their condition with that of others, to improve it whenever it is worse, and whenever it is better to enjoy it.

No. 100. Saturday, 15 March 1760.

[A Good Sort of Woman]

TO THE IDLER.

SIR,

The uncertainty and defects of language have produced very frequent complaints among the learned; yet there still remain many words among us undefined, which are very necessary to be rightly understood, and which produce very mischievous mistakes when they are erroneously interpreted.

I lived in a state of celibacy beyond the usual time. In the hurry first of pleasure and afterwards of business, I felt no want of a domestick companion; but becoming weary of labour I soon grew more weary of idleness, and thought it reasonable to follow the custom of life, and to seek some solace of my cares in female tenderness, and some amusement of my leisure in female chearfulness.

The choice which has been long delayed is commonly made at last with great caution. My resolution was to keep my passions neutral, and to marry only in compliance with my reason. I drew upon a page of my pocket book a scheme of all female virtues and vices, with the vices which border upon every virtue, and the virtues which are allied to every vice. I considered that wit was sarcastick, and magnanimity imperious; that avarice was economical, and ignorance obsequious; and having estimated the good and evil of every quality, employed my own diligence and that of my friends to find the lady in whom nature and reason had reached that happy medi-

[35] *policy:* system of government or administration.

ocrity which is equally remote from exuberance and deficience.

Every woman had her admirers and her censurers, and the expectations which one raised were by another quickly depressed: yet there was one in whose favour almost all suffrages concurred. Miss Gentle was universally allowed to be a good sort of woman. Her fortune was not large, but so prudently managed, that she wore finer cloaths and saw more company than many who were known to be twice as rich. Miss Gentle's visits were everywhere welcome, and whatever family she favoured with her company, she always left behind her such a degree of kindness as recommended her to others; every day extended her acquaintance, and all who knew her declared that they never met with a better sort of woman.

To Miss Gentle I made my addresses, and was received with great equality of temper. She did not in the days of courtship assume the privilege of imposing rigorous commands, or resenting slight offences. If I forgot any of her injunctions I was gently reminded, if I missed the minute of appointment I was easily forgiven. I foresaw nothing in marriage but a halcyon calm, and longed for the happiness which was to be found in the inseparable society of a good sort of woman.

The jointure was soon settled by the intervention of friends, and the day came in which Miss Gentle was made mine for ever. The first month was passed easily enough in receiving and repaying the civilities of our friends. The bride practised with great exactness all the niceties of ceremony, and distributed her notice in the most punctilious proportions to the friends who surrounded us with their happy auguries.

But the time soon came when we were left to ourselves, and were to receive our pleasures from each other, and I then began to perceive that I was not formed to be much delighted by a good sort of woman. Her great principle is, that the orders of a family must not be broken. Every hour of the day has its employment inviolably appropriated, nor will any importunity persuade her to walk in the garden, at the time which she has devoted to her needlework, or to sit up stairs in that part of the forenoon, which she has accustomed herself to spend in the back parlour. She allows herself to sit half an hour after breakfast, and an hour after dinner; while I am talking or reading to her, she keeps her eye upon her watch, and when the minute of departure comes, will leave an argument unfinished, or the intrigue of a play unravelled. She once called me to supper when I was watching an eclipse, and summoned me at another time to bed when I was going to give directions at a fire.

Her conversation is so habitually cautious, that she never talks to me but in general terms, as to one whom it is dangerous to trust. For discriminations of character she has no names; all whom she mentions are honest men and agreeable women. She smiles not by sensation but by practice. Her laughter is never excited but by a joke, and her notion of a joke is not very delicate. The repetition of a good joke does not weaken its effect; if she has laughed once, she will laugh again.

She is an enemy to nothing but ill nature and pride, but she has frequent reason to lament that they are so frequent in the world. All who are not equally pleased with the good and bad, with the elegant and gross, with the witty and the dull, all who distinguish excellence from defect she considers as ill-natured; and she condemns as proud all who repress impertinence or quell presumption, or expect respect from any other eminence than that of fortune, to which she is always willing to pay homage.

There are none whom she openly hates; for if once she suffers, or believes herself to suffer, any contempt or insult, she never dismisses it from her mind but takes all opportunities to tell how easily she can forgive. There are none whom she loves much better than others; for when any of her acquaintance decline in the opinion of the world she always finds it inconvenient to visit them; her affection continues unaltered but it is impossible to be intimate with the whole town.

She daily exercises her benevolence by pitying every misfortune that happens to every family within her circle of notice; she is in hourly terrors lest one should catch cold in the rain, and another be frighted by the high wind. Her charity she shews by lamenting that so many poor wretches should languish in the streets, and by wondering what the great can think on that they do so little good with such large estates.

Her house is elegant and her table dainty though she has little taste of elegance, and is wholly free from vicious luxury; but she comforts herself that nobody can say that her house is dirty, or that her dishes are not well drest.

This, Mr. Idler, I have found by long experience to be the character of a good sort of woman, which I have sent you for the information of those by whom "a good sort of woman" and "a good woman" may happen to be used as equivalent terms, and who may suffer by the mistake like

Your humble servant,
TIM WARNER.

No. 103. Saturday, 5 April 1760.

[A Horror of the Last]

Much of the pain and pleasure of mankind arises from the conjectures which every one makes of the thoughts of others; we all enjoy praise which we do not hear, and resent contempt which we do not see. The Idler may therefore be forgiven, if he suffers his imagination to represent to him what his readers will say or think when they are informed that they have now his last paper in their hands.

Value is more frequently raised by scarcity than by use. That which lay neglected when it was common, rises in estimation as its quantity becomes less. We seldom learn the true want of what we have till it is discovered that we can have no more.

This essay will, perhaps, be read with care even by those who have not yet attended to any other; and he that finds this late attention recompensed, will not forbear to wish that he had bestowed it sooner.

Though the Idler and his readers have contracted no close friendship they are perhaps both unwilling to part. There are few things not purely evil, of which we can say, without some emotion of uneasiness, "this is the last." Those who never could agree together, shed tears when mutual discontent has determined them to final separation; of a place which has been frequently visited, tho' without pleasure, the last look is taken with heaviness of heart; and the Idler, with all his chilness of tranquillity, is not wholly unaffected by the thought that his last essay is now before him.

This secret horrour of the last is inseparable from a thinking being whose life is limited, and to whom death is dreadful. We always make a secret comparison between a part and the whole; the termination of any period of life reminds us that life itself has likewise its termination; when we have done any thing for the last time, we involuntarily reflect that a part of the days allotted us is past, and that as more is past there is less remaining.

It is very happily and kindly provided, that in every life there are certain pauses and interruptions, which force consideration upon the careless, and seriousness upon the light; points of time where one course of action ends and another begins; and by vicissitude of fortune, or alteration of employment, by change of place, or loss of friendship, we are forced to say of something, "this is the last."

An even and unvaried tenour of life always hides from our apprehension the approach of its end. Succession is not perceived but by variation; he that lives to-day as he lived yesterday, and expects that, as the present day is, such will be the morrow, easily conceives time as running in a circle and returning to itself. The uncertainty of our duration is impressed commonly by dissimilitude of condition; it is only by finding life changeable that we are reminded of its shortness.

This conviction, however forcible at every new impression, is every moment fading from the mind; and partly by the inevitable incursion of new images, and partly by voluntary exclusion of unwelcome thoughts, we are again exposed to the universal fallacy; and we must do another thing for the last time, before we consider that the time is nigh when we shall do no more.

As the last *Idler* is published in that solemn week[36] which the Christian world has always set apart for the examination of the conscience, the review of life, the extinction of earthly desires and the renovation of holy purposes, I hope that my readers are already disposed to view every incident with seriousness, and improve it by meditation; and that when they see this series of trifles brought to a conclusion, they will consider that by outliving the *Idler*, they have past weeks, months, and years which are now no longer in their power; that an end must in time be put to every thing great as to every thing little; that to life must come its last hour, and to this system of

[36] Holy Week, the week before Easter.

being its last day, the hour at which probation ceases, and repentance will be vain; the day in which every work of the hand, and imagination of the heart shall be brought to judgment, and an everlasting futurity shall be determined by the past.

From "A Review of *A Free Enquiry into the Nature and Origin of Evil*"

[Jenyns's book aimed to deal with the problem of evil by explaining it away, in the manner of many eighteenth-century optimistic systems which maintained that this was the "best of all possible worlds." The most famous expression of such a theory in England was Alexander Pope's *Essay on Man* (1733–34). This was based on the theories of Pope's friend Henry St. John, Viscount Bolingbroke, who was (unlike Pope) consciously opposed to orthodox Christianity. Note that Johnson demolishes Jenyns's system not by asserting the orthodox Christian position based on faith, but by turning Jenyns's own weapon of logical argument against him. Some of Johnson's lengthy quotations from Jenyns have been simply omitted; others, summarized.]

This is a treatise consisting of six letters upon a very difficult and important question, which I am afraid this author's endeavours will not free from the perplexity, which has intangled the speculatists of all ages, and which must always continue while *we see* but *in part*. He calls it a *Free* enquiry, and indeed his *freedom* is, I think, greater than his modesty. Though he is far from the contemptible arrogance, or the impious licentiousness of *Bolingbroke*, yet he decides too easily upon questions out of the reach of human determination, with too little consideration of mortal weakness, and with too much vivacity for the necessary caution.

In the first letter *on evil in general*, he observes, that, "it is the solution of this important question, *whence came evil*, alone, that can ascertain the moral characteristic of God, without which there is an end of all distinction between good and evil." Yet he begins this enquiry by this declaration. "That there is a supreme being, infinitely powerful, wise and benevolent, the great creator and preserver of all things, is a truth so clearly demonstrated, that it shall be here taken for granted." What is this but to say, that we have already reason to grant the existence of those attributes of God, which the present enquiry is designed to prove? The present enquiry is then surely made to no purpose. The attributes to the demonstration of which the solution of this great question is necessary, have been demonstrated without any solution, or by means of the solution of some former writer. . . .

[Johnson quotes Jenyns's argument—really a series of unsupported statements—that what appears evil to individuals contributes to the good of the whole.]

This is elegant and acute, but will by no means calm discontent or silence curiosity; for whether evil can be wholly separated from good or not, it is plain that they may be mixed in various degrees, and as far as human eyes can judge, the degree of evil might have been less without any impediment to good.

The second Letter *on the Evils of Imperfection*, is little more than a paraphrase of *Pope*'s epistles, or yet less than a paraphrase, a mere translation of poetry into prose. This is surely to attack difficulty with very disproportionate abilities, to cut the *Gordian* knot with very blunt instruments. When we are told of the insufficiency of former solutions, why is one of the latest, which no man can have forgotten, given us again? I am told, that this pamphlet is not the effort of hunger; What can it be then but the product of vanity? and yet how can vanity be gratified by plagiarism, or transcription? When this speculatist finds himself prompted to another performance, let him consider whether he is about to disburthen his mind or employ his fingers; and if I might venture to offer him a subject, I should wish that he would solve this question, Why he that has nothing to write, should desire to be a writer?

Yet is not this letter without some sentiments, which though not new, are of great importance, and may be read with pleasure in the thousandth repetition.

"Whatever we enjoy is purely a free gift from our Creator; but that we enjoy no more, can never sure be deemed an injury, or a just reason to question his infinite benevolence. All our happiness is owing to his goodness; but that it is no greater, is owing only to ourselves, that is, to our not having any inherent right to any happiness, or even to any existence at all. This is no more to be imputed to God, than the wants of a beggar to the person who has relieved him: that he had something was owing to his benefactor: but that he had no more, only to his own original poverty."

Thus far he speaks what every man must approve, and what every wise man has said before him. He then gives us the system of subordination, not invented, for it was known I think to the *Arabian* metaphysicians, but adopted by *Pope*; and from him borrowed by the diligent researches of this great investigator.

"No system can possibly be formed, even in imagination, without a subordination of parts. Every animal body must have different members, subservient to each other; every picture must be composed of various colours, and of light and shade; all harmony must be formed of trebles, tenors, and basses; every beautiful and useful edifice must consist of higher and lower, more and less magnificent apartments. This is in the very essence of all created things, and therefore cannot be prevented by any means whatever, unless by not creating them at all."

These instances are used instead of *Pope*'s *Oak* and *weeds*, or *Jupiter* and his *satellites*; but neither *Pope*, nor this writer have much contributed to solve the difficulty. Perfection or imperfection of unconscious beings has no meaning as referred to themselves; the *bass* and the *treble* are equally perfect; the mean and magnificent apartments feel no pleasure or pain from the comparison. *Pope* might ask the *weed*, why it was less than the *Oak*, but the *weed* would never ask the question for itself. The *bass* and *treble* differ only to the hearer, meanness and magnificence only to the inhabitant. There is no evil but must inhere in a conscious being, or be referred to it; that is, evil must be felt before it is evil. Yet even on this subject many questions might be offered which human understanding has not yet answered, and which the present haste of this extract will not suffer me to dilate. . . .

[Johnson quotes Jenyns's recapitulation of the theory of the Great Chain of Being: that God's goodness necessarily created the greatest possible variety of beings, which range (like links on a chain) from the highest to the lowest possible degree of perfection; thus man's imperfections result necessarily from his position on the scale of existence.]

This doctrine of the regular subordination of beings, the scale of existence, and the chain of nature, I have often considered, but always left the Inquiry in doubt and uncertainty.

That every being not infinite, compared with infinity, must be imperfect, is evident to intuition; that whatever is imperfect must have a certain line which it cannot pass, is equally certain. But the reason which determined this limit, and for which such being was suffered to advance thus far and no further, we shall never be able to discern. Our discoveries tell us, the Creator has made beings of all orders, and that therefore one of them must be such a man. But this system seems to be established on a concession which if it be refused cannot be extorted.

Every reason which can be brought to prove, that there are beings of every possible sort, will provide that there is the greatest number possible of every sort of beings; but this with respect to man we know, if we know any thing, not to be true.

It does not appear even to the imagination, that of three orders of being, the first and the third receive any advantage from the imperfection of the second, or that indeed they may not equally exist, though the second had never been, or should cease to be, and why should that be concluded necessary, which cannot be proved even to be useful?

The scale of existence from infinity to nothing, cannot possibly have being. The highest being not infinite must be, as has been often observed, at an infinite distance below infinity. *Cheyne*, who, with the desire inherent in mathematicians to reduce every thing to mathematical images, considers all existence as a *cone*, allows that the basis is at an infinite distance from the body.[1] And in this distance between finite and infinite, there will be room for ever for an infinite series of indefinable existence.

Between the lowest positive existence and nothing, wherever we suppose positive existence to cease, is another chasm infinitely deep; where there is room again for endless orders of subordinate nature, continued for ever and for ever, and yet infinitely superior to non-existence.

To these meditations humanity is unequal. But yet we may ask, not of our maker, but of each other, since on the one side creation, wherever it stops, must stop infinitely below infinity, and on the other infinitely above nothing, what necessity there is that it should proceed so far either way, that beings so high or so low should ever have existed. We may ask; but I believe no created wisdom can give an adequate answer.

Nor is this all. In the scale, wherever it begins or ends, are

---

[1] George Cheyne, *Philosophical Principles of Natural Religion* (1705–15).

infinite vacuities. At whatever distance we suppose the next
order of beings to be above man, there is room for an intermediate order of beings between them; and if for one order
then for infinite orders; since every thing that admits of more
or less, and consequently all the parts of that which admits
them, may be infinitely divided. So that, as far as we can
judge, there may be room in the vacuity between any two
steps of the scale, or between any two points of the cone of
being for infinite exertion of infinite power.

Thus it appears how little reason those who repose their
reason upon the scale of being have to triumph over them who
recur to any other expedient of solution, and what difficulties
arise on every side to repress the rebellions of presumptuous
decision. *Qui pauca considerat, facile pronunciat* [He who
considers little, easily pronounces judgment]. In our passage
through the boundless ocean of disquisition we often take
fogs for land, and after having long toiled to approach them
find, instead of repose and harbours, new storms of objection
and fluctuations of uncertainty.

We are next entertained with *Pope*'s alleviations of those
evils which we are doomed to suffer.

"Poverty, or the want of riches, is generally compensated
by having more hopes and fewer fears, by a greater share of
health, and a more exquisite relish of the smallest enjoyments,
than those who possess them are usually bless'd with. The
want of taste and genius, with all the pleasures that arise from
them, are commonly recompensed by a more useful kind of
common sense, together with a wonderful delight, as well as
success, in the busy pursuits of a scrambling world. The sufferings of the sick are greatly relieved by many trifling gratifications imperceptible to others, and sometimes almost repaid
by the inconceivable transports occasioned by the return of
health and vigour. Folly cannot be very grievous, because
imperceptible; and I doubt not but there is some truth in
that rant of a mad poet, that there is a pleasure in being mad,
which none but madmen know. Ignorance, or the want of
knowledge and literature, the appointed lot of all born to
poverty, and the drudgeries of life, is the only opiate capable
of infusing that insensibility which can enable them to endure
the miseries of the one, and the fatigues of the other. It is a
cordial administered by the gracious hand of providence; of
which they ought never to be deprived by an ill-judged and

improper education. It is the basis of all subordination, the support of society, and the privilege of individuals: and I have ever thought it a most remarkable instance of the divine wisdom, that whereas in all animals, whose individuals rise little above the rest of their species, knowledge is instinctive; in man, whose individuals are so widely different, it is acquired by education; by which means the prince and the labourer, the philosopher and the peasant, are in some measure fitted for their respective situations."

Much of these positions is perhaps true, and the whole paragraph might well pass without censure, were not objections necessary to the establishment of knowledge. *Poverty* is very gently paraphrased by *want of riches*. In that sense almost every man may in his own opinion be poor. But there is another poverty which is *want of competence*, of all that can soften the miseries of life, of all that can diversify attention, or delight imagination. There is yet another poverty which is want of *necessaries*, a species of poverty which no care of the publick, no charity of particulars, can preserve many from feeling openly, and many secretly.

That hope and fear are inseparably or very frequently connected with poverty, and riches, my surveys of life have not informed me. The milder degrees of poverty are sometimes supported by hope, but the more severe often sink down in motionless despondence. Life must be seen before it can be known. This author and *Pope* perhaps never saw the miseries which they imagine thus easy to be born. The poor indeed are insensible of many little vexations which sometimes imbitter the possessions and pollute the enjoyments of the rich. They are not pained by casual incivility, or mortified by the mutilation of a compliment; but this happiness is like that of a malefactor who ceases to feel the cords that bind him when the pincers are tearing his flesh.

That want of taste for one enjoyment is supplied by the pleasures of some other, may be fairly allowed. But the compensations of sickness I have never found near to equivalence, and the transports of recovery only prove the intenseness of the pain.

With folly no man is willing to confess himself very intimately acquainted, and therefore its pains and pleasures are kept secret. But what the author says of its happiness seems applicable only to fatuity, or gross dulness, for that inferiority of understanding which makes one man without any other reason the slave, or tool, or property of another, which makes him sometimes useless, and sometimes ridiculous, is often felt with very quick sensibility. On the happiness of madmen, as the case is not very frequent, it is not necessary to raise a disquisition, but I cannot forbear to observe, that I never yet knew disorders of mind encrease felicity: every madman is either arrogant and irascible, or gloomy and suspicious, or possessed by some passion or notion destructive to his quiet. He has always discontent in his look, and malignity in his bosom. And, if we had the power of choice, he would soon repent who should resign his reason to secure his peace.

Concerning the portion of ignorance necessary to make the condition of the lower classes of mankind safe to the public and tolerable to themselves, both morals and policy exact a nicer enquiry than will be very soon or very easily made. There is undoubtedly a degree of knowledge which will direct a man to refer all to providence, and to acquiesce in the condition which omniscient goodness has determined to allot him; to consider this world as a phantom that must soon glide from before his eyes, and the distresses and vexations that encompass him, as dust scattered in his path, as a blast that chills him for a moment, and passes off for ever.

Such wisdom, arising from the comparison of a part with the whole of our existence, those that want it most cannot possibly obtain from philosophy, nor unless the method of education, and the general tenour of life are changed, will very easily receive it from religion. The bulk of mankind is not likely to be very wise or very good: and I know not whether there are not many states of life, in which all knowledge less than the highest wisdom, will produce discontent and danger. I believe it may be sometimes found, that a *little learning* is to a poor man a *dangerous thing*. But such is the condition of humanity, that we easily see, or quickly feel the wrong, but cannot always distinguish the right. Whatever knowledge is superfluous, in irremediable poverty, is hurtful, but the difficulty is to determine when poverty is irremediable, and at what point superfluity begins. Gross ignorance every man has found equally dangerous with perverted knowledge. Men left wholly to their appetites and their instincts, with little sense of moral or religious obligation, and with very faint distinctions of right and wrong, can never be safely employed, or confidently trusted: they can be honest only by obstinacy, and diligent only by compulsion or caprice. Some instruction, therefore, is necessary, and much perhaps may be dangerous.

Though it should be granted that those who are *born to poverty and drudgery* should not be *deprived* by an *improper education* of the *opiate* of *ignorance*; even this concession will not be of much use to direct our practice, unless it be determined who are those that are *born to poverty*. To entail irreversible poverty upon generation after generation only because the ancestor happened to be poor, is in itself cruel, if not unjust, and is wholly contrary to the maxims of a commercial nation, which always suppose and promote a rotation of property, and offer every individual a chance of mending his condition by his diligence. Those who communicate literature to the son of a poor man, consider him as one not born to poverty, but to the necessity of deriving a better fortune from himself. In this attempt, as in others, many fail, and many succeed. Those that fail will feel their misery more acutely; but since poverty is now confessed to be such a calamity as cannot be born without the opiate of insensibility, I hope the happiness of those whom education enables to escape from it, may turn the ballance against that exacerbation which the others suffer.

I am always afraid of determining on the side of envy or cruelty. The privileges of education may sometimes be improperly bestowed, but I shall always fear to with-hold them, lest I should be yielding to the suggestions of pride, while I persuade myself that I am following the maxims of policy; and under the appearance of salutary restraints, should be indulging the lust of dominion, and that malevolence which delights in seeing others depressed.

Pope's doctrine is at last exhibited in a comparison, which, like other proofs of the same kind, is better adapted to delight the fancy than convince the reason.

"Thus the universe resembles a large and well-regulated family, in which all the officers and servants, and even the domestic animals, are subservient to each other in a proper subordination: each enjoys the privileges and perquisites peculiar to his place, and at the same time contributes by that just subordination to the magnificence and happiness of the whole."

The magnificence of a house is of use or pleasure always to

the master, and sometimes to the domestics. But the magnificence of the universe adds nothing to the supreme Being; for any part of its inhabitants with which human knowledge is acquainted, an universe much less spacious or splendid would have been sufficient; and of happiness it does not appear that any is communicated from the Beings of a lower world to those of a higher.

The enquiry after the cause of *natural evil* is continued in the third letter, in which, as in the former, there is mixture of borrowed truth, and native folly, of some notions just and trite, with others uncommon and ridiculous.

His opinion of the value and importance of happiness is certainly just, and I shall insert it, not that it will give any information to any reader, but it may serve to shew how the most common notion may be swelled in sound, and diffused in bulk, till it shall perhaps astonish the author himself.

"Happiness is the only thing of real value in existence; neither riches, nor power, nor wisdom, nor learning, nor strength, nor beauty, nor virtue, nor religion, nor even life itself, being of any importance, but as they contribute to its production. All these are in themselves neither good nor evil; happiness alone is their great end, and they are desireable only as they tend to promote it." . . .

In all this there is nothing that can silence the enquiries of curiosity, or calm the perturbations of doubt. Whether subordination implies imperfection may be disputed. The means respecting themselves, may be as perfect as the end. The weed as a weed is no less perfect than the oak as an oak. That *imperfection implies evil and evil suffering*, is by no means evident. Imperfection may imply privative evil, or the absence of some good, but this privation produces no suffering, but by the help of knowledge. An infant at the breast is yet an imperfect man, but there is no reason for belief that he is unhappy by his immaturity, unless some positive pain be superadded.

When this author presumes to speak of the universe, I would advise him a little to distrust his own faculties, however large and comprehensive. Many words easily understood on common occasion, become uncertain and figurative when applied to the works of Omnipotence. Subordination in human affairs is well understood, but when it is attributed to the universal system, its meaning grows less certain, like the petty distinctions of locality, which are of good use upon our own globe, but have no meaning with regard to infinite space, in which nothing is *high* or *low*.

That if a man, by exaltation to a higher nature were exempted from the evils which he now suffers, some other being must suffer them; that if man were not man, some other being must be man, is a position arising from his established notion of the scale of being. A notion to which *Pope* has given some importance by adopting it, and of which I have therefore endeavoured to show the uncertainty and inconsistency. This scale of being I have demonstrated to be raised by presumptuous imagination, to rest on nothing at the bottom, to lean on nothing at the top, and to have vacuities from step to step through which any order of being may sink into nihility without any inconvenience, so far as we can judge to the next rank above or below it. We are therefore little enlightened by a writer who tells us that any being in the state of man must suffer what man suffers, when the only question, that requires to be resolved is, Why any being is in this state?

Of poverty and labour he gives just and elegant representations, which yet do not remove the difficulty of the first and fundamental question, though supposing the present state of man necessary, they may supply some motives to content.

"Poverty is what all could not possibly have been exempted from, not only by reason of the fluctuating nature of human possessions, but because the world could not subsist without it; for had all been rich, none could have submitted to the commands of another, or the necessary drudgeries of life; thence all governments must have been dissolved, arts neglected, and lands uncultivated, and so an universal penury have overwhelmed all, instead of now and then pinching a few. Hence, by the by, appears the great excellence of charity, by which men are enabled by a particular distribution of the blessings and enjoyments of life, on proper occasions, to prevent that poverty which by a general one omnipotence itself could never have prevented: so that, by inforcing this duty, God as it were demands our assistance to promote universal happiness, and to shut out misery at every door, where it strives to intrude itself.

"Labour, indeed, God might easily have excused us from, since at his command, the earth would readily have poured forth all her treasures without our inconsiderable assistance:

but if the severest labour cannot sufficiently subdue the malignity of human nature, what plots and machinations, what wars, rapine and devastation, what profligacy and licentiousness must have been the consequences of universal idleness! so that labour ought only to be looked upon as a task kindly imposed upon us by our indulgent creator, necessary to preserve our health, our safety, and our innocence."

I am afraid that *the latter end of his commonwealth forgets the beginning.* If God *could easily have excused us from labour,* I do not comprehend why *he could not possibly have exempted all from poverty.* For poverty, in its easier and more tolerable degree, is little more than necessity of labour, and, in its more severe and deplorable state, little more than inability for labour. To be poor is to work for others, or to want the succour of others without work. And the same exuberant fertility which would make work unnecessary might make poverty impossible.

Surely a man who seems not completely master of his own opinion, should have spoken more cautiously of omnipotence, nor have presumed to say what it could perform, or what it could prevent. I am in doubt whether those who stand highest in *the scale of being* speak thus confidently of the dispensations of their maker.

For fools rush in, where angels fear to tread.[2]

Of our inquietudes of mind his account is still less reasonable. "Whilst men are injured, they must be inflamed with anger; and whilst they see cruelties, they must be melted with pity; whilst they perceive danger, they must be sensible of fear." This is to give a reason for all evil, by showing that one evil produces another. If there is danger there ought to be fear; but if fear is an evil, why should there be danger? His vindication of pain is of the same kind: pain is useful to alarm us, that we may shun greater evils, but those greater evils must be presupposed that the fitness of pain may appear. . . .

Having thus dispatched the consideration of particular evils, he comes at last to a general reason for which *evil* may be said to be *our good.*[3] He is of opinion that there is some inconceivable benefit in pain abstractedly considered; that pain

---

[2] Pope, *Essay on Criticism*, line 625.
[3] Johnson ironically applies the words of Milton's Satan: "Evil, be thou my good" (*Paradise Lost*, IV, 110).

however inflicted, or wherever felt, communicates some good to the general system of being, and that every animal is some way or other the better for the pain of every other animal. This opinion he carries so far as to suppose that there passes some principle of union through all animal life, as attraction is communicated to all corporeal nature, and that the evils suffered on this globe, may by some inconceivable means contribute to the felicity of the inhabitants of the remotest planet.

How the origin of evil is brought nearer to human conception by any *inconceivable* means, I am not able to discover. We believed that the present system of creation was right, though we could not explain the adaptation of one part to the other, or for the whole succession of causes and consequences. Where has this enquirer added to the little knowledge that we had before. He has told us of the benefits of evil, which no man feels, and relations between distant parts of the universe, which he cannot himself conceive. There was enough in this question inconceivable before, and we have little advantage from a new inconceivable solution.

I do not mean to reproach this author for not knowing what is equally hidden from learning and from ignorance. The shame is to impose words for ideas upon ourselves or others. To imagine that we are going forward when we are only turning round. To think that there is any difference between him that gives no reason, and him that gives a reason, which by his own confession cannot be conceived.

But that he may not be thought to conceive nothing but things inconceivable, he has at last thought on a way by which human sufferings may produce good effects. He imagines that as we have not only animals for food, but choose some for our diversion, the same privilege may be allowed to some beings above us, *who may deceive, torment, or destroy us for the ends only of their own pleasure or utility*. This he again finds impossible to be conceived, *but that impossibility lessens not the probability of the conjecture, which by analogy is so strongly confirmed*.

I cannot resist the temptation of contemplating this analogy, which I think he might have carried further very much to the advantage of his argument. He might have shewn that these *hunters whose game is man* have many sports analogous to our own. As we drown whelps and kittens, they amuse themselves now and then with sinking a ship, and stand round the fields of *Blenheim* or the walls of *Prague*, as we encircle a cock-pit. As we shoot a bird flying, they take a man in the midst of his business or pleasure, and knock him down with an apoplexy. Some of them, perhaps, are virtuosi, and delight in the operations of an asthma, as a human philosopher in the effects of the air pump. To swell a man with a tympany is as good sport as to blow a frog. Many a merry bout have these frolic beings at the vicissitudes of an ague, and good sport it is to see a man tumble with an epilepsy, and revive and tumble again, and all this he knows not why. As they are wiser and more powerful than we, they have more exquisite diversions, for we have no way of procuring any sport so brisk and so lasting as the paroxysms of the gout and stone which undoubtedly must make high mirth, especially if the play be a little diversified with the blunders and puzzles of the blind and deaf. We know not how far their sphere of observation may extend. Perhaps now and then a merry being may place himself in such a situation as to enjoy at once all the varieties of an epidemical disease, or amuse his leisure with the tossings and contortions of every possible pain exhibited together.

One sport the merry malice of these beings has found means of enjoying to which we have nothing equal or similar. They now and then catch a mortal proud of his parts,[4] and flattered either by the submission of those who court his kindness, or the notice of those who suffer him to court theirs. A head thus prepared for the reception of false opinions, and the projection of vain designs, they easily fill with idle notions, till in time they make their plaything an author: their first diversion commonly begins with an Ode or an epistle, then rises perhaps to a political irony, and is at last brought to its height, by a treatise of philosophy. Then begins the poor animal to entangle himself in sophisms, and flounder in absurdity, to talk confidently of the scale of being, and to give solutions which himself confesses impossible to be understood. Sometimes, however, it happens that their pleasure is without much mischief. The author feels no pain, but while they are wondering at the extravagance of his opinion, and pointing him out to one another as a new example of human folly, he is enjoying his own applause, and that of his companions, and perhaps is elevated with the hope of standing at the head of a new sect.

[4] *parts:* intellectual ability.

Many of the books which now croud the world, may be justly suspected to be written for the sake of some invisible order of beings, for surely they are of no use to any of the corporeal inhabitants of the world. Of the productions of the last bounteous year, how many can be said to serve any purpose of use or pleasure. The only end of writing is to enable the readers better to enjoy life, or better to endure it: and how will either of those be put more in our power by him who tells us, that we are puppets, of which some creature not much wiser than ourselves manages the wires. That a set of beings unseen and unheard, are hovering about us, trying experiments upon our sensibility, putting us in agonies to see our limbs quiver, torturing us to madness, that they may laugh at our vagaries, sometimes obstructing the bile, that they may see how a man looks when he is yellow: sometimes breaking a traveller's bones to try how he will get home; sometimes wasting a man to a skeleton, and sometimes killing him fat for the greater elegance of his hide.

This is an account of natural evil, which though, like the rest, not quite new is very entertaining, though I know not how much it may contribute to patience. The only reason why we should contemplate evil is, that we may bear it better, and I am afraid nothing is much more placidly endured, for the sake of making others sport. . . .

[After quoting and approving Jenyns's discussion of "the essence and the end of virtue," Johnson summarizes his trite explanations for the evils in human government and religion.]

Religion has been, he says, corrupted by the wickedness of those to whom it was communicated, and has lost part of its efficacy by its connection with temporal interest and human passion.

He justly observes, that from all this, no conclusion can be drawn against the divine original of christianity, since the objections arise not from the nature of the revelation, but of him to whom it is communicated.

All this is known, and all this is true, but why, we have not yet discovered. Our author, if I understand him right, pursues the argument thus: The religion of man produces evils, because the morality of man is imperfect; his morality is imperfect, that he may be justly a subject of punishment: he is made subject to punishment because the pain of part is necessary to the happiness of the whole; pain is necessary to happiness no mortal can tell why or how. . . .

The History of Rasselas, Prince of Abyssinia

[Johnson had been interested in Abyssinia since he translated Father Lobo's *Voyage* in 1735, and he included a philosophical tale about Seged, Lord of Ethiopia, in *The Rambler* (Numbers 204 and 205). He had read several books on the subject, from which he got the name Rasselas (*ras* is the root word for "chief" in Amharic, and there was a prince named Rasselach), the tradition that the Abyssinian princes were kept in a secluded paradise, and the story that the fourth child of one emperor escaped. With this background in his mind, Johnson was able to compose *Rasselas* quickly—in the evenings of one week—in order to pay the expenses occasioned by his mother's death.]

I
Description of a Palace in a Valley

Ye who listen with credulity to the whispers of fancy, and pursue with eagerness the phantoms of hope; who expect that age will perform the promises of youth, and that the deficiencies of the present day will be supplied by the morrow; attend to the history of Rasselas prince of Abyssinia.

Rasselas was the fourth son of the mighty emperor in whose dominions the Father of Waters[1] begins his course; whose bounty pours down the streams of plenty, and scatters over half the world the harvests of Egypt.

According to the custom which has descended from age to age among the monarchs of the torrid zone, Rasselas was confined in a private palace, with the other sons and daughters of Abyssinian royalty, till the order of succession should call him to the throne.

The place, which the wisdom or policy of antiquity had destined for the residence of the Abyssinian princes, was a spacious valley in the kingdom of Amhara, surrounded on every side by mountains, of which the summits overhang the middle part. The only passage by which it could be entered was a cavern that passed under a rock, of which it has long been disputed whether it was the work of nature or of human industry. The outlet of the cavern was concealed by a thick wood, and the mouth which opened into the valley was closed with gates of iron, forged by the artificers of ancient days, so massy that no man could, without the help of engines, open or shut them.

From the mountains on every side, rivulets descended that filled all the valley with verdure and fertility, and formed a

[1] *Father of Waters:* the Nile.

lake in the middle inhabited by fish of every species, and
frequented by every fowl whom nature has taught to dip
the wing in water. This lake discharged its superfluities by a
stream which entered a dark cleft of the mountain on the
northern side, and fell with dreadful noise from precipice to
precipice till it was heard no more.

The sides of the mountains were covered with trees, the
banks of the brooks were diversified with flowers; every blast
shook spices from the rocks, and every month dropped fruits
upon the ground. All animals that bite the grass, or browse
the shrub, whether wild or tame, wandered in this extensive
circuit, secured from beasts of prey by the mountains which
confined them. On one part were flocks and herds feeding
in the pastures, on another all the beasts of chase frisking in
the lawns; the sprightly kid was bounding on the rocks, the
subtle monkey frolicking in the trees, and the solemn ele-
phant reposing in the shade. All the diversities of the world
were brought together, the blessings of nature were collected,
and its evils extracted and excluded.

The valley, wide and fruitful, supplied its inhabitants with
the necessaries of life, and all delights and superfluities were
added at the annual visit which the emperor paid his children,
when the iron gate was opened to the sound of music; and
during eight days every one that resided in the valley was
required to propose whatever might contribute to make
seclusion pleasant, to fill up the vacancies of attention, and
lessen the tediousness of time. Every desire was immediately
granted. All the artificers of pleasure were called to gladden
the festivity; the musicians exerted the power of harmony,
and the dancers showed their activity before the princes, in
hope that they should pass their lives in this blissful captivity,
to which these only were admitted whose performance was
thought able to add novelty to luxury. Such was the appearance of security and delight which this retirement afforded
that they to whom it was new always desired that it might be
perpetual; and as those on whom the iron gate had once
closed were never suffered to return, the effect of longer
experience could not be known. Thus every year produced
new schemes of delight, and new competitors for imprisonment.

The palace stood on an eminence raised about thirty paces
above the surface of the lake. It was divided into many
squares or courts, built with greater or less magnificence

according to the rank of those for whom they were designed. The roofs were turned into arches of massy stone joined with a cement that grew harder by time, and the building stood from century to century, deriding the solstitial rains and equinoctial hurricanes, without need of reparation.

This house, which was so large as to be fully known to none but some ancient officers who successively inherited the secrets of the place, was built as if suspicion herself had dictated the plan. To every room there was an open and secret passage, every square had a communication with the rest, either from the upper stories by private galleries, or by subterranean passages from the lower apartments. Many of the columns had unsuspected cavities, in which a long race of monarchs had reposited their treasures. They then closed up the opening with marble, which was never to be removed but in the utmost exigencies of the kingdom; and recorded their accumulations in a book which was itself concealed in a tower not entered but by the emperor, attended by the prince who stood next in succession.

II
The Discontent of Rasselas in the Happy Valley

Here the sons and daughters of Abyssinia lived only to know the soft vicissitudes² of pleasure and repose, attended by all that were skillful to delight, and gratified with whatever the senses can enjoy. They wandered in gardens of fragrance, and slept in the fortresses of security. Every art was practiced to make them pleased with their own condition. The sages who instructed them told them of nothing but the miseries of public life, and described all beyond the mountains as regions of calamity, where discord was always raging, and where man preyed upon man.

To heighten their opinion of their own felicity, they were daily entertained with songs, the subject of which was the *happy valley*. Their appetites were excited by frequent enumerations of different enjoyments, and revelry and merriment was the business of every hour from the dawn of morning to the close of even.

These methods were generally successful; few of the princes

---

² *vicissitudes:* alternations.

had ever wished to enlarge their bounds, but passed their lives in full conviction that they had all within their reach that art or nature could bestow, and pitied those whom fate had excluded from this seat of tranquillity, as the sport of chance, and the slaves of misery.

Thus they rose in the morning and lay down at night, pleased with each other and with themselves, all but Rasselas, who, in the twenty-sixth year of his age, began to withdraw himself from their pastimes and assemblies, and to delight in solitary walks and silent meditation. He often sat before tables covered with luxury, and forgot to taste the dainties that were placed before him: he rose abruptly in the midst of the song, and hastily retired beyond the sound of music. His attendants observed the change and endeavored to renew his love of pleasure: he neglected their officiousness, repulsed their invitations, and spent day after day on the banks of rivulets sheltered with trees, where he sometimes listened to the birds in the branches, sometimes observed the fish playing in the stream, and anon cast his eyes upon the pastures and mountains filled with animals, of which some were biting the herbage, and some sleeping among the bushes.

This singularity of his humor made him much observed. One of the sages, in whose conversation he had formely delighted, followed him secretly, in hope of discovering the cause of his disquiet. Rasselas, who knew not that any one was near him, having for some time fixed his eyes upon the goats that were browsing among the rocks, began to compare their condition with his own.

"What," said he, "makes the difference between man and all the rest of the animal creation? Every beast that strays beside me has the same corporal necessities with myself; he is hungry and crops the grass, he is thirsty and drinks the stream, his thirst and hunger are appeased, he is satisfied and sleeps; he rises again and is hungry, he is again fed and is at rest. I am hungry and thirsty like him, but when thirst and hunger cease I am not at rest; I am, like him, pained with want, but am not, like him, satisfied with fullness. The intermediate hours are tedious and gloomy; I long again to be hungry that I may again quicken my attention. The birds peck the berries or the corn, and fly away to the groves where they sit in seeming happiness on the branches, and waste their lives in tuning one unvaried series of sounds. I likewise can call the lutanist and the singer, but the sounds that pleased me yesterday weary me today, and will grow yet more wearisome tomorrow. I can discover within me no power of perception which is not glutted with its proper[3] pleasure, yet I do not feel myself delighted. Man has surely some latent sense of which this place affords no gratification, or he has some desires distinct from sense which must be satisfied before he can be happy."

After this he lifted up his head and, seeing the moon rising, walked towards the palace. As he passed through the fields, and saw the animals around him, "Ye," said he, "are happy, and need not envy me that walk thus among you, burthened with myself; nor do I, ye gentle beings, envy your felicity; for it is not the felicity of man. I have many distresses from which ye are free; I fear pain when I do not feel it; I sometimes shrink at evils recollected, and sometimes start at evils anticipated: surely the equity of providence has balanced peculiar sufferings with peculiar enjoyments."

With observations like these the prince amused himself as he returned, uttering them with a plaintive voice, yet with a look that discovered[4] him to feel some complacence in his own perspicacity, and to receive some solace of the miseries of life from consciousness of the delicacy with which he felt, and the eloquence with which he bewailed them. He mingled cheerfully in the diversions of the evening, and all rejoiced to find that his heart was lightened.

III
The Wants of Him That Wants Nothing

On the next day his old instructor, imagining that he had now made himself acquainted with his disease of mind, was in hope of curing it by counsel, and officiously sought an opportunity of conference, which the prince, having long considered him as one whose intellects were exhausted, was not very willing to afford: "Why," said he, "does this man thus intrude upon me; shall I be never suffered to forget those lectures which pleased only while they were new, and to become new again must be forgotten?" He then walked into the wood, and composed himself to his usual meditations,

[3] *proper:* appropriate.
[4] *discovered:* revealed.

when, before his thoughts had taken any settled form, he perceived his pursuer at his side, and was at first prompted by his impatience to go hastily away; but, being unwilling to offend a man whom he had once reverenced and still loved, he invited him to sit down with him on the bank.

The old man, thus encouraged, began to lament the change which had been lately observed in the prince, and to inquire why he so often retired from the pleasures of the palace, to loneliness and silence. "I fly from pleasure," said the prince, "because pleasure has ceased to please; I am lonely because I am miserable, and am unwilling to cloud with my presence the happiness of others." "You, sir," said the sage, "are the first who has complained of misery in the *happy valley*. I hope to convince you that your complaints have no real cause. You are here in full possession of all that the emperor of Abyssinia can bestow; here is neither labor to be endured nor danger to be dreaded, yet here is all that labor or danger can procure or purchase. Look round and tell me which of your wants is without supply: if you want nothing, how are you unhappy?"

"That I want nothing," said the prince, "or that I know not what I want, is the cause of my complaint; if I had any known want, I should have a certain wish; that wish would excite endeavor, and I should not then repine to see the sun move so slowly towards the western mountain, or lament when the day breaks and sleep will not longer hide me from myself. When I see the kids and the lambs chasing one another, I fancy that I should be happy if I had something to pursue. But, possessing all that I can want, I find one day and one hour exactly like another, except that the latter is still more tedious than the former. Let your experience inform me how the day may now seem as short as in my childhood, while nature was yet fresh, and every moment showed me what I never had observed before. I have already enjoyed too much; give me something to desire."

The old man was surprised at this new species of affliction, and knew not what to reply, yet was unwilling to be silent. "Sir," said he, "if you had seen the miseries of the world, you would know how to value your present state." "Now," said the prince, "you have given me something to desire; I shall long to see the miseries of the world, since the sight of them is necessary to happiness."

IV
The Prince Continues to Grieve and Muse

At this time the sound of music proclaimed the hour of repast, and the conversation was concluded. The old man went away sufficiently discontented to find that his reasonings had produced the only conclusion which they were intended to prevent. But in the decline of life shame and grief are of short duration; whether it be that we bear easily what we have borne long, or that, finding ourselves in age less regarded, we less regard others; or that we look with slight regard upon afflictions, to which we know that the hand of death is about to put an end.

The prince, whose views were extended to a wider space, could not speedily quiet his emotions. He had been before terrified at the length of life which nature promised him, because he considered that in a long time much must be endured; he now rejoiced in his youth, because in many years much might be done.

This first beam of hope that had been ever darted into his mind rekindled youth in his cheeks, and doubled the luster of his eyes. He was fired with the desire of doing something, though he knew not yet with distinctness either end or means.

He was now no longer gloomy and unsocial; but, considering himself as master of a secret stock of happiness, which he could enjoy only by concealing it, he affected to be busy in all schemes of diversion, and endeavored to make others pleased with the state of which he himself was weary. But pleasures never can be so multiplied or continued as not to leave much of life unemployed; there were many hours, both of the night and day, which he could spend without suspicion in solitary thought. The load of life was much lightened: he went eagerly into the assemblies, because he supposed the frequency of his presence necessary to the success of his purposes; he retired gladly to privacy, because he had now a subject of thought.

His chief amusement was to picture to himself that world which he had never seen; to place himself in various conditions; to be entangled in imaginary difficulties, and to be engaged in wild adventures: but his benevolence always terminated his projects in the relief of distress, the detection of fraud, the defeat of oppression, and the diffusion of happiness.

Thus passed twenty months of the life of Rasselas. He busied himself so intensely in visionary bustle that he forgot his real solitude; and, amidst hourly preparations for the various incidents of human affairs, neglected to consider by what means he should mingle with mankind.

One day, as he was sitting on a bank, he feigned to himself an orphan virgin robbed of her little portion[5] by a treacherous lover, and crying after him for restitution and redress. So strongly was the image impressed upon his mind, that he started up in the maid's defense, and ran forward to seize the plunderer with all the eagerness of real pursuit. Fear naturally quickens the flight of guilt. Rasselas could not catch the fugitive with his utmost efforts; but, resolving to weary, by perseverance, him whom he could not surpass in speed, he pressed on till the foot of the mountain stopped his course.

Here he recollected himself, and smiled at his own useless impetuosity. Then raising his eyes to the mountain, "This," said he, "is the fatal obstacle that hinders at once the enjoyment of pleasure, and the exercise of virtue. How long is it that my hopes and wishes have flown beyond this boundary of my life, which yet I never have attempted to surmount!"

Struck with this reflection, he sat down to muse, and remembered that since he first resolved to escape from his confinement the sun had passed twice over him in his annual course. He now felt a degree of regret with which he had never been before acquainted. He considered how much might have been done in the time which had passed, and left nothing real behind it. He compared twenty months with the life of man. "In life," said he, "is not to be counted the ignorance of infancy, or imbecility[6] of age. We are long before we are able to think, and we soon cease from the power of acting. The true period of human existence may be reasonably estimated as forty years, of which I have mused away the four and twentieth part. What I have lost was certain, for I have certainly possessed it; but of twenty months to come who can assure me?"

The consciousness of his own folly pierced him deeply, and he was long before he could be reconciled to himself. "The

---

[5] *portion:* inheritance.
[6] *imbecility:* weakness, mental or physical.

rest of my time," said he, "has been lost by the crime or folly of my ancestors, and the absurd institutions of my country; I remember it with disgust, yet without remorse: but the months that have passed since new light darted into my soul, since I formed a scheme of reasonable felicity, have been squandered by my own fault. I have lost that which can never be restored: I have seen the sun rise and set for twenty months, an idle gazer on the light of heaven: in this time the birds have left the nest of their mother, and committed themselves to the woods and to the skies: the kid has forsaken the teat, and learned by degrees to climb the rocks in quest of independent sustenance. I only have made no advances, but am still helpless and ignorant. The moon by more than twenty changes admonished me of the flux of life; the stream that rolled before my feet upbraided my inactivity. I sat feasting on intellectual luxury, regardless alike of the examples of the earth and the instructions of the planets. Twenty months are passed, who shall restore them!"

These sorrowful meditations fastened upon his mind; he passed four months in resolving to lose no more time in idle resolves, and was awakened to more vigorous exertion by hearing a maid, who had broken a porcelain cup, remark that what cannot be repaired is not to be regretted.

This was obvious; and Rasselas reproached himself that he had not discovered it, having not known, or not considered, how many useful hints are obtained by chance, and how often the mind, hurried by her own ardor to distant views, neglects the truths that lie open before her. He, for a few hours, regretted his regret, and from that time bent his whole mind upon the means of escaping from the valley of happiness.

V
The Prince Meditates His Escape

He now found that it would be very difficult to effect that which it was very easy to suppose effected. When he looked round about him, he saw himself confined by the bars of nature which had never yet been broken, and by the gate, through which none that once had passed it were ever able to return. He was now impatient as an eagle in a grate.[7] He

---

[7] *grate:* cage.

passed week after week in clambering the mountains to see if there was any aperture which the bushes might conceal, but found all the summits inaccessible by their prominence. The iron gate he despaired to open; for it was not only secured with all the power of art, but was always watched by successive sentinels, and was by its position exposed to the perpetual observation of all the inhabitants.

He then examined the cavern through which the waters of the lake were discharged; and, looking down at a time when the sun shone strongly upon its mouth, he discovered it to be full of broken rocks, which, though they permitted the stream to flow through many narrow passages, would stop any body of solid bulk. He returned discouraged and dejected; but, having now known the blessing of hope, resolved never to despair.

In these fruitless searches he spent ten months. The time, however, passed cheerfully away: in the morning he rose with new hope, in the evening applauded his own diligence, and in the night slept sound after his fatigue. He met a thousand amusements which beguiled his labor, and diversified his thoughts. He discerned the various instincts of animals, and properties of plants, and found the place replete with wonders, of which he purposed to solace himself with the contemplation if he should never be able to accomplish his flight; rejoicing that his endeavors, though yet unsuccessful, had supplied him with a source of inexhaustible inquiry.

But his original curiosity was not yet abated; he resolved to obtain some knowledge of the ways of men. His wish still continued, but his hope grew less. He ceased to survey any longer the walls of his prison, and spared to search by new toils for interstices which he knew could not be found, yet determined to keep his design always in view and lay hold on any expedient that time should offer.

VI
A Dissertation on the Art of Flying

Among the artists[8] that had been allured into the happy valley, to labor for the accommodation and pleasure of its inhabitants, was a man eminent for his knowledge of the

[8] *artists:* people skilled in practical science.

mechanic powers, who had contrived many engines both of use and recreation. By a wheel, which the stream turned, he forced the water into a tower, whence it was distributed to all the apartments of the palace. He erected a pavilion in the garden, around which he kept the air always cool by artificial showers. One of the groves, appropriated to the ladies, was ventilated by fans, to which the rivulet that run through it gave a constant motion; and instruments of soft music were placed at proper distances, of which some played by the impulse of the wind and some by the power of the stream.

This artist was sometimes visited by Rasselas, who was pleased with every kind of knowledge, imagining that the time would come when all his acquisitions should be of use to him in the open world. He came one day to amuse himself in his usual manner, and found the master busy in building a sailing chariot: he saw that the design was practicable upon a level surface, and with expressions of great esteem solicited its completion. The workman was pleased to find himself so much regarded by the prince, and resolved to gain yet higher honors. "Sir," said he, "you have seen but a small part of what the mechanic sciences can perform. I have been long of opinion that, instead of the tardy conveyance of ships and chariots, man might use the swifter migration of wings; that the fields of air are open to knowledge, and that only ignorance and idleness need crawl upon the ground."

This hint rekindled the prince's desire of passing the mountains: having seen what the mechanist had already performed, he was willing to fancy that he could do more; yet resolved to inquire further before he suffered hope to afflict him by disappointment. "I am afraid," said he to the artist, "that your imagination prevails over your skill, and that you now tell me rather what you wish than what you know. Every animal has his element assigned him; the birds have the air, and man and beasts the earth." "So," replied the mechanist, "fishes have the water, in which yet beasts can swim by nature, and men by art. He that can swim needs not despair to fly: to swim is to fly in a grosser fluid, and to fly is to swim in a subtler. We are only to proportion our power of resistance to the different density of the matter through which we are to pass. You will be necessarily upborne by the air, if you can renew any impulse upon it faster than the air can recede from the pressure."

"But the exercise of swimming," said the prince, "is very

laborious; the strongest limbs are soon wearied; I am afraid the act of flying will be yet more violent, and wings will be of no great use, unless we can fly further than we can swim."

"The labor of rising from the ground," said the artist, "will be great, as we see it in the heavier domestic fowls; but, as we mount higher, the earth's attraction, and the body's gravity, will be gradually diminished, till we shall arrive at a region where the man will float in the air without any tendency to fall: no care will then be necessary but to move forwards, which the gentlest impulse will effect. You, sir, whose curiosity is so extensive, will easily conceive with what pleasure a philosopher, furnished with wings and hovering in the sky, would see the earth and all its inhabitants rolling beneath him, and presenting to him successively, by its diurnal motion, all the countries within the same parallel. How must it amuse the pendent spectator to see the moving scene of land and ocean, cities, and deserts! To survey with equal security the marts of trade and the fields of battle; mountains infested by barbarians, and fruitful regions gladdened by plenty and lulled by peace! How easily shall we then trace the Nile through all his passage; pass over to distant regions, and examine the face of nature from one extremity of the earth to the other!"

"All this," said the prince, "is much to be desired, but I am afraid that no man will be able to breathe in these regions of speculation and tranquillity. I have been told that respiration is difficult upon lofty mountains, yet from these precipices, though so high as to produce great tenuity of the air, it is very easy to fall: therefore I suspect that from any height where life can be supported, there may be danger of too quick descent."

"Nothing," replied the artist, "will ever be attempted, if all possible objections must be first overcome. If you will favor my project I will try the first flight at my own hazard. I have considered the structure of all volant animals, and find the folding continuity of the bat's wings most easily accommodated to the human form. Upon this model I shall begin my task tomorrow, and in a year expect to tower into the air beyond the malice or pursuit of man. But I will work only on this condition that the art shall not be divulged, and that you shall not require me to make wings for any but ourselves."

"Why," said Rasselas, "should you envy others so great an

advantage? All skill ought to be exerted for universal good; every man has owed much to others, and ought to repay the kindness that he has received."

"If men were all virtuous," returned the artist, "I should with great alacrity teach them all to fly. But what would be the security of the good if the bad could at pleasure invade them from the sky? Against any army sailing through the clouds neither walls nor mountains nor seas could afford any security. A flight of northern savages might hover in the wind, and light at once with irresistible violence upon the capital of a fruitful region that was rolling under them. Even this valley, the retreat of princes, the abode of happiness, might be violated by the sudden descent of some of the naked nations that swarm on the coast of the southern sea."

The prince promised secrecy, and waited for the performance, not wholly hopeless of success. He visited the work from time to time, observed its progress, and remarked many ingenious contrivances to facilitate motion, and unite levity with strength. The artist was every day more certain that he should leave vultures and eagles behind him, and the contagion of his confidence seized upon the prince.

In a year the wings were finished, and, on a morning appointed, the maker appeared furnished for flight on a little promontory: he waved his pinions a while to gather air, then leaped from his stand, and in an instant dropped into the lake. His wings, which were of no use in the air, sustained him in the water, and the prince drew him to land, half dead with terror and vexation.

VII
The Prince Finds a Man of Learning

The prince was not much afflicted by this disaster, having suffered himself to hope for a happier event only because he had no other means of escape in view. He still persisted in his design to leave the happy valley by the first opportunity.

His imagination was now at a stand; he had no prospect of entering into the world; and, notwithstanding all his endeavors to support himself, discontent by degrees preyed upon him and he began again to lose his thoughts in sadness, when the rainy season, which in these countries is periodical, made it inconvenient to wander in the woods.

The rain continued longer and with more violence than had been ever known: the clouds broke on the surrounding mountains, and the torrents streamed into the plain on every side, till the cavern was too narrow to discharge the water. The lake overflowed its banks, and all the level of the valley was covered with the inundation. The eminence, on which the palace was built, and some other spots of rising ground, were all that the eye could now discover. The herds and flocks left the pastures, and both the wild beasts and the tame retreated to the mountains.

This inundation confined all the princes to domestic amusements, and the attention of Rasselas was particularly seized by a poem which Imlac rehearsed upon the various conditions of humanity. He commanded the poet to attend him in his apartment, and recite his verses a second time; then entering into familiar talk, he thought himself happy in having found a man who knew the world so well, and could so skillfully paint the scenes of life. He asked a thousand questions about things to which, though common to all other mortals, his confinement from childhood had kept him a stranger. The poet pitied his ignorance and loved his curiosity, and entertained him from day to day with novelty and instruction, so that the prince regretted the necessity of sleep, and longed till the morning should renew his pleasure.

As they were sitting together, the prince commanded Imlac to relate his history, and to tell by what accident he was forced, or by what motive induced, to close his life in the happy valley. As he was going to begin his narrative, Rasselas was called to a concert, and obliged to restrain his curiosity till the evening.

VIII
The History of Imlac

The close of the day is, in the regions of the torrid zone, the only season of diversion and entertainment, and it was therefore midnight before the music ceased, and the princesses retired. Rasselas then called for his companion and required him to begin the story of his life.

"Sir," said Imlac, "my history will not be long: the life that is devoted to knowledge passes silently away, and is very little diversified by events. To talk in public, to think in solitude, to read and to hear, to inquire and answer inquiries, is the business of a scholar. He wanders about the world without pomp or terror, and is neither known nor valued but by men like himself.

"I was born in the kingdom of Goiama, at no great distance from the fountain[9] of the Nile. My father was a wealthy merchant, who traded between the inland countries of Africk and the ports of the Red Sea. He was honest, frugal, and diligent, but of mean sentiments and narrow comprehension: he desired only to be rich, and to conceal his riches lest he should be spoiled[10] by the governors of the province."

"Surely," said the prince, "my father must be negligent of his charge if any man in his dominions dares take that which belongs to another. Does he not know that kings are accountable for injustice permitted as well as done? If I were emperor, not the meanest of my subjects should be oppressed with impunity. My blood boils when I am told that a merchant durst not enjoy his honest gains for fear of losing them by the rapacity of power. Name the governor who robbed the people, that I may declare his crimes to the emperor."

"Sir," said Imlac, "your ardor is the natural effect of virtue animated by youth: the time will come when you will acquit your father, and perhaps hear with less impatience of the governor. Oppression is, in the Abyssinian dominions, neither frequent nor tolerated; but no form of government has been yet discovered by which cruelty can be wholly prevented. Subordination supposes power on one part and subjection on the other; and if power be in the hands of men it will sometimes be abused. The vigilance of the supreme magistrate may do much, but much will still remain undone. He can never know all the crimes that are committed, and can seldom punish all that he knows."

"This," said the prince, "I do not understand, but I had rather hear thee than dispute. Continue thy narration."

"My father," proceeded Imlac, "originally intended that I should have no other education than such as might qualify me for commerce; and discovering in me great strength of memory and quickness of apprehension often declared his hope that I should be some time the richest man in Abyssinia."

"Why," said the prince, "did thy father desire the increase

9 *fountain:* source.
10 *spoiled:* plundered.

of his wealth, when it was already greater than he durst discover or enjoy? I am unwilling to doubt thy veracity, yet inconsistencies cannot both be true."

"Inconsistencies," answered Imlac, "cannot both be right, but, imputed to man, they may both be true. Yet diversity is not inconsistency. My father might expect a time of greater security. However, some desire is necessary to keep life in motion, and he whose real wants are supplied must admit those of fancy."

"This," said the prince, "I can in some measure conceive. I repent that I interrupted thee."

"With this hope," proceeded Imlac, "he sent me to school; but when I had once found the delight of knowledge, and felt the pleasure of intelligence and the pride of invention, I began silently to despise riches, and determined to disappoint the purpose of my father, whose grossness of conception raised my pity. I was twenty years old before my tenderness would expose me to the fatigue of travel, in which time I had been instructed, by successive masters, in all the literature[11] of my native country. As every hour taught me something new, I lived in a continual course of gratifications; but, as I advanced towards manhood, I lost much of the reverence with which I had been used to look on my instructors; because, when the lesson was ended, I did not find them wiser or better than common men.

"At length my father resolved to initiate me in commerce, and, opening one of his subterranean treasuries, counted out ten thousand pieces of gold. 'This, young man,' said he, 'is the stock with which you must negotiate. I began with less than the fifth part, and you see how diligence and parsimony have increased it. This is your own to waste or to improve. If you squander it by negligence or caprice, you must wait for my death before you will be rich: if, in four years, you double your stock, we will thenceforward let subordination cease, and live together as friends and partners; for he shall always be equal with me, who is equally skilled in the art of growing rich.'

"We laid our money upon camels, concealed in bales of cheap goods, and travelled to the shore of the Red Sea. When I cast my eye on the expanse of waters my heart bounded like that of a prisoner escaped. I felt an unextinguishable

[11] *literature:* learning.

curiosity kindle in my mind, and resolved to snatch this opportunity of seeing the manners[12] of other nations, and of learning sciences unknown in Abyssinia.

"I remembered that my father had obliged me to the improvement of my stock, not by a promise which I ought not to violate but by a penalty which I was at liberty to incur; and therefore determined to gratify my predominant desire, and by drinking at the fountains of knowledge to quench the thirst of curiosity.

"As I was supposed to trade without connection with my father, it was easy for me to become acquainted with the master of a ship and procure a passage to some other country. I had no motives of choice to regulate my voyage; it was sufficient for me that, wherever I wandered, I should see a country which I had not seen before. I therefore entered a ship bound for Surat, having left a letter for my father declaring my intention.

IX
The History of Imlac Continued

"When I first entered upon the world of waters and lost sight of land, I looked round about me with pleasing terror, and thinking my soul enlarged by the boundless prospect imagined that I could gaze round for ever without satiety; but, in a short time, I grew weary of looking on barren uniformity, where I could only see again what I had already seen. I then descended into the ship, and doubted for a while whether all my future pleasures would not end like this in disgust and disappointment. Yet surely, said I, the ocean and the land are very different; the only variety of water is rest and motion, but the earth has mountains and valleys, deserts and cities: it is inhabited by men of different customs and contrary opinions; and I may hope to find variety in life, though I should miss it in nature.

"With this thought I quieted my mind; and amused myself during the voyage, sometimes by learning from the sailors the art of navigation, which I have never practiced, and sometimes by forming schemes for my conduct in different situations, in not one of which I have been ever placed.

[12] *manners*: ways of acting.

"I was almost weary of my naval amusements when we landed safely at Surat. I secured my money, and purchasing some commodities for show joined myself to a caravan that was passing into the inland country. My companions, for some reason or other conjecturing that I was rich, and, by my inquiries and admiration,[13] finding that I was ignorant, considered me as a novice whom they had a right to cheat, and who was to learn at the usual expense the art of fraud. They exposed me to the theft of servants and the exaction of officers, and saw me plundered upon false pretenses, without any advantage to themselves but that of rejoicing in the superiority of their own knowledge."

"Stop a moment," said the prince. "Is there such depravity in man as that he should injure another without benefit to himself? I can easily conceive that all are pleased with superiority; but your ignorance was merely accidental, which, being neither your crime nor your folly, could afford them no reason to applaud themselves; and the knowledge which they had, and which you wanted,[14] they might as effectually have shown by warning, as betraying you."

"Pride," said Imlac, "is seldom delicate, it will please itself with very mean advantages; and envy feels not its own happiness but when it may be compared with the misery of others. They were my enemies because they grieved to think me rich, and my oppressors because they delighted to find me weak."

"Proceed," said the prince. "I doubt not of the facts which you relate, but imagine that you impute them to mistaken motives."

"In this company," said Imlac, "I arrived at Agra, the capital of Indostan, the city in which the great Mogul commonly resides. I applied myself to the language of the country, and in a few months was able to converse with the learned men; some of whom I found morose and reserved, and others easy and communicative; some were unwilling to teach another what they had with difficulty learned themselves; and some showed that the end of their studies was to gain the dignity of instructing.

"To the tutor of the young princes I recommended myself so much that I was presented to the emperor as a man of

---

[13] *admiration:* wondering.
[14] *wanted:* lacked.

uncommon knowledge. The emperor asked me many questions concerning my country and my travels; and though I cannot now recollect anything that he uttered above the power of a common man, he dismissed me astonished at his wisdom and enamored of his goodness.

"My credit was now so high, that the merchants with whom I had travelled applied to me for recommendations to the ladies of the court. I was surprised at their confidence of solicitation, and gently reproached them with their practices on the road. They heard me with cold indifference and showed no tokens of shame or sorrow.

"They then urged their request with the offer of a bribe; but what I would not do for kindness I would not do for money; and refused them, not because they had injured me, but because I would not enable them to injure others; for I knew they would have made use of my credit to cheat those who should buy their wares.

"Having resided at Agra till there was no more to be learned, I traveled into Persia, where I saw many remains of ancient magnificence, and observed many new accommodations[15] of life. The Persians are a nation eminently social, and their assemblies afforded me daily opportunities of remarking characters and manners, and of tracing human nature through all its variations.

"From Persia I passed into Arabia, where I saw a nation at once pastoral and warlike; who live without any settled habitation; whose only wealth is their flocks and herds; and who have yet carried on, through all ages, an hereditary war with all mankind, though they neither covet nor envy their possessions.

X
Imlac's History Continued. A Dissertation upon Poetry

"Wherever I went, I found that poetry was considered as the highest learning, and regarded with a veneration somewhat approaching to that which man would pay to the angelic nature. And it yet fills me with wonder, that, in almost all countries, the most ancient poets are considered as the best:

---

[15] *accommodations:* conveniences.

whether it be that every other kind of knowledge is an acquisition gradually attained, and poetry is a gift conferred at once; or that the first poetry of every nation surprised them as a novelty, and retained the credit by consent which it received by accident at first: or whether, as the province of poetry is to describe nature and passion, which are always the same, the first writers took possession of the most striking objects for description and the most probable occurrences for fiction, and left nothing to those that followed them but transcription of the same events and new combinations of the same images. Whatever be the reason, it is commonly observed that the early writers are in possession of nature, and their followers of art: that the first excel in strength and invention, and the latter in elegance and refinement.

"I was desirous to add my name to this illustrious fraternity. I read all the poets of Persia and Arabia, and was able to repeat by memory the volumes[16] that are suspended in the mosque of Mecca. But I soon found that no man was ever great by imitation. My desire of excellence impelled me to transfer my attention to nature and to life. Nature was to be my subject, and men to be my auditors: I could never describe what I had not seen: I could not hope to move those with delight or terror, whose interests and opinions I did not understand.

"Being now resolved to be a poet, I saw everything with a new purpose; my sphere of attention was suddenly magnified: no kind of knowledge was to be overlooked. I ranged mountains and deserts for images and resemblances, and pictured upon my mind every tree of the forest and flower of the valley. I observed with equal care the crags of the rock and the pinnacles of the palace. Sometimes I wandered along the mazes of the rivulet, and sometimes watched the changes of the summer clouds. To a poet nothing can be useless. Whatever is beautiful, and whatever is dreadful, must be familiar to his imagination: he must be conversant with all that is awfully vast or elegantly little. The plants of the garden, the animals of the wood, the minerals of the earth, and meteors of the sky, must all concur to store his mind with inexhaustible variety: for every idea is useful for the enforcement or

---

[16] The seven "golden" volumes hung in the mosque are considered the masterpieces of Arabic poetry.

decoration of moral or religious truth; and he who knows most will have most power of diversifying his scenes, and of gratifying his reader with remote allusions and unexpected instruction.

"All the appearances of nature I was therefore careful to study, and every country which I have surveyed has contributed something to my poetical powers."

"In so wide a survey," said the prince, "you must surely have left much unobserved. I have lived, till now, within the circuit of these mountains, and yet cannot walk abroad without the sight of something which I had never beheld before, or never heeded."

"The business of a poet," said Imlac, "is to examine not the individual but the species; to remark general properties and large appearances: he does not number the streaks of the tulip, or describe the different shades in the verdure of the forest. He is to exhibit in his portraits of nature such prominent and striking features, as recall the original to every mind; and must neglect the minuter discriminations, which one may have remarked and another have neglected, for those characteristics which are alike obvious to vigilance and carelessness.

"But the knowledge of nature is only half the task of a poet; he must be acquainted likewise with all the modes of life. His character requires that he estimate the happiness and misery of every condition; observe the power of all the passions in all their combinations, and trace the changes of the human mind as they are modified by various institutions and accidental influences of climate or custom, from the sprightliness of infancy to the despondence of decrepitude. He must divest himself of the prejudices of his age or country; he must consider right and wrong in their abstracted and invariable state; he must disregard present laws and opinions, and rise to general and transcendental truths, which will always be the same: he must therefore content himself with the slow progress of his name; contemn the applause of his own time, and commit his claims to the justice of posterity. He must write as the interpreter of nature, and the legislator of mankind, and consider himself as presiding over the thoughts and manners of future generations; as a being superior to time and place.

"His labor is not yet at an end: he must know many languages and many sciences; and, that his style may be worthy of his thoughts, must, by incessant practice, familiarize to himself every delicacy of speech and grace of harmony."

XI
Imlac's Narrative Continued. A Hint on Pilgrimage

Imlac now felt the enthusiastic fit and was proceeding to aggrandize his own profession, when the prince cried out, "Enough! Thou hast convinced me, that no human being can ever be a poet. Proceed with thy narration."

"To be a poet," said Imlac, "is indeed very difficult." "So difficult," returned the prince, "that I will at present hear no more of his labors. Tell me whither you went when you had seen Persia."

"From Persia," said the poet, "I traveled through Syria, and for three years resided in Palestine, where I conversed with great numbers of the northern and western nations of Europe; the nations which are now in possession of all power and all knowledge; whose armies are irresistible and whose fleets command the remotest parts of the globe. When I compared these men with the natives of our own kingdom and those that surround us, they appeared almost another order of beings. In their countries it is difficult to wish for anything that may not be obtained: a thousand arts, of which we never heard, are continually laboring for their convenience and pleasure; and whatever their own climate has denied them is supplied by their commerce."

"By what means," said the prince, "are the Europeans thus powerful? or why, since they can easily visit Asia and Africa for trade or conquest, cannot the Asiatics and Africans invade their coasts, plant colonies in their ports, and give laws to their natural princes? The same wind that carries them back would bring us thither."

"They are more powerful, sir, than we," answered Imlac, "because they are wiser; knowledge will always predominate over ignorance, as man governs the other animals. But why their knowledge is more than ours, I know not what reason can be given, but the unsearchable will of the Supreme Being."

"When," said the prince with a sigh, "shall I be able to visit Palestine, and mingle with this mighty confluence of nations? Till that happy moment shall arrive, let me fill up the time with such representations as thou canst give me. I am not ignorant of the motive that assembles such numbers in that place, and cannot but consider it as the center of wisdom and piety, to which the best and wisest men of every land must be continually resorting."

"There are some nations," said Imlac, "that send few visitants to Palestine; for many numerous and learned sects in Europe concur to censure pilgrimage as superstitious, or deride it as ridiculous."

"You know," said the prince, "how little my life has made me acquainted with diversity of opinions: it will be too long to hear the arguments on both sides; you, that have considered them, tell me the result."

"Pilgrimage," said Imlac, "like many other acts of piety, may be reasonable or superstitious, according to the principles upon which it is performed. Long journeys in search of truth are not commanded. Truth, such as is necessary to the regulation of life, is always found where it is honestly sought. Change of place is no natural cause of the increase of piety, for it inevitably produces dissipation of mind. Yet, since men go every day to view the fields where great actions have been performed, and return with stronger impressions of the event, curiosity of the same kind may naturally dispose us to view that country whence our religion had its beginning; and I believe no man surveys those awful scenes without some confirmation of holy resolutions. That the Supreme Being may be more easily propitiated in one place than in another is the dream of idle superstition; but that some places may operate upon our own minds in an uncommon manner is an opinion which hourly experience will justify. He who supposes that his vices may be more successfully combated in Palestine will, perhaps, find himself mistaken, yet he may go thither without folly: he who thinks they will be more freely pardoned dishonors at once his reason and religion."

"These," said the prince, "are European distinctions. I will consider them another time. What have you found to be the effect of knowledge? Are those nations happier than we?"

"There is so much infelicity," said the poet, "in the world, that scarce any man has leisure from his own distresses to estimate the comparative happiness of others. Knowledge is certainly one of the means of pleasure, as is confessed by the natural desire which every mind feels of increasing its ideas. Ignorance is mere privation, by which nothing can be produced: it is a vacuity in which the soul sits motionless and torpid for want of attraction; and, without knowing why, we always rejoice when we learn, and grieve when we forget. I am therefore inclined to conclude that, if nothing counteracts the natural consequence of learning, we grow more happy as our minds take a wider range.

"In enumerating the particular comforts of life we shall find many advantages on the side of the Europeans. They cure wounds and diseases with which we languish and perish. We suffer inclemencies of weather which they can obviate. They have engines for the despatch of many laborious works, which we must perform by manual industry. There is such communication between distant places that one friend can hardly be said to be absent from another. Their policy removes all public inconveniences: they have roads cut through their mountains and bridges laid upon their rivers. And, if we descend to the privacies of life, their habitations are more commodious, and their possessions are more secure."

"They are surely happy," said the prince, "who have all these conveniences, of which I envy none so much as the facility with which separated friends interchange their thoughts."

"The Europeans," answered Imlac, "are less unhappy than we, but they are not happy. Human life is everywhere a state in which much is to be endured, and little to be enjoyed."

XII
The Story of Imlac Continued

"I am not yet willing," said the prince, "to suppose that happiness is so parsimoniously distributed to mortals; nor can believe but that, if I had the choice of life, I should be able to fill every day with pleasure. I would injure no man, and should provoke no resentment: I would relieve every distress, and should enjoy the benedictions of gratitude. I would choose my friends among the wise, and my wife among the virtuous; and therefore should be in no danger from treachery or unkindness. My children should, by my care, be learned and pious, and would repay to my age what their childhood had received. What would dare to molest him who might call on every side to thousands enriched by his bounty or assisted by his power? And why should not life glide quietly away in the soft reciprocation of protection and reverence? All this may be done without the help of European refinements, which appear by their effects to be rather specious than useful. Let us leave them and pursue our journey."

"From Palestine," said Imlac, "I passed through many regions of Asia; in the more civilized kingdoms as a trader, and among the barbarians of the mountains as a pilgrim. At last I began to long for my native country, that I might repose after my travels and fatigues in the places where I had spent my earliest years, and gladden my old companions with the recital of my adventures. Often did I figure to myself those, with whom I had sported away the gay hours of dawning life, sitting round me in its evening, wondering at my tales and listening to my counsels.

"When this thought had taken possession of my mind, I considered every moment as wasted which did not bring me nearer to Abyssinia. I hastened into Egypt and, notwithstanding my impatience, was detained ten months in the contemplation of its ancient magnificence, and in inquiries after the remains of its ancient learning. I found in Cairo a mixture of all nations; some brought thither by the love of knowledge, some by the hope of gain, and many by the desire of living after their own manner without observation, and of lying hid in the obscurity of multitudes: for, in a city populous as Cairo, it is possible to obtain at the same time the gratifications of society and the secrecy of solitude.

"From Cairo I travelled to Suez, and embarked on the Red Sea, passing along the coast till I arrived at the port from which I had departed twenty years before. Here I joined myself to a caravan and re-entered my native country.

"I now expected the caresses of my kinsmen and the congratulations of my friends, and was not without hope that my father, whatever value he had set upon riches, would own with gladness and pride a son who was able to add to the felicity and honor of the nation. But I was soon convinced that my thoughts were vain. My father had been dead fourteen years, having divided his wealth among my brothers, who were removed to some other provinces. Of my companions the greater part was in the grave, of the rest some could with difficulty remember me, and some considered me as one corrupted by foreign manners.

"A man used to vicissitudes is not easily dejected. I forgot, after a time, my disappointment, and endeavored to recommend myself to the nobles of the kingdom: they admitted me to their tables, heard my story, and dismissed me. I opened a school, and was prohibited to teach. I then resolved to sit down in the quiet of domestic life, and addressed a lady that was fond of my conversation, but rejected my suit because my father was a merchant.

"Wearied at last with solicitation and repulses, I resolved to hide myself forever from the world, and depend no longer on the opinion or caprice of others. I waited for the time when the gate of the *happy valley* should open that I might bid farewell to hope and fear: the day came; my performance was distinguished with favor, and I resigned myself with joy to perpetual confinement."

"Hast thou here found happiness at last?" said Rasselas. "Tell me without reserve; art thou content with thy condition? or, dost thou wish to be again wandering and inquiring? All the inhabitants of this valley celebrate their lot, and, at the annual visit of the emperor, invite others to partake of their felicity."

"Great prince," said Imlac, "I shall speak the truth: I know not one of all your attendants who does not lament the hour when he entered this retreat. I am less unhappy than the rest, because I have a mind replete with images, which I can vary and combine at pleasure. I can amuse my solitude by the renovation of the knowledge which begins to fade from my memory, and by recollection of the accidents[17] of my past life. Yet all this ends in the sorrowful consideration that my acquirements are now useless, and that none of my pleasures can be again enjoyed. The rest, whose minds have no impression but of the present moment, are either corroded by malignant passions, or sit stupid in the gloom of perpetual vacancy."

"What passions can infest those," said the prince, "who have no rivals? We are in a place where impotence precludes malice, and where all envy is repressed by community of enjoyments."

"There may be community," said Imlac, "of material possessions, but there can never be community of love or of

---

[17] *accidents:* events.

esteem. It must happen that one will please more than another; he that knows himself despised will always be envious; and still more envious and malevolent if he is condemned to live in the presence of those who despise him. The invitations, by which they allure others to a state which they feel to be wretched, proceed from the natural malignity of hopeless misery. They are weary of themselves and of each other, and expect to find relief in new companions. They envy the liberty which their folly has forfeited, and would gladly see all mankind imprisoned like themselves.

"From this crime, however, I am wholly free. No man can say that he is wretched by my persuasion. I look with pity on the crowds who are annually soliciting admission to captivity, and wish that it were lawful for me to warn them of their danger."

"My dear Imlac," said the prince, "I will open to thee my whole heart. I have long meditated an escape from the happy valley. I have examined the mountains on every side, but find myself insuperably barred: teach me the way to break my prison; thou shalt be the companion of my flight, the guide to my rambles, the partner of my fortune, and my sole director in the *choice of life*."

"Sir," answered the poet, "your escape will be difficult and, perhaps, you may soon repent your curiosity. The world, which you figure to yourself smooth and quiet as the lake in the valley, you will find a sea foaming with tempests and boiling with whirlpools: you will be sometimes overwhelmed by the waves of violence, and sometimes dashed against the rocks of treachery. Amidst wrongs and frauds, competitions and anxieties, you will wish a thousand times for these seats of quiet, and willingly quit hope to be free from fear."

"Do not seek to deter me from my purpose," said the prince, "I am impatient to see what thou hast seen; and, since thou art thyself weary of the valley, it is evident that thy former state was better than this. Whatever be the consequence of my experiment, I am resolved to judge with my own eyes of the various conditions of men, and then to make deliberately my *choice of life*."

"I am afraid," said Imlac, "you are hindered by stronger restraints than my persuasions; yet, if your determination is fixed, I do not counsel you to despair. Few things are impossible to diligence and skill."

XIII
Rasselas Discovers the Means of Escape

The prince now dismissed his favorite to rest, but the narrative of wonders and novelties filled his mind with perturbation. He revolved[18] all that he had heard, and prepared innumerable questions for the morning.

Much of his uneasiness was now removed. He had a friend to whom he could impart his thoughts, and whose experience could assist him in his designs. His heart was no longer condemned to swell with silent vexation. He thought that even the *happy valley* might be endured with such a companion, and that, if they could range the world together, he should have nothing further to desire.

In a few days the water was discharged, and the ground dried. The prince and Imlac then walked out together to converse without the notice of the rest. The prince, whose thoughts were always on the wing, as he passed by the gate said, with a countenance of sorrow, "Why art thou so strong, and why is man so weak?"

"Man is not weak," answered his companion, "knowledge is more than equivalent to force. The master of mechanics laughs at strength. I can burst the gate, but cannot do it secretly. Some other expedient must be tried."

As they were walking on the side of the mountain, they observed that the conies, which the rain had driven from their burrows, had taken shelter among the bushes, and formed holes behind them, tending upwards in an oblique line. "It has been the opinion of antiquity," said Imlac, "that human reason borrowed many arts from the instinct of animals; let us, therefore, not think ourselves degraded by learning from the cony. We may escape by piercing the mountain in the same direction. We will begin where the summit hangs over the middle part, and labor upward till we shall issue out beyond the prominence."

The eyes of the prince, when he heard this proposal, sparkled with joy. The execution was easy, and the success certain.

No time was now lost. They hastened early in the morning to choose a place proper for their mine. They clambered

---

[18] *revolved:* thought about.

with great fatigue among crags and brambles, and returned without having discovered any part that favored their design. The second and the third day were spent in the same manner, and with the same frustration. But, on the fourth, they found a small cavern concealed by a thicket, where they resolved to make their experiment.

Imlac procured instruments proper to hew stone and remove earth, and they fell to their work on the next day with more eagerness than vigor. They were presently exhausted by their efforts, and sat down to pant upon the grass. The prince, for a moment, appeared to be discouraged. "Sir," said his companion, "practice will enable us to continue our labor for a longer time; mark, however, how far we have advanced, and you will find that our toil will some time have an end. Great works are performed not by strength, but perseverance: yonder palace was raised by single stones, yet you see its height and spaciousness. He that shall walk with vigor three hours a day will pass in seven years a space equal to the circumference of the globe."

They returned to their work day after day, and, in a short time, found a fissure in the rock, which enabled them to pass far with very little obstruction. This Rasselas considered as a good omen. "Do not disturb your mind," said Imlac, "with other hopes or fears than reason may suggest: if you are pleased with prognostics of good, you will be terrified likewise with tokens of evil, and your whole life will be prey to superstition. Whatever facilitates our work is more than an omen, it is a cause of success. This is one of those pleasing surprises which often happen to active resolution. Many things difficult to design prove easy to performance."

XIV
Rasselas and Imlac Receive an Unexpected Visit

They had now wrought their way to the middle, and solaced their toil with the approach of liberty, when the prince, coming down to refresh himself with air, found his sister Nekayah standing before the mouth of the cavity. He started and stood confused, afraid to tell his design, and yet hopeless to conceal it. A few moments determined him to repose on her fidelity, and secure her secrecy by a declaration without reserve.

"Do not imagine," said the princess, "that I came hither as a spy: I had long observed from my window that you and Imlac directed your walk every day towards the same point, but I did not suppose you had any better reason for the preference than a cooler shade or more fragrant bank; nor followed you with any other design than to partake of your conversation. Since then not suspicion but fondness has detected you, let me not lose the advantage of my discovery. I am equally weary of confinement with yourself, and not less desirous of knowing what is done or suffered in the world. Permit me to fly with you from this tasteless tranquillity, which will yet grow more loathsome when you have left me. You may deny me to accompany you, but cannot hinder me from following."

The prince, who loved Nekayah above his other sisters, had no inclination to refuse her request, and grieved that he had lost an opportunity of showing his confidence by a voluntary communication. It was therefore agreed that she should leave the valley with them; and that, in the meantime, she should watch lest any other straggler should, by chance or curiosity, follow them to the mountain.

At length their labor was at an end; they saw light beyond the prominence and, issuing to the top of the mountain, beheld the Nile, yet a narrow current, wandering beneath them.

The prince looked round with rapture, anticipated all the pleasures of travel, and in thought was already transported beyond his father's dominions. Imlac, though very joyful at his escape, had less expectation of pleasure in the world, which he had before tried and of which he had been weary.

Rasselas was so much delighted with a wider horizon that he could not soon be persuaded to return into the valley. He informed his sister that the way was open, and that nothing now remained but to prepare for their departure.

XV
The Prince and Princess Leave the Valley, and See Many Wonders

The prince and princess had jewels sufficient to make them rich whenever they came into a place of commerce, which, by Imlac's direction, they hid in their clothes and, on the night of the next full moon, all left the valley. The princess was followed only by a single favorite, who did not know whither she was going.

They clambered through the cavity, and began to go down on the other side. The princess and her maid turned their eyes towards every part and, seeing nothing to bound their prospect, considered themselves as in danger of being lost in a dreary vacuity. They stopped and trembled. "I am almost afraid," said the princess, "to begin a journey of which I cannot perceive an end, and to venture into this immense plain where I may be approached on every side by men whom I never saw." The prince felt nearly the same emotions, though he thought it more manly to conceal them.

Imlac smiled at their terrors, and encouraged them to proceed; but the princess continued irresolute till she had been imperceptibly drawn forward too far to return.

In the morning they found some shepherds in the field, who set milk and fruits before them. The princess wondered that she did not see a palace ready for her reception, and a table spread with delicacies; but, being faint and hungry, she drank the milk and eat the fruits, and thought them of a higher flavor than the products of the valley.

They traveled forward by easy journeys, being all unaccustomed to toil or difficulty and knowing, that though they might be missed, they could not be pursued. In a few days they came into a more populous region, where Imlac was diverted with the admiration which his companions expressed at the diversity of manners, stations, and employments.

Their dress was such as might not bring upon them the suspicion of having anything to conceal, yet the prince, wherever he came, expected to be obeyed, and the princess was frightened, because those that came into her presence did not prostrate themselves before her. Imlac was forced to observe them with great vigilance, lest they should betray their rank by their unusual behavior, and detained them several weeks in the first village to accustom them to the sight of common mortals.

By degrees the royal wanderers were taught to understand that they had for a time laid aside their dignity, and were to expect only such regard as liberality and courtesy could procure. And Imlac, having by many admonitions prepared them to endure the tumults of a port and the ruggedness of the commercial race, brought them down to the seacoast.

The prince and his sister, to whom everything was new, were gratified equally at all places, and therefore remained for some months at the port without any inclination to pass further. Imlac was content with their stay, because he did not think it safe to expose them, unpracticed in the world, to the hazards of a foreign country.

At last he began to fear lest they should be discovered, and proposed to fix a day for their departure. They had no pretensions to judge for themselves, and referred the whole scheme to his direction. He therefore took passage in a ship to Suez; and, when the time came, with great difficulty prevailed on the princess to enter the vessel. They had a quick and prosperous voyage, and from Suez travelled by land to Cairo.

XVI
They Enter Cairo, and Find Every Man Happy

As they approached the city, which filled the strangers with astonishment, "This," said Imlac to the prince, "is the place where travelers and merchants assemble from all the corners of the earth. You will here find men of every character and every occupation. Commerce is here honorable: I will act as a merchant, and you shall live as strangers who have no other end of travel than curiosity; it will soon be observed that we are rich; our reputation will procure us access to all whom we shall desire to know; you will see all the conditions of humanity, and enable yourself at leisure to make your *choice of life*."

They now entered the town, stunned by the noise, and offended by the crowds. Instruction had not yet so prevailed over habit, but that they wondered to see themselves pass undistinguished along the street, and met by the lowest of the people without reverence or notice. The princess could not at first bear the thought of being leveled with the vulgar and, for some days, continued in her chamber, where she was served by her favorite Pekuah as in the palace of the valley.

Imlac, who understood traffic,[19] sold part of the jewels the

---

[19] *traffic:* trade.

next day, and hired a house, which he adorned with such magnificence that he was immediately considered as a merchant of great wealth. His politeness attracted many acquaintance, and his generosity made him courted by many dependents. His table was crowded by men of every nation, who all admired his knowledge, and solicited his favor. His companions, not being able to mix in the conversation, could make no discovery of their ignorance or surprise, and were gradually initiated in the world as they gained knowledge of the language.

The prince had, by frequent lectures, been taught the use and nature of money; but the ladies could not, for a long time, comprehend what the merchants did with small pieces of gold and silver, or why things of so little use should be received as equivalent to the necessaries of life.

They studied the language two years, while Imlac was preparing to set before them the various ranks and conditions of mankind. He grew acquainted with all who had anything uncommon in their fortune[20] or conduct. He frequented the voluptuous and the frugal, the idle and the busy, the merchants and the men of learning.

The prince, being now able to converse with fluency, and having learned the caution necessary to be observed in his intercourse with strangers, began to accompany Imlac to places of resort, and to enter into all assemblies, that he might make his *choice of life*.

For some time he thought choice needless, because all appeared to him equally happy. Wherever he went he met gaiety and kindness, and heard the song of joy, or the laugh of carelessness. He began to believe that the world overflowed with universal plenty, and that nothing was withheld either from want or merit; that every hand showered liberality, and every heart melted with benevolence: "And who then," says he, "will be suffered to be wretched?"

Imlac permitted the pleasing delusion, and was unwilling to crush the hope of inexperience; till one day, having sat a while silent, "I know not," said the prince, "what can be the reason that I am more unhappy than any of our friends. I see them perpetually and unalterably cheerful, but feel my own mind restless and uneasy. I am unsatisfied with those

[20] *fortune:* situation.

pleasures which I seem most to court; I live in the crowds of jollity not so much to enjoy the company as to shun myself, and am only loud and merry to conceal my sadness."

"Every man," said Imlac, "may, by examining his own mind, guess what passes in the minds of others: when you feel that your own gaiety is counterfeit, it may justly lead you to suspect that of your companions not to be sincere. Envy is commonly reciprocal. We are long before we are convinced that happiness is never to be found, and each believes it possessed by others, to keep alive the hope of obtaining it for himself. In the assembly, where you passed the last night, there appeared such sprightliness of air and volatility of fancy, as might have suited beings of an higher order, formed to inhabit serener regions inaccessible to care or sorrow: yet, believe me, prince, there was not one who did not dread the moment when solitude should deliver him to the tyranny of reflection."

"This," said the prince, "may be true of others, since it is true of me; yet, whatever be the general infelicity of man, one condition is more happy than another, and wisdom surely directs us to take the least evil in the *choice of life*."

"The causes of good and evil," answered Imlac, "are so various and uncertain, so often entangled with each other, so diversified by various relations, and so much subject to accidents which cannot be foreseen, that he who would fix his conditions upon incontestable reasons of preference, must live and die inquiring and deliberating."

"But surely," said Rasselas, "the wise men, to whom we listen with reverence and wonder, chose that mode of life for themselves which they thought most likely to make them happy."

"Very few," said the poet, "live by choice. Every man is placed in his present condition by causes which acted without his foresight, and with which he did not always willingly cooperate; and therefore you will rarely meet one who does not think the lot of his neighbor better than his own."

"I am pleased to think," said the prince, "that my birth has given me at least one advantage over others by enabling me to determine for myself. I have here the world before me; I will review it at leisure: surely happiness is somewhere . to be found."

XVII
The Prince Associates with
Young Men of Spirit and Gaiety

Rasselas rose next day, and resolved to begin his experiments upon life. "Youth," cried he, "is the time of gladness: I will join myself to the young men, whose only business is to gratify their desires, and whose time is all spent in a succession of enjoyments."

To such societies he was readily admitted, but a few days brought him back weary and disgusted. Their mirth was without images,[21] their laughter without motive; their pleasures were gross and sensual, in which the mind had no part; their conduct was at once wild and mean; they laughed at order and at law, but the frown of power dejected, and the eye of wisdom abashed them.

The prince soon concluded that he should never be happy in a course of life of which he was ashamed. He thought it unsuitable to a reasonable being to act without a plan, and to be sad or cheerful only by chance. "Happiness," said he, "must be something solid and permanent, without fear and without uncertainty."

But his young companions had gained so much of his regard by their frankness and courtesy, that he could not leave them without warning and remonstrance. "My friends," said he, "I have seriously considered our manners and our prospects, and find that we have mistaken our own interest. The first years of man must make provision for the last. He that never thinks never can be wise. Perpetual levity must end in ignorance; and intemperance, though it may fire the spirits for an hour, will make life short or miserable. Let us consider that youth is of no long duration, and that in maturer age, when the enchantments of fancy shall cease and phantoms of delight dance no more about us, we shall have no comforts but the esteem of wise men, and the means of doing good. Let us, therefore, stop, while to stop is in our power: let us live as men who are sometime to grow old, and to whom it will be the most dreadful of all evils not to count their past years but by follies, and to be reminded of their

[21] *images:* ideas.

former luxuriance of health only by the maladies which riot has produced."

They stared a while in silence one upon another and, at last, drove him away by a general chorus of continued laughter.

The consciousness that his sentiments were just, and his intentions kind, was scarcely sufficient to support him against the horror of derision. But he recovered his tranquillity, and pursued his search.

XVIII
The Prince Finds a Wise and Happy Man

As he was one day walking in the street, he saw a spacious building which all were, by the open doors, invited to enter: he followed the stream of people, and found it a hall or school of declamation, in which professors read lectures to their auditory. He fixed his eye upon a sage raised above the rest, who discoursed with great energy on the government of the passions. His look was venerable, his action graceful, his pronunciation clear, and his diction elegant. He showed, with great strength of sentiment, and variety of illustration, that human nature is degraded and debased, when the lower faculties predominate over the higher; that when fancy, the parent of passion, usurps the dominion of the mind, nothing ensues but the natural effect of unlawful government, perturbation and confusion; that she betrays the fortresses of the intellect to rebels, and excites her children to sedition against reason, their lawful sovereign. He compared reason to the sun, of which the light is constant, uniform, and lasting; and fancy to a meteor, of bright but transitory luster, irregular in its motion, and delusive in its direction.

He then communicated the various precepts given from time to time for the conquest of passion, and displayed the happiness of those who had obtained the important victory, after which man is no longer the slave of fear nor the fool of hope; is no more emaciated by envy, inflamed by anger, emasculated by tenderness, or depressed by grief; but walks on calmly through the tumults or the privacies of life, as the sun pursues alike his course through the calm or the stormy sky.

He enumerated many examples of heroes immovable by

pain or pleasure, who looked with indifference on those modes or accidents to which the vulgar give the names of good and evil. He exhorted his hearers to lay aside their prejudices, and arm themselves against the shafts of malice or misfortune by invulnerable patience, concluding, that this state only was happiness, and that this happiness was in everyone's power.

Rasselas listened to him with the veneration due to the instructions of a superior being and, waiting for him at the door, humbly implored the liberty of visiting so great a master of true wisdom. The lecturer hesitated a moment, when Rasselas put a purse of gold into his hand, which he received with a mxture of joy and wonder.

"I have found," said the prince at his return to Imlac, "a man who can teach all that is necessary to be known, who, from the unshaken throne of rational fortitude, looks down on the scenes of life changing beneath him. He speaks, and attention watches his lips. He reasons, and conviction closes his periods. This man shall be my future guide: I will learn his doctrines, and imitate his life."

"Be not too hasty," said Imlac, "to trust, or to admire, the teachers of morality: they discourse like angels, but they live like men."

Rasselas, who could not conceive how any man could reason so forcibly without feeling the cogency of his own arguments, paid his visit in a few days, and was denied admission. He had now learned the power of money, and made his way by a piece of gold to the inner apartment, where he found the philosopher in a room half darkened, with his eyes misty and his face pale. "Sir," said he, "you are come at a time when all human friendship is useless; what I suffer cannot be remedied, what I have lost cannot be supplied. My daughter, my only daughter, from whose tenderness I expected all the comforts of my age, died last night of a fever. My views, my purposes, my hopes are at an end: I am now a lonely being disunited from society."

"Sir," said the prince, "mortality is an event by which a wise man can never be surprised: we know that death is always near, and it should therefore always be expected." "Young man," answered the philosopher, "you speak like one that has never felt the pangs of separation." "Have you then forgot the precepts," said Rasselas, "which you so powerfully enforced? Has wisdom no strength to arm the heart against calamity? Consider, that external things are naturally variable, but truth and reason are always the same." "What comfort," said the mourner, "can truth and reason afford me? of what effect are they now, but to tell me that my daughter will not be restored?"

The prince, whose humanity would not suffer him to insult misery with reproof, went away convinced of the emptiness of rhetorical sound, and the inefficacy of polished periods and studied sentences.

XIX
A Glimpse of Pastoral Life

He was still eager upon the same inquiry; and, having heard of a hermit that lived near the lowest cataract of the Nile, and filled the whole country with the fame of his sanctity, resolved to visit his retreat, and inquire whether that felicity, which public life could not afford, was to be found in solitude; and whether a man whose age and virtue made him venerable could teach any peculiar art of shunning evils or enduring them.

Imlac and the princess agreed to accompany him and, after the necessary preparations, they began their journey. Their way lay through fields, where shepherds tended their flocks, and the lambs were playing upon the pasture. "This," said the poet, "is the life which has been often celebrated for its innocence and quiet: let us pass the heat of the day among the shepherds' tents, and know whether all our searches are not to terminate in pastoral simplicity."

The proposal pleased them, and they induced the shepherds, by small presents and familiar questions, to tell their opinion of their own state: they were so rude[22] and ignorant, so little able to compare the good with the evil of the occupation, and so indistinct in their narratives and descriptions, that very little could be learned from them. But it was evident that their hearts were cankered with discontent; that they considered themselves as condemned to labor for the luxury of the rich, and looked up with stupid malevolence toward those that were placed above them.

The princess pronounced with vehemence that she would

---

[22] *rude:* boorish.

never suffer these envious savages to be her companions, and that she should not soon be desirous of seeing any more specimens of rustic happiness; but could not believe that all the accounts of primeval pleasures were fabulous, and was yet in doubt whether life had anything that could be justly preferred to the placid gratifications of fields and woods. She hoped that the time would come, when with a few virtuous and elegant companions she should gather flowers planted by her own hand, fondle the lambs of her own ewe, and listen, without care, among brooks and breezes, to one of her maidens reading in the shade.

XX
The Danger of Prosperity

On the next day they continued their journey, till the heat compelled them to look round for shelter. At a small distance they saw a thick wood, which they no sooner entered than they perceived that they were approaching the habitations of men. The shrubs were diligently cut away to open walks where the shades were darkest; the boughs of opposite trees were artificially interwoven; seats of flowery turf were raised in vacant spaces, and a rivulet, that wantoned along the side of a winding path, had its banks sometimes opened into small basins and its stream sometimes obstructed by little mounds of stone heaped together to increase its murmurs.

They passed slowly through the wood, delighted with such unexpected accommodations, and entertained each other with conjecturing what, or who, he could be that, in those rude and unfrequented regions, had leisure and art for such harmless luxury.

As they advanced, they heard the sound of music, and saw youths and virgins dancing in the grove; and, going still further, beheld a stately palace built upon a hill surrounded with woods. The laws of eastern hospitality allowed them to enter, and the master welcomed them like a man liberal and wealthy.

He was skillful enough in appearances soon to discern that they were no common guests, and spread his table with magnificence. The eloquence of Imlac caught his attention, and the lofty courtesy of the princess excited his respect. When they offered to depart he entreated their stay, and was the next day still more unwilling to dismiss them than before. They were easily persuaded to stop, and civility grew up in time to freedom and confidence.

The prince now saw all the domestics cheerful, and all the face of nature smiling round the place, and could not forbear to hope that he should find here what he was seeking; but when he was congratulating the master upon his possessions, he answered with a sigh, "My condition has indeed the appearance of happiness, but appearances are delusive. My prosperity puts my life in danger; the Bassa of Egypt is my enemy, incensed only by my wealth and popularity. I have been hitherto protected against him by the princes of the country; but, as the favor of the great is uncertain, I know not how soon my defenders may be persuaded to share the plunder with the Bassa. I have sent my treasures into a distant country, and upon the first alarm am prepared to follow them. Then will my enemies riot in my mansion, and enjoy the gardens which I have planted."

They all joined in lamenting his danger and deprecating his exile; and the princess was so much disturbed with the tumult of grief and indignation that she retired to her apartment. They continued with their kind inviter a few days longer, and then went forward to find the hermit.

XXI
The Happiness of Solitude. The Hermit's History

They came on the third day, by the direction of the peasants, to the hermit's cell: it was a cavern in the side of a mountain, overshadowed with palm trees; at such a distance from the cataract that nothing more was heard than a gentle uniform murmur, such as composed the mind to pensive meditation, especially when it was assisted by the wind whistling among the branches. The first rude essay of nature had been so much improved by human labor that the cave contained several apartments, appropriated to different uses, and often afforded lodging to travelers whom darkness or tempests happened to overtake.

The hermit sat on a bench at the door to enjoy the coolness of the evening. On one side lay a book with pens and papers, on the other mechanical instruments of various kinds.

As they approached him unregarded, the princess observed that he had not the countenance of a man that had found, or could teach, the way to happiness.

They saluted him with great respect, which he repaid like a man not unaccustomed to the forms of courts. "My children," said he, "if you have lost your way, you shall be willingly supplied with such conveniencies for the night as this cavern will afford. I have all that nature requires, and you will not expect delicacies in a hermit's cell."

They thanked him and, entering, were pleased with the neatness and regularity of the place. The hermit set flesh and wine before them, though he fed only upon fruits and water. His discourse was cheerful without levity, and pious without enthusiasm.[23] He soon gained the esteem of his guests, and the princess repented of her hasty censure.

At last Imlac began thus: "I do not now wonder that your reputation is so far extended; we have heard at Cairo of your wisdom, and came hither to implore your direction for this young man and maiden in the *choice of life*."

"To him that lives well," answered the hermit, "every form of life is good; nor can I give any other rule for choice than to remove from all apparent evil."

"He will remove most certainly from evil," said the prince, "who shall devote himself to that solitude which you have recommended by your example."

"I have indeed lived fifteen years in solitude," said the hermit, "but have no desire that my example should gain any imitators. In my youth I professed arms, and was raised by degrees to the highest military rank. I have traversed wide countries at the head of my troops, and seen many battles and sieges. At last, being disgusted by the preferment of a younger officer, and feeling that my vigor was beginning to decay, I resolved to close my life in peace, having found the world full of snares, discord, and misery. I had once escaped from the pursuit of the enemy by the shelter of this cavern, and therefore chose it for my final residence. I employed artificers to form it into chambers, and stored it with all that I was likely to want.

"For some time after my retreat, I rejoiced like a tempest-beaten sailor at his entrance into the harbor, being delighted

---

[23] *enthusiasm:* extravagant religious fervor.

with the sudden change of the noise and hurry of war to stillness and repose. When the pleasure of novelty went away, I employed my hours in examining the plants which grow in the valley, and the minerals which I collected from the rocks. But that inquiry is now grown tasteless and irksome. I have been for some time unsettled and distracted: my mind is disturbed with a thousand perplexities of doubt and vanities of imagination, which hourly prevail upon me, because I have no opportunities of relaxation or diversion. I am sometimes ashamed to think that I could not secure myself from vice but by retiring from the exercise of virtue, and begin to suspect that I was rather impelled by resentment, than led by devotion, into solitude. My fancy riots in scenes of folly, and I lament that I have lost so much and have gained so little. In solitude, if I escape the example of bad men, I want likewise the counsel and conversation of the good. I have been long comparing the evils with the advantages of society, and resolve to return into the world tomorrow. The life of a solitary man will be certainly miserable, but not certainly devout."

They heard his resolution with surprise but, after a short pause, offered to conduct him to Cairo. He dug up a considerable treasure which he had hid among the rocks, and accompanied them to the city, on which, as he approached it, he gazed with rapture.

XXII
The Happiness of a Life Led According to Nature

Rasselas went often to an assembly of learned men, who met at stated times to unbend their minds and compare their opinions. Their manners were somewhat coarse, but their conversation was instructive, and their disputations acute though sometimes too violent, and often continued till neither controvertist remembered upon what question they began. Some faults were almost general among them: every one was desirous to dictate to the rest, and every one was pleased to hear the genius or knowledge of another depreciated.

In this assembly Rasselas was relating his interview with the hermit, and the wonder with which he heard him censure a course of life which he had so deliberately chosen and so laudably followed. The sentiments of the hearers were various.

Some were of opinion that the folly of his choice had been[24] justly punished by condemnation to perpetual perseverance. One of the youngest among them, with great vehemence, pronounced him an hypocrite. Some talked of the right of society to the labor of individuals, and considered retirement as a desertion of duty. Others readily allowed that there was a time when the claims of the public were satisfied, and when a man might properly sequester himself to review his life and purify his heart.

One, who appeared more affected with the narrative than the rest, thought it likely, that the hermit would, in a few years, go back to his retreat and, perhaps, if shame did not restrain, or death intercept him, return once more from his retreat into the world: "For the hope of happiness," said he, "is so strongly impressed that the longest experience is not able to efface it. Of the present state, whatever it be, we feel, and are forced to confess, the misery, yet, when the same state is again at a distance, imagination paints it as desirable. But the time will surely come, when desire will be no longer our torment, and no man shall be wretched but by his own fault."

"This," said a philosopher, who had heard him with tokens of great impatience, "is the present condition of a wise man. The time is already come when none are wretched but by their own fault. Nothing is more idle than to inquire after happiness, which nature has kindly placed within our reach. The way to be happy is to live according to nature, in obedience to that universal and unalterable law with which every heart is originally impressed; which is not written on it by precept but engraven by destiny, not instilled by education but infused at our nativity. He that lives according to nature will suffer from the delusions of hope or importunities of desire: he will receive and reject with equability of temper; and act or suffer as the reason of things shall alternately prescribe. Other men may amuse themselves with subtle definitions, or intricate ratiocination. Let them learn to be wise by easier means: let them observe the hind of the forest and the linnet of the grove: let them consider the life of animals, whose motions are regulated by instinct; they obey their guide and are happy. Let us therefore, at length, cease to dispute and learn to live; throw away the incumbrance of

[24] *had been:* would have been.

precepts, which they who utter them with so much pride and pomp do not understand, and carry with us this simple and intelligible maxim, that deviation from nature is deviation from happiness."

When he had spoken, he looked round him with a placid air, and enjoyed the consciousness of his own beneficence. "Sir," said the prince, with great modesty, "as I, like all the rest of mankind, am desirous of felicity, my closest attention has been fixed upon your discourse: I doubt not the truth of a position which a man so learned has so confidently advanced. Let me only know what it is to live according to nature."

"When I find young men so humble and so docile," said the philosopher, "I can deny them no information which my studies have enabled me to afford. To live according to nature is to act always with due regard to the fitness arising from the relations and qualities of causes and effects; to concur with the great and unchangeable scheme of universal felicity; to cooperate with the general disposition and tendency of the present system of things."

The prince soon found that this was one of the sages whom he should understand less as he heard him longer. He therefore bowed and was silent, and the philosopher, supposing him satisfied and the rest vanquished, rose up and departed with the air of a man that had cooperated with the present system.

XXIII
The Prince and His Sister Divide between Them

Rasselas returned home full of reflections, doubtful how to direct his future steps. Of the way to happiness he found the learned and simple equally ignorant; but, as he was yet young, he flattered himself that he had time remaining for more experiments, and further inquiries. He communicated to Imlac his observations and his doubts, but was answered by him with new doubts, and remarks that gave him no comfort. He therefore discoursed more frequently and freely with his sister, who had yet the same hope with himself, and always assisted him to give some reason why, though he had been hitherto frustrated, he might succeed at last.

"We have hitherto," said she, "known but little of the world: we have never yet been either great or mean. In our own country though we had royalty we had no power, and in this we have not yet seen the private recesses of domestic peace. Imlac favors not our search, lest we should in time find him mistaken. We will divide the task between us: you shall try what is to be found in the splendor of courts, and I will range the shades of humbler life. Perhaps command and authority may be the supreme blessings, as they afford most opportunities of doing good; or perhaps what this world can give may be found in the modest habitations of middle fortune: too low for great designs and too high for penury and distress."

XXIV
The Prince Examines the Happiness of High Stations

Rasselas applauded the design, and appeared next day with a splendid retinue at the court of the Bassa. He was soon distinguished for his magnificence, and admitted, as a prince whose curiosity had brought him from distant countries, to an intimacy with the great officers and frequent conversation with the Bassa himself.

He was at first inclined to believe that the man must be pleased with his own condition whom all approached with reverence and heard with obedience, and who had the power to extend his edicts to a whole kingdom. "There can be no pleasure," said he, "equal to that of feeling at once the joy of thousands all made happy by wise administration. Yet, since, by the law of subordination, this sublime delight can be in one nation but the lot of one, it is surely reasonable to think that there is some satisfaction more popular and accessible, and that millions can hardly be subjected to the will of a single man, only to fill his particular breast with incommunicable content."

These thoughts were often in his mind, and he found no solution of the difficulty. But as presents and civilities gained him more familiarity, he found that almost every man who stood high in employment hated all the rest and was hated by them, and that their lives were a continual succession of plots and detections, stratagems and escapes, faction and treachery. Many of those who surrounded the Bassa were sent only to watch and report his conduct; every tongue was muttering censure and every eye was searching for a fault.

At last the letters of revocation arrived, the Bassa was carried in chains to Constantinople, and his name was mentioned no more.

"What are we now to think of the prerogatives of power," said Rasselas to his sister; "is it without any efficacy to good? or is the subordinate degree only dangerous, and the supreme safe and glorious? Is the Sultan the only happy man in his dominions? or is the Sultan himself subject to the torments of suspicion, and the dread of enemies?"

In a short time the second Bassa was deposed. The Sultan, that had advanced him, was murdered by the Janissaries, and his successor had other views and different favorites.

XXV
The Princess Pursues Her Inquiry
with More Diligence Than Success

The princess, in the meantime, insinuated herself into many families; for there are few doors through which liberality, joined with good humor, cannot find its way. The daughters of many houses were airy and cheerful, but Nekayah had been too long accustomed to the conversation of Imlac and her brother to be much pleased with childish levity and prattle which had no meaning. She found their thoughts narrow, their wishes low, and their merriment often artificial. Their pleasures, poor as they were, could not be preserved pure, but were embittered by petty competitions and worthless emulation. They were always jealous of the beauty of each other; of a quality to which solicitude can add nothing, and from which detraction can take nothing away. Many were in love with triflers like themselves, and many fancied that they were in love when in truth they were only idle. Their affection was seldom fixed on sense or virtue, and therefore seldom ended but in vexation. Their grief, however, like their joy, was transient; everything floated in their mind unconnected with the past or future, so that one desire easily gave way to another, as a second stone cast into the water effaces and confounds the circles of the first.

With these girls she played as with inoffensive animals, and found them proud of her countenance,[25] and weary of her company.

But her purpose was to examine more deeply, and her affability easily persuaded the hearts that were swelling with sorrow to discharge their secrets in her ear: and those whom hope flattered, or prosperity delighted, often courted her to partake their pleasures.

The princess and her brother commonly met in the evening in a private summer house on the bank of the Nile, and related to each other the occurrences of the day. As they were sitting together, the princess cast her eyes upon the river that flowed before her. "Answer," said she, "great Father of Waters, thou that rollest thy floods through eighty nations, to the invocations of the daughter of thy native king. Tell me if thou waterest, through all thy course, a single habitation from which thou dost not hear the murmurs of complaint?"

"You are then," said Rasselas, "not more successful in private houses than I have been in courts." "I have, since the last partition of our provinces," said the princess, "enabled myself to enter familiarly into many families where there was the fairest show of prosperity and peace, and know not one house that is not haunted by some fury that destroys its quiet.

"I did not seek ease among the poor, because I concluded that there it could not be found. But I saw many poor whom I had supposed to live in affluence. Poverty has, in large cities, very different appearances: it is often concealed in splendor and often in extravagance. It is the care of a very great part of mankind to conceal their indigence from the rest: they support themselves by temporary expedients, and every day is lost in contriving for the morrow.

"This, however, was an evil which, though frequent, I saw with less pain because I could relieve it. Yet some have refused my bounties, more offended with my quickness to detect their wants, than pleased with my readiness to succor them: and others, whose exigencies compelled them to admit my kindness, have never been able to forgive their benefactress. Many, however, have been sincerely grateful without the ostentation of gratitude or the hope of other favors."

[25] *countenance:* appearance of favor.

XXVI
The Princess Continues Her Remarks
upon Private Life

Nekayah, perceiving her brother's attention fixed, proceeded in her narrative.

"In families where there is or is not poverty, there is commonly discord: if a kingdom be, as Imlac tells us, a great family, a family likewise is a little kingdom, torn with factions and exposed to revolutions. An unpracticed observer expects the love of parents and children to be constant and equal; but this kindness seldom continues beyond the years of infancy: in a short time the children become rivals to their parents. Benefits are allayed by reproaches, and gratitude debased by envy.

"Parents and children seldom act in concert: each child endeavors to appropriate the esteem or fondness of the parents, and the parents, with yet less temptation, betray each other to their children; thus some place their confidence in the father and some in the mother, and, by degrees, the house is filled with artifices and feuds.

"The opinions of children and parents, of the young and the old, are naturally opposite, by the contrary effects of hope and despondence, of expectation and experience, without crime or folly on either side. The colors of life in youth and age appear different, as the face of nature in spring and winter. And how can children credit the assertions of parents, which their own eyes show them to be false?

"Few parents act in such a manner as much to enforce their maxims by the credit of their lives. The old man trusts wholly to slow contrivance and gradual progression: the youth expects to force his way by genius, vigor, and precipitance. The old man pays regard to riches, and the youth reverences virtue. The old man deifies prudence; the youth commits himself to magnanimity and chance. The young man, who intends no ill, believes that none is intended, and therefore acts with openness and candor:[26] but his father, having suffered the injuries of fraud, is impelled to suspect, and too often allured to practice it. Age looks with anger on the

---

[26] *candor:* readiness to believe the best.

temerity of youth, and youth with contempt on the scrupulosity of age. Thus parents and children, for the greatest part,
live on to love less and less: and, if those whom nature has
thus closely united are the torments of each other, where
shall we look for tenderness and consolation?"

"Surely," said the prince, "you must have been unfortunate
in your choice of acquaintance: I am unwilling to believe
that the most tender of all relations is thus impeded in its
effects by natural necessity."

"Domestic discord," answered she, "is not inevitably and
fatally necessary; but yet is not easily avoided. We seldom see
that a whole family is virtuous: the good and evil cannot well
agree; and the evil can yet less agree with one another: even
the virtuous fall sometimes to variance, when their virtues are
of different kinds and tending to extremes. In general, those
parents have most reverence who most deserve it: for he that
lives well cannot be despised.

"Many other evils infest private life. Some are the slaves
of servants whom they have trusted with their affairs. Some
are kept in continual anxiety to the caprice of rich relations,
whom they cannot please and dare not offend. Some husbands are imperious, and some wives perverse: and, as it is
always more easy to do evil than good, though the wisdom
or virtue of one can very rarely make many happy, the folly
or vice of one may often make many miserable."

"If such be the general effect of marriage," said the prince,
"I shall, for the future, think it dangerous to connect my
interest with that of another, lest I should be unhappy by my
partner's fault."

"I have met," said the princess, "with many who live
single for that reason; but I never found that their prudence
ought to raise envy. They dream away their time without
friendship, without fondness, and are driven to rid themselves of the day, for which they have no use, by childish
amusements or vicious delights. They act as beings under the
constant sense of some known inferiority, that fills their minds
with rancor and their tongues with censure. They are peevish
at home, and malevolent abroad; and, as the outlaws of
human nature, make it their business and their pleasure to
disturb that society which debars them from its privileges.
To live without feeling or exciting sympathy, to be fortunate
without adding to the felicity of others, or afflicted without

tasting the balm of pity, is a state more gloomy than solitude: it is not retreat but exclusion from mankind. Marriage has many pains, but celibacy has no pleasures."

"What then is to be done?" said Rasselas, "the more we inquire, the less we can resolve. Surely he is most likely to please himself that has no other inclination to regard."

XXVII
Disquisition upon Greatness

The conversation had a short pause. The prince, having considered his sister's observations, told her that she had surveyed life with prejudice, and supposed misery where she did not find it. "Your narrative," says he, "throws yet a darker gloom upon the prospects of futurity: the predictions of Imlac were but faint sketches of the evils painted by Nekayah. I have been lately convinced that quiet is not the daughter of grandeur or of power: that her presence is not to be bought by wealth nor enforced by conquest. It is evident that as any man acts in a wider compass, he must be more exposed to opposition from enmity or miscarriage from chance; whoever has many to please or to govern must use the ministry of many agents, some of whom will be wicked and some ignorant; by some he will be misled and by others betrayed. If he gratifies one he will offend another: those that are not favored will think themselves injured; and, since favors can be conferred but upon few, the greater number will be always discontented."

"The discontent," said the princess, "which is thus unreasonable, I hope that I shall always have spirit to despise, and you, power to repress."

"Discontent," answered Rasselas, "will not always be without reason under the most just or vigilant administration of public affairs. None, however attentive, can always discover that merit which indigence or faction may happen to obscure; and none, however powerful, can always reward it. Yet he that sees inferior desert advanced above him will naturally impute that preference to partiality or caprice; and, indeed, it can scarcely be hoped that any man, however magnanimous by nature or exalted by condition, will be able to persist forever in fixed and inexorable justice of distribution: he will sometimes indulge his own affections, and sometimes those of his favorites; he will permit some to please him who can never serve him; he will discover in those whom he loves qualities which in reality they do not possess; and to those, from whom he receives pleasure, he will in his turn endeavor to give it. Thus will recommendations sometimes prevail which were purchased by money, or by the more destructive bribery of flattery and servility.

"He that has much to do will do something wrong, and of that wrong must suffer the consequences; and, if it were possible that he should always act rightly, yet when such numbers are to judge of his conduct, the bad will censure and obstruct him by malevolence, and the good sometimes by mistake.

"The highest stations cannot therefore hope to be the abodes of happiness, which I would willingly believe to have fled from thrones and palaces to seats of humble privacy and placid obscurity. For what can hinder the satisfaction, or intercept the expectations, of him whose abilities are adequate to his employments, who sees with his own eyes the whole circuit of his influence, who chooses by his own knowledge all whom he trusts, and whom none are tempted to deceive by hope or fear? Surely he has nothing to do but to love and to be loved, to be virtuous and to be happy."

"Whether perfect happiness would be procured by perfect goodness," said Nekayah, "this world will never afford an opportunity of deciding. But this, at least, may be maintained, that we do not always find visible happiness in proportion to visible virtue. All natural and almost all political evils are incident alike to the bad and good: they are confounded in the misery of a famine, and not much distinguished in the fury of a faction; they sink together in a tempest, and are driven together from their country by invaders. All that virtue can afford is quietness of conscience, a steady prospect of a happier state; this may enable us to endure calamity with patience; but remember that patience must suppose pain."

XXVIII
Rasselas and Nekayah Continue Their Conversation

"Dear princess," said Rasselas, "you fall into the common errors of exaggeratory declamation by producing, in a familiar disquisition,[27] examples of national calamities and scenes of extensive misery which are found in books rather than in the world, and which, as they are horrid,[28] are ordained to be rare. Let us not imagine evils which we do not feel, nor injure life by misrepresentations. I cannot bear that querulous eloquence which threatens every city with a siege like that of Jerusalem, that makes famine attend on every flight of locusts, and suspends pestilence on the wing of every blast that issues from the south.

"On necessary and inevitable evils, which overwhelm kingdoms at once, all disputation is vain: when they happen they must be endured. But it is evident that these bursts of universal distress are more dreaded than felt: thousands and ten thousands flourish in youth and wither in age, without the knowledge of any other than domestic evils, and share the same pleasures and vexations whether their kings are mild or cruel, whether the armies of their country pursue their enemies, or retreat before them. While courts are disturbed with intestine competitions, and ambassadors are negotiating in foreign countries, the smith still plies his anvil, and the husbandman drives his plow forward; the necessaries of life are required and obtained, and the successive business of the seasons continues to make its wonted revolutions.

"Let us cease to consider what, perhaps, may never happen, and what, when it shall happen, will laugh at human speculation. We will not endeavor to modify the motions of the elements, or to fix the destiny of kingdoms. It is our business to consider what beings like us may perform, each laboring for his own happiness by promoting within his circle, however narrow, the happiness of others.

"Marriage is evidently the dictate of nature; men and women were made to be companions of each other, and therefore I cannot be persuaded but that marriage is one of the means of happiness."

"I know not," said the princess, "whether marriage be more than one of the innumerable modes of human misery. When I see and reckon the various forms of connubial infelicity, the unexpected causes of lasting discord, the diversities of temper, the oppositions of opinion, the rude collisions of contrary desire where both are urged by violent impulses, the

[27] *familiar disquisition:* examination of domestic life.
[28] *horrid:* dreadful.

obstinate contests of disagreeing virtues, where both are supported by consciousness of good intention, I am sometimes disposed to think with the severer casuists of most nations that marriage is rather permitted than approved, and that none, but by the instigation of a passion too much indulged, entangle themselves with indissoluble compacts."

"You seem to forget," replied Rasselas, "that you have, even now, represented celibacy as less happy than marriage. Both conditions may be bad, but they cannot both be worst. Thus it happens when wrong opinions are entertained that they mutually destroy each other, and leave the mind open to truth."

"I did not expect," answered the princess, "to hear that imputed to falsehood which is the consequence only of frailty. To the mind, as to the eye, it is difficult to compare with exactness objects vast in their extent, and various in their parts. Where we see or conceive the whole at once we readily note the discriminations and decide the preference: but of two systems, of which neither can be surveyed by any human being in its full compass of magnitude and multiplicity of complication, where is the wonder that, judging of the whole by parts, I am alternately affected by one and the other as either presses on my memory or fancy? We differ from ourselves just as we differ from each other when we see only part of the question, as in the multifarious relations of politics and morality: but when we perceive the whole at once, as in numerical computations, all agree in one judgment and none ever varies his opinion."

"Let us not add," said the prince, "to the other evils of life the bitterness of controversy, nor endeavor to vie with each other in subtleties of argument. We are employed in a search, of which both are equally to enjoy the success, or suffer by the miscarriage. It is therefore fit that we assist each other. You surely conclude too hastily from the infelicity of marriage against its institution; will not the misery of life prove equally that life cannot be the gift of heaven? The world must be peopled by marriage, or peopled without it."

"How the world is to be peopled," returned Nekayah, "is not my care and needs not be yours. I see no danger that the present generation should omit to leave successors behind them: we are not now inquiring for the world but for ourselves."

XXIX
The Debate on Marriage Continued

"The good of the whole," says Rasselas, "is the same with the good of all its parts. If marriage be best for mankind it must be evidently best for individuals, or a permanent and necessary duty must be the cause of evil, and some must be inevitably sacrificed to the convenience of others. In the estimate which you have made of the two states, it appears that the incommodities of a single life are, in a great measure, necessary and certain, but those of the conjugal state accidental and avoidable."

"I cannot forbear to flatter myself that prudence and benevolence will make marriage happy. The general folly of mankind is the cause of general complaint. What can be expected but disappointment and repentance from a choice made in the immaturity of youth, in the ardor of desire, without judgment, without foresight, without inquiry after conformity of opinions, similarity of manners, rectitude of judgment, or purity of sentiment.

"Such is the common process of marriage. A youth and maiden meeting by chance, or brought together by artifice, exchange glances, reciprocate civilities, go home, and dream of one another. Having little to divert attention or diversify thought, they find themselves uneasy when they are apart, and therefore conclude that they shall be happy together. They marry, and discover what nothing but voluntary blindness had before concealed; they wear out life in altercations, and charge nature with cruelty.

"From those early marriages proceeds likewise the rivalry of parents and children: the son is eager to enjoy the world before the father is willing to forsake it, and there is hardly room at once for two generations. The daughter begins to bloom before the mother can be content to fade, and neither can forbear to wish for the absence of the other.

"Surely all these evils may be avoided by that deliberation and delay which prudence prescribes to irrevocable choice. In the variety and jollity of youthful pleasures life may be well enough supported without the help of a partner. Longer time will increase experience, and wider views will allow better opportunities of inquiry and selection: one advantage, at least, will be certain; the parents will be visibly older than their children."

"What reason cannot collect," said Nekayah, "and what experiment has not yet taught, can be known only from the report of others. I have been told that late marriages are not eminently happy. This is a question too important to be neglected, and I have often proposed it to those, whose accuracy of remark, and comprehensiveness of knowledge, made their suffrages worthy of regard. They have generally determined that it is dangerous for a man and woman to suspend their fate upon each other, at a time when opinions are fixed and habits are established; when friendships have been contracted on both sides, when life has been planned into method, and the mind has long enjoyed the contemplation of its own prospects.

"It is scarcely possible that two traveling through the world under the conduct of chance should have been both directed to the same path, and it will not often happen that either will quit the track which custom has made pleasing. When the desultory levity of youth has settled into regularity, it is soon succeeded by pride ashamed to yield, or obstinacy delighting to contend. And even though mutual esteem produces mutual desire to please, time itself, as it modifies unchangeably the external mien, determines likewise the direction of the passions, and gives an inflexible rigidity to the manners. Long customs are not easily broken: he that attempts to change the course of his own life very often labors in vain; and how shall we do that for others which we are seldom able to do for ourselves?"

"But surely," interposed the prince, "you suppose the chief motive of choice forgotten or neglected. Whenever I shall seek a wife, it shall be my first question whether she be willing to be led by reason?"

"Thus it is," said Nekayah, "that philosophers are deceived. There are a thousand familiar disputes which reason never can decide; questions that elude investigation and make logic ridiculous; cases where something must be done, and where little can be said. Consider the state of mankind, and inquire how few can be supposed to act upon any occasions, whether small or great, with all the reasons of action present to their minds. Wretched would be the pair above all names of wretchedness who should be doomed to adjust by reason every morning all the minute detail of a domestic day.

"Those who marry at an advanced age will probably escape the encroachments of their children; but, in diminution of this advantage, they will be likely to leave them, ignorant and helpless, to a guardian's mercy: or, if that should not happen, they must at least go out of the world before they see those whom they love best either wise or great.

"From their children, if they have less to fear, they have less also to hope, and they lose, without equivalent, the joys of early love, and the convenience of uniting with manners pliant, and minds susceptible of new impressions, which might wear away their dissimilitudes by long cohabitation, as soft bodies, by continual attrition, conform their surfaces to each other.

"I believe it will be found that those who marry late are best pleased with their children, and those who marry early with their partners."

"The union of these two affections," said Rasselas, "would produce all that could be wished. Perhaps there is a time when marriage might unite them, a time neither too early for the father, nor too late for the husband."

"Every hour," answered the princess, "confirms my prejudice in favor of the position so often uttered by the mouth of Imlac, 'That nature sets her gifts on the right hand and on the left.' Those conditions, which flatter hope and attract desire, are so constituted that, as we approach one, we recede from another. There are goods so opposed that we cannot seize both but, by too much prudence, may pass between them at too great a distance to reach either. This is often the fate of long consideration; he does nothing who endeavors to do more than is allowed to humanity. Flatter not yourself with contrarieties of pleasure. Of the blessings set before you make your choice, and be content. No man can taste the fruits of autumn while he is delighting his scent with the flowers of the spring: no man can, at the same time, fill his cup from the source and the mouth of the Nile."

XXX
Imlac Enters, and Changes the Conversation

Here Imlac entered, and interrupted them. "Imlac," said Rasselas, "I have been taking from the princess the dismal history of private life, and am almost discouraged from further search."

"It seems to me," said Imlac, "that while you are making the choice of life, you neglect to live. You wander about a single city which, however large and diversified, can now afford few novelties, and forget that you are in a country famous among the earliest monarchies for the power and wisdom of its inhabitants; a country where the sciences first dawned that illuminate the world, and beyond which the arts cannot be traced of civil society or domestic life.

"The old Egyptians have left behind them monuments of industry and power before which all European magnificence is confessed to fade away. The ruins of their architecture are the schools of modern builders, and from the wonders which time has spared we may conjecture, though uncertainly, what it has destroyed."

"My curiosity," said Rasselas, "does not very strongly lead me to survey piles of stone or mounds of earth; my business is with man. I came hither not to measure fragments of temples or trace choked aqueducts, but to look upon the various scenes of the present world."

"The things that are now before us," said the princess, "require attention, and deserve it. What have I to do with the heroes or the monuments of ancient times? with times which never can return, and heroes, whose form of life was different from all that the present condition of mankind requires or allows."

"To know anything," returned the poet, "we must know its effects; to see men we must see their works, that we may learn what reason has dictated or passion has incited, and find what are the most powerful motives of action. To judge rightly of the present we must oppose it to the past; for all judgment is comparative, and of the future nothing can be known. The truth is that no mind is much employed upon the present: recollection and anticipation fill up almost all our moments. Our passions are joy and grief, love and hatred, hope and fear. Of joy and grief the past is the object, and the future of hope and fear; even love and hatred respect the past, for the cause must have been before the effect.

"The present state of things is the consequence of the former, and it is natural to inquire what were the sources of the good that we enjoy or of the evil that we suffer. If we act only for ourselves, to neglect the study of history is not prudent: if we are entrusted with the care of others, it is not just. Ignorance, when it is voluntary, is criminal; and he may properly be charged with evil who refused to learn how he might prevent it.

"There is no part of history so generally useful as that which relates the progress of the human mind, the gradual improvement of reason, the successive advances of science, the vicissitudes of learning and ignorance which are the light and darkness of thinking beings, the extinction and resuscitation of arts, and all the revolutions of the intellectual world. If accounts of battles and invasions are peculiarly the business of princes, the useful or elegant arts are not to be neglected; those who have kingdoms to govern, have understandings to cultivate.

"Example is always more efficacious than precept. A soldier is formed in war, and a painter must copy pictures. In this, contemplative life has the advantage: great actions are seldom seen; but the labors of art are always at hand for those who desire to know what art has been able to perform.

"When the eye or the imagination is struck with any uncommon work the next transition of an active mind is to the means by which it was performed. Here begins the true use of such contemplation; we enlarge our comprehension by new ideas, and perhaps recover some art lost to mankind, or learn what is less perfectly known in our own country. At least we compare our own with former times, and either rejoice at our improvements or, what is the first motion towards good, discover our defects."

"I am willing," said the prince, "to see all that can deserve my search." "And I," said the princess, "shall rejoice to learn something of the manners of antiquity."

"The most pompous[29] monument of Egyptian greatness, and one of the most bulky works of manual industry," said Imlac, "are the pyramids; fabrics raised before the time of history, and of which the earliest narratives afford us only

[29] *pompous:* magnificent.

uncertain traditions. Of these the greatest is still standing, very little injured by time."

"Let us visit them tomorrow," said Nekayah. "I have often heard of the pyramids, and shall not rest till I have seen them within and without with my own eyes."

XXXI
They Visit the Pyramids

The resolution being thus taken, they set out the next day. They laid tents upon their camels, being resolved to stay among the pyramids till their curiosity was fully satisfied. They traveled gently, turned aside to everything remarkable, stopped from time to time and conversed with the inhabitants, and observed the various appearances of towns, ruined and inhabited, of wild and cultivated nature.

When they came to the great pyramid they were astonished at the extent of the base, and the height of the top. Imlac explained to them the principles upon which the pyramidal form was chosen for a fabric intended to coextend its duration with that of the world: he showed that its gradual diminution gave it such stability as defeated all the common attacks of the elements, and could scarcely be overthrown by earthquakes themselves, the least resistible of natural violence. A concussion that should shatter the pyramid would threaten the dissolution of the continent.

They measured all its dimensions, and pitched their tents at its foot. Next day they prepared to enter its interior apartments, and having hired the common guides climbed up to the first passage, when the favorite of the princess, looking into the cavity, stepped back and trembled. "Pekuah," said the princess, "of what art thou afraid?" "Of the narrow entrance," answered the lady, "and of the dreadful gloom. I dare not enter a place which must surely be inhabited by unquiet souls. The original possessors of these dreadful vaults will start up before us, and, perhaps, shut us in forever." She spoke, and threw her arms round the neck of her mistress.

"If all your fear be of apparitions," said the prince, "I will promise you safety: there is no danger from the dead; he that is once buried will be seen no more."

"That the dead are seen no more," said Imlac, "I will not

undertake to maintain against the concurrent and unvaried testimony of all ages and of all nations. There is no people, rude or learned, among whom apparitions of the dead are not related and believed. This opinion, which perhaps prevails as far as human nature is diffused, could become universal only by its truth: those that never heard of one another would not have agreed in a tale which nothing but experience can make credible. That it is doubted by single cavilers can very little weaken the general evidence, and some who deny it with their tongues confess it by their fears.

"Yet I do not mean to add new terrors to those which have already seized upon Pekuah. There can be no reason why specters should haunt the pyramid more than other places, or why they should have power or will to hurt innocence and purity. Our entrance is no violation of their privileges; we can take nothing from them, how then can we offend them?"

"My dear Pekuah," said the princess, "I will always go before you, and Imlac shall follow you. Remember that you are the companion of the princess of Abyssinia."

"If the princess is pleased that her servant should die," returned the lady, "let her command some death less dreadful than enclosure in this horrid cavern. You know I dare not disobey you: I must go if you command me; but if I once enter, I never shall come back."

The princess saw that her fear was too strong for expostulation or reproof, and embracing her, told her that she should stay in the tent till their return. Pekuah was yet not satisfied, but entreated the princess not to pursue so dreadful a purpose as that of entering the recesses of the pyramid. "Though I cannot teach courage," said Nekayah, "I must not learn cowardice; nor leave at last undone what I came hither only to do."

XXXII
They Enter the Pyramid

Pekuah descended to the tents, and the rest entered the pyramid: they passed through the galleries, surveyed the vaults of marble, and examined the chest in which the body of the founder is supposed to have been reposited. They then sat down in one of the most spacious chambers to rest a while before they attempted to return.

"We have now," said Imlac, "gratified our minds with an exact view of the greatest work of man, except the wall of China.

"Of the wall it is very easy to assign the motives. It secured a wealthy and timorous nation from the incursions of barbarians, whose unskillfulness in arts made it easier for them to supply their wants by rapine than by industry, and who from time to time poured in upon the habitations of peaceful commerce, as vultures descend upon domestic fowl. Their celerity and fierceness made the wall necessary, and their ignorance made it efficacious.

"But for the pyramids no reason has ever been given adequate to the cost and labor of the work. The narrowness of the chambers proves that it could afford no retreat from enemies, and treasures might have been reposited at far less expense with equal security. It seems to have been erected only in compliance with that hunger of imagination which preys incessantly upon life, and must be always appeased by some employment. Those who have already all that they can enjoy, must enlarge their desires. He that has built for use, till use is supplied, must begin to build for vanity, and extend his plan to the utmost power of human performance, that he may not be soon reduced to form another wish.

"I consider this mighty structure as a monument of the insufficiency of human enjoyments. A king whose power is unlimited, and whose treasures surmount all real and imaginary wants, is compelled to solace, by the erection of a pyramid, the satiety of dominion and tastelessness of pleasures, and to amuse the tediousness of declining life by seeing thousands laboring without end, and one stone, for no purpose, laid upon another. Whoever thou art that, not content with a moderate condition, imaginest happiness in royal magnificence, and dreamest that command or riches can feed the appetite of novelty with perpetual gratifications, survey the pyramids and confess thy folly!"

XXXIII
The Princess Meets with an Unexpected Misfortune

They rose up, and returned through the cavity at which they had entered, and the princess prepared for her favorite a long narrative of dark labyrinths and costly rooms, and of the different impressions which the varieties of the way had made upon her. But, when they came to their train,[30] they found everyone silent and dejected: the men discovered shame and fear in their countenances, and the women were weeping in the tents.

What had happened they did not try to conjecture, but immediately inquired. "You had scarcely entered into the pyramid," said one of the attendants, "when a troop of Arabs rushed upon us: we were too few to resist them and too slow to escape. They were about to search the tents, set us on our camels, and drive us along before them, when the approach of some Turkish horsemen put them to flight; but they seized the lady Pekuah with her two maids, and carried them away: the Turks are now pursuing them by our instigation, but I fear they will not be able to overtake them."

The princess was overpowered with surprise and grief. Rasselas, in the first heat of his resentment, ordered his servants to follow him, and prepared to pursue the robbers with his saber in his hand. "Sir," said Imlac, "what can you hope from violence or valor? the Arabs are mounted on horses trained to battle and retreat; we have only beasts of burden. By leaving our present station we may lose the princess, but cannot hope to regain Pekuah."

In a short time the Turks returned, having not been able to reach the enemy. The princess burst out into new lamentations, and Rasselas could scarcely forbear to reproach them with cowardice; but Imlac was of opinion that the escape of the Arabs was no addition to their misfortune, for, perhaps, they would have killed their captives rather than have resigned them.

XXXIV
They Return to Cairo without Pekuah

There was nothing to be hoped from longer stay. They returned to Cairo repenting of their curiosity, censuring the negligence of the government, lamenting their own rashness which had neglected to procure a guard, imagining many expedients by which the loss of Pekuah might have been

[30] *train:* retinue.

prevented, and resolving to do something for her recovery, though none could find anything proper to be done.

Nekayah retired to her chamber, where her women attempted to comfort her by telling her that all had their troubles, and that lady Pekuah had enjoyed much happiness in the world for a long time, and might reasonably expect a change of fortune. They hoped that some good would befall her wheresoever she was, and that their mistress would find another friend who might supply her place.

The princess made them no answer, and they continued the form of condolence, not much grieved in their hearts that the favorite was lost.

Next day the prince presented to the Bassa a memorial[31] of the wrong which he had suffered, and a petition for redress. The Bassa threatened to punish the robbers, but did not attempt to catch them, nor, indeed, could any account or description be given by which he might direct the pursuit.

It soon appeared that nothing would be done by authority. Governors, being accustomed to hear of more crimes than they can punish and more wrongs than they can redress, set themselves at ease by indiscriminate negligence, and presently[32] forget the request when they lose sight of the petitioner.

Imlac then endeavored to gain some intelligence by private agents. He found many who pretended to an exact knowledge of all the haunts of the Arabs and to regular correspondence with their chiefs, and who readily undertook the recovery of Pekuah. Of these, some were furnished with money for their journey, and came back no more; some were liberally paid for accounts which a few days discovered to be false. But the princess would not suffer any means, however improbable, to be left untried. While she was doing something she kept her hope alive. As one expedient failed, another was suggested; when one messenger returned unsuccessful, another was despatched to a different quarter.

Two months had now passed, and of Pekuah nothing had been heard; the hopes which they had endeavored to raise in each other grew more languid, and the princess, when she saw nothing more to be tried, sunk down inconsolable in

---

[31] *memorial:* statement of the facts, with a petition for action.
[32] *presently:* at once.

hopeless dejection. A thousand times she reproached herself with the easy compliance by which she permitted her favorite to stay behind her. "Had not my fondness," said she, "lessened my authority, Pekuah had not dared to talk of her terrors. She ought to have feared me more than specters. A severe look would have overpowered her; a peremptory command would have compelled obedience. Why did foolish indulgence prevail upon me? Why did I not speak and refuse to hear?"

"Great princess," said Imlac, "do not reproach yourself for your virtue, or consider that as blamable by which evil has accidentally been caused. Your tenderness for the timidity of Pekuah was generous and kind. When we act according to our duty, we commit the event to Him by whose laws our actions are governed, and who will suffer none to be finally punished for obedience. When in prospect of some good, whether natural or moral, we break the rules prescribed us, we withdraw from the direction of superior wisdom, and take all consequences upon ourselves. Man cannot so far know the connection of causes and events as that he may venture to do wrong in order to do right. When we pursue our end by lawful means, we may always console our miscarriage by the hope of future recompense. When we consult only our own policy, and attempt to find a nearer way to good by over-leaping the settled boundaries of right and wrong, we cannot be happy even by success, because we cannot escape the consciousness of our fault; but if we miscarry, the disappointment is irremediably embittered. How comfortless is the sorrow of him who feels at once the pangs of guilt, and the vexation of calamity which guilt has brought upon him?

"Consider, princess, what would have been your condition, if the lady Pekuah had entreated to accompany you and, being compelled to stay in the tents, had been carried away; or how would you have borne the thought, if you had forced her into the pyramid, and she had died before you in agonies of terror."

"Had either happened," said Nekayah, "I could not have endured life till now: I should have been tortured to madness by the remembrance of such cruelty, or must have pined away in abhorrence of myself."

"This at least," said Imlac, "is the present reward of virtuous conduct, that no unlucky consequence can oblige us to repent it."

XXXV
The Princess Languishes for Want of Pekuah

Nekayah, being thus reconciled to herself, found that no evil is insupportable but that which is accompanied with consciousness of wrong. She was, from that time, delivered from the violence of tempestuous sorrow, and sunk into silent pensiveness and gloomy tranquillity. She sat from morning to evening recollecting all that had been done or said by her Pekuah, treasured up with care every trifle on which Pekuah had set an accidental value, and which might recall to mind any little incident or careless conversation. The sentiments of her whom she now expected to see no more were treasured in her memory as rules of life, and she deliberated to no other end than to conjecture on any occasion what would have been the opinion and counsel of Pekuah.

The women, by whom she was attended, knew nothing of her real condition, and therefore she could not talk to them but with caution and reserve. She began to remit her curiosity, having no great care to collect notions which she had no convenience of uttering. Rasselas endeavored first to comfort and afterwards to divert her; he hired musicians, to whom she seemed to listen but did not hear them, and procured masters to instruct her in various arts, whose lectures, when they visited her again, were again to be repeated. She had lost her taste of pleasure and her ambition of excellence. And her mind, though forced into short excursions, always recurred to the image of her friend.

Imlac was every morning earnestly enjoined to renew his inquiries, and was asked every night whether he had yet heard of Pekuah, till not being able to return the princess the answer that she desired, he was less and less willing to come into her presence. She observed his backwardness, and commanded him to attend her. "You are not," said she, "to confound impatience with resentment, or to suppose that I charge you with negligence because I repine at your unsuccessfulness. I do not much wonder at your absence; I know that the unhappy are never pleasing, and that all naturally avoid the contagion of misery. To hear complaints is wearisome alike to the wretched and the happy; for who would cloud by adventitious grief the short gleams of gaiety which life allows us? or who that is struggling under his own evils will add to them the miseries of another?

"The time is at hand when none shall be disturbed any longer by the sighs of Nekayah: my search after happiness is now at an end. I am resolved to retire from the world with all its flatteries and deceits, and will hide myself in solitude, without any other care than to compose my thoughts and regulate my hours by a constant succession of innocent occupations, till, with a mind purified from all earthly desires, I shall enter into that state to which all are hastening, and in which I hope again to enjoy the friendship of Pekuah."

"Do not entangle your mind," said Imlac, "by irrevocable determinations, nor increase the burthen of life by a voluntary accumulation of misery: the weariness of retirement will continue or increase when the loss of Pekuah is forgotten. That you have been deprived of one pleasure is no very good reason for rejection of the rest."

"Since Pekuah was taken from me," said the princess, "I have no pleasure to reject or to retain. She that has no one to love or trust has little to hope. She wants the radical[33] principle of happiness. We may, perhaps, allow that what satisfaction this world can afford, must arise from the conjunction of wealth, knowledge, and goodness: wealth is nothing but as it is bestowed, and knowledge nothing but as it is communicated: they must therefore be imparted to others, and to whom could I now delight to impart them? Goodness affords the only comfort which can be enjoyed without a partner, and goodness may be practiced in retirement."

"How far solitude may admit goodness or advance it, I shall not," replied Imlac, "dispute at present. Remember the confession of the pious hermit. You will wish to return into the world, when the image of your companion has left your thoughts." "That time," said Nekayah, "will never come. The generous frankness, the modest obsequiousness,[34] and the faithful secrecy of my dear Pekuah, will always be more missed as I shall live longer to see vice and folly."

"The state of a mind oppressed with a sudden calamity," said Imlac, "is like that of the fabulous inhabitants of the

---

[33] *radical:* fundamental.
[34] *obsequiousness:* promptness to serve and please.

new-created earth, who, when the first night came upon them, supposed that day never would return. When the clouds of sorrow gather over us we see nothing beyond them, nor can imagine how they will be dispelled: yet a new day succeeded to the night, and sorrow is never long without a dawn of ease. But they who restrain themselves from receiving comfort do as the savages would have done, had they put out their eyes when it was dark. Our minds, like our bodies, are in continual flux; something is hourly lost and something acquired. To lose much at once is inconvenient to either, but while the vital powers remain uninjured, nature will find the means of reparation. Distance has the same effect on the mind as on the eye, and while we glide along the stream of time, whatever we leave behind us is always lessening and that which we approach increasing in magnitude. Do not suffer life to stagnate; it will grow muddy for want of motion: commit yourself again to the current of the world; Pekuah will vanish by degrees; you will meet in your way some other favorite, or learn to diffuse yourself in general conversation."[35]

"At least," said the prince, "do not despair before all remedies have been tried: the inquiry after the unfortunate lady is still continued, and shall be carried on with yet greater diligence on condition that you will promise to wait a year for the event, without any unalterable resolution."

Nekayah thought this a reasonable demand, and made the promise to her brother, who had been advised by Imlac to require it. Imlac had, indeed, no great hope of regaining Pekuah, but he supposed that if he could secure the interval of a year, the princess would be then in no danger of a cloister.

XXXVI
Pekuah Is Still Remembered. The Progress of Sorrow

Nekayah, seeing that nothing was omitted for the recovery of her favorite, and having by her promise set her intention of retirement at a distance, began imperceptibly to return to common cares and common pleasures. She rejoiced without her own consent at the suspension of her sorrows, and some-

[35] I.e., extend your interests by participating in society.

times caught herself with indignation in the act of turning away her mind from the remembrance of her, whom yet she resolved never to forget.

She then appointed a certain hour of the day for meditation on the merits and fondness of Pekuah, and for some weeks retired constantly at the time fixed, and returned with her eyes swollen and her countenance clouded. By degrees she grew less scrupulous, and suffered any important and pressing avocation to delay the tribute of daily tears. She then yielded to less occasions; sometimes forgot what she was indeed afraid to remember, and at last wholly released herself from the duty of periodical affliction.

Her real love of Pekuah was yet not diminished. A thousand occurrences brought her back to memory, and a thousand wants, which nothing but the confidence of friendship can supply, made her frequently regretted. She, therefore, solicited Imlac never to desist from inquiry, and to leave no art of intelligence untried that, at least, she might have the comfort of knowing that she did not suffer by negligence or sluggishness. "Yet what," said she, "is to be expected from our pursuit of happiness, when we find the state of life to be such, that happiness itself is the cause of misery? Why should we endeavor to attain that of which the possession cannot be secured? I shall henceforward fear to yield my heart to excellence however bright, or to fondness however tender, lest I should lose again what I have lost in Pekuah."

XXXVII
The Princess Hears News of Pekuah

In seven months, one of the messengers, who had been sent away upon the day when the promise was drawn from the princess, returned, after many unsuccessful rambles, from the borders of Nubia, with an account that Pekuah was in the hands of an Arab chief, who possessed a castle or fortress on the extremity of Egypt. The Arab, whose revenue was plunder, was willing to restore her with her two attendants for two hundred ounces of gold.

The price was no subject of debate. The princess was in ecstasies when she heard that her favorite was alive, and might so cheaply be ransomed. She could not think of delaying for a moment Pekuah's happiness or her own, but entreated her brother to send back the messenger with the sum required. Imlac, being consulted, was not very confident of the veracity of the relator, and was still more doubtful of the Arab's faith, who might, if he were too liberally trusted, detain at once the money and the captives. He thought it dangerous to put themselves in the power of the Arab by going into his district, and could not expect that the rover would so much expose himself as to come into the lower country, where he might be seized by the forces of the Bassa.

It is difficult to negotiate where neither will trust. But Imlac, after some deliberation, directed the messenger to propose that Pekuah should be conducted by ten horsemen to the monastery of St. Anthony, which is situated in the deserts of Upper Egypt, where she should be met by the same number, and her ransom should be paid.

That no time might be lost, as they expected that the proposal would not be refused, they immediately began their journey to the monastery; and, when they arrived, Imlac went forward with the former messenger to the Arab's fortress. Rasselas was desirous to go with them, but neither his sister nor Imlac would consent. The Arab, according to the custom of his nation, observed the laws of hospitality with great exactness to those who put themselves into his power, and in a few days brought Pekuah with her maids by easy journeys to their place appointed, where receiving the stipulated price he restored her with great respect to liberty and her friends, and undertook to conduct them back towards Cairo beyond all danger of robbery or violence.

The princess and her favorite embraced each other with transport too violent to be expressed, and went out together to pour the tears of tenderness in secret, and exchange professions of kindness and gratitude. After a few hours they returned into the refectory of the convent, where, in the presence of the prior and his brethren, the prince required of Pekuah the history of her adventures.

XXXVIII
The Adventures of the Lady Pekuah

"At what time, and in what manner, I was forced away," said Pekuah, "your servants have told you. The suddenness of the event struck me with surprise, and I was at first rather stupified than agitated with any passion of either fear or sorrow. My confusion was increased by the speed and tumult of our flight while we were followed by the Turks, who, as it seemed, soon despaired to overtake us, or were afraid of those whom they made a show of menacing.

"When the Arabs saw themselves out of danger they slackened their course, and, as I was less harassed by external violence, I began to feel more uneasiness in my mind. After some time we stopped near a spring shaded with trees in a pleasant meadow, where we were set upon the ground and offered such refreshments as our masters were partaking. I was suffered to sit with my maids apart from the rest, and none attempted to comfort or insult us. Here I first began to feel the full weight of my misery. The girls sat weeping in silence, and from time to time looked on me for succor. I knew not to what condition we were doomed, nor could conjecture where would be the place of our captivity, or whence to draw any hope of deliverance. I was in the hands of robbers and savages, and had no reason to suppose that their pity was more than their justice, or that they would forbear the gratification of any ardor of desire or caprice of cruelty. I, however, kissed my maids, and endeavored to pacify them by remarking, that we were yet treated with decency, and that, since we were now carried beyond pursuit, there was no danger of violence to our lives.

"When we were to be set again on horseback, my maids clung round me and refused to be parted, but I commanded them not to irritate those who had us in their power. We traveled the remaining part of the day through an unfrequented and pathless country, and came by moonlight to the side of a hill where the rest of the troop was stationed. Their tents were pitched and their fires kindled, and our chief was welcomed as a man much beloved by his dependents.

"We were received into a large tent, where we found women who had attended their husbands in the expedition. They set before us the supper which they had provided, and I eat it rather to encourage my maids than to comply with any appetite of my own. When the meat was taken away they spread the carpets for repose. I was weary, and hoped to find in sleep that remission of distress which nature seldom denies. Ordering myself therefore to be undressed, I observed that the women looked very earnestly upon me, not expecting, I suppose, to see me so submissively attended. When my upper

vest was taken off, they were apparently struck with the
splendor of my clothes, and one of them timorously laid her
hand upon the embroidery. She then went out and, in a
short time, came back with another woman, who seemed to
be of higher rank and greater authority. She did, at her
entrance, the usual act of reverence, and, taking me by the
hand, placed me in a smaller tent spread with finer carpets,
where I spent the night quietly with my maids.

"In the morning as I was sitting on the grass, the chief of
the troop came towards me. I rose up to receive him, and he
bowed with great respect. 'Illustrious lady,' said he, 'my
fortune is better than I had presumed to hope: I am told by
my women that I have a princess in my camp.' 'Sir,'
answered I, 'your women have deceived themselves and you;
I am not a princess, but an unhappy stranger who intended
soon to have left this country, in which I am now to be
imprisoned forever.' 'Whoever, or whencesoever, you are,'
returned the Arab, 'your dress and that of your servants
show your rank to be high and your wealth to be great. Why
should you, who can so easily procure your ransom, think
yourself in danger of perpetual captivity? The purpose of my
incursions is to increase my riches, or more properly to
gather tribute. The sons of Ishmael are the natural and hereditary lords of this part of the continent, which is usurped by
late invaders and low-born tyrants, from whom we are
compelled to take by the sword what is denied to justice. The
violence of war admits no distinction; the lance that is lifted
at guilt and power will sometimes fall on innocence and
gentleness.'

'How little,' said I, 'did I expect that yesterday it should
have fallen upon me.'

'Misfortunes,' answered the Arab, 'should always be expected. If the eye of hostility could learn reverence or pity,
excellence like yours had been exempt from injury. But the
angels of affliction spread their toils alike for the virtuous
and the wicked, for the mighty and the mean. Do not be
disconsolate; I am not one of the lawless and cruel rovers of
the desert; I know the rules of civil life: I will fix your
ransom, give a passport to your messenger, and perform my
stipulation with nice[36] punctuality.'

"You will easily believe that I was pleased with his courtesy;

---

[36] *nice*: precise.

and finding that his predominant passion was desire of money, I began now to think my danger less, for I knew that no sum would be thought too great for the release of Pekuah. I told him that he should have no reason to charge me with ingratitude if I was used with kindness, and that any ransom, which could be expected for a maid of common rank, would be paid, but that he must not persist to rate me as a princess. He said, he would consider what he should demand, and then, smiling, bowed and retired.

"Soon after the women came about me, each contending to be more officious than the other, and my maids themselves were served with reverence. We traveled onward by short journeys. On the fourth day the chief told me, that my ransom must be two hundred ounces of gold, which I not only promised him, but told him that I would add fifty more if I and my maids were honorably treated.

"I never knew the power of gold before. From that time I was the leader of the troop. The march of every day was longer or shorter as I commanded, and the tents were pitched where I chose to rest. We now had camels and other conveniencies for travel, my own women were always at my side, and I amused myself with observing the manners of the vagrant nations, and with viewing remains of ancient edifices with which these deserted countries appear to have been, in some distant age, lavishly embellished.

"The chief of the band was a man far from illiterate: he was able to travel by the stars or the compass, and had marked in his erratic expeditions such places as are most worthy the notice of a passenger. He observed to me that buildings are always best preserved in places little frequented and difficult of access: for, when once a country declines from its primitive splendor, the more inhabitants are left, the quicker ruin will be made. Walls supply stones more easily than quarries, and palaces and temples will be demolished to make stables of granite and cottages of porphyry.

XXXIX
The Adventures of Pekuah Continued

"We wandered about in this manner for some weeks whether, as our chief pretended, for my gratification, or, as I rather suspected, for some convenience of his own. I endeavored to appear contented where sullenness and resentment would have been of no use, and that endeavor conduced much to the calmness of my mind; but my heart was always with Nekayah, and the troubles of the night much overbalanced the amusements of the day. My women, who threw all their cares upon their mistress, set their minds at ease from the time when they saw me treated with respect, and gave themselves up to the incidental alleviations of our fatigue without solicitude or sorrow. I was pleased with their pleasure, and animated with their confidence. My condition had lost much of its terror, since I found that the Arab ranged the country merely to get riches. Avarice is an uniform and tractable vice: other intellectual distempers are different in different constitutions of mind; that which soothes the pride of one will offend the pride of another; but to the favor of the covetous there is a ready way, bring money and nothing is denied.

"At last we came to the dwelling of our chief, a strong and spacious house built with stone in an island of the Nile, which lies, as I was told, under the tropic. "Lady," said the Arab, "you shall rest after your journey a few weeks in this place, where you are to consider yourself as sovereign. My occupation is war: I have therefore chosen this obscure residence, from which I can issue unexpected and to which I can retire unpursued. You may now repose in security: here are few pleasures, but here is no danger." He then led me into the inner apartments, and seating me on the richest couch, bowed to the ground. His women, who considered me as a rival, looked on me with malignity; but being soon informed that I was a great lady detained only for my ransom, they began to vie with each other in obsequiousness and reverence.

"Being again comforted with new assurances of speedy liberty, I was for some days diverted from impatience by the novelty of the place. The turrets overlooked the country to a great distance, and afforded a view of many windings of the stream. In the day I wandered from one place to another as the course of the sun varied the splendor of the prospect, and saw many things which I had never seen before. The crocodiles and river-horses[37] are common in this unpeopled region, and I often looked upon them with terror though I knew that

[37] *river-horses:* hippopotamuses.

they could not hurt me. For some time I expected to see mermaids and tritons, which, as Imlac has told me, the European travelers have stationed in the Nile, but no such beings ever appeared, and the Arab, when I inquired after them, laughed at my credulity.

"At night the Arab always attended me to a tower set apart for celestial observations, where he endeavored to teach me the names and courses of the stars. I had no great inclination to this study, but an appearance of attention was necessary to please my instructor, who valued himself for his skill, and, in a little while, I found some employment requisite to beguile the tediousness of time, which was to be passed always amidst the same objects. I was weary of looking in the morning on things from which I had turned away weary in the evening: I therefore was at last willing to observe the stars rather than do nothing, but could not always compose my thoughts, and was very often thinking on Nekayah when others imagined me contemplating the sky. Soon after the Arab went upon another expedition, and then my only pleasure was to talk with my maids about the accident by which we were carried away, and the happiness that we should all enjoy at the end of our captivity."

"There were women in your Arab's fortress," said the princess, "why did you not make them your companions, enjoy their conversation, and partake their diversions? In a place where they found business or amusement, why should you alone sit corroded with idle melancholy or why could not you bear for a few months that condition to which they were condemned for life?"

"The diversions of the women," answered Pekuah, "were only childish play, by which the mind accustomed to stronger operations could not be kept busy. I could do all which they delighted in doing by powers merely sensitive,[38] while my intellectual faculties were flown to Cairo. They ran from room to room as a bird hops from wire to wire in his cage. They danced for the sake of motion, as lambs frisk in a meadow. One sometimes pretended to be hurt that the rest might be alarmed, or hid herself that another might seek her. Part of their time passed in watching the progress of light bodies that floated on the river, and part in marking the various forms into which clouds broke in the sky.

[38] *sensitive:* of the senses.

"Their business was only needlework, in which I and my maids sometimes helped them; but you know that the mind will easily straggle from the fingers, nor will you suspect that captivity and absence from Nekayah could receive solace from silken flowers.

"Nor was much satisfaction to be hoped from their conversation: for of what could they be expected to talk? They had seen nothing; for they had lived from early youth in that narrow spot: of what they had not seen they could have no knowledge, for they could not read. They had no ideas but of the few things that were within their view, and had hardly names for anything but their clothes and their food. As I bore a superior character, I was often called to terminate their quarrels, which I decided as equitably as I could. If it could have amused me to hear the complaints of each against the rest, I might have been often detained by long stories, but the motives of their animosity were so small that I could not listen without intercepting the tale."

"How," said Rasselas, "can the Arab, whom you represented as a man of more than common accomplishments, take any pleasure in his seraglio, when it is filled only with women like these? Are they exquisitely beautiful?"

"They do not," said Pekuah, "want that unaffecting and ignoble beauty which may subsist without sprightliness or sublimity, without energy of thought or dignity of virtue. But to a man like the Arab such beauty was only a flower casually plucked and carelessly thrown away. Whatever pleasures he might find among them, they were not those of friendship or society. When they were playing about him he looked on them with inattentive superiority: when they vied for his regard he sometimes turned away disgusted. As they had no knowledge, their talk could take nothing from the tediousness of life: as they had no choice, their fondness, or appearance of fondness, excited in him neither pride nor gratitude; he was not exalted in his own esteem by the smiles of a woman who saw no other man, nor was much obliged by that regard of which he could never know the sincerity, and which he might often perceive to be exerted not so much to delight him as to pain a rival. That which he gave, and they received, as love, was only a careless distribution of superfluous time, such love as man can bestow upon that which he despises, such as has neither hope nor fear, neither joy nor sorrow."

"You have reason, lady, to think yourself happy," said Imlac, "that you have been thus easily dismissed. How could a mind, hungry for knowledge, be willing, in an intellectual famine, to lose such a banquet as Pekuah's conversation?"

"I am inclined to believe," answered Pekuah, "that he was for some time in suspense; for, notwithstanding his promise, whenever I proposed to dispatch a messenger to Cairo, he found some excuse for delay. While I was detained in his house he made many incursions into the neighboring countries, and, perhaps, he would have refused to discharge me, had his plunder been equal to his wishes. He returned always courteous, related his adventures, delighted to hear my observations, and endeavored to advance my acquaintance with the stars. When I importuned him to send away my letters, he soothed me with professions of honor and sincerity; and, when I could be no longer decently denied, put his troop again in motion, and left me to govern in his absence. I was much afflicted by this studied procrastination, and was sometimes afraid that I should be forgotten; that you would leave Cairo, and I must end my days in an island of the Nile.

"I grew at last hopeless and dejected, and cared so little to entertain him that he for a while more frequently talked with my maids. That he should fall in love with them, or with me, might have been equally fatal, and I was not much pleased with the growing friendship. My anxiety was not long; for, as I recovered some degree of cheerfulness, he returned to me, and I could not forbear to despise my former uneasiness.

"He still delayed to send for my ransom, and would, perhaps, never have determined, had not your agent found his way to him. The gold which he would not fetch he could not reject when it was offered. He hastened to prepare for our journey hither, like a man delivered from the pain of an intestine conflict. I took leave of my companions in the house, who dismissed me with cold indifference."

Nekayah, having heard her favorite's relation, rose and embraced her, and Rasselas gave her an hundred ounces of gold, which she presented to the Arab for the fifty that were promised.

XL
The History of a Man of Learning

They returned to Cairo, and were so well pleased at finding themselves together that none of them went much abroad. The prince began to love learning, and one day declared to Imlac, that he intended to devote himself to science,[39] and pass the rest of his days in literary solitude.

"Before you make your final choice," answered Imlac, "you ought to examine its hazards, and converse with some of those who are grown old in the company of themselves. I have just left the observatory of one of the most learned astronomers in the world, who has spent forty years in unwearied attention to the motions and appearances of the celestial bodies, and has drawn out his soul in endless calculations. He admits a few friends once a month to hear his deductions and enjoy his discoveries. I was introduced as a man of knowledge worthy of his notice. Men of various ideas and fluent conversation are commonly welcome to those whose thoughts have been long fixed upon a single point, and who find the images of other things stealing away. I delighted him with my remarks, he smiled at the narrative of my travels, and was glad to forget the constellations, and descend for a moment into the lower world.

"On the next day of vacation I renewed my visit, and was so fortunate as to please him again. He relaxed from that time the severity of his rule, and permitted me to enter at my own choice. I found him always busy, and always glad to be relieved. As each knew much which the other was desirous of learning, we exchanged our notions with great delight. I perceived that I had every day more of his confidence, and always found new cause of admiration in the profundity of his mind. His comprehension is vast, his memory capacious and retentive, his discourse is methodical, and his expression clear.

"His integrity and benevolence are equal to his learning. His deepest researches and most favorite studies are willingly interrupted for any opportunity of doing good by his counsel or his riches. To his closest[40] retreat, at his most busy mo-

[39] *science:* learning.
[40] *closest:* most private.

ments, all are admitted that want his assistance: 'For though I exclude idleness and pleasure, I will never,' says he, 'bar my doors against charity. To man is permitted the contemplation of the skies, but the practice of virtue is commanded.' "

"Surely," said the princess, "this man is happy."

"I visited him," said Imlac, "with more and more frequency, and was every time more enamored of his conversation: he was sublime without haughtiness, courteous without formality, and communicative without ostentation. I was at first, great princess, of your opinion, thought him the happiest of mankind, and often congratulated him on the blessing that he enjoyed. He seemed to hear nothing with indifference but the praises of his condition, to which he always returned a general answer, and diverted the conversation to some other topic.

"Amidst this willingness to be pleased, and labor to please, I had quickly reason to imagine that some painful sentiment pressed upon his mind. He often looked up earnestly towards the sun, and let his voice fall in the midst of his discourse. He would sometimes, when we were alone, gaze upon me in silence with the air of a man who longed to speak what he was yet resolved to suppress. He would often send for me with vehement injunctions of haste, though, when I came to him, he had nothing extraordinary to say. And sometimes, when I was leaving him, would call me back, pause a few moments and then dismiss me.

XLI
The Astronomer Discovers the Cause of His Uneasiness

"At last the time came when the secret burst his reserve. We were sitting together last night in the turret of his house, watching the emersion of a satellite of Jupiter. A sudden tempest clouded the sky, and disappointed our observation. We sat a while silent in the dark, and then he addressed himself to me in these words: 'Imlac, I have long considered thy friendship as the greatest blessing of my life. Integrity without knowledge is weak and useless, and knowledge without integrity is dangerous and dreadful. I have found in thee all the qualities requisite for trust: benevolence, experience, and fortitude. I have long discharged an office which I must soon quit at the call of nature, and shall rejoice in the hour of imbecility and pain to devolve it upon thee.'

"I thought my self honored by this testimony, and protested that whatever could conduce to his happiness would add likewise to mine.

" 'Hear, Imlac, what thou wilt not without difficulty credit. I have possessed for five years the regulation of weather and the distribution of the seasons: the sun has listened to my dictates, and passed from tropic to tropic by my direction; the clouds, at my call, have poured their waters, and the Nile has overflowed at my command; I have restrained the rage of the Dog Star and mitigated the fervors of the Crab.[41] The winds alone, of all the elemental powers, have hitherto refused my authority, and multitudes have perished by equinoctial tempests which I found myself unable to prohibit or restrain. I have administered this great office with exact justice, and made to the different nations of the earth an impartial dividend of rain and sunshine. What must have been the misery of half the globe if I had limited the clouds to particular regions, or confined the sun to either side of the equator?'

XLII
The Opinion of the Astronomer
Is Explained and Justified

"I suppose he discovered in me, through the obscurity of the room, some tokens of amazement and doubt, for after a short pause he proceeded thus:

" 'Not to be easily credited will neither surprise nor offend me; for I am probably the first of human beings to whom this trust has been imparted. Nor do I know whether to deem this distinction a reward or punishment; since I have possessed it I have been far less happy than before, and nothing but the consciousness of good intention could have enabled me to support the weariness of unremitted vigilance.'

" 'How long sir,' said I, 'has this great office been in your hands?'

[1] The ascendance of the Dog Star (Sirius) in late summer and of the constellation Cancer (the Crab) in late June and July marked hot weather—very severe in Egypt.

" 'About ten years ago,' said he, 'my daily observations of the changes of the sky led me to consider whether, if I had the power of the seasons, I could confer greater plenty upon the inhabitants of the earth. This contemplation fastened on my mind, and I sat days and nights in imaginary dominion, pouring upon this country and that the showers of fertility, and seconding every fall of rain with a due proportion of sunshine. I had yet only the will to do good, and did not imagine that I should ever have the power.

" 'One day as I was looking on the fields withering with heat, I felt in my mind a sudden wish that I could send rain on the southern mountains and raise the Nile to an inundation. In the hurry of my imagination I commanded rain to fall, and, by comparing the time of my command, with that of the inundation, I found that the clouds had listened to my lips.'

" 'Might not some other cause,' said I, 'produce this concurrence? the Nile does not always rise on the same day.'

" 'Do not believe,' said he with impatience, 'that such objections could escape me: I reasoned long against my own conviction, and labored against truth with the utmost obstinacy. I sometimes suspected myself of madness, and should not have dared to impart this secret but to a man like you, capable of distinguishing the wonderful from the impossible, and the incredible from the false.'

" 'Why, sir,' said I, 'do you call that incredible, which you know or think you know, to be true?'

" 'Because,' said he, 'I cannot prove it by any external evidence; and I know too well the laws of demonstration to think that my conviction ought to influence another who cannot, like me, be conscious of my force. I, therefore, shall not attempt to gain credit by disputation. It is sufficient that I feel this power that I have long possessed, and every day exerted it. But the life of man is short, the infirmities of age increase upon me, and the time will soon come when the regulator of the year must mingle with the dust. The care of appointing a successor has long disturbed me; the night and the day have been spent in comparisons of all the characters which have come to my knowledge, and I have yet found none so worthy as thyself.

XLIII
The Astronomer Leaves Imlac His Directions

" 'Hear therefore what I shall impart with attention, such as the welfare of a world requires. If the task of a king be considered as difficult, who has the care only of a few millions to whom he cannot do much good or harm, what must be the anxiety of him, on whom depend the action of the elements, and the great gifts of light and heat!——Hear me therefore with attention.

" 'I have diligently considered the position of the earth and sun, and formed innumerable schemes in which I changed their situation. I have sometimes turned aside the axis of the earth, and sometimes varied the ecliptic of the sun: but I have found it impossible to make a disposition by which the world may be advantaged; what one region gains, another loses by any imaginable alteration, even without considering the distant parts of the solar system with which we are unacquainted. Do not, therefore, in thy administration of the year, indulge thy pride by innovation; do not please thyself with thinking that thou canst make thyself renowned to all future ages by disordering the seasons. The memory of mischief is no desirable fame. Much less will it become thee to let kindness or interest[42] prevail. Never rob other countries of rain to pour it on thine own. For us the Nile is sufficient.'

"I promised that when I possessed the power, I would use it with inflexible integrity, and he dismissed me, pressing my hand. 'My heart,' said he, 'will be now at rest, and my benevolence will no more destroy my quiet: I have found a man of wisdom and virtue to whom I can cheerfully bequeath the inheritance of the sun.' "

The prince heard this narration with very serious regard, but the princess smiled, and Pekuah convulsed herself with laughter. "Ladies," said Imlac, "to mock the heaviest of human afflictions is neither charitable nor wise. Few can attain this man's knowledge and few practice his virtues; but all may suffer his calamity. Of the uncertainties of our present state the most dreadful and alarming is the uncertain continuance of reason."

[42] *interest:* self-interest.

The princess was recollected, and the favorite was abashed. Rasselas, more deeply affected, inquired of Imlac, whether he thought such maladies of the mind frequent, and how they were contracted.

XLIV
The Dangerous Prevalence of Imagination

"Disorders of intellect," answered Imlac, "happen much more often than superficial observers will easily believe. Perhaps, if we speak with rigorous exactness, no human mind is in its right state. There is no man whose imagination does not sometimes predominate over his reason, who can regulate his attention wholly by his will, and whose ideas will come and go at his command. No man will be found in whose mind airy notions do not sometimes tyrannize, and force him to hope or fear beyond the limits of sober probability. All power of fancy over reason is a degree of insanity; but while this power is such as we can control and repress, it is not visible to others nor considered as any depravation of the mental faculties; it is not pronounced madness but when it comes ungovernable, and apparently[43] influences speech or action.

"To indulge the power of fiction, and send imagination out upon the wing, is often the sport of those who delight too much in silent speculation. When we are alone we are not always busy; the labor of excogitation is too violent to last long; the ardor of inquiry will sometimes give way to idleness or satiety. He who has nothing external that can divert him must find pleasure in his own thoughts, and must conceive himself what he is not; for who is pleased with what he is? He then expatiates in boundless futurity, and culls from all imaginable conditions that which for the present moment he should most desire, amuses his desires with impossible enjoyments, and confers upon his pride unattainable dominion. The mind dances from scene to scene, unites all pleasures in all combinations, and riots in delights which nature and fortune, with all their bounty, cannot bestow.

"In time some particular train of ideas fixes the attention,

---

[43] *apparently*: visibly.

all other intellectual gratifications are rejected, the mind, in weariness or leisure, recurs constantly to the favorite conception, and feasts on the luscious falsehood whenever she is offended with the bitterness of truth. By degrees the reign of fancy is confirmed; she grows first imperious and in time despotic. Then fictions begin to operate as realities, false opinions fasten upon the mind, and life passes in dreams of rapture or of anguish.

"This, sir, is one of the dangers of solitude, which the hermit has confessed not always to promote goodness, and the astronomer's misery has proved to be not always propitious to wisdom."

"I will no more," said the favorite, "imagine myself the queen of Abyssinia. I have often spent the hours which the princess gave to my own disposal in adjusting ceremonies and regulating the court; I have repressed the pride of the powerful and granted the petitions of the poor; I have built new palaces in more happy situations, planted groves upon the tops of mountains, and have exulted in the beneficence of royalty, till, when the princess entered, I had almost forgotten to bow down before her."

"And I," said the princess, "will not allow myself any more to play the shepherdess in my waking dreams. I have often soothed my thoughts with the quiet and innocence of pastoral employments, till I have in my chamber heard the winds whistle and the sheep bleat; sometimes freed the lamb entangled in the thicket, and sometimes with my crook encountered the wolf. I have a dress like that of the village maids which I put on to help my imagination, and a pipe on which I play softly, and suppose myself followed by my flocks."

"I will confess," said the prince, "an indulgence of fantastic delight more dangerous than yours. I have frequently endeavored to image the possibility of a perfect government by which all wrong should be restrained, all vice reformed, and all the subjects preserved in tranquillity and innocence. This thought produced innumerable schemes of reformation, and dictated many useful regulations and salutary edicts. This has been the sport and sometimes the labor of my solitude; and I start when I think with how little anguish I once supposed the death of my father and my brothers."

"Such," says Imlac, "are the effects of visionary schemes:

when we first form them we know them to be absurd, but familiarize them by degrees, and in time lose sight of their folly."

XLV
They Discourse with an Old Man

The evening was now far past, and they rose to return home. As they walked along the bank of the Nile, delighted with the beams of the moon quivering on the water, they saw at a small distance an old man whom the prince had often heard in the assembly of the sages. "Yonder," said he, "is one whose years have calmed his passions, but not clouded his reason: let us close the disquisitions of the night, by inquiring what are his sentiments of his own state, that we may know whether youth alone is to struggle with vexation, and whether any better hope remains for the latter part of life."

Here the sage approached and saluted them. They invited him to join their walk, and prattled awhile as acquaintance that had unexpectedly met one another. The old man was cheerful and talkative, and the way seemed short in his company. He was pleased to find himself not disregarded, accompanied them to their house and, at the prince's request, entered with them. They placed him in the seat of honor, and set wine and conserves before him.

"Sir," said the princess, "an evening walk must give to a man of learning, like you, pleasures which ignorance and youth can hardly conceive. You know the qualities and the causes of all that you behold, the laws by which the river flows, the periods in which the planets perform their revolutions. Every thing must supply you with contemplation, and renew the consciousness of your own dignity."

"Lady," answered he, "let the gay and the vigorous expect pleasure in their excursions, it is enough that age can obtain ease. To me the world has lost its novelty: I look round, and see what I remember to have seen in happier days. I rest against a tree, and consider that in the same shade I once disputed upon the annual overflow of the Nile with a friend who is now silent in the grave. I cast my eyes upwards, fix them on the changing moon, and think with pain on the vicissitudes of life. I have ceased to take much delight in physical truth;[44] for what have I to do with those things which I am soon to leave?"

"You may at least recreate yourself," said Imlac, "with the recollection of an honorable and useful life, and enjoy the praise which all agree to give you."

"Praise," said the sage with a sigh, "is to an old man an empty sound. I have neither mother to be delighted with the reputation of her son, nor wife to partake the honors of her husband. I have outlived my friends and my rivals. Nothing is now of much importance; for I cannot extend my interest beyond myself. Youth is delighted with applause, because it is considered as the earnest of some future good, and because the prospect of life is far extended: but to me, who am now declining to decrepitude, there is little to be feared from the malevolence of men, and yet less to be hoped from their affection or esteem. Something they may yet take away, but they can give me nothing. Riches would now be useless, and high employment would be pain. My retrospect of life recalls to my view many opportunities of good neglected, much time squandered upon trifles, and more lost in idleness and vacancy. I leave many great designs unattempted, and many great attempts unfinished. My mind is burthened with no heavy crime, and therefore I compose myself to tranquillity; endeavor to abstract my thoughts from hopes and cares which, though reason knows them to be vain, still try to keep their old possession of the heart; expect with serene humility that hour which nature cannot long delay; and hope to possess in a better state that happiness which here I could not find, and that virtue which here I have not attained."

He rose and went away, leaving his audience not much elated with the hope of long life. The prince consoled himself with remarking that it was not reasonable to be disappointed by this account; for age had never been considered as the season of felicity, and if it was possible to be easy in decline and weakness, it was likely that the days of vigor and alacrity might be happy: that the noon of life might be bright, if the evening could be calm.

The princess suspected that age was querulous and malignant, and delighted to repress the expectations of those who

[44] *physical truth:* scientific knowledge.

had newly entered the world. She had seen the possessors of estates look with envy on their heirs, and known many who enjoy pleasure no longer than they can confine it to themselves.

Pekuah conjectured that the man was older than he appeared, and was willing to impute his complaints to delirious[45] dejection; or else supposed that he had been unfortunate, and was therefore discontented: "For nothing," said she, "is more common than to call our own condition, the condition of life."

Imlac, who had no desire to see them depressed, smiled at the comforts which they could so readily procure to themselves, and remembered, that at the same age, he was equally confident of unmingled prosperity, and equally fertile of consolatory expedients. He forbore to force upon them unwelcome knowledge, which time itself would too soon impress. The princess and her lady retired; the madness of the astronomer hung upon their minds, and they desired Imlac to enter upon his office,[46] and delay next morning the rising of the sun.

XLVI
The Princess and Pekuah Visit the Astronomer

The princess and Pekuah, having talked in private of Imlac's astronomer, thought his character at once so amiable and so strange that they could not be satisfied without a nearer knowledge, and Imlac was requested to find the means of bringing them together.

This was somewhat difficult; the philosopher had never received any visits from women, though he lived in a city that had in it many Europeans who followed the manners of their own countries, and many from other parts of the world that lived there with European liberty. The ladies would not be refused, and several schemes were proposed for the accomplishment of their design. It was proposed to introduce them as strangers in distress, to whom the sage was always accessible; but, after some deliberation, it appeared, that by

[45] *delirious:* crazy.
[46] I.e., take up his duties.

this artifice no acquaintance could be formed, for their conversation would be short, and they could not decently importune him often. "This," said Rasselas, "is true; but I have
yet a stronger objection against the misrepresentation of your
state. I have always considered it as treason against the great
republic of human nature to make any man's virtues the
means of deceiving him, whether on great or little occasions.
All imposture weakens confidence and chills benevolence.
When the sage finds that you are not what you seemed, he
will feel the resentment natural to a man who, conscious of
great abilities, discovers that he has been tricked by understandings meaner than his own, and perhaps the distrust,
which he can never afterwards wholly lay aside, may stop
the voice of counsel and close the hand of charity; and where
will you find the power of restoring his benefactions to mankind or his peace to himself?"

To this no reply was attempted, and Imlac began to hope
that their curiosity would subside; but, next day, Pekuah told
him she had now found an honest pretense for a visit to the
astronomer, for she would solicit permission to continue
under him the studies in which she had been initiated by the
Arab, and the princess might go with her either as a fellow-
student, or because a woman could not decently come alone.
"I am afraid," said Imlac, "that he will be soon weary of your
company: men advanced far in knowledge do not love to
repeat the elements of their art, and I am not certain that
even of the elements, as he will deliver them connected with
inferences and mingled with reflections, you are a very
capable auditress." "That," said Pekuah, "must be my care:
I ask of you only to take me thither. My knowledge is perhaps more than you imagine it, and by concurring always
with his opinions I shall make him think it greater than it is."

The astronomer, in pursuance of this resolution, was told
that a foreign lady, traveling in search of knowledge, had
heard of his reputation and was desirous to become his
scholar. The uncommonness of the proposal raised at once
his surprise and curiosity and when, after a short deliberation, he consented to admit her, he could not stay without
impatience till the next day.

The ladies dressed themselves magnificently, and were
attended by Imlac to the astronomer, who was pleased to
see himself approached with respect by persons of so splendid

an appearance. In the exchange of the first civilities he was timorous and bashful; but when the talk became regular, he recollected his powers, and justified the character which Imlac had given. Inquiring of Pekuah what could have turned her inclination towards astronomy, he received from her a history of her adventure at the pyramid, and of the time passed in the Arab's island. She told her tale with ease and elegance, and her conversation took possession of his heart. The discourse was then turned to astronomy: Pekuah displayed what she knew; he looked upon her as a prodigy of genius, and entreated her not to desist from a study which she had so happily begun.

They came again and again, and were every time more welcome than before. The sage endeavored to amuse them that they might prolong their visits, for he found his thoughts grow brighter in their company; the clouds of solicitude vanished by degrees as he forced himself to entertain them, and he grieved when he was left at their departure to his old employment of regulating the seasons.

The princess and her favorite had now watched his lips for several months, and could not catch a single word from which they could judge whether he continued or not in the opinion of his preternatural commission. They often contrived to bring him to an open declaration, but he easily eluded all their attacks, and on which side soever they pressed him escaped from them to some other topic.

As their familiarity increased they invited him often to the house of Imlac, where they distinguished him by extraordinary respect. He began gradually to delight in sublunary pleasures. He came early and departed late; labored to recommend himself by assiduity and compliance; excited their curiosity after new arts that they might still want his assistance; and when they made any excursion of pleasure or inquiry entreated to attend them.

By long experience of his integrity and wisdom, the prince and his sister were convinced that he might be trusted without danger; and lest he should draw any false hopes from the civilities which he received, discovered to him their condition, with the motives of their journey, and required his opinion on the choice of life.

"Of the various conditions which the world spreads before you, which you shall prefer," said the sage, "I am not able to instruct you. I can only tell that I have chosen wrong. I have passed my time in study without experience; in the attainment of sciences which can, for the most part, be but remotely useful to mankind. I have purchased knowledge at the expense of all the common comforts of life: I have missed the endearing elegance of female friendship, and the happy commerce[47] of domestic tenderness. If I have obtained any prerogatives above other students, they have been accompanied with fear, disquiet, and scrupulosity; but even of these prerogatives, whatever they were, I have, since my thoughts have been diversified by more intercourse with the world, begun to question the reality. When I have been for a few days lost in pleasing dissipation, I am always tempted to think that my inquiries have ended in error, and that I have suffered much, and suffered it in vain."

Imlac was delighted to find that the sage's understanding was breaking through its mists, and resolved to detain him from the planets till he should forget his task of ruling them, and reason should recover its original influence.

From this time the astronomer was received into familiar friendship, and partook of all their projects and pleasures: his respect kept him attentive, and the activity of Rasselas did not leave much time unengaged. Something was always to be done; the day was spent in making observations which furnished talk for the evening, and the evening was closed with a scheme for the morrow.

The sage confessed to Imlac that since he had mingled in the gay tumults of life, and divided his hours by a succession of amusements, he found the conviction of his authority over the skies fade gradually from his mind, and began to trust less to an opinion which he never could prove to others, and which he now found subject to variation from causes in which reason had no part. "If I am accidentally left alone for a few hours," said he, "my inveterate persuasion rushes upon my soul, and my thoughts are chained down by some irresistible violence, but they are soon disentangled by the prince's conversation, and instantaneously released at the entrance of Pekuah. I am like a man habitually afraid of specters, who is set at ease by a lamp, and wonders at the dread which harassed him in the dark, yet, if his lamp be

---

[47] *commerce:* social relationships.

extinguished, feels again the terrors which he knows that when it is light he shall feel no more. But I am sometimes afraid lest I indulge my quiet by criminal negligence, and voluntarily forget the great charge with which I am entrusted. If I favor myself in a known error, or am determined by my own ease in a doubtful question of this importance, how dreadful is my crime!"

"No disease of the imagination," answered Imlac, "is so difficult of cure as that which is complicated with the dread of guilt: fancy and conscience then act interchangeably upon us, and so often shift their places that the illusions of one are not distinguished from the dictates of the other. If fancy presents images not moral or religious, the mind drives them away when they give it pain, but when melancholic notions take the form of duty, they lay hold on the faculties without opposition, because we are afraid to exclude or banish them. For this reason the superstitious are often melancholy, and the melancholy almost always superstitious.

"But do not let the suggestions of timidity overpower your better reason: the danger of neglect can be but as the probability of the obligation, which when you consider it with freedom, you find very little, and that little growing every day less. Open your heart to the influence of the light, which, from time to time, breaks in upon you: when scruples importune you which you in your lucid moments know to be vain, do not stand to parley, but fly to business or to Pekuah, and keep this thought always prevalent, that you are only one atom of the mass of humanity, and have neither such virtue nor vice as that you should be singled out for supernatural favors or afflictions."

XLVII
The Prince Enters and Brings a New Topic

"All this," said the astronomer, "I have often thought, but my reason has been so long subjugated by an uncontrollable and overwhelming idea that it durst not confide in its own decisions. I now see how fatally I betrayed my quiet, by suffering chimeras to prey upon me in secret; but melancholy shrinks from communication, and I never found a man before, to whom I could impart my troubles, though I had been certain of relief. I rejoice to find my own sentiments confirmed by yours, who are not easily deceived and can have no motive or purpose to deceive. I hope that time and variety will dissipate the gloom that has so long surrounded me, and the latter part of my days will be spent in peace."

"Your learning and virtue," said Imlac, "may justly give you hopes."

Rasselas then entered with the princess and Pekuah, and inquired whether they had contrived any new diversion for the next day. "Such," said Nekayah, "is the state of life that none are happy but by the anticipation of change: the change itself is nothing; when we have made it, the next wish is to change again. The world is not yet exhausted; let me see something tomorrow which I never saw before."

"Variety," said Rasselas, "is so necessary to content that even the happy valley disgusted me by the recurrence of its luxuries; yet I could not forbear to reproach myself with impatience when I saw the monks of St. Anthony support without complaint a life, not of uniform delight, but uniform hardship."

"Those men," answered Imlac, "are less wretched in their silent convent than the Abyssinian princes in their prison of pleasure. Whatever is done by the monks is incited by an adequate and reasonable motive. Their labor supplies them with necessaries; it therefore cannot be omitted, and is certainly rewarded. Their devotion prepares them for another state, and reminds them of its approach while it fits them for it. Their time is regularly distributed; one duty succeeds another, so that they are not left open to the distraction of unguided choice nor lost in the shades of listless inactivity. There is a certain task to be performed at an appropriated hour; and their toils are cheerful, because they consider them as acts of piety by which they are always advancing towards endless felicity."

"Do you think," said Nekayah, "that the monastic rule is a more holy and less imperfect state than any other? May not he equally hope for future happiness who converses openly with mankind, who succors the distressed by his charity, instructs the ignorant by his learning, and contributes by his industry to the general system of life; even though he should omit some of the mortifications which are practiced in the cloister, and allow himself such harmless delights as his condition may place within his reach?"

"This," said Imlac, "is a question which has long divided

the wise and perplexed the good. I am afraid to decide on either part. He that lives well in the world is better than he that lives well in a monastery. But perhaps everyone is not able to stem the temptations of public life; and, if he cannot conquer, he may properly retreat. Some have little power to do good and have likewise little strength to resist evil. Many are weary of their conflicts with adversity, and are willing to eject those passions which have long busied them in vain. And many are dismissed by age and diseases from the more laborious duties of society. In monasteries the weak and timorous may be happily sheltered, the weary may repose, and the penitent may meditate. Those retreats of prayer and contemplation have something so congenial to the mind of man that perhaps there is scarcely one that does not purpose to close his life in pious abstraction[48] with a few associates serious as himself."

"Such," said Pekuah, "has often been my wish, and I have heard the princess declare that she should not willingly die in a crowd."

"The liberty of using harmless pleasures," proceeded Imlac, "will not be disputed; but it is still to be examined what pleasures are harmless. The evil of any pleasure that Nekayah can image is not in the act itself but in its consequences. Pleasure, in itself harmless, may become mischievous by endearing to us a state which we know to be transient and probatory, and withdrawing our thoughts from that, of which every hour brings us nearer to the beginning, and of which no length of time will bring us to the end. Mortification is not virtuous in itself, nor has any other use but that it disengages us from the allurements of sense. In the state of future perfection to which we all aspire, there will be pleasure without danger and security without restraint."

The princess was silent and Rasselas, turning to the astronomer, asked him whether he could not delay her retreat by showing her something which she had not seen before.

"Your curiosity," said the sage, "has been so general, and your pursuit of knowledge so vigorous, that novelties are not now very easily to be found: but what you can no longer procure from the living may be given by the dead. Among the wonders of this country are the catacombs, or the ancient

---

[48] *abstraction:* seclusion.

repositories in which the bodies of the earliest generations were lodged, and where, by the virtue of the gums which embalmed them, they yet remain without corruption."

"I know not," said Rasselas, "what pleasure the sight of the catacombs can afford; but, since nothing else is offered, I am resolved to view them, and shall place this with many other things which I have done because I would do something."

They hired a guard of horsemen, and the next day visited the catacombs. When they were about to descend into the sepulchral caves, "Pekuah," said the princess, "we are now again invading the habitations of the dead; I know that you will stay behind; let me find you safe when I return." "No, I will not be left," answered Pekuah, "I will go down between you and the prince."

They then all descended, and roved with wonder through the labyrinth of subterraneous passages where the bodies were laid in rows on either side.

XLVIII
Imlac Discourses on the Nature of the Soul

"What reason," said the prince, "can be given why the Egyptians should thus expensively preserve those carcasses which some nations consume with fire, others lay to mingle with the earth, and all agree to remove from their sight as soon as decent rites can be performed?"

"The original of ancient customs," said Imlac, "is commonly unknown; for the practice often continues when the cause has ceased; and concerning superstitious ceremonies it is vain to conjecture; for what reason did not dictate reason cannot explain. I have long believed that the practice of embalming arose only from tenderness to the remains of relations or friends, and to this opinion I am more inclined because it seems impossible that this care should have been general: had all the dead been embalmed, their repositories must in time have been more spacious than the dwellings of the living. I suppose only the rich or honorable were secured from corruption, and the rest left to the course of nature.

"But it is commonly supposed that the Egyptians believed the soul to live as long as the body continued undissolved, and therefore tried this method of eluding death."

"Could the wise Egyptians," said Nekayah, "think so grossly of the soul? If the soul could once survive its separation, what could it afterwards receive or suffer from the body?"

"The Egyptians would doubtless think erroneously," said the astronomer, "in the darkness of heathenism, and the first dawn of philosophy. The nature of the soul is still disputed amidst all our opportunities of clearer knowledge: some yet say that it may be material, who nevertheless believe it to be immortal."

"Some," answered Imlac, "have indeed said that the soul is material, but I can scarcely believe that any man has thought it who knew how to think; for all the conclusions of reason enforce the immateriality of mind, and all the notices of sense and investigations of science concur to prove the unconsciousness of matter.

"It was never supposed that cogitation is inherent in matter, or that every particle is a thinking being. Yet, if any part of matter be devoid of thought, what part can we suppose to think? Matter can differ from matter only in form, density, bulk, motion, and direction of motion: to which of these, however varied or combined, can consciousness be annexed? To be round or square, to be solid or fluid, to be great or little, to be moved slowly or swiftly one way or another, are modes of material existence, all equally alien from the nature of cogitation. If matter be once without thought, it can only be made to think by some new modification, but all the modifications which it can admit are equally unconnected with cogitative powers."

"But the materialists," said the astronomer, "urge that matter may have qualities with which we are unacquainted."

"He who will determine," returned Imlac, "against that which he knows, because there may be something which he knows not; he that can set hypothetical possibility against acknowledged certainty, is not to be admitted among reasonable beings. All that we know of matter is that matter is inert, senseless, and lifeless; and if this conviction cannot be opposed but by referring us to something that we know not, we have all the evidence that human intellect can admit. If that which is known may be overruled by that which is unknown, no being, not omniscient, can arrive at certainty."

"Yet let us not," said the astronomer, "too arrogantly limit the Creator's power."

"It is no limitation of omnipotence," replied the poet, "to suppose that one thing is not consistent with another, that the same proposition cannot be at once true and false, that the same number cannot be even and odd, that cogitation cannot be conferred on that which is created incapable of cogitation."

"I know not," said Nekayah, "any great use of this question. Does that immateriality which, in my opinion, you have sufficiently proved, necessarily include eternal duration?"

"Of immateriality," said Imlac, "our ideas are negative and therefore obscure. Immateriality seems to imply a natural power of perpetual duration as a consequence of exemption from all causes of decay: whatever perishes is destroyed by the solution of its contexture, and separation of its parts; nor can we conceive how that which has no parts, and therefore admits no solution, can be naturally corrupted or impaired."

"I know not," said Rasselas, "how to conceive any thing without extension: what is extended must have parts, and you allow that whatever has parts may be destroyed."

"Consider your own conceptions," replied Imlac, "and the difficulty will be less. You will find substance without extension. An ideal form is no less real than material bulk: yet an ideal form has no extension. It is no less certain, when you think on a pyramid, that your mind possesses the idea of a pyramid, than that the pyramid itself is standing. What space does the idea of a pyramid occupy more than the idea of a grain of corn? or how can either idea suffer laceration? As is the effect such is the cause; as thought is, such is the power that thinks; a power impassive and indiscerptible."[49]

"But the Being," said Nekayah, "whom I fear to name, the Being which made the soul can destroy it."

"He, surely, can destroy it," answered Imlac, "since, however unperishable, it receives from a superior nature its power of duration. That it will not perish by any inherent cause of decay, or principle of corruption, may be shown by philosophy; but philosophy can tell no more. That it will not be annihilated by Him that made it, we must humbly learn from higher authority."

The whole assembly stood awhile silent and collected. "Let us return," said Rasselas, "from this scene of mortality. How gloomy would be these mansions of the dead to him who did

---

[49] *impassive and indiscerptible:* invulnerable and indivisible.

not know that he shall never die; that what now acts shall continue its agency, and what now thinks shall think on for ever. Those that lie here stretched before us, the wise and the powerful of ancient times, warn us to remember the shortness of our present state: they were perhaps snatched away while they were busy, like us, in the choice of life."

"To me," said the princess, "the choice of life is become less important: I hope hereafter to think only on the choice of eternity."

They then hastened out of the caverns and, under the protection of their guard, returned to Cairo.

XLIX
The Conclusion, in Which Nothing Is Concluded

It was now the time of the inundation of the Nile: a few days after their visit to the catacombs, the river began to rise.

They were confined to their house. The whole region being under water gave them no invitation to any excursions and, being well supplied with materials for talk, they diverted themselves with comparisons of the different forms of life which they had observed, and with various schemes of happiness which each of them had formed.

Pekuah was never so much charmed with any place as the convent of St. Anthony, where the Arab restored her to the princess, and wished only to fill it with pious maidens, and to be made prioress of the order: she was weary of expectation and disgust, and would gladly be fixed in some unvariable state.

The princess thought that of all sublunary things knowledge was the best: she desired first to learn all sciences, and then purposed to found a college of learned women in which she would preside, that, by conversing with the old and educating the young, she might divide her time between the acquisition and communication of wisdom, and raise up for the next age models of prudence and patterns of piety.

The prince desired a little kingdom in which he might administer justice in his own person, and see all the parts of government with his own eyes; but he could never fix the limits of his dominion, and was always adding to the number of his subjects.

Imlac and the astronomer were contented to be driven

along the stream of life without directing their course to any particular port.

Of these wishes that they had formed they well knew that none could be obtained. They deliberated awhile what was to be done and resolved, when the inundation should cease, to return to Abyssinia.

From the Edition of Shakespeare

[Early in the eighteenth century, it was recognized that Shakespeare's plays required editing. Since Shakespeare did not publish them himself, there was no authoritative text—only some pirated quartos of individual plays and a handsome but inaccurate folio collected edition, published by two friends in his acting company seven years after his death (1623). The folio was reissued in three increasingly inaccurate editions during the seventeenth century. To get back to what Shakespeare wrote, it was necessary to collate the text of the First Folio with those of the better quartos and sometimes, when no surviving text made sense, to try to guess what Shakespeare had written. For example, the existing text of *Henry V* included the nonsensical phrase "a table of green fields" in the Hostess's description of Falstaff's death (II, iii, 17). Lewis Theobald, the third eighteenth-century editor, conjectured that Shakespeare must have written " 'a [an Elizabethan colloquialism for *he*] babled [babbled] of green fields" —the reading universally accepted today. Other conjectures were not so happy, however, as eighteenth-century editors before Johnson, ignorant of Elizabethan English or impatient with Shakespeare's obscurities, freely "restored" lines that did not suit their taste. Johnson, the sixth eighteenth-century editor of Shakespeare, produced a far better text than his predecessors. Although not a textual scholar, he had learned much about Elizabethan English through his work on the *Dictionary*. But it is his Preface and critical Notes that remain significant today.

In his Preface, Johnson definitively disposed of the arguments of neoclassical critics who condemned Shakespeare's negligence of the traditional rules for dramatic composition. The first rule Johnson challenges is that dramatic characters must conform to some *a priori* idea of what is typical for their group. John Dennis, for example, condemned Shakespeare's characterization of Menenius in *Coriolanus* because it was beneath the dignity of a Roman senator to indulge in buffoonery (*An Essay on the Genius and Writings of Shakespeare*, 1712). All the neoclassical critics agreed that comic and tragic elements must not be mixed in a play, as they cancel each other out. They also insisted that plays must be unified not only in action (plot), but in time and place: the action could cover no more than twenty-four hours, and must be limited at least to the same city. Thomas Rymer derided Shakespeare's violation of unity of place in *Othello*, as well as his violation of tragic decorum in making Iago shout coarsely to Brabantio and letting Brutus and Cassius quarrel realistically in *Julius Caesar*, IV, iii (*A Short View of Tragedy*, 1693). Voltaire found the jokes of the gravediggers offensively out of place in *Hamlet*, as were those of the plebeians in *Julius Caesar*, and could not understand how the English could admire Shakespeare when they had Addison's frigid but correct tragedy *Cato* before their eyes (*Letters Concerning the English Nation*, 1734).]

From the Preface

That praises are without reason lavished on the dead, and that the honors due only to excellence are paid to antiquity, is a complaint likely to be always continued by those who, being able to add nothing to truth, hope for eminence from the heresies of paradox; or those who, being forced by disappointment upon consolatory expedients, are willing to hope from posterity what the present age refuses and flatter themselves that the regard which is yet denied by envy will be at last bestowed by time.

Antiquity, like every other quality that attracts the notice of mankind, has undoubtedly votaries that reverence it not from reason, but from prejudice. Some seem to admire indiscriminately whatever has been long preserved, without considering that time has sometimes cooperated with chance; all perhaps are more willing to honor past than present excellence; and the mind contemplates genius through the shades of age, as the eye surveys the sun through artificial opacity. The great contention of criticism is to find the faults of the moderns and the beauties of the ancients. While an author is yet living, we estimate his powers by his worst performance; and when he is dead, we rate them by his best.

To works, however, of which the excellence is not absolute and definite, but gradual and comparative; to works not raised upon principles demonstrative and scientific but appealing wholly to observation and experience, no other test can be applied than length of duration and continuance of esteem. What mankind have long possessed they have often examined and compared; and if they persist to value the possession, it is because frequent comparisons have confirmed opinion in its favor. As among the works of nature no man can properly call a river deep or a mountain high, without the knowledge of many mountains and many rivers; so, in the productions of genius, nothing can be styled excellent till it has been compared with other works of the same kind. Demonstration immediately displays its power and has nothing to hope or fear from the flux of years; but works tentative and experimental must be estimated by their proportion to the general and collective ability of man, as it is discovered in a long succession of endeavors. Of the first building that was raised, it might be with certainty determined that it was round or square, but whether it was spacious or lofty must have been referred to time. The Pythagorean scale of numbers[1] was at once discovered to be perfect; but the poems of Homer we yet know not to transcend the common limits of human intelligence but by remarking that nation after nation, and century after century, has been able to do little more than transpose his incidents, new-name his characters, and paraphrase his sentiments.

The reverence due to writings that have long subsisted arises, therefore, not from any credulous confidence in the superior wisdom of past ages or gloomy persuasion of the degeneracy of mankind, but is the consequence of acknowledged and indubitable positions that what has been longest known has been most considered, and what is most considered is best understood.

The poet of whose works I have undertaken the revision[2] may now begin to assume the dignity of an ancient and claim the privilege of established fame and prescriptive veneration. He has long outlived his century, the term commonly fixed as the test of literary merit. Whatever advantages he might once derive from personal allusions, local customs, or temporary opinions have for many years been lost; and every topic of merriment or motive of sorrow which the modes of artificial[3] life afforded him now only obscure the scenes which they once illuminated. The effects of favor and competition are at an end; the tradition of his friendships and his enmities have perished; his works support no opinion with arguments nor supply any faction with invectives; they can neither indulge vanity nor gratify malignity, but are read without any other reason than the desire of pleasure and are therefore praised only as pleasure is obtained; yet, thus unassisted by

[1] The Greek philosopher Pythagoras discovered the absolute relationship between numbers and the intervals of the musical scale.
[2] *revision:* editing.
[3] *artificial:* created by people (of a particular time), as opposed to natural (inherent and unchanging).

interest[4] or passion, they have passed through variations of taste and changes of manners, and, as they devolved from one generation to another, have received new honors at every transmission.

But because human judgment, though it be gradually gaining upon certainty, never becomes infallible; and approbation, though long continued, may yet be only the approbation of prejudice or fashion; it is proper to inquire by what peculiarities of excellence Shakespeare has gained and kept the favor of his countrymen.

Nothing can please many, and please long, but just representations of general nature. Particular manners can be known to few, and therefore few only can judge how nearly they are copied. The irregular combinations of fanciful invention may delight awhile by that novelty of which the common satiety of life sends us all in quest; but the pleasures of sudden wonder are soon exhausted, and the mind can only repose on the stability of truth.

Shakespeare is, above all writers, at least above all modern writers, the poet of nature, the poet that holds up to his readers a faithful mirror of manners and of life. His characters are not modified by the customs of particular places, unpracticed by the rest of the world; by the peculiarities of studies or professions which can operate but upon small numbers: they are the genuine progeny of common humanity, such as the world will always supply, and observation will always find. His persons act and speak by the influence of those general passions and principles by which all minds are agitated and the whole system of life is continued in motion. In the writings of other poets a character is too often an individual; in those of Shakespeare it is commonly a species.

It is from this wide extension of design that so much instruction is derived. It is this which fills the plays of Shakespeare with practical axioms and domestic wisdom. It was said of Euripides that every verse was a precept; and it may be said of Shakespeare that from his works may be collected a system of civil and economical prudence.[5] Yet his real power is not shown in the splendor of particular passages, but by the progress of his fable[6] and the tenor of his dialogue;

---

[4] *interest:* self-interest.

[5] *civil and economical prudence:* practical wisdom in public and private life.

[6] *fable:* plot.

and he that tries to recommend him by select quotations will succeed like the pedant in Hierocles, who, when he offered his house for sale, carried a brick in his pocket as a specimen.

It will not easily be imagined how much Shakespeare excels in accommodating his sentiments to real life but by comparing him with other authors. It was observed of the ancient schools of declamation that the more diligently they were frequented, the more was the student disqualified for the world, because he found nothing there which he should ever meet in any other place.[7] The same remark may be applied to every stage but that of Shakespeare. The theater, when it is under any other direction, is peopled by such characters as were never seen, conversing in a language which was never heard, upon topics which will never arise in the commerce of mankind. But the dialogue of this author is often so evidently determined by the incident which produces it, and is pursued with so much ease and simplicity, that it seems scarcely to claim the merit of fiction, but to have been gleaned by diligent selection out of common conversation and common occurrences.

Upon every other stage the universal agent is love, by whose power all good and evil is distributed and every action quickened or retarded. To bring a lover, a lady, and a rival into the fable; to entangle them in contradictory obligations, perplex them with oppositions of interest, and harass them with violence of desires inconsistent with each other; to make them meet in rapture and part in agony, to fill their mouths with hyperbolical joy and outrageous sorrow, to distress them as nothing human ever was distressed, to deliver them as nothing human ever was delivered, is the business of a modern dramatist.[8] For this, probability is violated, life is misrepresented, and language is depraved. But love is only one of many passions; and as it has no great influence upon the sum of life, it has little operation in the dramas of a poet who caught his ideas from the living world and exhibited only what he saw before him. He knew that any other passion, as it was regular or exorbitant, was a cause of happiness or calamity.

Characters thus ample and general were not easily discriminated and preserved, yet perhaps no poet ever kept his personages more distinct from each other. I will not say with

[7] Petronius, *Satyricon* (first century A. D.), I, i.
[8] Johnson's criticism applies equally to the heroic tragedy of the Restoration and the sentimental comedy of his own time.

Pope that every speech may be assigned to the proper speaker,[9] because many speeches there are which have nothing characteristical; but, perhaps, though some may be equally adapted to every person, it will be difficult to find any that can be properly transferred from the present possessor to another claimant. The choice is right, when there is reason for choice.

Other dramatists can only gain attention by hyperbolical or aggravated characters, by fabulous and unexampled excellence or depravity, as the writers of barbarous romances invigorated the reader by a giant and a dwarf; and he that should form his expectations of human affairs from the play, or from the tale, would be equally deceived. Shakespeare has no heroes; his scenes are occupied only by men, who act and speak as the reader thinks that he should himself have spoken or acted on the same occasion. Even where the agency is supernatural, the dialogue is level with life. Other writers disguise the most natural passions and most frequent incidents, so that he who contemplates them in the book will not know them in the world. Shakespeare approximates the remote and familiarizes the wonderful; the event which he represents will not happen but, if it were possible, its effects would probably be such as he has assigned; and it may be said that he has not only shown human nature as it acts in real exigences, but as it would be found in trials to which it cannot be exposed.

This, therefore, is the praise of Shakespeare, that his drama is the mirror of life; that he who has mazed his imagination in following the phantoms which other writers raise up before him may here be cured of his delirious ecstasies by reading human sentiments in human language, by scenes from which a hermit may estimate the transactions of the world and a confessor predict the progress of the passions.

His adherence to general nature has exposed him to the censure of critics who form their judgments upon narrower principles. Dennis and Rymer think his Romans not sufficiently Roman and Voltaire censures his kings as not completely royal. Dennis is offended that Menenius, a senator of Rome, should play the buffoon; and Voltaire perhaps thinks

---

[9] Pope wrote in the Preface to his edition: ". . . had all the speeches been printed without the very names of the persons, I believe one might have applied them with a certainty to every speaker."

decency violated when the Danish usurper is represented as a drunkard.[10] But Shakespeare always makes nature predominate over accident; and, if he preserves the essential character, is not very careful of distinctions superinduced and adventitious. His story requires Romans or kings, but he thinks only on men. He knew that Rome, like every other city, had men of all dispositions; and wanting a buffoon, he went into the senate house for that which the senate house would certainly have afforded him. He was inclined to show an usurper and a murderer not only odious, but despicable; he therefore added drunkenness to his other qualities, knowing that kings love wine like other men, and that wine exerts its natural power upon kings. These are the petty cavils of petty minds; a poet overlooks the casual distinction of country and condition, as a painter, satisfied with the figure, neglects the drapery.

The censure which he has incurred by mixing comic and tragic scenes, as it extends to all his works, deserves more consideration. Let the fact be first stated and then examined.

Shakespeare's plays are not in the rigorous and critical sense either tragedies or comedies, but compositions of a distinct kind; exhibiting the real state of sublunary nature, which partakes of good and evil, joy and sorrow, mingled with endless variety of proportion and innumerable modes of combination; and expressing the course of the world, in which the loss of one is the gain of another; in which, at the same time, the reveler is hasting to his wine, and the mourner burying his friend; in which the malignity of one is sometimes defeated by the frolic of another; and many mischiefs and many benefits are done and hindered without design.

Out of this chaos of mingled purposes and casualties[11] the ancient poets, according to the laws which custom had prescribed, selected some the crimes of men and some their absurdities; some the momentous vicissitudes of life, and some the lighter occurrences; some the terrors of distress, and some the gaieties of prosperity. Thus rose the two modes of imitation, known by the names of *tragedy* and *comedy*, compositions intended to promote different ends by contrary means, and considered as so little allied that I do not recollect

---

[10] Menenius describes himself as a buffoon (*Coriolanus*, II, i, 49ff), and Hamlet calls attention to King Claudius's drinking (I, iv, 8–9).
[11] *casualties:* chance events.

among the Greeks or Romans a single writer who attempted both.

Shakespeare has united the powers of exciting laughter and sorrow not only in one mind but in one composition. Almost all his plays are divided between serious and ludicrous characters, and, in the successive evolutions of the design, sometimes produce seriousness and sorrow, and sometimes levity and laughter.

That this is a practice contrary to the rules of criticism will be readily allowed; but there is always an appeal open from criticism to nature. The end of writing is to instruct; the end of poetry is to instruct by pleasing.[12] That the mingled drama may convey all the instruction of tragedy or comedy cannot be denied, because it includes both in its alternations of exhibition and approaches nearer than either to the appearance of life, by showing how great machinations and slender designs may promote or obviate one another, and the high and the low cooperate in the general system by unavoidable concatenation.

It is objected that by this change of scenes the passions are interrupted in their progression, and that the principal event, being not advanced by a due gradation of preparatory incidents, wants at last the power to move, which constitutes the perfection of dramatic poetry. This reasoning is so specious that it is received as true even by those who in daily experience feel it to be false. The interchanges of mingled scenes seldom fail to produce the intended vicissitudes[13] of passion. Fiction cannot move so much but that the attention may be easily transferred; and though it must be allowed that pleasing melancholy be sometimes interrupted by unwelcome levity, yet let it be considered likewise that melancholy is often not pleasing, and that the disturbance of one man may be the relief of another; that different auditors have different habitudes; and that, upon the whole, all pleasure consists in variety.

The players, who in their edition divided our author's works into comedies, histories, and tragedies, seem not to have distinguished the three kinds by any very exact or definite ideas.

An action which ended happily to the principal persons, however serious or distressful through its intermediate inci-

---

[12] A critical axiom originally from Horace (*Art of Poetry*, lines 343–44).
[13] *vicissitudes:* alternations.

dents, in their opinion constituted a comedy. This idea of a comedy continued long amongst us; and plays were written which, by changing the catastrophe, were tragedies today and comedies tomorrow.

Tragedy was not in those times a poem of more general dignity or elevation than comedy; it required only a calamitous conclusion, with which the common criticism of the age was satisfied, whatever lighter pleasure it afforded in its progress.

History was a series of actions with no other than chronological succession, independent on each other, and without any tendency to introduce or regulate the conclusion. It is not always very nicely distinguished from tragedy. There is not much nearer approach to unity of action in the tragedy of *Antony and Cleopatra* than in the history of *Richard the Second.* But a history might be continued through many plays; as it had no plan, it had no limits.

Through all these denominations of the drama, Shakespeare's mode of composition is the same: an interchange of seriousness and merriment, by which the mind is softened at one time and exhilarated at another. But whatever be his purpose, whether to gladden or depress, or to conduct the story, without vehemence or emotion, through tracts of easy and familiar dialogue, he never fails to attain his purpose; as he commands us, we laugh or mourn, or sit silent with quiet expectation, in tranquillity without indifference.

When Shakespeare's plan is understood, most of the criticisms of Rymer and Voltaire vanish away. The play of *Hamlet* is opened, without impropriety, by two sentinels; Iago bellows at Brabantio's window without injury to the scheme of the play, though in terms which a modern audience would not easily endure; the character of Polonius is seasonable and useful; and the gravediggers themselves may be heard with applause.

Shakespeare engaged in dramatic poetry with the world open before him; the rules of the ancients were yet known to few; the public judgment was unformed; he had no example of such fame as might force him upon imitation, nor critics of such authority as might restrain his extravagance; he therefore indulged his natural disposition; and his disposition, as Rymer has remarked, led him to comedy. In tragedy he often writes, with great appearance of toil and study, what is written at last with little felicity; but in his comic scenes he seems to produce, without labor, what no labor can improve. In tragedy he is always struggling after some occasion to be comic; but in comedy he seems to repose, or to luxuriate, as in a mode of thinking congenial to his nature. In his tragic scenes there is always something wanting, but his comedy often surpasses expectation or desire. His comedy pleases by the thoughts and the language, and his tragedy for the greater part by incident and action. His tragedy seems to be skill, his comedy to be instinct.

The force of his comic scenes has suffered little diminution, from the changes made by a century and a half, in manners or in words. As his personages act upon principles arising from genuine passion very little modified by particular forms, their pleasures and vexations are communicable to all times and to all places; they are natural and therefore durable. The adventitious peculiarities of personal habits are only superficial dyes, bright and pleasing for a little while, yet soon fading to a dim tinct, without any remains of former luster; but the discriminations of true passion are the colors of nature; they pervade the whole mass and can only perish with the body that exhibits them. The accidental compositions of heterogeneous modes are dissolved by the chance which combined them; but the uniform simplicity of primitive[14] qualities neither admits increase nor suffers decay. The sand heaped by one flood is scattered by another, but the rock always continues in its place. The stream of time, which is continually washing the dissoluble fabrics of other poets, passes without injury by the adamant of Shakespeare.

If there be, what I believe there is, in every nation a style which never becomes obsolete, a certain mode of phraseology so consonant and congenial to the analogy and principles of its respective language as to remain settled and unaltered; this style is probably to be sought in the common intercourse of life, among those who speak only to be understood without ambition of elegance. The polite are always catching modish innovations, and the learned depart from established forms of speech in hope of finding or making better; those who wish for distinction forsake the vulgar[15] when the vulgar is right; but there is a conversation above grossness and below refinement where propriety resides, and where this poet seems to

---

[14] *primitive:* primary.
[15] *vulgar:* common, popular.

have gathered his comic dialogue. He is therefore more agreeable to the ears of the present age than any other author equally remote, and among his other excellencies deserves to be studied as one of the original masters of our language.

These observations are to be considered not as unexceptionably constant, but as containing general and predominant truth. Shakespeare's familiar dialogue is affirmed to be smooth and clear, yet not wholly without ruggedness or difficulty; as a country may be eminently fruitful though it has spots unfit for cultivation; his characters are praised as natural, though their sentiments are sometimes forced and their actions improbable; as the earth upon the whole is spherical, though its surface is varied with protuberances and cavities.

Shakespeare with his excellencies has likewise faults, and faults sufficient to obscure and overwhelm any other merit. I shall show them in the proportion in which they appear to me, without envious malignity or superstitious veneration. No question can be more innocently discussed than a dead poet's pretensions to renown; and little regard is due to that bigotry which sets candor[16] higher than truth.

His first defect is that to which may be imputed most of the evil in books or in men. He sacrifices virtue to convenience and is so much more careful to please than to instruct that he seems to write without any moral purpose. From his writings indeed a system of social duty may be selected, for he that thinks reasonably must think morally; but his precepts and axioms drop casually from him; he makes no just distribution of good or evil, nor is always careful to show in the virtuous a disapprobation of the wicked; he carries his persons indifferently through right and wrong and at the close dismisses them without further care and leaves their examples to operate by chance. This fault the barbarity of his age cannot extenuate; for it is always a writer's duty to make the world better, and justice is a virtue independent on time or place.

The plots are often so loosely formed that a very slight consideration may improve them, and so carelessly pursued that he seems not always to comprehend his own design. He omits opportunities of instructing or delighting which the train of his story seems to force upon him, and apparently rejects those exhibitions which would be more affecting, for the sake of those which are more easy.

---

[16] *candor:* kindly reluctance to criticize.

It may be observed that in many of his plays the latter part is evidently neglected. When he found himself near the end of his work and in view of his reward, he shortened the labor to snatch the profit. He therefore remits his efforts where he should most vigorously exert them, and his catastrophe is improbably produced or imperfectly represented.

He had no regard to distinction of time or place but gives to one age or nation, without scruple, the customs; institutions, and opinions of another, at the expense not only of likelihood but of possibility. These faults Pope has endeavored, with more zeal than judgment, to transfer to his imagined interpolators.[17] We need not wonder to find Hector quoting Aristotle, when we see the loves of Theseus and Hippolyta combined with the Gothic mythology of fairies.[18] Shakespeare, indeed, was not the only violator of chronology, for in the same age Sidney, who wanted not[19] the advantages of learning, has, in his *Arcadia*, confounded the pastoral with the feudal times, the days of innocence, quiet, and security, with those of turbulence, violence, and adventure.

In his comic scenes he is seldom very successful when he engages his characters in reciprocations of smartness and contests of sarcasm; their jests are commonly gross and their pleasantry licentious; neither his gentlemen nor his ladies have much delicacy nor are sufficiently distinguished from his clowns by any appearance of refined manners. Whether he represented the real conversation of his time is not easy to determine. The reign of Elizabeth is commonly supposed to have been a time of stateliness, formality, and reserve; yet perhaps the relaxations of that severity were not very elegant. There must, however, have been always some modes of gaiety preferable to others, and a writer ought to choose the best.

In tragedy his performance seems constantly to be worse as his labor is more. The effusions of passion which exigence forces out are for the most part striking and energetic; but

---

[17] In the Preface to his edition, Pope attributed anachronisms such as Hector's quoting Aristotle to the ignorance of the actors who first published his plays. Whenever Pope found a passage "excessively bad," he decided it was an interpolation and demoted it to the bottom of the page.
[18] Hector (c. 1200 B.C.) quotes Aristotle (fourth century, B.C.) in *Troilus and Cressida* (II, ii, 166–67); ancient Greek is combined with Gothic mythology in *A Midsummer Night's Dream*.
[19] *wanted not:* did not lack.

whenever he solicits his invention or strains his faculties, the offspring of his throes is tumor, meanness, tediousness, and obscurity.

In narration he affects a disproportionate pomp of diction and a wearisome train of circumlocution and tells the incident imperfectly in many words which might have been more plainly delivered in few. Narration[20] in dramatic poetry is naturally tedious, as it is unanimated and inactive and obstructs the progress of the action; it should therefore always be rapid and enlivened by frequent interruption. Shakespeare found it an encumbrance and, instead of lightening it by brevity, endeavored to recommend it by dignity and splendor.

His declamations or set speeches are commonly cold and weak, for his power was the power of nature; when he endeavored, like other tragic writers, to catch opportunities of amplification and, instead of inquiring what the occasion demanded, to show how much his stores of knowledge could supply, he seldom escapes without the pity or resentment of his reader.

It is incident to him to be now and then entangled with an unwieldy sentiment, which he cannot well express and will not reject; he struggles with it awhile and, if it continues stubborn, comprises it in words such as occur and leaves it to be disentangled and evolved[21] by those who have more leisure to bestow upon it.

Not that always where the language is intricate the thought is subtle, or the image always great where the line is bulky; the equality of words to things is very often neglected, and trivial sentiments and vulgar ideas disappoint the attention to which they are recommended by sonorous epithets and swelling figures.[22]

But the admirers of this great poet have most reason to complain when he approaches nearest to his highest excellence and seems fully resolved to sink them in dejection and mollify them with tender emotions by the fall of greatness, the danger of innocence, or the crosses of love. What he does best, he soon ceases to do. He is not long soft and pathetic without some idle conceit[23] or contemptible equivocation. He no

---

[20] *Narration:* relating, rather than dramatizing, action.
[21] *evolved:* ordered.
[22] *swelling figures:* inflated figures of speech.
[23] *conceit:* strained figure of speech.

sooner begins to move than he counteracts himself; and terror and pity, as they are rising in the mind, are checked and blasted by sudden frigidity.

A quibble[24] is to Shakespeare what luminous vapors[25] are to the traveler; he follows it at all adventures; it is sure to lead him out of his way and sure to engulf him in the mire. It has some malignant power over his mind, and its fascinations are irresistible. Whatever be the dignity or profundity of his disquisition, whether he be enlarging knowledge or exalting affection, whether he be amusing attention with incidents or enchaining it in suspense, let but a quibble spring up before him and he leaves his work unfinished. A quibble is the golden apple for which he will always turn aside from his career or stoop from his elevation.[26] A quibble, poor and barren as it is, gave him such delight that he was content to purchase it by the sacrifice of reason, propriety, and truth. A quibble was to him the fatal Cleopatra for which he lost the world and was content to lose it.

It will be thought strange that in enumerating the defects of this writer I have not yet mentioned his neglect of the unities, his violation of those laws which have been instituted and established by the joint authority of poets and critics.

For his other deviations from the art of writing, I resign him to critical justice without making any other demand in his favor than that which must be indulged to all human excellence: that his virtues be rated with his failings. But from the censure which this irregularity may bring upon him, I shall, with due reverence to that learning which I must oppose, adventure to try how I can defend him.

His histories, being neither tragedies nor comedies, are not subject to any of their laws; nothing more is necessary to all the praise which they expect than that the changes of action be so prepared as to be understood, that the incidents be various and affecting, and the characters consistent, natural, and distinct. No other unity is intended, and therefore none is to be sought.

In his other works he has well enough preserved the unity of action. He has not, indeed, an intrigue regularly perplexed and regularly unraveled; he does not endeavor to hide his

---

[24] *quibble:* pun.
[25] *vapors:* will-o'-the-wisps.
[26] In Greek mythology, Atalanta lost a crucial race because she turned aside to pick up three golden apples.

design only to discover[27] it, for this is seldom the order of real events, and Shakespeare is the poet of nature; but his plan has commonly, what Aristotle requires, a beginning, a middle, and an end, one event is concatenated with another, and the conclusion follows by easy consequence. There are perhaps some incidents that might be spared, as in other poets there is much talk that only fills up time upon the stage; but the general system makes gradual advances, and the end of the play is the end of expectation.

To the unities of time and place he has shown no regard; and perhaps a nearer view of the principles on which they stand will diminish their value and withdraw from them the veneration which, from the time of Corneille,[28] they have very generally received, by discovering that they have given more trouble to the poet than pleasure to the auditor.

The necessity of observing the unities of time and place arises from the supposed necessity of making the drama credible. The critics hold it impossible that an action of months or years can be possibly believed to pass in three hours; or that the spectator can suppose himself to sit in the theater while ambassadors go and return between distant kings, while armies are levied and towns besieged, while an exile wanders and returns, or till he whom they saw courting his mistress shall lament the untimely fall of his son. The mind revolts from evident falsehood, and fiction loses its force when it departs from the resemblance of reality.

From the narrow limitation of time necessarily arises the contraction of place. The spectator, who knows that he saw the first act at Alexandria, cannot suppose that he sees the next at Rome, at a distance to which not the dragons of Medea could, in so short a time, have transported him; he knows with certainty that he has not changed his place; and he knows that place cannot change itself; that what was a house cannot become a plain; that what was Thebes can never be Persepolis.

Such is the triumphant language with which a critic exults over the misery of an irregular poet and exults commonly without resistance or reply. It is time, therefore, to tell him by the authority of Shakespeare, that he assumes, as an un-

---

[27] *discover:* reveal.
[28] The seventeenth-century dramatist Pierre Corneille observed the rules in his plays and argued for them in his "Essay on the Three Unities" (1660).

questionable principle, a position which, while his breath is forming it into words, his understanding pronounces to be false. It is false, that any representation is mistaken for reality; that any dramatic fable in its materiality was ever credible, or, for a single moment, was ever credited.

The objection arising from the impossibility of passing the first hour at Alexandria and the next at Rome supposes that when the play opens the spectator really imagines himself at Alexandria and believes that his walk to the theater has been a voyage to Egypt, and that he lives in the days of Antony and Cleopatra. Surely he that imagines this may imagine more. He that can take the stage at one time for the palace of the Ptolemies may take it in half an hour for the promontory of Actium. Delusion, if delusion be admitted, has no certain limitation; if the spectator can be once persuaded that his old acquaintance are Alexander and Caesar, that a room illuminated with candles is the plain of Pharsalia or the bank of Granicus, he is in a state of elevation above the reach of reason or of truth, and from the heights of empyrean poetry may despise the circumscriptions of terrestrial nature. There is no reason why a mind thus wandering in ecstasy should count the clock, or why an hour should not be a century in that calenture of the brains that can make the stage a field.

The truth is that the spectators are always in their senses and know from the first act to the last that the stage is only a stage, and that the players are only players. They come to hear a certain number of lines recited with just gesture and elegant modulation. The lines relate to some action, and an action must be in some place; but the different actions that complete a story may be in places very remote from each other; and where is the absurdity of allowing that space to represent first Athens and then Sicily which was always known to be neither Sicily nor Athens, but a modern theater.

By supposition, as place is introduced, time may be extended; the time required by the fable elapses for the most part between the acts; for, of so much of the action as is represented, the real and poetical duration is the same. If in the first act preparations for war against Mithridates are represented to be made in Rome, the event of the war may, without absurdity, be represented in the catastrophe as happening in Pontus; we know that there is neither war nor preparation for war; we know that we are neither in Rome nor Pontus; that neither Mithridates nor Lucullus are before us.

The drama exhibits successive imitations of successive actions; and why may not the second imitation represent an action that happened years after the first if it be so connected with it that nothing but time can be supposed to intervene? Time is, of all modes of existence, most obsequious to the imagination; a lapse of years is as easily conceived as a passage of hours. In contemplation we easily contract the time of real actions and therefore willingly permit it to be contracted when we only see their imitation.

It will be asked how the drama moves if it is not credited. It is credited with all the credit due to a drama. It is credited, whenever it moves, as a just picture of a real original; as representing to the auditor what he would himself feel if he were to do or suffer what is there feigned to be suffered or to be done. The reflection that strikes the heart is not that the evils before us are real evils, but that they are evils to which we ourselves may be exposed. If there be any fallacy, it is not that we fancy the players, but that we fancy ourselves unhappy for a moment; but we rather lament the possibility than suppose the presence of misery, as a mother weeps over her babe when she remembers that death may take it from her. The delight of tragedy proceeds from our consciousness of fiction; if we thought murders and treasons real, they would please no more.

Imitations produce pain or pleasure not because they are mistaken for realities, but because they bring realities to mind. When the imagination is recreated by a painted landscape, the trees are not supposed capable to give us shade, or the fountains coolness; but we consider how we should be pleased with such fountains playing beside us and such woods waving over us. We are agitated in reading the history of *Henry the Fifth*, yet no man takes his book for the field of Agincourt. A dramatic exhibition is a book recited with concomitants that increase or diminish its effect. Familiar[29] comedy is often more powerful in the theater than on the page; imperial tragedy is always less. The humor of Petruchio may be heightened by grimace; but what voice or what gesture can hope to add dignity or force to the soliloquy of Cato?[30]

A play read affects the mind like a play acted. It is therefore

---

[29] *Familiar:* domestic.
[30] Petruchio is the hero of Shakespeare's farcical *Taming of the Shrew*; Addison's noble hero Cato contemplates suicide in his soliloquy in V, i.

evident that the action is not supposed to be real; and it follows that between the acts a longer or shorter time may be
allowed to pass, and that no more account of space or duration is to be taken by the auditor of a drama than by the
reader of a narrative, before whom may pass in an hour the
life of a hero or the revolutions of an empire.

Whether Shakespeare knew the unities and rejected them
by design, or deviated from them by happy ignorance, it is,
I think, impossible to decide and useless to inquire. We may
reasonably suppose that when he rose to notice, he did not
want the counsels and admonitions of scholars and critics,
and that he at last deliberately persisted in a practice which
he might have begun by chance. As nothing is essential to the
fable but unity of action, and as the unities of time and place
arise evidently from false assumptions, and, by circumscribing
the extent of the drama, lessen its variety, I cannot think it
much to be lamented that they were not known by him, or
not observed; nor, if such another poet could arise, should I
very vehemently reproach him that his first act passed at
Venice and his next in Cyprus.[31] Such violations of rules
merely positive[32] become the comprehensive genius of Shakespeare, and such censures are suitable to the minute and
slender criticism of Voltaire:

> Non usque adeo permiscuit imis
> Longus summa dies, ut non, si voce Metelli
> Serventur leges, malint a Caesare tolli.[33]
> [The course of time has not wrought such
> confusion that the laws would not rather be
> trampled on by Caesar than saved by Metel-
> lus.[33]]

Yet when I speak thus slightly of dramatic rules, I cannot
but recollect how much wit and learning may be produced
against me; before such authorities I am afraid to stand, not
that I think the present question one of those that are to be
decided by mere authority, but because it is to be suspected
that these precepts have not been so easily received but for

---

[31] Rymer ridiculed Shakespeare for moving the action of *Othello* from
Venice (I) to Cyprus (II–V).
[32] Arbitrary, conventional.
[33] Lucan, *Pharsalia*, III, 138–40.

better reasons than I have yet been able to find. The result of my inquiries, in which it would be ludicrous to boast of impartiality, is that the unities of time and place are not essential to a just drama; that, though they may sometimes conduce to pleasure, they are always to be sacrificed to the nobler beauties of variety and instruction; and that a play written with nice observation of critical rules is to be contemplated as an elaborate curiosity, as the product of superfluous and ostentatious art, by which is shown rather what is possible than what is necessary.

He that, without diminution of any other excellence, shall preserve all the unities unbroken deserves the like applause with the architect who shall display all the orders of architecture in a citadel without any deduction from its strength; but the principal beauty of a citadel is to exclude the enemy, and the greatest graces of a play are to copy nature and instruct life.

Perhaps what I have here not dogmatically but deliberatively written may recall the principles of the drama to a new examination. I am almost frightened at my own temerity and, when I estimate the fame and the strength of those that maintain the contrary opinion, am ready to sink down in reverential silence; as Aeneas withdrew from the defense of Troy when he saw Neptune shaking the wall and Juno heading the besiegers.[34]

Those whom my arguments cannot persuade to give their approbation to the judgment of Shakespeare will easily, if they consider the condition of his life, make some allowance for his ignorance.

Every man's performances, to be rightly estimated, must be compared with the state of the age in which he lived and with his own particular opportunities; and though to a reader a book be not worse or better for the circumstances of the author, yet as there is always a silent reference of human works to human abilities, and as the inquiry how far man may extend his designs, or how high he may rate his native force, is of far greater dignity than in what rank we shall place any particular performance, curiosity is always busy to discover the instruments as well as to survey the workmanship, to know how much is to be ascribed to original powers and how

[34] Virgil, *Aeneid*, II, 610–14.

much to casual and adventitious help. The palaces of Peru or Mexico were certainly mean and incommodious habitations if compared to the houses of European monarchs; yet who could forbear to view them with astonishment who remembered that they were built without the use of iron?

The English nation, in the time of Shakespeare, was yet struggling to emerge from barbarity. The philology[35] of Italy had been transplanted hither in the reign of Henry the Eighth; and the learned languages had been successfully cultivated by Lily, Linacre, and More; by Pole, Cheke, and Gardiner; and afterwards by Smith, Clerk, Haddon, and Ascham. Greek was now taught to boys in the principal schools; and those who united elegance with learning read with great diligence the Italian and Spanish poets. But literature was yet confined to professed scholars, or to men and women of high rank. The public was gross and dark; and to be able to read and write was an accomplishment still valued for its rarity.

Nations, like individuals, have their infancy. A people newly awakened to literary curiosity, being yet unacquainted with the true state of things, knows not how to judge of that which is proposed as its resemblance. Whatever is remote from common appearances is always welcome to vulgar, as to childish, credulity; and of a country unenlightened by learning, the whole people is the vulgar. The study of those who then aspired to plebeian learning was laid out upon adventures, giants, dragons, and enchantments. *The Death of Arthur* was the favorite volume.

The mind which has feasted on the luxurious wonders of fiction has no taste for the insipidity of truth. A play which imitated only the common occurrences of the world would, upon the admirers of *Palmerin* and *Guy of Warwick*, have made little impression; he that wrote for such an audience was under the necessity of looking round for strange events and fabulous transactions; and that incredibility by which maturer knowledge is offended was the chief recommendation of writings to unskillful curiosity.

Our author's plots are generally borrowed from novels; and it is reasonable to suppose that he chose the most popular, such as were read by many and related by more; for his audience could not have followed him through the intricacies of

---

[35] *philology:* literary scholarship.

the drama had they not held the thread to the story in their hands.

The stories which we now find only in remoter authors were in his time accessible and familiar. The fable of *As You Like It*, which is supposed to be copied from Chaucer's *Gamelyn*,[36] was a little pamphlet of those times; and old Mr. Cibber[37] remembered the tale of *Hamlet* in plain English prose, which the critics have now to seek in Saxo Grammaticus.[38]

His English histories he took from English chronicles and English ballads; and as the ancient writers were made known to his countrymen by versions,[39] they supplied him with new subjects; he dilated some of Plutarch's lives into plays, when they had been translated by North.

His plots, whether historical or fabulous, are always crowded with incidents by which the attention of a rude people was more easily caught than by sentiment or argumentation; and such is the power of the marvelous, even over those who despise it, that every man finds his mind more strongly seized by the tragedies of Shakespeare than of any other writer. Others please us by particular speeches; but he always makes us anxious for the event and has perhaps excelled all but Homer in securing the first purpose of a writer, by exciting restless and unquenchable curiosity and compelling him that reads his work to read it through.

The shows and bustle with which his plays abound have the same original.[40] As knowledge advances, pleasure passes from the eye to the ear, but returns, as it declines, from the ear to the eye. Those to whom our author's labors were exhibited had more skill in pomps or processions than in poetical language and perhaps wanted[41] some visible and discriminated[42] events as comments on the dialogue. He knew how he should most please; and whether his practice is more

---

[36] A verse romance (c. 1350), then attributed to Chaucer, which was the source of Thomas Lodge's *Rosalynde* (1590), Shakespeare's source for *As You Like It*.
[37] Colley Cibber, actor, dramatist, and theater manager, here distinguished from his son, Theophilus.
[38] A thirteenth-century historian who wrote in Latin.
[39] *versions*: translations.
[40] *original*: origin.
[41] *wanted*: needed.
[42] *discriminated*: distinct.

agreeable to nature, or whether his example has prejudiced the nation, we still find that on our stage something must be done as well as said, and inactive declamation is very coldly heard, however musical or elegant, passionate or sublime.

Voltaire expresses his wonder that our author's extravagances are endured by a nation which has seen the tragedy of *Cato*. Let him be answered that Addison speaks the language of poets; and Shakespeare, of men. We find in *Cato* innumerable beauties which enamor us of its author, but we see nothing that acquaints us with human sentiments or human actions; we place it with the fairest and the noblest progeny which judgment propagates by conjunction with learning; but *Othello* is the vigorous and vivacious offspring of observation impregnated by genius. *Cato* affords a splendid exhibition of artificial and fictitious manners and delivers just and noble sentiments, in diction easy, elevated, and harmonious, but its hopes and fears communicate no vibration to the heart; the composition refers us only to the writer; we pronounce the name of *Cato*, but we think on Addison.

The work of a correct and regular writer is a garden accurately formed and diligently planted, varied with shades, and scented with flowers; the composition of Shakespeare is a forest, in which oaks extend their branches, and pines tower in the air, interspersed sometimes with weeds and brambles, and sometimes giving shelter to myrtles and to roses; filling the eye with awful pomp and gratifying the mind with endless diversity. Other poets display cabinets of precious rarities, minutely finished, wrought into shape, and polished into brightness. Shakespeare opens a mine which contains gold and diamonds in unexhaustible plenty, though clouded by incrustations, debased by impurities, and mingled with a mass of meaner minerals.

It has been much disputed whether Shakespeare owed his excellence to his own native force, or whether he had the common helps of scholastic education, the precepts of critical science, and the examples of ancient authors.

There has always prevailed a tradition that Shakespeare wanted learning, that he had no regular education, nor much skill in the dead languages. Jonson, his friend, affirms that "he had small Latin, and less Greek," who, besides that he had no imaginable temptation to falsehood, wrote at a time when the character and acquisitions of Shakespeare were known to multitudes. His evidence ought therefore to decide the controversy, unless some testimony of equal force could be opposed.

Some have imagined that they have discovered deep learning in many imitations of old writers; but the examples which I have known urged were drawn from books translated in his time; or were such easy coincidences of thought as will happen to all who consider the same subjects; or such remarks on life or axioms of morality as float in conversation and are transmitted through the world in proverbial sentences.

I have found it remarked that in this important sentence, "Go before, I'll follow," we read a translation of, *I prae, sequar*.[43] I have been told that when Caliban, after a pleasing dream, says, "I cried to sleep again,"[44] the author imitates Anacreon, who had, like every other man, the same wish on the same occasion.

There are a few passages which may pass for imitations, but so few that the exception only confirms the rule; he obtained them from accidental quotations or by oral communication and, as he used what he had, would have used more if he had obtained it.

The *Comedy of Errors* is confessedly taken from the *Menaechmi* of Plautus; from the only play of Plautus which was then in English. What can be more probable than that he who copied that would have copied more; but that those which were not translated were inaccessible?

Whether he knew the modern languages is uncertain. That his plays have some French scenes proves but little; he might easily procure them to be written, and probably, even though he had known the language in the common degree, he could not have written it without assistance. In the story of *Romeo and Juliet* he is observed to have followed the English translation, where it deviates from the Italian; but this on the other part proves nothing against his knowledge of the original. He was to copy, not what he knew himself, but what was known to his audience.

It is most likely that he had learned Latin sufficiently to make him acquainted with construction, but that he never advanced to an easy perusal of the Roman authors. Concern-

---

[43] Zachary Grey had suggested that Shakespeare's line was translated from Terence (*Critical, Historical, and Explanatory Notes on Shakespeare*, 1754).

[44] *The Tempest*, III, ii, 149.

ing his skill in modern languages, I can find no sufficient ground of determination; but as no imitations of French or Italian authors have been discovered, though the Italian poetry was then high in esteem, I am inclined to believe that he read little more than English and chose for his fables only such tales as he found translated.

That much knowledge is scattered over his works is very justly observed by Pope; but it is often such knowledge as books did not supply. He that will understand Shakespeare must not be content to study him in the closet,[45] he must look for his meaning sometimes among the sports of the field, and sometimes among the manufactures of the shop.

There is, however, proof enough that he was a very diligent reader, nor was our language then so indigent of books but that he might very liberally indulge his curiosity without excursion into foreign literature. Many of the Roman authors were translated, and some of the Greek; the Reformation had filled the kingdom with theological learning; most of the topics of human disquisition had found English writers; and poetry had been cultivated not only with diligence but success. This was a stock of knowledge sufficient for a mind so capable of appropriating and improving it.

But the greater part of his excellence was the product of his own genius. He found the English stage in a state of the utmost rudeness; no essays either in tragedy or comedy had appeared from which it could be discovered to what degree of delight either one or other might be carried. Neither character nor dialogue were yet understood. Shakespeare may be truly said to have introduced them both amongst us and in some of his happier scenes to have carried them both to the utmost height.

By what gradations of improvement he proceeded is not easily known; for the chronology of his works is yet unsettled. Rowe is of opinion that "perhaps we are not to look for his beginning, like those of other writers, in his least perfect works; art had so little and nature so large a share in what he did, that for aught I know," says he, "the performances of his youth, as they were the most vigorous, were the best."[46] But the power of nature is only the power of using to any

---

[45] *closet:* small private room.
[46] Nicholas Rowe, in the life of Shakespeare prefixed to his edition (1709).

certain purpose the materials which diligence procures or opportunity supplies. Nature gives no man knowledge, and, when images are collected by study and experience, can only assist in combining or applying them. Shakespeare, however favored by nature, could impart only what he had learned; and as he must increase his ideas, like other mortals, by gradual acquisition, he, like them, grew wiser as he grew older, could display life better, as he knew it more, and instruct with more efficacy, as he was himself more amply instructed.

There is a vigilance of observation and accuracy of distinction which books and precepts cannot confer; from this almost all original and native excellence proceeds. Shakespeare must have looked upon mankind with perspicacity, in the highest degree curious and attentive. Other writers borrow their characters from preceding writers and diversify them only by the accidental appendages of present manners; the dress is a little varied, but the body is the same. Our author had both matter and form to provide; for, except the characters of Chaucer, to whom I think he is not much indebted, there were no writers in English, and perhaps not many in other modern languages, which showed life in its native colors. . . .

[After further praising Shakespeare's wonderful achievement in depicting human and inanimate nature—all drawn from his own observation—Johnson discusses the task of editing Shakespeare: he explains the particular difficulties presented by Shakespeare's text, evaluates the five editors who preceded him (Nicholas Rowe, Alexander Pope, Lewis Theobald, Sir Thomas Hanmer, and William Warburton), and describes his own procedure in annotating, explicating, and emending. He has become increasingly cautious about conjectural emendation because he reflects that, whatever their deficiencies, the editors of the First Folio "who had the copy before their eyes were more likely to read it right than we who read it only by imagination." He was also modest about the value of annotation:]

Notes are often necessary, but they are necessary evils. Let him that is yet unacquainted with the power of Shakespeare and who desires to feel the highest pleasure that the drama can give, read every play, from the first scene to the last, with utter negligence of all his commentators. When his fancy is once on the wing, let it not stoop at correction or explanation. When his attention is strongly engaged, let it disdain alike to turn aside to the name of Theobald and of Pope. Let him read on through brightness and obscurity, through integrity and corruption; let him preserve his comprehension of the dialogue and his interest in the fable. And when the pleasures of novelty have ceased, let him attempt exactness and read the commentators.

Particular passages are cleared by notes, but the general effect of the work is weakened. The mind is refrigerated by interruption; the thoughts are diverted from the principal subject; the reader is weary, he suspects not why, and at last throws away the book which he has too diligently studied.

Parts are not to be examined till the whole has been surveyed; there is a kind of intellectual remoteness necessary for the comprehension of any great work in its full design and in its true proportions; a close approach shows the smaller niceties, but the beauty of the whole is discerned no longer.

It is not very grateful[47] to consider how little the succession of editors has added to this author's power of pleasing. He was read, admired, studied, and imitated, while he was yet deformed with all the improprieties which ignorance and neglect could accumulate upon him; while the reading was yet not rectified nor his allusions understood; yet then did Dryden pronounce that "Shakespeare was the man who of all modern and perhaps ancient poets had the largest and most comprehensive soul."

All the images of nature were still present to him, and he drew them not laboriously but luckily; when he describes anything, you more than see it, you feel it too. Those who accuse him to have wanted learning give him the greater commendation; he was naturally learned; he needed not the spectacles of books to read nature; he looked inwards and found her there. I cannot say he is everywhere alike; were he so, I should do him injury to compare him with the greatest of mankind. He is many times flat and insipid; his comic wit degenerating into clenches,[48] his serious swelling into bombast. But he is always great when some great occasion is presented to him; no man can say he ever had a fit subject for his wit and did not then raise himself as high above the rest of poets,

---

[47] *grateful:* gratifying.

[48] *clenches:* puns.

Quantum lenta solent inter viburna cupressi.
[As much as cypresses do among the bending osiers.][49]

It is to be lamented that such a writer should want a commentary; that his language should become obsolete or his sentiments obscure. But it is vain to carry wishes beyond the condition of human things; that which must happen to all has happened to Shakespeare, by accident and time; and more than has been suffered by any other writer since the use of types[50] has been suffered by him through his own negligence of fame, or perhaps by that superiority of mind which despised its own performances when it compared them with its powers, and judged those works unworthy to be preserved which the critics of following ages were to contend for the fame of restoring and explaining.

Among these candidates of inferior fame, I am now to stand the judgment of the public; and wish that I could confidently produce my commentary as equal to the encouragement which I have had the honor of receiving. Every work of this kind is by its nature deficient, and I should feel little solicitude about the sentence were it to be pronounced only by the skillful and the learned.

---

[49] John Dryden, *An Essay of Dramatic Poesy* (1668). He quotes Virgil's *Eclogues*, I, 25.
[50] I.e., the use of movable types; printing.

Selection of Johnson's Notes to the Plays

Measure for Measure

[On III, i, 32–34, where the Duke tries to persuade Claudio that life is not worth prizing:]

> DUKE. Thou hast nor youth nor age;
> But as it were an after-dinner's sleep,
> Dreaming on both.

This is exquisitely imagined. When we are young we busy ourselves in forming schemes for succeeding time, and miss the gratifications that are before us; when we are old we amuse the languour of age with the recollection of youthful pleasures or performances; so that our life, of which no part is filled with the business of the present time, resembles our dreams after dinner, when the events of the morning are mingled with the designs of the evening.

[On the ending of the play, where Isabella pleads for Angelo, the villain who has tried to force her into sexual relations and has (she believes) executed her brother:]

The Duke has justly observed that Isabel is "importuned against all sense" to solicit for Angelo, yet here "against all sense" she solicits for him. Her argument is extraordinary.

> A due sincerity govern'd his deeds,
> Till he did look on me; since it is so,
> Let him not die.   [V, i, 449–51]

That Angelo had committed all the crimes charged against him, as far as he could commit them, is evident. The only "intent" which "his act did not overtake," was the defilement of Isabel. Of this Angelo was only intentionally guilty.

Angelo's crimes were such, as must sufficiently justify punishment, whether its end be to secure the innocent from wrong, or to deter guilt by example; and I believe every reader feels some indignation when he finds him spared. From what extenuation of his crime can Isabel, who yet supposes her brother dead, form any plea in his favour. "Since he was good till he looked on me, let him not die." I am afraid our varlet poet intended to inculcate, that women think ill of nothing that raises the credit of their beauty, and are ready, however virtuous, to pardon any act which they think incited by their own charms.

[On the Duke's refusal to pardon Lucio, whose only offense has been slandering him (V, i, 495ff):]

After the pardon of two murderers Lucio might be treated by the good Duke with less harshness; but perhaps the poet intended to show, what is too often seen "that men easily forgive wrongs which are not committed against themselves."

The Merchant of Venice

[On IV, i, 90–94, Shylock's retort to the Christians who beg him to show mercy to Antonio:]

> You have among you many a purchas'd slave,
> Which, like your asses and your dogs and mules,
> You use in abject and in slavish parts,
> Because you bought them: shall I say to you,
> Let them be free, marry them to your heirs?

This argument considered as used to the particular persons, seems conclusive. I see not how Venetians or Englishmen, while they practice the purchase and sale of slaves, can much enforce or demand the law of "doing to others as we would that they should do unto us."

As You Like It

[Johnson's concluding comment on *As You Like It*:]

Of this play the fable is wild and pleasing. I know not how the ladies will approve the facility with which both Rosalind and Celia give away their hearts. To Celia much may be forgiven for the heroism of her friendship. The character of Jaques is natural and well preserved. The comick dialogue is very sprightly, with less mixture of low buffoonery than in some other plays; and the graver part is elegant and harmonious. By hastening to the end of his work Shakespeare suppressed the dialogue between the usurper and the hermit, and lost an opportunity of exhibiting a moral lesson in which he might have found matter worthy of his highest powers.

Much Ado About Nothing

[On IV, i, 248–49, Leonato's acquiescence to a plan suggested immediately after his daughter has been publicly disgraced:]

> Being that I flow in grief,
> The smallest twine may lead me.

This is one of our author's observations upon life. Men overpowered with distress eagerly listen to the first offers of relief, close with every scheme, and believe every promise. He that has no longer any confidence in himself, is glad to repose his trust in any other that will undertake to guide him.

King John

[On II, ii, 68–71, Lady Constance's defiance of two kings, when she has learned that her son is to be dispossessed of his rightful throne:]

> I will instruct my sorrows to be proud;
> For grief is proud and makes his owner stoop.
> To me and to the state of my great grief
> Let kings assemble.

In *Much Ado About Nothing*, the father of Hero, depressed by her disgrace, declares himself so subdued by grief that "a thread may lead him." How is it that grief in Leonato and Lady Constance, produces effects directly opposite, and yet both agreeable to nature. Sorrow softens the mind while it is yet warmed by hope, but hardens it when it is congealed by despair. Distress, while there remains any prospect of relief, is weak and flexible, but when no succour remains, is fearless and stubborn; angry alike at those that injure, and at those that do not help; careless to please where nothing can be gained, and fearless to offend when there is nothing further to be dreaded. Such was this writer's knowledge of the passions.

Henry IV, Part 2

[On V, v, 64–66, the newly crowned Henry V's repudiation of Falstaff:]

> Till then, I banish thee, on pain of death,
> As I have done the rest of my misleaders,
> Not to come near our person by ten mile.

Mr. Rowe observes, that many readers lament to see Falstaff so hardly used by his old friend. But if it be considered that the fat knight has never uttered one sentiment of generosity, and with all his power of exciting mirth, has nothing in him that can be esteemed, no great pain will be suffered from the reflection that he is compelled to live honestly, and maintained by the king, with a promise of advancement when he shall deserve it.

I think the poet more blameable for Poins, who is always represented as joining some virtues with his vices, and is therefore treated by the Prince with apparent distinction, yet he does nothing in the time of action, and though after the bustle is over he is again a favourite, at last vanishes without notice. Shakespeare certainly lost him by heedlessness, in the multiplicity of his characters, the variety of his action, and his eagerness to end the play.

[On V, v, 92, the Chief Justice's order, "Go, carry Sir John Falstaff to the Fleet":]

I do not see why Falstaff is carried to the Fleet. We have never lost sight of him since his dismission from the king; he has committed no new fault, and therefore incurred no punishment; but the different agitations of fear, anger, and surprise in him and his company, made a good scene to the eye; and our author, who wanted them no longer on the stage, was glad to find this method of sweeping them away.

[Johnson's concluding comment on *Henry IV*, Part 2:]

I fancy every reader, when he ends this play, cries out with Desdemona, "O most lame and impotent conclusion!" As this play was not, to our knowledge, divided into acts by the author, I could be content to conclude it with the death of Henry the Fourth.

In that Jerusalem shall Harry dye.

These scenes which now make the fifth act of *Henry the Fourth*, might then be the first of *Henry the Fifth*; but the truth is, that they do unite very commodiously to either play. When these plays were represented, I believe they ended as they are now ended in the books; but Shakespeare seems to have designed that the whole series of action from the beginning of *Richard the Second*, to the end of *Henry the Fifth*, should be considered by the reader as one work, upon one plan, only broken into parts by the necessity of exhibition.

None of Shakespeare's plays are more read than the *First and Second Parts of Henry the Fourth*. Perhaps no author has ever in two plays afforded so much delight. The great events are interesting, for the fate of kingdoms depends upon them; the slighter occurrences are diverting, and, except one or two, sufficiently probable; the incidents are multiplied with wonderful fertility of invention, and the characters diversified with utmost nicety of discernment, and the profoundest skill in the nature of man.

The Prince, who is the hero both of the comick and tragick part, is a young man of great abilities and violent passions, whose virtues are obscured by negligence, and whose understanding is dissipated by levity. In his idle hours he is rather loose than wicked, and when the occasion forces out his latent qualities, he is great without effort, and brave without tumult.

The trifler is roused into a hero, and the hero again reposes in the trifler. This character is great, original, and just.

Percy is a rugged soldier, cholerick, and quarrelsome, and has only the soldier's virtues, generosity and courage.

But Falstaff unimitated, unimitable Falstaff, how shall I describe thee? Thou compound of sense and vice; of sense which may be admired but not esteemed, of vice which may be despised, but hardly detested. Falstaff is a character loaded with faults, and with those faults which naturally produce contempt. He is a thief, and a glutton, a coward, and a boaster, always ready to cheat the weak, and prey upon the poor; to terrify the timorous and insult the defenceless. At once obsequious and malignant, he satirises in their absence those whom he lives by flattering. He is familiar with the Prince only as an agent of vice, but of this familiarity he is so proud as not only to be supercilious and haughty with common men, but to think his interest of importance to the Duke of Lancaster. Yet the man thus corrupt, thus despicable, makes himself necessary to the prince that despises him, by the most pleasing of all qualities, perpetual gaiety, by an unfailing power of exciting laughter, which is the more freely indulged, as his wit is not of the splendid or ambitious kind, but consists in easy escapes and sallies of levity, which make sport but raise no envy. It must be observed that he is stained with no enormous or sanguinary crimes, so that his licentiousness is not so offensive but that it may be borne for his mirth.

The moral to be drawn from this representation is, that no man is more dangerous than he that with a will to corrupt, hath the power to please; and that neither wit nor honesty ought to think themselves safe with such a companion when they see Henry seduced by Falstaff.

Henry V

[On King Henry's clumsy wooing of Princess Katharine of France (V, ii, 123ff):]

I know not why Shakespeare now gives the King nearly such a character as he made him formerly ridicule in Percy. This military grossness and unskilfulness in all the softer arts, does not suit very well with the gaieties of his youth, with the general knowledge ascribed to him at his accession, or with the contemptuous message sent him by the Dauphin, who represents him as fitter for the ball room than the field, and tells him that he is not "to revel into dutchies," or win provinces "with a nimble galliard." The truth is, that the poet's matter failed him in the fifth act, and he was glad to fill it up with whatever he could get; and not even Shakespeare can write well without a proper subject. It is a vain endeavour for the most skilful hand to cultivate barrenness, or to paint upon vacuity.

King Lear

[On I, i, 173–74, Lear's refusal to listen to Kent's plea to withdraw his sentence on Cordelia:]

> Which nor our nature nor our place can bear, —
> Our potency made good . . .

Lear, who is characterized as hot, heady and violent, is, with very just observation of life, made to entangle himself with vows, upon any sudden provocation to vow revenge, and then to plead the obligation of a vow in defense of implacability.

[On Edgar's description of what is supposed to be Dover Cliff (IV, vi, 11ff):]

This description has been much admired since the time of Addison, who has remarked, with a poor attempt at pleasantry, that "he who can read it without being giddy has a very good head, or a very bad one." The description is certainly not mean, but I am far from thinking it wrought to the utmost excellence of poetry. He that looks from a precipice finds himself assailed by one great and dreadful image of irresistible destruction. But this overwhelming idea is dissipated and enfeebled from the instant that the mind can restore itself to the observation of particulars, and diffuse its attention to distinct objects. The enumeration of the choughs and crows, the samphire-man and the fishers, counteracts the great effect of the prospect, as it peoples the desert of intermediate vacuity, and stops the mind in the rapidity of its descent through emptiness and horrour.

[On V, iii, 265–66, the reactions when Lear comes on stage bearing the dead Cordelia in his arms:]

> KENT. Is this the promis'd end?
> EDGAR. Or image of that horror?
> ALBANY. Fall and cease.

These two exclamations are given to Edgar and Albany in the folio, to animate the dialogue, and employ all the persons on the stage, but they are very obscure.

[Johnson's concluding comment on *King Lear*:]

The tragedy of Lear is deservedly celebrated among the dramas of Shakespeare. There is perhaps no play which keeps the attention so strongly fixed; which so much agitates our passions and interests our curiosity. The artful involutions of distinct interests, the striking opposition of contrary characters, the sudden changes of fortune, and the quick succession of events, fill the mind with a perpetual tumult of indignation, pity, and hope. There is no scene which does not contribute to the aggravation of the distress or conduct of the action, and scarce a line which does not conduce to the progress of the scene. So powerful is the current of the poet's imagination, that the mind, which once ventures within it, is hurried irresistibly along.

On the seeming improbability of Lear's conduct it may be observed, that he is represented according to histories at that time vulgarly received as true. And perhaps if we turn our thoughts upon the barbarity and ignorance of the age to which this story is referred, it will appear not so unlikely as while we estimate Lear's manners by our own. Such preference of one daughter to another, or resignation of dominion on such conditions, would be yet credible, if told of a petty prince of Guinea or Madagascar. Shakespeare, indeed, by the mention of his earls and dukes, has given us the idea of times more civilised, and of life regulated by softer manners; and the truth is, that though he so nicely discriminates, and so minutely describes the characters of men, he commonly neglects and confounds the characters of ages, by mingling customs ancient and modern, English and foreign.

My learned friend Mr. Warton, who has in the *Adventurer* very minutely criticised this play, remarks, that the instances of cruelty are too savage and shocking, and that the intervention of Edmund destroys the simplicity of the story. These objections may, I think, be answered, by repeating, that the cruelty of the daughters is an historical fact, to which the poet has added little, having only drawn it into a series by dialogue and action. But I am not able to apologise with equal plausibility for the extrusion of Gloucester's eyes, which seems an act too horrid to be endured in dramatick exhibition, and such as must always compel the mind to relieve its distress by incredulity. Yet let it be remembered that our authour well knew what would please the audience for which he wrote.

The injury done by Edmund to the simplicity of the action is abundantly recompensed by the addition of variety, by the art with which he is made to co-operate with the chief design, and the opportunity which he gives the poet of combining perfidy with perfidy, and connecting the wicked son with the wicked daughters, to impress this important moral, that villainy is never at a stop, that crimes lead to crimes, and at last terminate in ruin.

But though this moral be incidentally enforced, Shakespeare has suffered the virtue of Cordelia to perish in a just cause, contrary to the natural ideas of justice, to the hope of the reader, and, what is yet more strange, to the faith of chronicles. Yet this conduct is justified by the Spectator, who blames Tate for giving Cordelia success and happiness in his alteration, and declares, that, in his opinion, "the tragedy has lost half its beauty." Dennis has remarked, whether justly or not, that, to secure the favourable reception of *Cato*, "the town was poisoned with much false and abominable criticism," and that endeavours had been used to discredit and decry poetical justice.[1] A play in which the wicked prosper, and the virtuous miscarry, may doubtless be good, because it is a just representation of the common events of human life; but since all reasonable beings naturally love justice, I cannot easily be persuaded, that the observation of justice makes a play worse; or, that if other excellencies are equal, the audience will not always rise better pleased from the final triumph of persecuted virtue.

In the present case the publick has decided. Cordelia, from

---

[1] Nahum Tate rewrote *King Lear* with a happy ending (1681), and his version actually held the stage through the eighteenth century. Joseph Addison was one of the few to deplore Tate's revision (*Spectator* No. 40, 1711); the point of John Dennis's charge is that the hero of Addison's tragedy, *Cato* (1713), is defeated although virtuous.

the time of Tate, has always retired with victory and felicity. And, if my sensations could add any thing to the general suffrage, I might relate, that I was many years ago so shocked by Cordelia's death, that I know not whether I ever endured to read again the last scenes of the play till I undertook to revise them as an editor.

There is another controversy among the criticks concerning this play. It is disputed whether the predominant image in Lear's disordered mind be the loss of his kingdom or the cruelty of his daughters. Mr. Murphy, a very judicious critick, has evinced by induction of particular passages, that the cruelty of his daughters is the primary source of his distress, and that the loss of royalty affects him only as a secondary and subordinate evil; he observes with great justness, that Lear would move our compassion but little, did we not rather consider the injured father than the degraded king.

Macbeth

[On I, vii, lines 28ff, from the entrance of Lady Macbeth:]

The arguments by which Lady Macbeth persuades her husband to commit the murder, afford a proof of Shakespeare's knowledge of human nature. She urges the excellence and dignity of courage, a glittering idea which has dazzled mankind from age to age, and animated sometimes the housebreaker, and sometimes the conqueror; but this sophism Macbeth has for ever destroyed by distinguishing true from false fortitude, in a line and a half; of which it may almost be said, that they ought to bestow immortality on the author, though all his other productions had been lost.

> I dare do all that may become a man,
> Who dares do more, is none.

This topic, which has been always employed with too much success, is used in this scene with peculiar propriety to a soldier by a woman. Courage is the distinguishing virtue of a soldier, and the reproach of cowardice cannot be borne by any man from a woman, without great impatience.

She then urges the oaths by which he had bound himself to murder Duncan, another art of sophistry by which men have sometimes deluded their consciences, and persuaded themselves that what would be criminal in others is virtuous in them; this argument Shakespeare, whose plan obliged him to make Macbeth yield, has not confuted, though he might easily have shown that a former obligation could not be vacated by a latter: that obligations laid on us by a higher power, could not be overruled by obligations which we lay upon ourselves.

[On II, iii, 113–14:]

> . . . Here lay Duncan,
> His silver skin lac'd with his golden blood;

Mr. Pope has endeavoured to improve one of these lines by substituting "goary blood" for "golden blood"; but it may easily be admitted that he who could on such an occasion talk of "lacing the silver skin," would "lace it" with "golden blood." No amendment can be made to this line, of which every word is equally faulty, but by a general blot.

It is not improbable, that Shakespeare put these forced and unnatural metaphors into the mouth of Macbeth as a mark of artifice and dissimulation, to show the difference between the studied language of hypocrisy, and the natural outcries of sudden passion. This whole speech so considered, is a remarkable instance of judgment, as it consists entirely of antithesis and metaphor.

[On IV, i, the great incantation scene:]

As this is the chief scene of enchantment in the play, it is proper in this place to observe, with how much judgment Shakespeare has selected all the circumstances of his infernal ceremonies, and how exactly he has conformed to common opinions and traditions.

> Thrice the brinded cat hath mew'd.
>
> [IV, i, 1]

The usual form in which familiar spirits are reported to converse with witches, is that of a cat. A witch, who was tried about half a century before the time of Shakespeare, had a cat named Rutterkin, as the spirit of one of those witches was Grimalkin; and when any mischief was to be done she used to bid Rutterkin "go and fly," but once when she would have sent Rutterkin to torment a daughter of the Countess of Rutland, instead of "going" or "flying," he only cried "mew," from whence she discovered that the lady was out of her power, the power of witches being not universal, but limited, as Shakespeare has taken care to inculcate.

> Though his bark cannot be lost,
> Yet it shall be tempest tost.

[I, iii, 24–25]

The common afflictions which the malice of witches produced were melancholy, fits, and loss of flesh, which are threatened by one of Shakespeare's witches.

> Weary sevnights, nine times nine,
> Shall he dwindle, peak and pine.

[I, iii, 22–23]

It was likewise their practice to destroy the cattle of their neighbors, and the farmers have to this day many ceremonies to secure their cows and other cattle from witchcraft; but they seem to have been most suspected of malice against swine. Shakespeare has accordingly made one of his witches declare that she has been "killing swine," and Dr. Harsenet observes, that about that time, "a sow could not be ill of the measles, nor a girl of the sullens, but some old woman was charged with witchcraft."

> Toad, that under cold stone,
> Days and nights has thirty-one
> Swelter'd venom sleeping got,
> Boil thou first i' th' charmed pot.

[IV, i, 6–9]

Toads have likewise long lain under the reproach of being by some means accessary to witchcraft, for which reason Shakespeare, in the first scene of this play, calls one of the spirits "Padocke" or "Toad," and now takes care to put a toad first into the pot. When Vaninus was seized at Toulouse, there was found at his lodgings *ingens bufo vitro inclusus*, "a great toad shut in a vial," upon which those that prosecuted him *veneficium ex probrabant*, "charged him," I suppose "with witchcraft."

> Fillet of a fenny snake,
> In the cauldron boil and bake;
> Eye of newt, and toe of frog;—
> For a charm, &c.

[IV, i, 12–14]

The propriety of these ingredients may be known by consulting the books *De Viribus Animalium* and *De Mirabilibus Mundi*, ascribed to Albertus Magnus, in which the reader, who has time and credulity, may discover very wonderful secrets.

> Finger of birth-strangled babe,
> Ditch-deliver'd by a drab;—

[IV, i, 30–31]

It has been already mentioned in the law against witches, that they are supposed to take up dead bodies to use in enchantments, which was confessed by the woman whom king James examined, and who had of a dead body that was divided in one of their assemblies, two fingers for her share. It is observable that Shakespeare, on this great occasion, which involves the fate of a king, multiplies all the circumstances of horror. The babe, whose finger is used, must be strangled in its birth; grease must not only be human, but must have dropped from a gibbet, the gibbet of a murderer; and even the sow, whose blood is used, must have offended nature by devouring her own farrow. These are touches of judgment and genius.

[Johnson's concluding comment on *Macbeth*:]

This play is deservedly celebrated for the propriety of its fictions, and solemnity, grandeur, and variety of its action; but it has no nice discriminations of character, the events are too great to admit the influence of particular dispositions, and the course of the action necessarily determines the conduct of the agents.

The danger of ambition is well described; and I know not whether it may not be said in defence of some parts which now seem improbable, that, in Shakespeare's time, it was necessary to warn credulity against vain and illusive predictions.

The passions are directed to their true end. Lady Macbeth

is merely detested; and though the courage of Macbeth preserves some esteem, yet every reader rejoices at his fall.

Cymbeline

[On I, v, 23–24, the attempt of Cornelius, a court physician, to dissuade the wicked Queen from experimenting on animals with poisons:]

> Your highness
> Shall from this practice but make hard your heart;

There is in this passage nothing that much requires a note, yet I cannot forbear to push it forward into observation. The thought would probably have been more amplified, had our author lived to be shocked with such experiments as have been published in later times, by a race of men that have practised tortures without pity, and related them without shame, and are yet suffered to erect their heads among human beings.

[Johnson's concluding comment on *Cymbeline*:]

This play has many just sentiments, some natural dialogues, and some pleasing scenes, but they are obtained at the expense of much incongruity.

To remark the folly of the fiction, the absurdity of the conduct, the confusion of the names and manners of different times, and the impossibility of the events in any system of life, were to waste criticism upon unresisting imbecility, upon faults too evident for detection, and too gross for aggravation.

Hamlet

[On II, i, 114–117, Polonius' realization that he has been too suspicious in telling Ophelia to repel Hamlet:]

> By heavens,
> It is as proper to our age
> To cast beyond ourselves in our opinions
> As it is common for the younger sort
> To lack discretion.

This is not the remark of a weak man. The vice of age is too much suspicion. Men long accustomed to the wiles of life "cast" commonly "beyond themselves," let their cunning go further than reason can attend it. This is always the fault of a little mind, made artful by long commerce with the world.

[On the character of Polonius, as illustrated particularly by his speech to the King and Queen:

> My liege, and madam, to expostulate
> What majesty should be, what duty is,
> Why day is day, night night, and time is time,
> Where nothing but to waste night, day, and time.
>
> (II, ii, 86–89)

and on Warburton's interpretation, that the speech is primarily a satire on the artificial oratory admired in Shakespeare's time:]

This account of the character of Polonius, though it sufficiently reconciles the seeming inconsistency of so much wisdom with so much folly, does not perhaps correspond exactly to the ideas of our authour. The commentator makes the character of Polonius, a character only of manners, discriminated by properties superficial, accidental, and acquired. The poet intended a nobler delineation of a mixed character of manners and of nature. Polonius is a man bred in courts, exercised in business, stored with observation, confident of his knowledge, proud of his eloquence, and declining into dotage. His mode of oratory is truly represented as designed to ridicule the practice of those times, of prefaces that made no introduction, and of method that embarrassed rather than explained. This part of his character is accidental, the rest is natural. Such a man is positive and confident, because he knows that his mind was once strong, and knows not that it is become weak. Such a man excels in general principles, but fails in the particular application. He is knowing in retrospect, and ignorant in foresight. While he depends upon his memory, and can draw from his repositories of knowledge, he utters weighty sentences, and gives useful counsel; but as the mind in its enfeebled state cannot be kept long busy and intent, the old man is subject to sudden dereliction of his faculties, he loses the order of his ideas, and entangles himself in his own thoughts, till he recovers the leading principle, and falls again into his former train. This idea of dotage encroaching upon wisdom, will solve all the phaenomena of the character of Polonius.

[Johnson's concluding comment on *Hamlet*:]

If the dramas of Shakespeare were to be characterized, each by the particular excellence which distinguishes it from the rest, we must allow to the tragedy of *Hamlet* the praise of variety. The incidents are so numerous, that the argument of the play would make a long tale. The scenes are interchangeably diversified with merriment and solemnity; with merriment that includes judicious and instructive observations, and solemnity, not strained by poetical violence above the natural sentiments of man. New characters appear from time to time in continual succession, exhibiting various forms of life and particular modes of conversation. The pretended madness of Hamlet causes much mirth, the mournful distraction of Ophelia fills the heart with tenderness, and every personage produces the effect intended, from the apparition that in the first act chills the blood with horror, to the fop in the last, that exposes affectation to just contempt.

The conduct is perhaps not wholly secure against objections. The action is indeed for the most part in continual progression, but there are some scenes which neither forward nor retard it. Of the feigned madness of Hamlet there appears no adequate cause, for he does nothing which he might not have done with the reputation of sanity. He plays the madman most, when he treats Ophelia with so much rudeness, which seems to be useless and wanton cruelty.

Hamlet is, through the whole play, rather an instrument than an agent. After he has, by the stratagem of the play, convicted the King, he makes no attempt to punish him, and his death is at last effected by an incident which Hamlet has no part in producing.

The catastrophe is not very happily produced; the exchange of weapons is rather an expedient of necessity, than a stroke of art. A scheme might easily have been formed, to kill Hamlet with the dagger, and Laertes with the bowl.

The poet is accused of having shewn little regard to poetical justice, and may be charged with equal neglect of poetical probability. The apparition left the regions of the dead to little purpose; the revenge which he demands is not obtained but by the death of him that was required to take it; and the gratification which would arise from the destruction of an usurper and a murderer, is abated by the untimely death of Ophelia, the young, the beautiful, the harmless, and the pious.

Othello

[On Othello's explanation of how he won Desdemona's love (I, iii, 127ff), specifically

> Wherein of antres vast and deserts idle,
> Rough quarries, rocks, and hills whose heads touch heaven

(lines 139–40), which had been ridiculed by neoclassical critics:]

Whoever ridicules this account of the progress of love, shows his ignorance, not only of history, but of nature and manners. It is not wonder that, in any age, or in any nation, a lady, recluse, timorous, and delicate, should desire to hear of events and scenes which she could never see, and should admire the man who had endured dangers, and performed actions, which, however great, were yet magnified by her timidity.

[On Pope's suggested emendation to "deserts wild":]

Every mind is liable to absence and inadvertency, else Pope could never have rejected a word so poetically beautiful. "Idle" is an epithet used to express the infertility of the chaotic state, in the Saxon translation of the Pentateuch.

[On III, iii, 206–8, Iago's argument against Desdemona's honesty:]

> She did deceive her father, marrying you;
> And when she seem'd to shake and fear your looks,
> She lov'd them most.

This and the following argument of Iago ought to be deeply impressed on every reader. Deceit and falsehood, whatever conveniences they may for a time promise or produce, are, in the sum of life, obstacles to happiness. Those who profit by the cheat, distrust the deceiver, and the act by which kindness was sought, puts an end to confidence.

The same objection may be made with a lower degree of strength against the imprudent generosity of disproportionate marriages. When the first heat of passion is over, it is easily succeeded by suspicion, that the same violence of inclination which caused one irregularity, may stimulate to another; and those who have shewn, that their passions are too powerful for their prudence, will, with very slight appearances against them, be censured, as not very likely to restrain them by their virtue.

[Johnson's concluding comment on *Othello*:]

The beauties of this play impress themselves so strongly upon the attention of the reader, that they can draw no aid from critical illustration. The fiery openness of Othello, magnanimous, artless, and credulous, boundless in his confidence, ardent in his affection, inflexible in his resolution, and obdurate in his revenge; the cool malignity of Iago, silent in his resentment, subtle in his designs, and studious at once of his interest and his vengeance; the soft simplicity of Desdemona, confident of merit, and conscious of innocence, her artless perseverance in her suit, and her slowness to suspect that she can be suspected, are such proof of Shakespeare's skill in human nature, as, I suppose, it is vain to seek in any modern writer. The gradual progress which Iago makes in the Moor's conviction, and the circumstances which he employs to inflame him, are so artfully natural, that, though it will perhaps not be said of him as he says of himself, that he is "a man not easily jealous," yet we cannot but pity him when at last we find him "perplexed in the extreme."

There is always danger lest wickedness conjoined with abilities should steal upon esteem, though it misses of approbation; but the character of Iago is so conducted, that he is from the first scene to the last hated and despised.

Even the inferior characters of this play would be very conspicuous in any other piece, not only for their justness but their strength. Cassio is brave, benevolent, and honest, ruined only by his want of stubbornness to resist an insidious invitation. Rodorigo's suspicious credulity, and impatient submission to the cheats which he sees practised upon him, and which by persuasion he suffers to be repeated, exhibit a strong picture of a weak mind betrayed by unlawful desires, to a false friend; and the virtue of Aemilia is such as we often find, worn loosely, but not cast off, easy to commit small crimes, but quickened and alarmed at atrocious villainies.

The scenes from the beginning to the end are busy, varied by happy interchanges, and regularly promoting the progression of the story; and the narrative in the end, though it tells but what is known already, yet is necessary to produce the death of Othello.

Had the scene opened in Cyprus, and the preceding incidents been occasionally related, there had been little wanting to a drama of the most exact and scrupulous regularity.

From Lives of the Poets

[When a Scottish firm issued a cheap edition of the standard English poets, a group of London booksellers resolved to protect their copyrights by bringing out a better edition, enhanced with biographical prefaces by Johnson. It was to start with Abraham Cowley, the last of the metaphysical poets, and end with Thomas Gray, a contemporary who had died in 1771. Johnson accepted their selection of poets, only adding four unimportant names, and originally planned to write "little prefaces." But many of these expanded as he grew interested in the work. The final great collection brought to a happy culmination Johnson's lifelong interest in biography and literature.

Though committed to truthfulness, Johnson was not so scrupulous a researcher as his disciple Boswell: he followed the best biographical accounts available and seldom bothered to check facts himself. Hence there are minor errors in dates and such in the *Lives*.]

John Milton
1608-1674

The life of Milton has been already written in so many forms, and with such minute inquiry, that I might perhaps more properly have contented myself with the addition of a few notes to Mr. Fenton's elegant abridgment,[1] but that a new narrative was thought necessary to the uniformity of this edition.

John Milton was by birth a gentleman, descended from the proprietors of Milton near Thame in Oxfordshire, one of whom forfeited his estate in the times of York and Lancaster. Which side he took I know not; his descendant inherited no veneration for the White Rose.[2]

His grandfather John was keeper of the forest of Shotover, a zealous papist, who disinherited his son because he had forsaken the religion of his ancestors.

His father, John, who was the son disinherited, had recourse for his support to the profession of a scrivener. He was a man eminent for his skill in music, many of his compositions being still to be found: and his reputation in his profession was such that he grew rich, and retired to an estate. He had probably more than common literature, as his son addresses him in one of his most elaborate Latin poems. He married a gentlewoman of the name of Caston, a Welsh family, by whom he had two sons, John the poet, and Christopher who studied the law, and adhered, as the law taught him, to the King's party, for which he was awhile persecuted: but having, by his brother's interest, obtained permission to live in quiet, he supported himself so honorably by chamber-practice,[3]

---

[1] Elijah Fenton's life of Milton, compiled for his edition of *Paradise Lost* (1725).
[2] Johnson thinks of the Stuarts (Charles I, etc.) as descendants of the House of York, symbolized by the White Rose.
[3] *chamber-practice:* practice in chambers (one's office) rather than in court.

that soon after the accession of King James, he was knighted and made a judge; but his constitution being too weak for business, he retired before any disreputable compliance became necessary.[4]

He had likewise a daughter Anne, whom he married with a considerable fortune to Edward Phillips, who came from Shrewsbury, and rose in the Crown Office to be secondary; by him she had two sons, John and Edward, who were educated by the poet, and from whom is derived the only authentic account of his domestic manners.[5]

John, the poet, was born in his father's house, at the Spread Eagle in Bread Street, December 9, 1608, between six and seven in the morning. His father appears to have been very solicitous about his education; for he was instructed at first by private tuition under the care of Thomas Young, who was afterwards chaplain to the English merchants at Hamburg; and of whom we have reason to think well, since his scholar considered him as worthy of an epistolary elegy.

He was then sent to St. Paul's School, under the care of Mr. Gill; and removed, in the beginning of his sixteenth year, to Christ's College in Cambridge, where he entered a sizar, February 12, 1624.[6]

He was at this time eminently skilled in the Latin tongue; and he himself, by annexing the dates to his first compositions, a boast of which the learned Politian had given him an example, seems to commend the earliness of his own proficiency to the notice of posterity. But the products of his vernal fertility have been surpassed by many, and particularly by his contemporary Cowley. Of the powers of the mind it is difficult to form an estimate: many have excelled Milton in their first essays who never rose to works like *Paradise Lost*.

At fifteen, a date which he uses till he is sixteen,[7] he translated or versified two Psalms, 114 and 136, which he thought worthy of the public eye; but they raise no great

---

[4] The tyrannical James II (reigned 1685–88) tried to sway judges' decisions.
[5] Edward wrote a biography of Milton for his edition of *Letters of State, written by Mr. John Milton* (1694).
[6] Actually, he entered as a commoner (a regular student), and in 1625.
[7] I.e., Milton considers himself fifteen rather than "in his sixteenth year," the usual phrase.

expectations; they would in any numerous school have obtained praise, but not excited wonder.

Many of his Elegies appear to have been written in his eighteenth year, by which it appears that he had then read the Roman authors with very nice discernment. I once heard Mr. Hampton, the translator of Polybius, remark what I think is true, that Milton was the first Englishman who, after the revival of letters, wrote Latin verses with classic elegance. If any exceptions can be made, they are very few: Haddon and Ascham, the pride of Elizabeth's reign, however they may have succeeded in prose, no sooner attempt verses than they provoke derision. If we produced anything worthy of notice before the Elegies of Milton, it was perhaps Alabaster's *Roxana.*

Of these exercises which the rules of the University required, some were published by him in his maturer years. They had been undoubtedly applauded: for they were such as few can perform: yet there is reason to suspect that he was regarded in his College with no great fondness. That he obtained no fellowship is certain; but the unkindness with which he was treated was not merely negative. I am ashamed to relate what I fear is true, that Milton was one of the last students in either university that suffered the public indignity of corporal correction.

It was, in the violence of controversial hostility, objected to him that he was expelled: this he steadily denies, and it was apparently not true; but it seems plain from his own verses to Diodati,[8] that he had incurred "rustication," a temporary dismission into the country, with perhaps the loss of a term . . .

He took both the usual degrees; that of Bachelor in 1628, and that of Master in 1632; but he left the university with no kindness for its institution, alienated either by the injudicious severity of his governors, or his own captious perverseness. The cause cannot now be known, but the effect appears in his writings. His scheme of education, inscribed to Hartlib,[9] supersedes all academical instruction, being intended to comprise the whole time which men usually spend in literature, from their entrance upon grammar, "till they proceed, as it

[8] Charles Diodati was a close friend of Milton's.
[9] Milton's *Of Education* (1644) is addressed to the writer Samuel Hartlib.

is called, masters of arts." And in his discourse *On the Likeliest Way to Remove Hirelings out of the Church*, he ingeniously proposes that

> the profits of the lands forfeited by the act for superstitious uses should be applied to such academies all over the land, where languages and arts may be taught together; so that youth may be at once brought up to a competency of learning and an honest trade, by which means such of them as had the gift, being enabled to support themselves (without tithes) by the latter, may, by the help of the former, become worthy preachers.

One of his objections to academical education, as it was then conducted, is that men designed for orders in the Church were permitted to act plays, "writhing and unboning their clergy limbs to all the antic and dishonest gestures of Trinculos, buffoons and bawds, prostituting the shame of that ministry which they had, or were near having, to the eyes of courtiers and court-ladies, their grooms and mademoiselles."

This is sufficiently peevish in a man, who, when he mentions his exile from the college, relates, with great luxuriance, the compensation which the pleasures of the theater afford him. Plays were therefore only criminal when they were acted by academics.

He went to the university with a design of entering into the church, but in time altered his mind; for he declared that whoever became a clergyman must "subscribe slave, and take an oath withal, which unless he took with a conscience that could retch, he must straight perjure himself. He thought it better to prefer a blameless silence before the [sacred] office of speaking, bought and begun with servitude and forswearing."[10]

These expressions are, I find, applied to the subscription of the Articles;[11] but it seems more probable that they relate to canonical obedience. I know not any of the Articles which seem to thwart his opinions; but the thoughts of obedience, whether canonical or civil, raised his indignation.

---

[10] *The Reason of Church Government* (1642), Bk. II.
[11] Anglican clergymen were required to subscribe to the Thirty-nine Articles, points of doctrine of the Church of England.

His unwillingness to engage in the ministry, perhaps not yet advanced to a settled resolution of declining it, appears in a letter to one of his friends, who had reproved his suspended and dilatory life, which he seems to have imputed to an insatiable curiosity, and fantastic luxury of various knowledge. To this he writes a cool and plausible answer, in which he endeavors to persuade him that the delay proceeds not from the delights of desultory study, but from the desire of obtaining more fitness for his task; and that he goes on, "not taking thought of being late, so it give advantage to be more fit."

When he left the university, he returned to his father, then residing at Horton in Buckinghamshire, with whom he lived five years; in which time he is said to have read all the Greek and Latin writers. With what limitations this universality is to be understood, who shall inform us?

It might be supposed that he who read so much should have done nothing else; but Milton found time to write the masque of *Comus*, which was presented at Ludlow, then the residence of the Lord President of Wales, in 1634; and had the honor of being acted by the Earl of Bridgewater's sons and daughters.[12] The fiction is derived from Homer's Circe;[13] but we never can refuse to any modern the liberty of borrowing from Homer. . . .

His next production was "Lycidas," an elegy, written in 1637, on the death of Mr. King, the son of Sir John King, secretary for Ireland in the time of Elizabeth, James, and Charles. King was much a favorite at Cambridge, and many of the wits joined to do honor to his memory. Milton's acquaintance with the Italian writers may be discovered by a mixture of longer and shorter verses, according to the rules of Tuscan poetry, and his malignity to the Church by some lines which are interpreted as threatening its extermination.

He is supposed about this time to have written his "Arcades"; for while he lived at Horton he used sometimes to steal from his studies a few days, which he spent at Harefield, the house of the Countess Dowager of Derby, where the "Arcades" made part of a dramatic entertainment.

---

[12] The Lord President of Wales was the Earl of Bridgewater.
[13] Circe, who turned men into pigs (*Odyssey*, Bk. X), was a symbol of sensuality.

He began now to grow weary of the country; and had some purpose of taking chambers in the Inns of Court, when the death of his mother set him at liberty to travel, for which he obtained his father's consent, and Sir Henry Wotton's directions, with the celebrated precept of prudence, "i pensieri stretti, ed il viso sciolto," "thoughts close, and looks loose."

In 1638 he left England, and went first to Paris; where, by the favor of Lord Scudamore, he had the opportunity of visiting Grotius,[14] then residing at the French court as ambassador from Christina of Sweden. From Paris he hasted into Italy, of which he had with particular diligence studied the language and literature; and, though he seems to have intended a very quick perambulation of the country, stayed two months at Florence; where he found his way into the academies, and produced his compositions with such applause as appears to have exalted him in his own opinion, and confirmed him in the hope, that, "by labor and intense study, which," says he, "I take to be my portion in this life, joined with a strong propensity of nature," he might "leave something so written to aftertimes, as they should not willingly let it die."[15]

It appears, in all his writings, that he had the usual concomitant of great abilities, a lofty and steady confidence in himself, perhaps not without some contempt of others; for scarcely any man ever wrote so much, and praised so few. Of his praise he was very frugal; as he set its value high, and considered his mention of a name as a security against the waste of time, and a certain preservative from oblivion.

At Florence he could not indeed complain that his merit wanted distinction. Carlo Dati presented him with an encomiastic inscription, in the tumid lapidary style; and Francini wrote him an ode, of which the first stanza is only empty noise; the rest are perhaps too diffuse on common topics, but the last is natural and beautiful.

From Florence he went to Siena, and from Siena to Rome, where he was again received with kindness by the learned and the great. Holstenius, the keeper of the Vatican Library, who had resided three years at Oxford, introduced him to Cardinal Barberini; and he, at a musical entertainment, waited

---

[14] Hugo Grotius, the founder of international law.
[15] *The Reason of Church Government*, Bk. II.

for him at the door, and led him by the hand into the assembly. Here Selvaggi praised him in a distich, and Salsilli in a tetrastich; neither of them of much value.[16] The Italians were gainers by this literary commerce; for the encomiums with which Milton repaid Salsilli, though not secure against a stern grammarian, turn the balance indisputably in Milton's favor.

Of these Italian testimonies, poor as they are, he was proud enough to publish them before his poems; though he says, he cannot be suspected but to have known that they were said "non tam de se, quam supra se [not so much about him as above him]."

At Rome, as at Florence, he stayed only two months; a time indeed sufficient if he desired only to ramble with an explainer of its antiquities or to view palaces and count pictures, but certainly too short for the contemplation of learning, policy, or manners.

From Rome he passed on to Naples, in company of a hermit; a companion from whom little could be expected, yet to him Milton owed his introduction to Manso, Marquis of Villa, who had been before the patron of Tasso. Manso was enough delighted with his accomplishments to honor him with a sorry distich, in which he commends him for everything but his religion; and Milton, in return, addressed him in a Latin poem, which must have raised an high opinion of English elegance and literature.

His purpose was now to have visited Sicily and Greece, but hearing of the differences between the king and parliament, he thought it proper to hasten home rather than pass his life in foreign amusements while his countrymen were contending for their rights. He therefore came back to Rome, though the merchants informed him of plots laid against him by the Jesuits, for the liberty of his conversations on religion. He had sense enough to judge that there was no danger, and therefore kept on his way, and acted as before, neither obtruding nor shunning controversy. He had perhaps given some offense by visiting Galileo, then a prisoner in the Inquisition for philosophical heresy; and at Naples he was told by Manso that, by his declarations on religious questions, he had excluded him-

---

[16] Dati's inscription, Francini's ode, and the epigrams of Selvaggi and Salsilli are prefixed to Milton's Latin poems (1645).

self from some distinctions which he should otherwise have paid him. But such conduct, though it did not please, was yet sufficiently safe; and Milton stayed two months more at Rome, and went on to Florence without molestation.

From Florence he visited Lucca. He afterwards went to Venice; and having sent away a collection of music and other books traveled to Geneva, which he probably considered as the metropolis of orthodoxy. Here he reposed, as in a congenial element, and became acquainted with John Diodati and Frederick Spanheim, two learned professors of divinity. From Geneva he passed through France, and came home, after an absence of a year and three months.

At his return he heard of the death of his friend Charles Diodati: a man whom it is reasonable to suppose of great merit, since he was thought by Milton worthy of a poem, entitled *Epitaphium Damonis* written with the common but childish imitation of pastoral life.

He now hired a lodging at the house of one Russell, a tailor in St. Bride's Churchyard, and undertook the education of John and Edward Phillips, his sister's sons. Finding his rooms too little, he took a house and garden in Aldersgate Street, which was not then so much out of the world as it is now; and chose his dwelling at the upper end of a passage that he might avoid the noise of the street. Here he received more boys, to be boarded and instructed.

Let not our veneration for Milton forbid us to look with some degree of merriment on great promises and small performance, on the man who hastens home because his countrymen are contending for their liberty, and, when he reaches the scene of action, vapors away his patriotism in a private boarding school. This is the period of his life from which all his biographers seem inclined to shrink. They are unwilling that Milton should be degraded to a schoolmaster; but, since it cannot be denied that he taught boys, one finds out that he taught for nothing, and another that his motive was only zeal for the propagation of learning and virtue; and all tell what they do not know to be true, only to excuse an act which no wise man will consider as in itself disgraceful. His father was alive; his allowance was not ample; and he supplied its deficiencies by an honest and useful employment.

It is told that in the art of education he performed wonders; and a formidable list is given of the authors, Greek and Latin, that were read in Aldersgate Street by youth between ten and fifteen or sixteen years of age. Those who tell or receive these stories should consider that nobody can be taught faster than he can learn. The speed of the horseman must be limited by the power of his horse. Every man that has ever undertaken to instruct others can tell what slow advances he has been able to make, and how much patience it requires to recall vagrant inattention, to stimulate sluggish indifference, and to rectify absurd misapprehension.

The purpose of Milton, as it seems, was to teach something more solid than the common literature of schools, by reading those authors that treat of physical subjects; such as the georgic,[17] and astronomical treatises of the ancients. This was a scheme of improvement which seems to have busied many literary projectors[18] of that age. Cowley, who had more means than Milton of knowing what was wanting to the embellishments of life, formed the same plan of education in his imaginary college.

But the truth is that the knowledge of external nature, and the sciences which that knowledge requires or includes, are not the great or the frequent business of the human mind. Whether we provide for action or conversation, whether we wish to be useful or pleasing, the first requisite is the religious and moral knowledge of right and wrong; the next is an acquaintance with the history of mankind, and with those examples which may be said to embody truth and prove by events the reasonableness of opinions. Prudence and justice are virtues and excellences of all times and of all places; we are perpetually moralists, but we are geometricians only by chance. Our intercourse with intellectual nature is necessary; our speculations upon matter are voluntary and at leisure. Physiological learning is of such rare emergence that one man may know another half his life without being able to estimate his skill in hydrostatics or astronomy, but his moral and prudential character immediately appears.

Those authors, therefore, are to be read at schools that supply most axioms of prudence, most principles of moral truth, and most materials for conversation; and these purposes are best served by poets, orators, and historians.

Let me not be censured for this digression as pedantic or paradoxical; for if I have Milton against me, I have Socrates

---

[17] *georgic:* agricultural.
[18] *projectors:* innovators of new methods (often derogatory).

on my side. It was his labor to turn philosophy from the study of nature to speculations upon life, but the innovators whom I oppose are turning off attention from life to nature. They seem to think that we are placed here to watch the growth of plants, or the motions of the stars. Socrates was rather of opinion that what we had to learn was how to do good, and avoid evil. . . .

Of institutions we may judge by their effects. From this wonder-working academy, I do not know that there ever proceeded any man very eminent for knowledge; its only genuine product, I believe, is a small history of poetry, written in Latin by his nephew Phillips, of which perhaps none of my readers has ever heard.

That in his school, as in everything else which he undertook, he labored with great diligence, there is no reason for doubting. One part of his method deserves general imitation. He was careful to instruct his scholars in religion. Every Sunday was spent upon theology, of which he dictated a short system, gathered from the writers that were then fashionable in the Dutch universities.

He set his pupils an example of hard study and spare diet; only now and then he allowed himself to pass a day of festivity and indulgence with some gay gentlemen of Gray's Inn.

He now began to engage in the controversies of the times, and lent his breath to blow the flames of contention. In 1641 he published a treatise *Of Reformation*, in two books, against the established Church: being willing to help the Puritans, who were, he says, "inferior to the prelates in learning."

Hall, Bishop of Norwich, had published an *Humble Remonstrance*, in defense of episcopacy; to which in 1641 ministers, of whose names the first letters made the celebrated word *Smectymnuus*, gave their answer. Of this answer a confutation was attempted by the learned Ussher;[19] and to the confutation Milton published a reply, entitled, *Of Prelatical Episcopacy, and whether It May Be Deduced from the Apostolical Times, by Virtue of those Testimonies which are Alleged to that Purpose in some Late Treatises, One whereof Goes under the Name of James Lord Bishop of Armagh.*

I have transcribed this title, to show, by his contemptuous mention of Ussher, that he had now adopted the puritanical

---

[19] James Ussher was the Archbishop of Armagh.

savageness of manners. His next work was *The Reason of Church Government Urged against Prelacy, by Mr. John Milton,* 1642. In this book he discovers, not with ostentatious exultation, but with calm confidence, his high opinion of his own powers; and promises to undertake something, he yet knows not what, that may be of use and honor to his country. "This," says he, "is not to be obtained but by devout prayers to that Eternal Spirit that can enrich with all utterance and knowledge, and sends out his seraphim with the hallowed fire of his altar, to touch and purify the lips of whom he pleases. To this must be added, industrious and select reading, steady observation, and insight into all seemly and generous arts and affairs; till which in some measure be compassed, I refuse not to sustain this expectation." From a promise like this, at once fervid, pious, and rational, might be expected the *Paradise Lost.*

He published the same year two more pamphlets, upon the same question. To one of his antagonists, who affirms that he was "vomited out of the university," he answers, in general terms: "The Fellows of the College wherein I spent some years, at my parting, after I had taken two degrees, as the manner is, signified many times how much better it would content them that I should stay. . . . As for the common approbation or dislike of that place, as now it is, that I should esteem or disesteem myself the more for that, too simple is the answerer, if he think to obtain with me. Of small practice were the physician who could not judge, by what she and her sister[20] have of long time vomited, that the worser stuff she strongly keeps in her stomach, but the better she is ever kecking at,[21] and is queasy: she vomits now out of sickness; but before it be well with her, she must vomit by strong physic. . . . The University, in the time of her better health, and my younger judgment, I never greatly admired, but now much less."

This is surely the language of a man who thinks that he has been injured. He proceeds to describe the course of his conduct, and the train of his thoughts; and, because he has been suspected of incontinence, gives an account of his own purity: "That if I be justly charged," says he, "with this crime, it may come upon me with tenfold shame."

---

[20] *sister:* i.e., Oxford University.
[21] *kecking at:* rejecting with disgust.

The style of his piece is rough, and such perhaps was that of his antagonist. This roughness he justifies, by great examples, in a long digression. Sometimes he tries to be humorous: "Lest I should take him for some chaplain in hand, some squire of the body to his prelate, one who serves not at the altar only but at the Court-cupboard,[22] he will bestow on us a pretty model of himself; and sets me out half a dozen phthisical mottoes, wherever he had them, hopping short in the measure of convulsion fits; in which labor the agony of his wit having scaped narrowly, instead of well-sized periods, he greets us with a quantity of thumb-ring posies. . . . And thus ends this section, or rather dissection of himself." Such is the controversial merriment of Milton; his gloomy seriousness is yet more offensive. Such is his malignity, "that hell grows darker at his frown."[23]

His father, after Reading was taken by Essex,[24] came to reside in his house; and his school increased. At Whitsuntide, in his thirty-fifth year, he married Mary, the daughter of Mr. Powell, a Justice of the Peace in Oxfordshire. He brought her to town with him, and expected all the advantages of a conjugal life. The lady, however, seems not much to have delighted in the pleasures of spare diet and hard study; for, as Phillips relates, "having for a month led a philosophical life, after having been used at home to a great house, and much company and joviality, her friends, possibly by her own desire, made earnest suit to have her company the remaining part of the summer; which was granted, upon a promise of her return at Michaelmas."

Milton was too busy to much miss his wife; he pursued his studies; and now and then visited the Lady Margaret Ley, whom he has mentioned in one of his sonnets. At last Michaelmas arrived; but the lady had no intention to return to the sullen gloom of her husband's habitation, and therefore very willingly forgot her promise. He sent her a letter, but had no answer; he sent more with the same success. It could be alleged that letters miscarry; he therefore dispatched a messenger, being by this time too angry to go himself. His mes-

---

[22] Milton calls the opposing author a chaplain to the archbishop, or rather a personal servant, one who serves not at the altar but at the sideboard (i.e., waits at table).
[23] A clever application of *Paradise Lost*, II, 719–20, where the description applies to Satan.
[24] The Earl of Essex, a Parliamentary general, captured Reading in 1643.

senger was sent back with some contempt. The family of the lady were Cavaliers.[25]

In a man whose opinion of his own merit was like Milton's, less provocation than this might have raised violent resentment. Milton soon determined to repudiate her for disobedience; and, being one of those who could easily find arguments to justify inclination, published (in 1644) *The Doctrine and Discipline of Divorce*; which was followed by *The Judgment of Martin Bucer, concerning Divorce*; and the next year, his *Tetrachordon: Expositions upon the Four Chief Places of Scripture which Treat of Marriage.*

This innovation was opposed, as might be expected, by the clergy, who, then holding their famous assembly at Westminster, procured that the author should be called before the Lords; "but that House," says Wood, "whether approving the doctrine, or not favoring his accusers, did soon dismiss him."

There seems not to have been much written against him, nor anything by any writers of eminence. The antagonist that appeared is styled by him, "a servingman turned solicitor." Howell in his *Letters* mentions the new doctrine with contempt; and it was, I suppose, thought more worthy of derision than of confutation. He complains of his neglect in two sonnets, of which the first is contemptible, and the second not excellent.

From this time it is observed that he became an enemy to the Presbyterians, whom he had favored before.[26] He that changes his party by his humor is not more virtuous than he that changes it by his interest; he loves himself rather than truth.

His wife and her relations now found that Milton was not an unresisting sufferer of injuries; and perceiving that he had begun to put his doctrine in practice, by courting a young woman of great accomplishments, the daughter of one Doctor Davis, who was however not ready to comply, they resolved to endeavor a reunion. He went sometimes to the house of one Blackborough, his relation, in the lane of St. Martin's-le-Grand, and at one of his usual visits was surprised to see his wife come from another room, and implore forgiveness on

---

[25] *Cavaliers:* Royalists, opposed to the Parliamentary party in the Civil War.
[26] He rejected the church discipline of the Presbyterians and became an Independent.

her knees. He resisted her entreaties for a while; "but partly," says Phillips, "his own generous nature, more inclinable to reconciliation than to perseverance in anger or revenge, and partly the strong intercession of friends on both sides, soon brought him to an act of oblivion and a firm league of peace." It were injurious to omit that Milton afterwards received her father and her brothers in his own house, when they were distressed, with other Royalists.

He published about the same time his *Areopagitica, a Speech of Mr. John Milton for the Liberty of Unlicensed Printing.* The danger of such unbounded liberty, and the danger of bounding it, have produced a problem in the science of government, which human understanding seems hitherto unable to solve. If nothing may be published but what civil authority shall have previously approved, power must always be the standard of truth; if every dreamer of innovations may propagate his projects, there can be no settlement; if every murmurer at government may teach his follies, there can be no religion. The remedy against these evils is to punish the authors; for it is yet allowed that every society may punish, though not prevent, the publication of opinions which that society shall think pernicious; but this punishment, though it may crush the author, promotes the book; and it seems not more reasonable to leave the right of printing unrestrained, because writers may be afterwards censured, than it would be to sleep with doors unbolted, because by our laws we can hang a thief.

But whatever were his engagements, civil or domestic, poetry was never long out of his thoughts. About this time (1645) a collection of his Latin and English poems appeared, in which the "Allegro" and "Penseroso," with some others, were first published.

He had taken a larger house in Barbican for the reception of scholars; but the numerous relations of his wife, to whom he generously granted refuge for a while, occupied his rooms. In time, however, they went away; "and the house again," says Phillips, "now looked like a house of the Muses only, though the accession of scholars was not great. Possibly his having proceeded so far in the education of youth, may have been the occasion of his adversaries calling him pedagogue and schoolmaster; whereas it is well known he never set up for a public school to teach all the young fry of a parish, but only was willing to impart his learning and knowledge to relations and the sons of gentlemen who were his intimate friends; and that neither his writings nor his way of teaching ever savored in the least of pedantry."

Thus laboriously does his nephew extenuate what cannot be denied, and what might be confessed without disgrace. Milton was not a man who could become mean by a mean employment. This, however, his warmest friends seem not to have found; they therefore shift and palliate. He did not sell literature to all comers at an open shop; he was a chamber-milliner, and measured his commodities only to his friends.

Phillips, evidently impatient of viewing him in this state of degradation, tells us that it was not long continued; and, to raise his character again, has a mind to invest him with military splendor: "He is much mistaken," he says, "if there was not about this time a design of making him an adjutant-general in Sir William Waller's army. But the new-modeling of the army proved an obstruction to the design." An event cannot be set at a much greater distance than by having been only "designed, about some time," if a man "be not much mistaken." Milton shall be a pedagogue no longer; for, if Phillips be not much mistaken, somebody at some time designed him for a soldier.

About the time that the army was new-modeled (1645) he removed to a smaller house in Holborn, which opened backward into Lincoln's Inn Fields. He is not known to have published anything afterwards till the King's death, when, finding his murderers condemned by the Presbyterians, he wrote a treatise to justify it, and "to compose the minds of the people."

He made some *Remarks on the Articles of Peace between Ormonde and the Irish Rebels*. While he contented himself to write, he perhaps did only what his conscience dictated; and if he did not very vigilantly watch the influence of his own passions, and the gradual prevalence of opinions, first willingly admitted then habitually indulged, if objections, by being overlooked, were forgotten, and desire superinduced conviction, he yet shared only the common weakness of mankind, and might be no less sincere than his opponents. But as faction seldom leaves a man honest, however it might find him, Milton is suspected of having interpolated the book called *Eikon Basilike*, which the Council of State, to whom he was now made Latin Secretary, employed him to censure, by inserting a prayer taken from Sidney's *Arcadia*, and imputing

it to the King; whom he charges, in his *Eikonoklastes*, with
the use of this prayer as with a heavy crime, in the indecent
language with which prosperity had emboldened the advocates
for rebellion to insult all that is venerable or great: "Who
would have imagined so little fear in him of the true all-seeing
Deity—as, immediately before his death, to pop into the hands
of the grave bishop that attended him, as a special relic of his
saintly exercises, a prayer stolen word for word from the
mouth of a heathen woman praying to a heathen god?"[27]

The papers which the King gave to Dr. Juxon on the scaf-
fold the regicides took away, so that they were at least the
publishers of this prayer; and Dr. Birch, who had examined
the question with great care, was inclined to think them the
forgers. The use of it by adaptation was innocent; and they
who could so noisily censure it, with a little extension of
their malice could contrive what they wanted to accuse.

King Charles the Second, being now sheltered in Holland,
employed Salmasius, Professor of Polite Learning at Leyden,
to write a defense of his father and of monarchy; and, to excite
his industry, gave him, as was reported, a hundred jacobuses.
Salmasius was a man of skill in languages, knowledge of
antiquity, and sagacity of emendatory criticism, almost ex-
ceeding all hope of human attainment; and having, by exces-
sive praises, been confirmed in great confidence of himself,
though he probably had not much considered the principles
of society or the rights of government, undertook the employment without distrust of his own qualifications; and, as
his expedition in writing was wonderful, in 1649 published
Defensio Regis.

To this Milton was required to write a sufficient answer;
which he performed (1651) in such a manner, that Hobbes
declared himself unable to decide whose language was best, or
whose arguments were worst. In my opinion, Milton's periods
are smoother, neater, and more pointed; but he delights
himself with teasing his adversary as much as with confuting
him. He makes a foolish allusion of Salmasius, whose doctrine
he considers as servile and unmanly, to the stream of Salmacis,
which whoever entered left half his virility behind him. Salmasius was a Frenchman, and was unhappily married to a

---

[27] *Eikon Basilike (The King's Image)*, which glorified Charles I, was
published immediately after his execution in 1649. Milton attacked it
in *Eikonoklastes (The Image Breaker)*, but probably did not interpolate
the prayer from Sidney.

scold. "Tu es Gallus," says Milton, "et, ut aiunt, nimium gallinaceus [you are a Frenchman and, so they say, excessively henpecked]." But his supreme pleasure is to tax his adversary, so renowned for criticism, with vicious[28] Latin. He opens his book with telling that he has used *persona*, which, according to Milton, signifies only a *mask*, in a sense not known to the Romans, by applying it as we apply *person*. But as Nemesis is always on the watch, it is memorable that he has enforced the charge of a solecism by an expression in itself grossly solecistical, when, for one of those supposed blunders, he says, as Ker, and I think some one before him, has remarked, "propino te grammatistis tuis *vapulandum* [I turn you over to your fellow grammarians to be beaten]." From *vapulo*, which has a passive sense, *vapulandus* can never be derived. No man forgets his original trade: the rights of nations, and of kings, sink into questions of grammar, if grammarians discuss them.

Milton when he undertook this answer was weak of body and dim of sight; but his will was forward, and what was wanting of health was supplied by zeal. He was rewarded with a thousand pounds, and his book was much read; for paradox, recommended by spirit and elegance, easily gains attention; and he who told every man that he was equal to his king could hardly want an audience.

That the performance of Salmasius was not dispersed with equal rapidity, or read with equal eagerness, is very credible. He taught only the stale doctrine of authority and the unpleasing duty of submission; and he had been so long not only the monarch but the tyrant of literature that almost all mankind were delighted to find him defied and insulted by a new name, not yet considered as anyone's rival. If Christina, as is said, commended the *Defense of the People*,[29] her purpose must be to torment Salmasius, who was then at her Court; for neither her civil station nor her natural character could dispose her to favor the doctrine, who was by birth a queen, and by temper despotic.

That Salmasius was, from the appearance of Milton's book, treated with neglect, there is not much proof; but to a man so long accustomed to admiration, a little praise of his antagonist would be sufficiently offensive, and might incline

---

[28] *vicious:* faulty.
[29] Milton's answer to Salmasius, *Pro Populo Anglicano Defensio.*

him to leave Sweden, from which, however, he was dismissed, not with any mark of contempt, but with a train of attendance scarce less than regal.

He prepared a reply, which, left as it was imperfect, was published by his son in the year of the Restoration. In the beginning, being probably most in pain for his Latinity, he endeavors to defend his use of the word *persona*; but, if I remember right, he misses a better authority than any that he has found, that of Juvenal in his fourth Satire:

> Quid agas cum dira et foedior omni
> Crimine *persona* est?

[What can you do when the person himself is more foul and monstrous than any charge you can bring against him?]

As Salmasius reproached Milton with losing his eyes in the quarrel, Milton delighted himself with the belief that he had shortened Salmasius's life, and both perhaps with more malignity than reason. Salmasius died at the Spa, September 3, 1653; and as controvertists are commonly said to be killed by their last dispute, Milton was flattered with the credit of destroying him.

Cromwell had now dismissed the parliament by the authority of which he had destroyed monarchy, and commenced monarch himself, under the title of Protector, but with kingly and more than kingly power. That his authority was lawful never was pretended; he himself founded his right only in necessity; but Milton, having now tasted the honey of public employment, would not return to hunger and philosophy, but, continuing to exercise his office under a manifest usurpation, betrayed to his power that liberty which he had defended. Nothing can be more just than that rebellion should end in slavery; that he, who had justified the murder of his king, for some acts which to him seemed unlawful, should now sell his services, and his flatteries, to a tyrant, of whom it was evident that he could do nothing lawful.

He had now been blind for some years; but his vigor of intellect was such that he was not disabled to discharge his office of Latin Secretary or continue his controversies. His mind was too eager to be diverted, and too strong to be subdued.

About this time his first wife died in childbed having left him three daughters. As he probably did not much love her, he did not long continue the appearance of lamenting her; but after a short time married Katherine, the daughter of one Captain Woodcock of Hackney; a woman doubtless educated in opinions like his own. She died within a year, of childbirth, or some distemper that followed it; and her husband has honored her memory with a poor sonnet.

The first reply to Milton's *Defensio Populi* was published in 1651, called *Apologia pro Rege et Populo Anglicano, contra Johannis Polypragmatici (alias Miltoni) Defensionem Destructivam Regis et Populi* [*Defense of the King and the English People, against John Busybody's (alias Milton's) Defense, which Would Destroy King and People*]. Of this the author was not known; but Milton and his nephew Phillips, under whose name he published an answer so much corrected by him that it might be called his own, imputed it to Bramhall; and, knowing him no friend to regicides, thought themselves at liberty to treat him as if they had known what they only suspected.

Next year appeared *Regii Sanguinis Clamor ad Coelum* [*The Cry of the King's Blood to Heaven*]. Of this the author was Peter du Moulin, who was afterwards prebendary of Canterbury; but Morus, or More, a French minister, having the care of its publication, was treated as the writer by Milton in his *Defensio Secunda*, and overwhelmed by such violence of invective that he began to shrink under the tempest, and gave his persecutors the means of knowing the true author. du Moulin was now in great danger; but Milton's pride operated against his malignity; and both he and his friends were more willing that du Moulin should escape than that he should be convicted of mistake.

In this *Second Defense* he shows that his eloquence is not merely satirical; the rudeness of his invective is equalled by the grossness of his flattery [of Cromwell]. . . .

Caesar, when he assumed the perpetual dictatorship, had not more servile or more elegant flattery. A translation may show its servility; but its elegance is less attainable. Having exposed the unskillfulness or selfishness of the former government, "We were left," says Milton, "to ourselves: the whole national interest fell into your hands, and subsists only in your abilities. To your virtue, overpowering and resistless, every man gives way, except some who, without equal qualifications, aspire to equal honors, who envy the distinctions of merit greater than their own; or who have yet to learn that in the coalition of human society nothing is more pleasing to God or more agreeable to reason than that the highest mind should have the sovereign power. Such, Sir, are you by general confession; such are the things achieved by you, the greatest and most glorious of our countrymen, the director of our public councils, the leader of unconquered armies, the father of your country; for by that title does every good man hail you, with sincere and voluntary praise."

Next year, having defended all that wanted defense, he found leisure to defend himself. He undertook his own vindication against More, whom he declares in his title to be justly called the author of the *Regii Sanguinis Clamor*. In this there is no want of vehemence nor eloquence, nor does he forget his wonted wit. "Morus es? an Momus? an uterque idem est [Are you Morus? or Momus? or are both one and the same]?"[30] . . .

With this piece ended his controversies; and he from this time gave himself up to his private studies and his civil employment.

As Secretary to the Protector he is supposed to have written the Declaration of the reasons for a war with Spain. His agency was considered as of great importance; for when a treaty with Sweden was artfully suspended, the delay was publicly imputed to Mr. Milton's indisposition; and the Swedish agent was provoked to express his wonder, that only one man in England could write Latin and that man blind.

Being now forty-seven years old, and seeing himself disencumbered from external interruptions, he seems to have recollected his former purposes, and to have resumed three great works which he had planned for his future employment: an epic poem, the history of his country, and a dictionary of the Latin tongue.

To collect a dictionary seems a work of all others least practicable in a state of blindness, because it depends upon perpetual and minute inspection and collation. Nor would Milton probably have begun it, after he had lost his eyes; but, having had it always before him, he continued it, says Phillips, "almost to his dying day; but the papers were so discomposed

---

[30] Momus was the classical god of irresponsible ridicule and fault-finding.

and deficient that they could not be fitted for the press." The compilers of the Latin dictionary printed at Cambridge had the use of those collections in three folios; but what was their fate afterwards is not known.

To compile a history from various authors, when they can only be consulted by other eyes, is not easy, nor possible but with more skillful and attentive help than can be commonly obtained; and it was probably the difficulty of consulting and comparing that stopped Milton's narrative at the Conquest; a period at which affairs were not yet very intricate, nor authors very numerous.

For the subject of his epic poem, after much deliberation, "long choosing, and beginning late,"[31] he fixed upon *Paradise Lost*; a design so comprehensive that it could be justified only by success. He had once designed to celebrate King Arthur, as he hints in his verses to Mansus: but "Arthur was reserved," says Fenton, "to another destiny."[32]

It appears by some sketches of poetical projects left in manuscript, and to be seen in a library at Cambridge, that he had digested his thoughts on this subject into one of those wild dramas which were anciently called mysteries; and Phillips had seen what he terms part of a tragedy, beginning with the first ten lines of Satan's address to the sun.[33] These mysteries consist of allegorical persons, such as Justice, Mercy, Faith. Of the tragedy or mystery of *Paradise Lost* there are two plans. . . .

[Johnson gives the two plans, for dramas which are not mysteries but morality plays.]

These are very imperfect rudiments of *Paradise Lost*; but it is pleasant to see great works in their seminal state, pregnant with latent possibilities of excellence; nor could there be any more delightful entertainment than to trace their gradual growth and expansion, and to observe how they are sometimes suddenly advanced by accidental hints, and sometimes slowly improved by steady meditation.

Invention is almost the only literary labor which blindness

---

[31] *Paradise Lost*, IX, 26.
[32] To be celebrated in two atrocious epics by Sir Richard Blackmore (1695, 1697).
[33] *Paradise Lost*, IV, 32–41.

cannot obstruct, and therefore he naturally solaced his solitude by the indulgence of his fancy and the melody of his numbers.[34] He had done what he knew to be necessarily previous to poetical excellence; he had made himself acquainted with "seemly arts and affairs"; his comprehension was extended by various knowledge, and his memory stored with intellectual treasures. He was skillful in many languages, and had by reading and composition attained the full mastery of his own. He would have wanted[35] little help from books, had he retained the power of perusing them.

But while his greater designs were advancing, having now, like many other authors, caught the love of publication, he amused himself, as he could, with little productions. He sent to the press (1658) a manuscript of Raleigh, called the *Cabinet Council*; and next year gratified his malevolence to the clergy, by a *Treatise of Civil Power in Ecclesiastical Cases*, and *The Means of Removing Hirelings out of the Church*.

Oliver was now dead; Richard was constrained to resign:[36] the system of extemporary government, which had been held together only by force, naturally fell into fragments when that force was taken away; and Milton saw himself and his cause in equal danger. But he had still hope of doing something. He wrote letters, which Toland has published, to such men as he thought friends to the new Commonwealth; and even in the year of the Restoration he "bated no jot of heart or hope,"[37] but was fantastical enough to think that the nation, agitated as it was, might be settled by a pamphlet, called *A Ready and Easy Way to Establish a Free Commonwealth*; which was, however, enough considered to be both seriously and ludicrously answered.

The obstinate enthusiasm of the commonwealthmen was very remarkable. When the King was apparently returning, Harrington, with a few associates as fanatical as himself, used to meet, with all the gravity of political importance, to settle an equal government by rotation; and Milton, kicking when he could strike no longer, was foolish enough to publish, a few weeks before the Restoration, notes upon a sermon preached by one Griffiths, entitled *The Fear of God and the*

[34] *numbers:* verses.
[35] *wanted:* needed.
[36] Richard Cromwell briefly succeeded his father as Protector (1658–59).
[37] See "To Mr. Cyriack Skinner," lines 7–8.

King. To these notes an answer was written by L'Estrange, in a pamphlet petulantly called *No Blind Guides*.

But whatever Milton could write, or men of greater activity could do, the King was now about to be restored with the irresistible approbation of the people. He was therefore no longer Secretary, and was consequently obliged to quit the house which he held by his office; and proportioning his sense of danger to his opinion of the importance of his writings, thought it convenient to seek some shelter, and hid himself for a time in Bartholomew Close by West Smithfield.

I cannot but remark a kind of respect, perhaps unconsciously, paid to this great man by his biographers: every house in which he resided is historically mentioned, as if it were an injury to neglect naming any place that he honored by his presence.

The King,[38] with lenity of which the world has had perhaps no other example, declined to be the judge or avenger of his own or his father's wrongs, and promised to admit into the Act of Oblivion all, except those whom the parliament should except; and the parliament doomed none to capital punishment but the wretches who had immediately cooperated in the murder of the King. Milton was certainly not one of them; he had only justified what they had done.

This justification was indeed sufficiently offensive; and (June 16) an order was issued to seize Milton's *Defense*, and Goodwin's *Obstructors of Justice*, another book of the same tendency, and burn them by the common hangman. The attorney general was ordered to prosecute the authors; but Milton was not seized, nor perhaps very diligently pursued.

Not long after (August 19) the flutter of innumerable bosoms was stilled by an Act which the King, that his mercy might want no recommendation of elegance, rather called an *act of oblivion* than of *grace*. Goodwin was named, with nineteen more, as incapacitated for any public trust; but of Milton there was no exception.

Of this tenderness shown to Milton, the curiosity of mankind has not forborne to inquire the reason. Burnet thinks he was forgotten; but this is another instance which may confirm Dalrymple's observation who says, "that whenever Burnet's narrations are examined, he appears to be mistaken."

[38] Charles II.

Forgotten he was not; for his prosecution was ordered; it must be therefore by design that he was included in the general oblivion. He is said to have had friends in the House[39] such as Marvell, Morrice, and Sir Thomas Clarges; and undoubtedly a man like him must have had influence. A very particular story of his escape is told by Richardson in his memoirs, which he received from Pope, as delivered by Betterton, who might have heard it from Davenant. In the war between the King and Parliament, Davenant was made prisoner, and condemned to die; but was spared at the request of Milton. When the turn of success brought Milton into the like danger, Davenant repaid the benefit by appearing in his favor. Here is a reciprocation of generosity and gratitude so pleasing that the tale makes its own way to credit. But if help were wanted, I know not where to find it. The danger of Davenant is certain from his own relations; but of his escape there is no account. Betterton's narration can be traced no higher; it is not known that he had it from Davenant. We are told that the benefit exchanged was life for life; but it seems not certain that Milton's life ever was in danger. Goodwin, who had committed the same kind of crime, escaped with incapacitation; and as exclusion from public trust is a punishment which the power of government can commonly inflict without the help of a particular law, it required no great interest to exempt Milton from a censure little more than verbal. Something may be reasonably ascribed to veneration and compassion—to veneration of his abilities, and compassion for his distresses—which made it fit to forgive his malice for his learning. He was now poor and blind; and who would pursue with violence an illustrious enemy, depressed by fortune, and disarmed by nature?

The publication of the Act of Oblivion put him in the same condition with his fellow subjects. He was, however, upon some pretense not now known, in the custody of the sergeant[40] in December; and, when he was released, upon his refusal of the fees demanded, he and the sergeant were called before the House. He was now safe within the shade of oblivion, and knew himself to be as much out of the power of a griping officer as any other man. How the question was determined is

---

[39] House of Commons.
[40] *sergeant:* the sergeant-at-arms of the House of Commons.

not known. Milton would hardly have contended, but that he knew himself to have right on his side.

He then removed to Jewin Street, near Aldersgate Street; and being blind, and by no means wealthy, wanted a domestic companion and attendant; and therefore, by the recommendation of Dr. Paget, married Elizabeth Minshull, of a gentleman's family in Cheshire, probably without a fortune. All his wives were virgins; for he has declared that he thought it gross and indelicate to be a second husband:[41] upon what other principles his choice was made cannot now be known, but marriage afforded not much of his happiness. The first wife left him in disgust, and was brought back only by terror; the second, indeed, seems to have been more a favorite, but her life was short. The third, as Phillips relates, oppressed his children in his lifetime, and cheated them at his death.

Soon after his marriage, according to an obscure story, he was offered the continuance of his employment, and, being pressed by his wife to accept it, answered, "You, like other women, want to ride in your coach; my wish is to live and die an honest man." If he considered the Latin Secretary as exercising any of the powers of government, he that had shared authority either with the Parliament or Cromwell, might have forborne to talk very loudly of his honesty; and if he thought the office purely ministerial, he certainly might have honestly retained it under the King. But this tale has too little evidence to deserve a disquisition; large offers and sturdy rejections are among the common topics of falsehood.

He had so much either of prudence or gratitude that he forebore to disturb the new settlement with any of his political or ecclesiastical opinions, and from this time devoted himself to poetry and literature. Of his zeal for learning in all its parts he gave a proof by publishing, the next year (1661), *Accidence Commenced Grammar*; a little book which has nothing remarkable, but that its author, who had been lately defending the supreme powers of his country and was then writing *Paradise Lost*, could descend from his elevation to rescue children from the perplexity of grammatical confusion, and the trouble of lessons unnecessarily repeated.

---

[41] *An Apology against a Pamphlet Called A Modest Confutation of the Animadversions upon the Remonstrant against Smectymnuus*. Johnson himself had married a widow.

About this time Ellwood the Quaker, being recommended to him as one who would read Latin to him, for the advantage of his conversation, attended him every afternoon, except on Sundays. Milton, who, in his letter to Hartlib, had declared, that "to read Latin with an English mouth is as ill a hearing as Law French," required that Ellwood should learn and practice the Italian pronunciation, which, he said, was necessary, if he would talk with foreigners. This seems to have been a task troublesome without use. There is little reason for preferring the Italian pronunciation to our own, except that it is more general; and to teach it to an Englishman is only to make him a foreigner at home. He who travels, if he speaks Latin, may so soon learn the sounds which every native gives it, that he need make no provision before his journey; and if strangers visit us, it is their business to practice such conformity to our modes as they expect from us in their own countries. Ellwood complied with the directions, and improved himself by his attendance; for he relates, that Milton, having a curious ear, knew by his voice when he read what he did not understand, and would stop him, and "open the most difficult passages."

In a short time he took a house in the Artillery Walk, leading to Bunhill Fields; the mention of which concludes the register of Milton's removals and habitations. He lived longer in this place than in any other.

He was now busied by *Paradise Lost*. Whence he drew the original design has been variously conjectured, by men who cannot bear to think themselves ignorant of that which, at last, neither diligence nor sagacity can discover. Some find the hint in an Italian tragedy. Voltaire tells a wild and unauthorized story of a farce seen by Milton in Italy, which opened thus: "Let the rainbow be the fiddlestick of the fiddle of Heaven." It has been already shown that the first conception was a tragedy or mystery, not of a narrative, but a dramatic work, which he is supposed to have begun to reduce to its present form about the time (1655) when he finished his dispute with the defenders of the King.

He long before had promised to adorn his native country by some great performance, while he had yet perhaps no settled design, and was stimulated only by such expectations as naturally arose from the survey of his attainments, and the consciousness of his powers. What he should undertake, it was difficult to determine. He was "long choosing, and began late."

While he was obliged to divide his time between his private studies and affairs of state, his poetical labor must have been often interrupted; and perhaps he did little more in that busy time than construct the narrative, adjust the episodes, proportion the parts, accumulate images and sentiments, and treasure in his memory, or preserve in writing, such hints as books or meditation would supply. Nothing particular is known of his intellectual operations while he was a statesman; for, having every help and accommodation at hand, he had no need of uncommon expedients.

Being driven from all public stations he is yet too great not to be traced by curiosity to his retirement, where he has been found by Mr. Richardson, the fondest of his admirers, sitting "before his door in a grey coat of coarse cloth, in warm sultry weather, to enjoy the fresh air; and so, as well as on his own room, receiving the visits of people of distinguished parts as well as quality." His visitors of high quality must now be imagined to be few; but men of parts might reasonably court the conversation of a man so generally illustrious, that foreigners are reported by Wood to have visited the house in Bread Street where he was born.

According to another account, he was seen in a small house, "neatly enough dressed in black clothes, sitting in a room hung with rusty green; pale but not cadaverous, with chalkstones in his hands. He said, that if it were not for the gout, his blindness would be tolerable."

In the intervals of his pain, being made unable to use the common exercises, he used to swing in a chair, and sometimes played upon an organ.

He was now confessedly and visibly employed upon his poem, of which the progress might be noted by those with whom he was familiar; for he was obliged, when he had composed as many lines as his memory would conveniently retain, to employ some friend in writing them, having, at least for part of the time, no regular attendant. This gave opportunity to observations and reports.

Mr. Phillips observes that there was a very remarkable circumstance in the composure of *Paradise Lost,* "which I have a particular reason," says he, "to remember; for whereas I had the perusal of it from the very beginning, for some years, as I went from time to time to visit him, in parcels of ten, twenty, or thirty verses at a time (which, being written by whatever hand came next, might possibly want correction as to the orthography and pointing[42]), having, as the summer came on, not been showed any for a considerable while, and desiring the reason thereof, was answered that his vein never happily flowed but from the autumnal equinox to the vernal; and that whatever he attempted at other times was never to his satisfaction, though he courted his fancy never so much; so that, in all the years he was about this poem, he may be said to have spent half his time therein."

Upon this relation Toland remarks that in his opinion Phillips has mistaken the time of the year; for Milton, in his elegies, declares that with the advance of the spring he feels the increase of his poetical force, "redeunt in carmina vires [strength comes back to my songs]." To this it is answered, that Phillips could hardly mistake time so well marked; and it may be added, that Milton might find different times of the year favorable to different parts of life. Mr. Richardson conceived it impossible that "such a work should be suspended for six months, or for one. It may go on faster or slower, but it must go on." By what necessity it must continually go on, or why it might not be laid aside and resumed, it is not easy to discover.

This dependance of the soul upon the seasons, those temporary and periodical ebbs and flows of intellect, may, I suppose, justly be derided as the fumes of vain imagination. "Sapiens dominabitur astris [The wise man is ruled by the stars]." The author that thinks himself weatherbound will find, with a little help from hellebore, that he is only idle or exhausted. But while this notion has possession of the head, it produces the inability which it supposes. Our powers owe much of their energy to our hopes; "possunt quia posse videntur [they are capable because they are thought to be capable]." When success seems attainable, diligence is enforced; but when it is admitted that the faculties are suppressed by a cross wind or a cloudy sky, the day is given up without resistance; for who can contend with the course of nature?

From such prepossessions Milton seems not to have been free. There prevailed in his time an opinion that the world was in its decay, and that we have had the misfortune to be

---

[42] *pointing:* punctuation.

produced in the decrepitude of nature. It was suspected that the whole creation languished, that neither trees nor animals had the height or bulk of their predecessors, and that everything was daily sinking by gradual diminution. Milton appears to suspect that souls partake of the general degeneracy, and is not without some fear that his book is to be written in "an age too late" for heroic poesy.

Another opinion wanders about the world, and sometimes finds reception among wise men—an opinion that restrains the operations of the mind to particular regions, and supposes that a luckless mortal may be born in a degree of latitude too high or too low for wisdom or for wit. From this fancy, wild as it is, he had not wholly cleared his head when he feared lest the "climate" of his country might be "too cold"[43] for flights of imagination.

Into a mind already occupied by such fancies, another not more reasonable might easily find its way. He that could fear lest his genius had fallen upon too old a world, or too chill a climate, might consistently magnify to himself the influence of the seasons, and believe his faculties to be vigorous only half the year.

His submission to the seasons was at least more reasonable than his dread of decaying nature, or a frigid zone, for general causes must operate uniformly in a general abatement of mental power; if less could be performed by the writer, less likewise would content the judges of his work. Among this lagging race of frosty grovelers he might still have risen into eminence by producing something which "they should not willingly let die." However inferior to the heroes who were born in better ages, he might still be great among his contemporaries, with the hope of growing every day greater in the dwindle of posterity: he might still be the giant of the pygmies, the one-eyed monarch of the blind.

Of his artifices of study or particular hours of composition we have little account, and there was perhaps little to be told. Richardson, who seems to have been very diligent in his inquiries, but discovers always a wish to find Milton discriminated from other men, relates that "he would sometimes lie awake whole nights, but not a verse could he make; and on a sudden his poetical faculty would rush upon him with an *impetus* or *oestrum*, and his daughter was immediately called

[43] *Paradise Lost*, IX, 44–45.

to secure what came. At other times he would dictate perhaps forty lines in a breath, and then reduce them to half the number."

These bursts of light and involutions of darkness, these transient and involuntary excursions and retrocessions of invention, having some appearance of deviation from the common train of nature, are eagerly caught by the lovers of a wonder. Yet something of this inequality happens to every man in every mode of exertion, manual or mental. The mechanic cannot handle his hammer and his file at all times with equal dexterity; there are hours, he knows not why, when "his hand is out." By Mr. Richardson's relation, casually conveyed, much regard cannot be claimed. That, in his intellectual hour, Milton called for his daughter "to secure what came," may be questioned; for unluckily it happens to be known that his daughters were never taught to write,[44] nor would he have been obliged, as is universally confessed, to have employed any casual visitor in disburthening his memory, if his daughter could have performed the office.

The story of reducing his exuberance has been told of other authors, and, though doubtless true of every fertile copious mind, seems to have been gratuitously transferred to Milton.

What he has told us, and we cannot now know more, is that he composed much of his poem in the night and morning, I suppose before his mind was disturbed with common business; and that he poured out with great fluency his "unpremeditated verse."[45] Versification free, like his, from the distresses of rhyme, must by a work so long be made prompt and habitual; and, when his thoughts were once adjusted, the words would come at his command.

At what particular times of his life the parts of his work were written cannot often be known. The beginning of the third book shows that he had lost his sight; and the introduction to the seventh that the return of the King had clouded him with discountenance, and that he was offended by the licentious festivity of the Restoration. There are no other internal notes of time. Milton, being now cleared from all effects of his disloyalty, had nothing required from him but the common duty of living in quiet, to be rewarded with the

---

[44] According to John Aubrey, Milton's daughter Deborah served as his scribe.
[45] *Paradise Lost*, IX, 24.

common right of protection; but this, which, when he skulked from the approach of his King, was perhaps more than he hoped, seems not to have satisfied him, for no sooner is he safe than he finds himself in danger, "fallen on evil days and evil tongues, and with darkness and with danger compassed round."[46] This darkness, had his eyes been better employed, had undoubtedly deserved compassion; but to add the mention of danger was ungrateful and unjust. He was fallen indeed on "evil days"; the time was come in which regicides could no longer boast their wickedness. But of "evil tongues" for Milton to complain required impudence at least equal to his other powers—Milton, whose warmest advocates must allow that he never spared any asperity of reproach or brutality of insolence.

But the charge itself seems to be false, for it would be hard to recollect any reproach cast upon him, either serious or ludicrous, through the whole remaining part of his life. He pursued his studies or his amusements without persecution, molestation, or insult. Such is the reverence paid to great abilities, however misused: they who contemplated in Milton the scholar and the wit were contented to forget the reviler of his King.

When the plague (1665) raged in London, Milton took refuge at Chalfont in Bucks, where Ellwood, who had taken the house for him, first saw a complete copy of *Paradise Lost*, and, having perused it, said to him, "Thou hast said a great deal upon *Paradise Lost*; what hast thou to say upon *Paradise Found*?"

Next year, when the danger of infection had ceased, he returned to Bunhill Fields, and designed the publication of his poem. A license was necessary, and he could expect no great kindness from a chaplain of the Archbishop of Canterbury. He seems, however, to have been treated with tenderness; for though objections were made to particular passages, and among them to the simile of the sun eclipsed in the first book, yet the license was granted; and he sold his copy, April 27, 1667, to Samuel Simmons, for an immediate payment of five pounds, with a stipulation to receive five pounds more when thirteen hundred should be sold of the first edition, and again, five pounds after the sale of the same number of the second edition, and another five pounds after the same

---

[46] See *Paradise Lost*, VII, 25–27.

sale of the third. None of the three editions were to be extended beyond fifteen hundred copies.

The first edition was ten books, in a small quarto. The titles were varied from year to year; and an advertisement and the arguments of the books[47] were omitted in some copies, and inserted in others.

The sale gave him in two years a right to his second payment, for which the receipt was signed April 26, 1669. The second edition was not given till 1674; it was printed small octavo, and the number of books was increased to twelve, by a division of the seventh and twelfth, and some other small improvements were made. The third edition was published in 1678; and the widow, to whom the copy was then to devolve, sold all her claims to Simmons for eight pounds, according to her receipt given Dec. 21, 1680. Simmons had already agreed to transfer the whole right to Brabazon Aylmer for twenty-five pounds; and Aylmer sold to Jacob Tonson half, August 17, 1683, and half, March 24, 1690, at a price considerably enlarged. In the history of *Paradise Lost* a deduction thus minute will rather gratify than fatigue.

The slow sale and tardy reputation of this poem have been always mentioned as evidences of neglected merit and of the uncertainty of literary fame, and inquiries have been made and conjectures offered about the causes of its long obscurity and late reception. But has the case been truly stated? Have not lamentation and wonder been lavished on an evil that was never felt?

That in the reigns of Charles and James the *Paradise Lost* received no public acclamations is readily confessed. Wit and literature were on the side of the court; and who that solicited favor or fashion would venture to praise the defender of the regicides? All that he himself could think his due, from "evil tongues" in "evil days," was that reverential silence which was generously preserved. But it cannot be inferred that his poem was not read or not, however unwillingly, admired.

The sale, if it be considered, will justify the public. Those who have no power to judge of past times but by their own should always doubt their conclusions. The call for books was not in Milton's age what it is in the present. To read was not then a general amusement; neither traders nor often gentlemen thought themselves disgraced by ignorance. The women had

---

[47] *arguments of the books:* prose summaries prefixed to each book.

not then aspired to literature, nor was every house supplied with a closet[48] of knowledge. Those, indeed, who professed learning were not less learned than at any other time; but of that middle race of students who read for pleasure or accomplishment and who buy the numerous products of modern typography, the number was then comparatively small. To prove the paucity of readers, it may be sufficient to remark that the nation had been satisfied, from 1623 to 1664, that is, forty-one years, with only two editions of the works of Shakespeare, which probably did not together make one thousand copies.

The sale of thirteen hundred copies in two years, in opposition to so much recent enmity and to a style of versification new to all and disgusting to many, was an uncommon example of the prevalence of genius. The demand did not immediately increase; for many more readers than were supplied at first the nation did not afford. Only three thousand were sold in eleven years; for it forced its way without assistance: its admirers did not dare to publish their opinion, and the opportunities now given of attracting notice by advertisements were then very few; the means of proclaiming the publication of new books have been produced by that general literature which now pervades the nation through all its ranks.

But the reputation and price of the copy still advanced, till the Revolution[49] put an end to the secrecy of love, and *Paradise Lost* broke into open view with sufficient security of kind reception.

Fancy can hardly forbear to conjecture with what temper Milton surveyed the silent progress of his work, and marked his reputation stealing its way in a kind of subterraneous current through fear and silence. I cannot but conceive him calm and confident, little disappointed, not at all dejected, relying on his own merit with steady consciousness, and waiting without impatience the vicissitudes of opinion, and the impartiality of a future generation.

In the meantime he continued his studies, and supplied the want of sight by a very odd expedient, of which Phillips gives the following account.

Mr. Phillips tells us, "that though our author had daily

---

[48] *closet:* study.
[49] The Glorious Revolution of 1688–89, in which the Roman Catholic absolutist James II was deposed and succeeded by William and Mary.

about him one or other to read, some persons of man's estate, who, of their own accord, greedily catched at the opportunity of being his readers that they might as well reap the benefit of what they read to him as oblige him by the benefit of their reading, and others of younger years were sent by their parents to the same end; yet excusing only the eldest daughter, by reason of her bodily infirmity and difficult utterance of speech (which, to say truth, I doubt[50] was the principal cause of excusing her), the other two were condemned to the performance of reading and exactly pronouncing of all the languages of whatever book he should at one time or other, think fit to peruse, viz. the Hebrew (and I think the Syriac), the Greek, the Latin, the Italian, Spanish, and French. All which sorts of books to be confined to read, without understanding one word, must needs be a trial of patience almost beyond endurance. Yet it was endured by both for a long time, though the irksomeness of this employment could not be always concealed, but broke out more and more into expressions of uneasiness; so that at length they were all, even the eldest also, sent out to learn some curious and ingenious sorts of manufacture that are proper for women to learn; particularly embroideries in gold or silver."

In the scene of misery which this mode of intellectual labor sets before our eyes, it is hard to determine whether the daughters or the father are most to be lamented. A language not understood can never be so read as to give pleasure, and very seldom so as to convey meaning. If few men would have had resolution to write books with such embarrassments, few likewise could have wanted ability to find some better expedient.

Three years after his *Paradise Lost* (1667), he published his *History of England*, comprising the whole fable of Geoffrey of Monmouth, and continued to the Norman invasion. Why he should have given the first part, which he seems not to believe, and which is universally rejected, it is difficult to conjecture. The style is harsh; but it has something of rough vigor, which perhaps may often strike, though it cannot please.

On this history the licenser again fixed his claws, and before he would transmit it to the press tore out several parts. Some censures of the Saxon monks were taken away, lest they

---

[50] *doubt:* suspect.

should be applied to the modern clergy; and a character of the Long Parliament, and Assembly of Divines, was excluded, of which the author gave a copy to the Earl of Anglesey, and which, being afterwards published, has been since inserted in its proper place.

The same year were printed *Paradise Regained* and *Samson Agonistes*, a tragedy written in imitation of the ancients, and never designed by the author for the stage. As these poems were published by another bookseller, it has been asked whether Simmons was discouraged from receiving them by the slow sale of the former. Why a writer changed his bookseller a hundred years ago I am far from hoping to discover. Certainly he who in two years sells thirteen hundred copies of a volume in quarto, bought for two payments of five pounds each, has no reason to repent his purchase.

When Milton showed *Paradise Regained* to Ellwood, "This," said he, "is owing to you; for you put it in my head by the question you put to me at Chalfont, which otherwise I had not thought of."

His last poetical offspring was his favorite. He could not, as Ellwood relates, endure to hear *Paradise Lost* preferred to *Paradise Regained*. Many causes may vitiate a writer's judgment of his own works. On that which has cost him much labor he sets a high value, because he is unwilling to think that he has been diligent in vain; what has been produced without toilsome efforts is considered with delight as a proof of vigorous faculties and fertile invention; and the last work, whatever it be, has necessarily most of the grace of novelty. Milton, however it happened, had this prejudice, and had it to himself.

To that multiplicity of attainments and extent of comprehension that entitle this great author to our veneration may be added a kind of humble dignity, which did not disdain the meanest services to literature. The epic poet, the controvertist, the politician, having already descended to accommodate children with a book of rudiments, now in the last years of his life composed a book of logic, for the initiation of students in philosophy, and published (1672) *Artis Logicae Plenior Institutio ad Petri Rami Methodum Concinnata*, that is, *A New Scheme of Logic, according to the Method of Ramus*. I know not whether even in this book he did not intend an act of hostility against the universities; for Ramus was one of the first oppugners of the old philosophy who disturbed with innovations the quiet of the schools.[51]

His polemical disposition again revived. He had now been safe so long that he forgot his fears and published a *Treatise of True Religion, Heresy, Schism, Toleration, and the Best Means to Prevent the Growth of Popery*.

But this little tract is modestly written, with respectful mention of the Church of England, and an appeal to the Thirtynine Articles. His principle of toleration is agreement in the sufficiency of the Scriptures, and he extends it to all who, whatever their opinions are, profess to derive them from the sacred books. The papists appeal to other testimonies, and are therefore in his opinion not to be permitted the liberty of either public or private worship; for though they plead conscience, "we have no warrant," he says, "to regard conscience which is not grounded in Scripture."

Those who are not convinced by his reasons may be perhaps delighted with his wit. The term "Roman Catholic" is, he says, "one of the Pope's bulls; it is particular universal, or catholic schismatic."[52]

He has, however, something better. As the best preservative against Popery he recommends the diligent perusal of the Scriptures; a duty from which he warns the busy part of mankind not to think themselves excused.

He now reprinted his juvenile poems with some additions.

In the last year of his life he sent to the press, seeming to take delight in publication, a collection of *Familiar Epistles* in Latin; to which, being too few to make a volume, he added some academical exercises, which perhaps he perused with pleasure, as they recalled to his memory the days of youth; but for which nothing but veneration for his name could now procure a reader.

When he had attained his sixty-sixth year, the gout, with which he had been long tormented, prevailed over the enfeebled powers of nature. He died by a quiet and silent expiration, about the tenth of November 1674, at his house in Bunhill Fields, and was buried next his father in the chancel

---

[51] Pierre la Ramée, called Petrus Ramus, was a sixteenth-century French philosopher who opposed the logic of Aristotle, then dominant in the universities.

[52] Milton puns on bull as (1) a papal edict and (2) a self-contradictory statement. "Catholic" originally meant "universal."

of St. Giles at Cripplegate. His funeral was very splendidly and numerously attended.

Upon his grave there is supposed to have been no memorial; but in our time a monument has been erected in Westminster Abbey "To the Author of Paradise Lost," by Mr. Benson, who has in the inscription bestowed more words upon himself than upon Milton.

When the inscription for the monument of Philips, in which he was said to be *soli Miltono secundus* [second only to Milton],[53] was exhibited to Dr. Sprat, then Dean of Westminster, he refused to admit it; the name of Milton was, in his opinion, too detestable to be read on the wall of a building dedicated to devotion. Atterbury, who succeeded him, being author of the inscription, permitted its reception. "And such has been the change of public opinion," said Dr. Gregory, from whom I heard this account, "that I have seen erected in the church a statue of that man, whose name I once knew considered as a pollution of its walls."

Milton has the reputation of having been in his youth eminently beautiful, so as to have been called the Lady of his college. His hair, which was of a light brown, parted at the foretop, and hung down upon his shoulders, according to the picture which he has given of Adam. He was, however, not of the heroic stature, but rather below the middle size, according to Mr. Richardson, who mentions him as having narrowly escaped from being "short and thick." He was vigorous and active, and delighted in the exercise of the sword, in which he is related to have been eminently skillful. His weapon was, I believe, not the rapier but the backsword, of which he recommends the use in his book on education.

His eyes are said never to have been bright; but, if he was a dexterous fencer, they must have been once quick.

His domestic habits, so far as they are known, were those of a severe student. He drank little strong drink of any kind, and fed without excess in quantity, and in his earlier years without delicacy of choice. In his youth he studied late at night; but afterwards changed his hours, and rested in bed from nine to four in the summer, and five in the winter. The course of his day was best known after he was blind. When

[53] John Philips wrote Miltonic parodies such as *The Splendid Shilling* (1705).

he first rose he heard a chapter in the Hebrew Bible, and then studied till twelve; then took some exercise for an hour; then dined; then played on the organ, and sung, or heard another sing; then studied to six; then entertained his visitors till eight; then supped, and, after a pipe of tobacco and a glass of water, went to bed.

So is his life described, but this even tenor appears attainable only in college. He that lives in the world will sometimes have the succession of his practice broken and confused. Visitors, of whom Milton is represented to have had great numbers, will come and stay unseasonably; business, of which every man has some, must be done when others will do it.

When he did not care to rise early, he had something read to him by his bedside; perhaps at this time his daughters were employed. He composed much in the morning, and dictated in the day, sitting obliquely in an elbow-chair with his leg thrown over the arm.

Fortune appears not to have had much of his care. In the Civil Wars he lent his personal estate to the Parliament; but when, after the contest was decided, he solicited repayment, he met not only with neglect, but "sharp rebuke"; and, having tired both himself and his friends, was given up to poverty and hopeless indignation, till he showed how able he was to do greater service. He was then made Latin Secretary, with two hundred pounds a year; and had a thousand pounds for his *Defense of the People*. His widow, who after his death, retired to Nantwich in Cheshire, and died about 1729, is said to have reported that he lost two thousand pounds by entrusting it to a scrivener; and that, in the general depredation upon the Church, he had grasped an estate of about sixty pounds a year belonging to Westminster Abbey, which, like other sharers of the plunder of rebellion, he was afterwards obliged to return. Two thousand pounds, which he had placed in the Excise Office,[54] were also lost. There is yet no reason to believe that he was ever reduced to indigence. His wants, being few, were competently supplied. He sold his library before his death, and left his family fifteen hundred pounds; on which his widow laid hold, and only gave one hundred to each of his daughters.

His literature was unquestionably great. He read all the languages which are considered either as learned or polite:

[54] A bank, which failed at the Restoration (1660).

Hebrew, with its two dialects, Greek, Latin, Italian, French, and Spanish. In Latin his skill was such as places him in the first rank of writers and critics; and he appears to have cultivated Italian with uncommon diligence. The books in which his daughter, who used to read to him, represented him as most delighting, after Homer, which he could almost repeat, were Ovid's *Metamorphoses* and Euripides. His Euripides is, by Mr. Cradock's kindness, now in my hands: the margin is sometimes noted; but I have found nothing remarkable.

Of the English poets he set most value upon Spenser, Shakespeare, and Cowley. Spenser was apparently his favorite; Shakespeare he may easily be supposed to like, with every other skillful reader, but I should not have expected that Cowley, whose ideas of excellence were different from his own, would have had much of his approbation. His character of Dryden, who sometimes visited him, was, that he was a good rhymist, but no poet.

His theological opinions are said to have been first Calvinistical; and afterwards, perhaps when he began to hate the Presbyterians, to have tended towards Arminianism.[55] In the mixed questions of theology and government, he never thinks that he can recede far enough from popery, or prelacy; but what Baudius says of Erasmus seems applicable to him, "magis habuit quod fugeret, quam quod sequeretur." He had determined rather what to condemn than what to approve. He has not associated himself with any denomination of Protestants: we know rather what he was not, than what he was. He was not of the Church of Rome; he was not of the Church of England.

To be of no church is dangerous. Religion, of which the rewards are distant and which is animated only by faith and hope, will glide by degrees out of the mind unless it be invigorated and reimpressed by external ordinances, by stated calls to worship, and the salutary influence of example. Milton, who appears to have had full conviction of the truth of Christianity, and to have regarded the Holy Scriptures with the profoundest veneration, to have been untainted by an heretical peculiarity of opinion, and to have lived in a confirmed belief of the immediate and occasional[56] agency of

---

[55] The doctrines of Jacobus Arminius, who modified Calvin's views on predestination.

[56] *immediate and occasional:* direct and indirect.

Providence, yet grew old without any visible worship. In the distribution of his hours, there was no hour of prayer, either solitary or with his household; omitting public prayers, he omitted all.

Of this omission the reason has been sought, upon a supposition which ought never to be made, that men live with their own approbation and justify their conduct to themselves. Prayer certainly was not thought superfluous by him, who represents our first parents as praying acceptably in the state of innocence, and efficaciously after their fall. That he lived without prayer can hardly be affirmed; his studies and meditations were an habitual prayer. The neglect of it in his family was probably a fault for which he condemned himself, and which he intended to correct, but that death, as too often happens, intercepted his reformation.

His political notions were those of an acrimonious and surly republican, for which it is not known that he gave any better reason than that "a popular government was the most frugal; for the trappings of a monarchy would set up an ordinary commonwealth." It is surely very shallow policy that supposes money to be the chief good; and even this, without considering that the support and expense of a court is for the most part only a particular kind of traffic, by which money is circulated without any national impoverishment.

Milton's republicanism was, I am afraid, founded in an envious hatred of greatness, and a sullen desire of independence; in petulance impatient of control, and pride disdainful of superiority. He hated monarchs in the state and prelates in the church; for he hated all whom he was required to obey. It is to be suspected that his predominant desire was to destroy rather than establish, and that he felt not so much the love of liberty as repugnance to authority.

It has been observed that they who most loudly clamor for liberty do not most liberally grant it. What we know of Milton's character in domestic relations is that he was severe and arbitrary. His family consisted of women; and there appears in his books something like a Turkish contempt of females, as subordinate and inferior beings. That his own daughters might not break the ranks, he suffered them to be depressed by a mean and penurious education. He thought woman made only for obedience, and man only for rebellion.

Of his family some account may be expected. His sister, first married to Mr. Phillips, afterwards married Mr. Agar,

a friend of her first husband, who succeeded him in the
Crown Office. She had by her first husband, Edward and John,
the two nephews whom Milton educated: and by her second,
two daughters.

His brother, Sir Christopher, had two daughters, Mary and
Catherine, and a son Thomas, who succeeded Agar in the
Crown Office, and left a daughter living in 1749 in Grosvenor
Street.

Milton had children only by his first wife: Anne, Mary,
and Deborah. Anne, though deformed, married a master
builder, and died of her first child. Mary died single. Deborah
married Abraham Clark, a weaver in Spitalfields, and lived
seventy-six years, to August, 1727. This is the daughter of
whom public mention has been made.[57] She could repeat the
first lines of Homer, the *Metamorphoses*, and some of
Euripides, by having often read them. Yet here incredulity
is ready to make a stand. Many repetitions are necessary to
fix in the memory lines not understood; and why should
Milton wish or want to hear them so often? These lines were
at the beginning of the poems. Of a book written in a language
not understood the beginning raises no more attention than
the end, and as those that understand it know commonly the
beginning best, its rehearsal will seldom be necessary. It is not
likely that Milton required any passage to be so much repeated
as that his daughter could learn it; nor likely that he desired
the initial lines to be read at all; nor that the daughter, weary
of the drudgery of pronouncing unideal sounds,[58] would
voluntarily commit them to memory.

To this gentlewoman Addison made a present, and promised
some establishment; but died soon after. Queen Caroline sent
her fifty guineas. She had seven sons and three daughters; but
none of them had any children, except her son Caleb and her
daughter Elizabeth. Caleb went to Fort St. George in the East
Indies, and had two sons, of whom nothing is now known.
Elizabeth married Thomas Foster, a weaver in Spitalfields,
and had seven children, who all died. She kept a petty grocer's
or chandler's shop, first at Holloway, and afterwards in Cock
Lane near Shoreditch Church. She knew little of her grandfather, and that little was not good. She told of his harshness

---

[57] A letter about her appeared in *The Gentleman's Magazine*, 46 (1776),
200.
[58] *unideal sounds:* sounds which meant nothing to her.

to his daughters, and his refusal to have them taught to write: and, in opposition to other accounts, represented him as delicate, though temperate, in his diet.

In 1750, April 5, *Comus* was played for her benefit. She had so little acquaintance with diversion or gaiety that she did not know what was intended when a benefit was offered her. The profits of the night were only one hundred and thirty pounds, though Dr. Newton brought a large contribution; and twenty pounds were given by Tonson,[59] a man who is to be praised as often as he is named. Of this sum one hundred pounds was placed in the stocks, after some debate between her and her husband in whose name it should be entered; and the rest augmented their little stock, with which they removed to Islington. This was the greatest benefaction that *Paradise Lost* ever procured the author's descendants; and to this he who has now attempted to relate his life had the honor of contributing a Prologue.

In the examination of Milton's poetical works I shall pay so much regard to time as to begin with his juvenile productions. For his early pieces he seems to have had a degree of fondness not very laudable: what he has once written he resolves to preserve, and gives to the public an unfinished poem, which he broke off because he was "nothing satisfied with what he had done," supposing his readers less nice[60] than himself. These preludes to his future labors are in Italian, Latin, and English. Of the Italian I cannot pretend to speak as a critic, but I have heard them commended by a man well qualified to decide their merit. The Latin pieces are lusciously elegant; but the delight which they afford is rather by the exquisite imitation of the ancient writers, by the purity of the diction, and the harmony of the numbers, than by any power of invention or vigor of sentiment. They are not all of equal value; the elegies excel the odes, and some of the exercises on Gunpowder Treason might have been spared.

The English poems, though they make no promises of *Paradise Lost*, have this evidence of genius, that they have a

---

[59] Thomas Newton, Bishop of Bristol, edited Milton; and Jacob Tonson was a publisher and great-nephew of the Tonson who bought the rights to *Paradise Lost*.
[60] *nice*: discriminating.

cast original and unborrowed. But their peculiarity is not excellence: if they differ from verses of others, they differ for the worse; for they are too often distinguished by repulsive harshness; the combination of words are new, but they are not pleasing; the rhymes and epithets seem to be laboriously sought and violently applied.

That in the early parts of his life he wrote with much care appears from his manuscripts, happily preserved at Cambridge, in which many of his smaller works are found as they were first written, with the subsequent corrections. Such relics show how excellence is acquired: what we hope ever to do with ease we may learn first to do with diligence.

Those who admire the beauties of this great poet sometimes force their own judgment into false approbation of his little pieces, and prevail upon themselves to think that admirable which is only singular. All that short compositions can commonly attain is neatness and elegance. Milton never learned the art of doing little things with grace; he overlooked the milder excellence of suavity and softness: he was a "lion" that had no skill "in dandling the kid."[61]

One of the poems on which much praise has been bestowed is "Lycidas"; of which the diction is harsh, the rhymes uncertain, and the numbers unpleasing. What beauty there is we must therefore seek in the sentiments and images. It is not to be considered as the effusion of real passion; for passion runs not after remote allusions and obscure opinions. Passion plucks no berries from the myrtle and ivy, nor calls upon Arethuse and Mincius, nor tells of rough "satyrs" and "fauns with clover heel."[62] Where there is leisure for fiction there is little grief.

In this poem there is no nature, for there is no truth; there is no art, for there is nothing new. Its form is that of a pastoral, easy, vulgar,[63] and therefore disgusting: whatever images it can supply, are long ago exhausted; and its inherent improbability always forces dissatisfaction on the mind. When Cowley tells of Hervey that they studied to-

---

[61] *Paradise Lost*, IV, 343–44.
[62] The fountain Arethuse, from an Idyl by Theocritus, and the river Mincius, from an Eclogue by Virgil, as well as satyrs and fauns, figure in "Lycidas."
[63] *vulgar:* commonly used.

gether,[64] it is easy to suppose how much he must miss the companion of his labors, and the partner of his discoveries; but what image of tenderness can be excited by these lines?

> We drove afield, and both together heard
> What time the grey fly winds her sultry horn,
> Battening our flocks with the fresh dews of night.

We know that they never drove afield, and that they had no flocks to batten; and though it be allowed that the representation may be allegorical, the true meaning is so uncertain and remote that it is never sought because it cannot be known when it is found.

Among the flocks and copses and flowers appear the heathen deities, Jove and Phoebus, Neptune and Aeolus, with a long train of mythological imagery, such as a college easily supplies. Nothing can less display knowledge or less exercise invention than to tell how a shepherd has lost his companion and must now feed his flocks alone, without any judge of his skill in piping; and how one god asks another god what is become of Lycidas, and how neither god can tell. He who thus grieves will excite no sympathy; he who thus praises will confer no honor.

This poem has yet a grosser fault. With these trifling fictions are mingled the most awful[65] and sacred truths, such as ought never to be polluted with such irreverend combinations. The shepherd likewise is now a feeder of sheep, and afterwards an ecclesiastical pastor, a superintendent of a Christian flock. Such equivocations are always unskillful; but here they are indecent, and at least approach to impiety, of which, however, I believe the writer not to have been conscious.

Such is the power of reputation justly acquired that its blaze drives away the eye from nice examination. Surely no man could have fancied that he read "Lycidas" with pleasure, had he not known its author.

Of the two pieces, "L'Allegro" and "Il Penseroso," I believe opinion is uniform; every man that reads them, reads them with pleasure. The author's design is not, what Theobald has remarked, merely to show how objects derive their colors

---

[64] Cowley's "On the Death of Mr. William Hervey," his friend at Cambridge.
[65] *awful:* awe-inspiring.

from the mind, by representing the operation of the same things upon the gay and the melancholy temper, or upon the same man as he is differently disposed; but rather how, among the successive variety of appearances, every disposition of mind takes hold on those by which it may be gratified.

The *cheerful* man hears the lark in the morning; the *pensive* man hears the nightingale in the evening. The *cheerful* man sees the cock strut, and hears the horn and hounds echo in the woods; then walks "not unseen" to observe the glory of the rising sun or listen to the singing milkmaid, and view the labors of the plowman and the mower; then casts his eyes about him over scenes of smiling plenty, and looks up to the distant tower, the residence of some fair inhabitant: thus he pursues rural gaiety through a day of labor or of play, and delights himself at night with the fanciful narratives of superstitious ignorance.

The *pensive* man at one time walks "unseen" to muse at midnight; and at another hears the sullen curfew. If the weather drives him home, he sits in a room lighted only by "glowing embers"; or by a lonely lamp outwatches the North Star to discover the habitation of separate souls, and varies the shades of meditation by contemplating the magnificent or pathetic scenes of tragic and epic poetry. When the morning comes, a morning gloomy with rain and wind, he walks into the dark trackless woods, falls asleep by some murmuring water, and with melancholy enthusiasm expects some dream of prognostication or some music played by aerial performers.

Both Mirth and Melancholy are solitary, silent inhabitants of the breast that neither receive nor transmit communication; no mention is therefore made of a philosophical friend or a pleasant companion. The seriousness does not arise from any participation of calamity, nor the gaiety from the pleasures of the bottle.

The man of *cheerfulness* having exhausted the country tries what "towered cities" will afford, and mingles with scenes of splendor, gay assemblies, and nuptial festivities, but he mingles a mere spectator as, when the learned comedies of Jonson or the wild dramas of Shakespeare are exhibited, he attends the theater.

The *pensive* man never loses himself in crowds, but walks the cloister or frequents the cathedral. Milton probably had not yet forsaken the Church.

Both his characters delight in music, but he seems to think

that cheerful notes would have obtained from Pluto a complete dismission of Eurydice, of whom solemn sounds only procured a conditional release.

For the old age of Cheerfulness he makes no provision; but Melancholy he conducts with great dignity to the close of life. His Cheerfulness is without levity, and his Pensiveness without asperity.

Through these two poems the images are properly selected and nicely distinguished, but the colors of the diction seem not sufficiently discriminated. I know not whether the characters are kept sufficiently apart. No mirth can, indeed, be found in his melancholy; but I am afraid that I always meet some melancholy in his mirth. They are two noble efforts of imagination.

The greatest of his juvenile performances is the masque of *Comus*, in which may very plainly be discovered the dawn or twilight of *Paradise Lost*. Milton appears to have formed very early that system of diction and mode of verse which his maturer judgment approved, and from which he never endeavored nor desired to deviate.

Nor does *Comus* afford only a specimen of his language: it exhibits likewise his power of description and his vigor of sentiment, employed in the praise and defense of virtue. A work more truly poetical is rarely found; allusions, images, and descriptive epithets, embellish almost every period[66] with lavish decoration. As a series of lines, therefore, it may be considered as worthy of all the admiration with which the votaries have received it.

As a drama it is deficient. The action is not probable. A masque, in those parts where supernatural intervention is admitted, must indeed be given up to all the freaks of imagination; but so far as the action is merely human it ought to be reasonable, which can hardly be said of the conduct of the two brothers, who, when their sister sinks with fatigue in a pathless wilderness, wander both away together in search of berries too far to find their way back, and leave a helpless lady to all the sadness and danger of solitude. This however is a defect overbalanced by its convenience.

What deserves more reprehension is that the prologue spoken in the wild wood by the Attendant Spirit is addressed

[66] *period:* sentence.

to the audience; a mode of communication so contrary to the nature of dramatic representation that no precedents can support it.

The discourse of the Spirit is too long, an objection that may be made to almost all the following speeches; they have not the spriteliness of a dialogue animated by reciprocal contention, but seem rather declamations deliberately composed and formally repeated on a moral question. The auditor therefore listens as to a lecture, without passion, without anxiety.

The song of Comus has airiness and jollity; but, what may recommend Milton's morals as well as his poetry, the invitations to pleasure are so general that they excite no distinct images of corrupt enjoyment, and take no dangerous hold on the fancy.

The following soliloquies of Comus and the Lady are elegant, but tedious. The song must owe much to the voice, if it ever can delight. At last the Brothers enter, with too much tranquillity; and when they have feared lest their sister should be in danger, and hoped that she is not in danger, the Elder makes a speech in praise of chastity, and the Younger finds how it is to be a philosopher.

Then descends the Spirit in form of a shepherd; and the Brother, instead of being in haste to ask his help, praises his singing, and inquires his business in that place. It is remarkable that at this interview the Brother is taken with a short fit of rhyming. The Spirit relates that the Lady is in the power of Comus, the Brother moralizes again, and the Spirit makes a long narration, of no use because it is false, and therefore unsuitable to a good being.

In all these parts the language is poetical and the sentiments are generous, but there is something wanting to allure attention.

The dispute between the Lady and Comus is the most animated and affecting scene of the drama, and wants nothing but a brisker reciprocation of objections and replies to invite attention and detain it.

The songs are vigorous, and full of imagery; but they are harsh in their diction, and not very musical in their numbers.

Throughout the whole the figures are too bold, and the language too luxuriant for dialogue: it is a drama in the epic style, inelegantly splendid, and tediously instructive.

The *Sonnets* were written in different parts of Milton's life upon different occasions. They deserve not any particular criticism; for of the best it can only be said that they are not bad, and perhaps only the eighth and the twenty-first are truly entitled to this slender commendation. The fabric of a sonnet, however adapted to the Italian language, has never succeeded in ours which, having greater variety of termination, requires the rhymes to be often changed.

Those little pieces may be dispatched without much anxiety; a greater work calls for greater care. I am now to examine *Paradise Lost*, a poem which, considered with respect to design, may claim the first place, and with respect to performance the second,[67] among the productions of the human mind.

By the general consent of critics the first praise of genius is due to the writer of an epic poem, as it requires an assemblage of all the powers which are singly sufficient for other compositions. Poetry is the art of uniting pleasure with truth, by calling imagination to the help of reason. Epic poetry undertakes to teach the most important truths by the most pleasing precepts, and therefore relates some great event in the most affecting manner. History must supply the writer with the rudiments of narration, which he must improve and exalt by a nobler art, must animate by dramatic energy, and diversify by retrospection and anticipation; morality must teach him the exact bounds and different shades of vice and virtue; from policy and practice of life he has to learn the discriminations of character and the tendency of the passions, either single or combined; and physiology[68] must supply him with illustrations and images. To put these materials to poetical use is required an imagination capable of painting nature and realizing fiction. Nor is he yet a poet till he has attained the whole extension of his language, distinguished all the delicacies of phrase, and all the colors of words, and learned to adjust their different sounds to all the varieties of metrical modulation.

Bossu is of opinion that the poet's first work is to find a *moral*, which his fable is afterwards to illustrate and establish. This seems to have been the process only of Milton: the moral of other poems is incidental and consequent; in Milton's only it is essential and intrinsic. His purpose was the most

---

[67] Second, presumably, to Homer's *Iliad*.
[68] *physiology:* natural science.

useful and the most arduous: "to vindicate the ways of God to man";[69] to show the reasonableness of religion, and the necessity of obedience to the Divine Law.

To convey this moral there must be a *fable*, a narration artfully constructed so as to excite curiosity and surprise expectation. In this part of his work Milton must be confessed to have equaled every other poet. He has involved in his account of the Fall of Man the events which preceded, and those that were to follow it: he has interwoven the whole system of theology with such propriety that every part appears to be necessary, and scarcely any recital is wished shorter for the sake of quickening the progress of the main action.

The subject of an epic poem is naturally an event of great importance. That of Milton is not the destruction of a city, the conduct of a colony, or the foundation of an empire.[70] His subject is the fate of worlds, the revolutions of heaven and of earth; rebellion against the Supreme King raised by the highest order of created beings; the overthrow of their host and the punishment of their crime; the creation of a new race of reasonable creatures; their original happiness and innocence; their forfeiture of immortality, and their restoration to hope and peace.

Great events can be hastened or retarded only by persons of elevated dignity. Before the greatness displayed in Milton's poem all other greatness shrinks away. The weakest of his agents are the highest and noblest of human beings, the original parents of mankind; with whose actions the elements consented, on whose rectitude or deviation of will depended the state of terrestrial nature and the condition of all the future inhabitants of the globe.

Of the other agents in the poem the chief are such as it is irreverence to name on slight occasions. The rest are lower powers,

> of which the least could wield
> Those elements, and arm him with the force
> Of all their regions; [VI, 221–23]

[69] *Paradise Lost*, I, 26, reads "justify the ways of God to man." Johnson quotes Pope, expressing his analogous purpose in *Essay on Man*, I, 16.
[70] Homer's *Iliad* describes the fall of Troy; Virgil's *Aeneid*, Aeneas's leading the survivors to Italy and founding the Roman Empire.

powers which only the control of Omnipotence restrains from laying creation waste, and filling the vast expanse of space with ruin and confusion. To display the motives and actions of beings thus superior, so far as human reason can examine them or human imagination represent them, is the task which this mighty poet has undertaken and performed.

In the examination of epic poems much speculation is commonly employed upon the *characters*. The characters in the *Paradise Lost* which admit of examination are those of angels and of man; of angels good and evil, of man in his innocent and sinful state.

Among the angels the virtue of Raphael is mild and placid, of easy condescension and free communication; that of Michael is regal and lofty, and, as may seem, attentive to the dignity of his own nature. Abdiel and Gabriel appear occasionally, and act as every incident requires; the solitary fidelity of Abdiel is very amiably painted.

Of the evil angels the characters are more diversified. To Satan, as Addison observes, such sentiments are given as suit "the most exalted and most depraved being." Milton has been censured, by Clarke, for the impiety which sometimes breaks from Satan's mouth. For there are thoughts, as he justly remarks, which no observation of character can justify, because no good man would willingly permit them to pass, however transiently, through his own mind. To make Satan speak as a rebel, without any such expressions as might taint the reader's imagination, was indeed one of the great difficulties in Milton's undertaking, and I cannot but think that he has extricated himself with great happiness. There is in Satan's speeches little that can give pain to a pious ear. The language of rebellion cannot be the same with that of obedience. The malignity of Satan foams in haughtiness and obstinacy; but his expressions are commonly general, and no otherwise offensive than as they are wicked.

The other chiefs of the celestial rebellion are very judiciously discriminated in the first and second books; and the ferocious character of Moloch appears, both in the battle and the council, with exact consistency.

To Adam and to Eve are given during their innocence such sentiments as innocence can generate and utter. Their love is pure benevolence and mutual veneration; their repasts are without luxury and their diligence without toil. Their addresses to their Maker have little more than the voice of admiration and gratitude. Fruition left them nothing to ask, and innocence left them nothing to fear.

But with guilt enter distrust and discord, mutual accusation, and stubborn self-defense; they regard each other with alienated minds, and dread their Creator as the avenger of their transgression. At last they seek shelter in his mercy, soften to repentance, and melt in supplication. Both before and after the Fall the superiority of Adam is diligently sustained.

Of the *probable* and the *marvelous*, two parts of a vulgar[71] epic poem which immerge the critic in deep consideration, the *Paradise Lost* requires little to be said. It contains the history of a miracle, of Creation and Redemption; it displays the power and the mercy of the Supreme Being; the probable therefore is marvelous, and the marvelous is probable. The substance of the narrative is truth; and as truth allows no choice, it is, like necessity, superior to rule. To the accidental or adventitious parts, as to everything human, some slight exceptions may be made. But the main fabric is immovably supported.

It is justly remarked by Addison that this poem has, by the nature of its subject, the advantage above all others, that it is universally and perpetually interesting. All mankind will, through all ages, bear the same relation to Adam and to Eve, and must partake of that good and evil which extend to themselves.

Of the *machinery*, so called from Θεὸς ἀπὸ μηχανῆς [god in the machine],[72] by which is meant the occasional interposition of supernatural power, another fertile topic of critical remarks, here is no room to speak, because everything is done under the immediate and visible direction of Heaven; but the rule is so far observed that no part of the action could have been accomplished by any other means.

Of *episodes*,[73] I think there are only two, contained in Raphael's relation of the war in heaven and Michael's prophetic account of the changes to happen in this world. Both are closely connected with the great action; one was necessary to Adam as a warning, the other as a consolation.

---

[71] *vulgar:* ordinary; i.e., secular.
[72] I.e., supernatural beings directly intervening in human affairs.
[73] *episodes:* digressions from the main action.

To the completeness or *integrity* of the design nothing can be objected; it has distinctly and clearly what Aristotle requires, a beginning, a middle, and an end. There is perhaps no poem of the same length from which so little can be taken without apparent mutilation. Here are no funeral games, nor is there any long description of a shield.[74] The short digressions at the beginning of the third, seventh, and ninth books, might doubtless be spared; but superfluities so beautiful who would take away? or who does not wish that the author of the *Iliad* had gratified succeeding ages with a little knowledge of himself? Perhaps no passages are more frequently or more attentively read than those extrinsic paragraphs; and, since the end of poetry is pleasure, that cannot be unpoetical with which all are pleased.

The questions, whether the action of the poem be strictly *one*, whether the poem can be properly termed *heroic*, and who is the hero, are raised by such readers as draw their principles of judgment rather from books than from reason. Milton, though he entitled *Paradise Lost* only a "poem," yet calls it himself "heroic song." Dryden, petulantly and indecently,[75] denies the heroism of Adam, because he was overcome; but there is no reason why the hero should not be unfortunate except established practice, since success and virtue do not go necessarily together. Cato is the hero of Lucan; but Lucan's authority will not be suffered by Quintilian to decide.[76] However, if success be necessary, Adam's deceiver was at last crushed; Adam was restored to his Maker's favor, and therefore may securely resume his human rank.

After the scheme and fabric of the poem must be considered its component parts, the sentiments and the diction.

The *sentiments*, as expressive of manners or appropriated to characters, are for the greater part unexceptionably just.

Splendid passages containing lessons of morality or precepts of prudence occur seldom. Such is the original formation

---

[74] Nothing comparable to the elaborate funeral games in the *Iliad* and the *Aeneid* nor the description of Achilles' shield in the *Iliad* (though Milton does briefly describe games conducted by the fallen angels in Bk. II).

[75] *indecently:* inappropriately.

[76] Cato, the virtuous hero of Lucan's *Pharsalia*, was defeated. But the critic Quintilian declared that Lucan was not a good model for the poet.

of this poem that as it admits no human manners till the Fall, it can give little assistance to human conduct. Its end is to raise the thoughts above sublunary cares or pleasures. Yet the praise of that fortitude, with which Abdiel maintained his singularity of virtue against the scorn of multitudes, may be accommodated to all times; and Raphael's reproof of Adam's curiosity after the planetary motions, with the answer returned by Adam,[77] may be confidently opposed[78] to any rule of life which any poet has delivered.

The thoughts which are occasionally called forth in the progress are such as could only be produced by an imagination in the highest degree fervid and active, to which materials were supplied by incessant study and unlimited curiosity. The heat of Milton's mind might be said to sublimate his learning, to throw off into his work the spirit of science,[79] unmingled with its grosser parts.

He had considered creation in its whole extent, and his descriptions are therefore learned. He had accustomed his imagination to unrestrained indulgence, and his conceptions therefore were extensive. The characteristic quality of his poem is sublimity. He sometimes descends to the elegant, but his element is the great. He can occasionally invest himself with grace; but his natural port[80] is gigantic loftiness. He can please when pleasure is required; but it is his peculiar power to astonish.

He seems to have been well acquainted with his own genius, and to know what it was that nature had bestowed upon him more bountifully than upon others: the power of displaying the vast, illuminating the splendid, enforcing the awful, darkening the gloomy, and aggravating the dreadful: he therefore chose a subject on which too much could not be said, on which he might tire his fancy without the censure of extravagance.

The appearances of nature and the occurrences of life did not satiate his appetite of greatness. To paint things as they

[77] Abdiel, alone among Satan's legions, opposed his rebellion against God (V, 803–907); Raphael rebuked Adam for questioning God's purpose in creating the heavens, telling him to confine his inquiries to what concerned him, and Adam gracefully acknowledged his error (VIII, 66–197).
[78] *opposed:* set against.
[79] *science:* knowledge.
[80] *port:* manner.

are requires a minute attention, and employs the memory rather than the fancy. Milton's delight was to sport in the wide regions of possibility; reality was a scene too narrow for his mind. He sent his faculties out upon discovery into worlds where only imagination can travel, and delighted to form new modes of existence, and furnish sentiment and action to superior beings, to trace the counsels of hell, or accompany the choirs of heaven.

But he could not be always in other worlds: he must sometimes revisit earth, and tell of things visible and known. When he cannot raise wonder by the sublimity of his mind, he gives delight by its fertility.

Whatever be his subject he never fails to fill the imagination. But his images and descriptions of the scenes or operations of nature do not seem to be always copied from original form, nor to have the freshness, raciness, and energy of immediate observation. He saw nature, as Dryden expresses it, "through the spectacles of books"; and on most occasions calls learning to his assistance. The garden of Eden brings to his mind the vale of Enna, where Proserpine was gathering flowers. Satan makes his way through fighting elements, like Argo between the Cyanean rocks, or Ulysses between the two Sicilian whirlpools, when he shunned Charybdis "on the larboard." The mythological allusions have been justly censured, as not being always used with notice of their vanity; but they contribute variety to the narration, and produce an alternate exercise of the memory and the fancy.

His similes are less numerous and more various than those of his predecessors. But he does not confine himself within the limits of rigorous comparison: his great excellence is amplitude, and he expands the adventitious image beyond the dimensions which the occasion required. Thus, comparing the shield of Satan to the orb of the Moon, he crowds the imagination with the discovery of the telescope and all the wonders which the telescope discovers.[81]

Of his moral sentiments it is hardly praise to affirm that they excel those of all other poets; for this superiority he was indebted to his acquaintance with the sacred writings. The ancient epic poets, wanting the light of Revelation, were very unskillful teachers of virtue: their principal characters may be

[81] *discovers:* reveals (*Paradise Lost* I, 284–91).

great, but they are not amiable. The reader may rise from their works with a greater degree of active or passive fortitude, and sometimes of prudence; but he will be able to carry away few precepts of justice, and none of mercy.

From the Italian writers it appears that the advantages of even Christian knowledge may be possessed in vain. Ariosto's pravity is generally known; and though the *Deliverance of Jerusalem* may be considered as a sacred subject, the poet has been very sparing of moral instruction.[82]

In Milton every line breathes sanctity of thought and purity of manners, except when the train of the narration requires the introduction of the rebellious spirits; and even they are compelled to acknowledge their subjection to God in such a manner as excites reverence and confirms piety.

Of human beings there are but two; but those two are the parents of mankind, venerable before their fall for dignity and innocence, and amiable after it for repentance and submission. In their first state their affection is tender without weakness, and their piety sublime without presumption. When they have sinned they show how discord begins in mutual frailty, and how it ought to cease in mutual forbearance; how confidence of the divine favor is forfeited by sin, and how hope of pardon may be obtained by penitence and prayer. A state of innocence we can only conceive, if indeed in our present misery it be possible to conceive it; but the sentiments and worship proper to a fallen and offending being we have all to learn, as we have all to practice.

The poet, whatever be done, is always great. Our progenitors in their first state conversed with angels; even when folly and sin had degraded them, they had not in their humiliation "the port of mean suitors"; and they rise again to reverential regard, when we find that their prayers were heard.

As human passions did not enter the world before the Fall, there is in the *Paradise Lost* little opportunity for the pathetic; but what little there is has not been lost. That passion which is peculiar to rational nature, the anguish arising from the consciousness of transgression and the horrors attending the sense of the divine displeasure, are very justly described and forcibly

---

[82] Ludovico Ariosto showed little or no concern for moral instruction in *Orlando Furioso* (1532); Torquato Tasso's *Deliverance of Jerusalem* (1575) is about the first crusade, but is not so moral as *Paradise Lost*.

impressed. But the passions are moved only on one occasion; sublimity is the general prevailing quality in this poem—sublimity variously modified, sometimes descriptive, sometimes argumentative.

The defects and faults of *Paradise Lost*, for faults and defects every work of man must have, it is the business of impartial criticism to discover. As in displaying the excellence of Milton I have not made long quotations, because of selecting beauties there had been no end, I shall in the same general manner mention that which seems to deserve censure; for what Englishman can take delight in transcribing passages, which, if they lessen the reputation of Milton, diminish in some degree the honor of our country?

The generality of my scheme does not admit the frequent notice of verbal inaccuracies; which Bentley, perhaps better skilled in grammar than in poetry, has often found, though he sometimes made them, and which he imputed to the obtrusions of a reviser whom the author's blindness obliged him to employ.[88] A supposition rash and groundless, if he thought it true; and vile and pernicious if, as is said, he in private allowed it to be false.

The plan of *Paradise Lost* has this inconvenience, that it comprises neither human actions nor human manners. The man and woman who act and suffer are in a state which no other man or woman can ever know. The reader finds no transaction in which he can be engaged, beholds no condition in which he can by any effort of imagination place himself; he has, therefore, little natural curiosity or sympathy.

We all, indeed, feel the effects of Adam's disobedience; we all sin like Adam, and like him must all bewail our offenses; we have restless and insidious enemies in the fallen angels, and in the blessed spirits we have guardians and friends; in the redemption of mankind we hope to be included: in the description of heaven and hell we are surely interested, as we are all to reside hereafter either in the regions of horror or of bliss.

But these truths are too important to be new: they have been taught to our infancy; they have mingled with our soli-

---

[88] In his edition of *Paradise Lost* (1732), the great classical scholar Richard Bentley freely emended lines which he considered faulty, on the grounds that the blind Milton was not able to revise his own copy.

tary thoughts and familiar conversation, and are habitually interwoven with the whole texture of life. Being therefore not new, they raise no unaccustomed emotion in the mind; what we knew before, we cannot learn; what is not unexpected, cannot surprise.

Of the ideas suggested by these awful scenes, from some we recede with reverence, except when stated hours require their association; and from others we shrink with horror, or admit them only as salutary inflictions, as counterpoises to our interests and passions. Such images rather obstruct the career of fancy than incite it.

Pleasure and terror are indeed the genuine sources of poetry; but poetical pleasure must be such as human imagination can at least conceive, and poetical terror such as human strength and fortitude may combat. The good and evil of eternity are too ponderous for the wings of wit; the mind sinks under them in passive helplessness, content with calm belief and humble adoration.

Known truths, however, may take a different appearance, and be conveyed to the mind by a new train of intermediate images. This Milton has undertaken, and performed with pregnancy and vigor of mind peculiar to himself. Whoever considers the few radical positions[84] which the Scriptures afforded him will wonder by what energetic operation he expanded them to such extent and ramified them to so much variety, restrained as he was by religious reverence from licentiousness of fiction.

Here is a full display of the united force of study and genius; of a great accumulation of materials, with judgment to digest and fancy to combine them: Milton was able to select from nature, or from story, from ancient fable or from modern science, whatever could illustrate or adorn his thoughts. An accumulation of knowledge impregnated his mind, fermented by study and exalted by imagination.

It has been therefore said, without an indecent hyperbole, by one of his encomiasts, that in reading *Paradise Lost* we read a book of universal knowledge.

But original deficience cannot be supplied. The want of human interest is always felt. *Paradise Lost* is one of the books which the reader admires and lays down, and forgets

---

[84] *few radical positions:* small foundation.

to take up again. None ever wished it longer than it is. Its perusal is a duty rather than a pleasure. We read Milton for instruction, retire harassed and overburdened, and look elsewhere for recreation; we desert our master, and seek for companions.

Another inconvenience of Milton's design is that it requires the description of what cannot be described, the agency of spirits. He saw that immateriality supplied no images, and that he could not show angels acting but by instruments of action; he therefore invested them with form and matter. This, being necessary, was therefore defensible; and he should have secured the consistency of his system by keeping immateriality out of sight, and enticing his reader to drop it from his thoughts. But he has unhappily perplexed his poetry with his philosophy. His infernal and celestial powers are sometimes pure spirit and sometimes animated body. When Satan walks with his lance upon the "burning marl," he has a body; when, in his passage between hell and the new world he is in danger of sinking in the vacuity and is supported by a gust of rising vapors, he has a body; when he animates the toad, he seems to be mere spirit that can penetrate matter at pleasure; when he "starts up in his own shape," he has at least a determined form; and when he is brought before Gabriel he has "a spear and a shield," which he had the power of hiding in the toad, though the arms of the contending angels are evidently material.

The vulgar inhabitants of Pandaemonium, being "incorporeal spirits," are "at large though without number" in a limited space; yet in the battle when they were overwhelmed by mountains their armour hurt them, "crushed in upon their substance, now grown gross by sinning." This likewise happened to the uncorrupted angels, who were overthrown "the sooner for their arms, for unarmed they might easily as spirits have evaded by contraction or remove." Even as spirits they are hardly spiritual; for "contraction" and "remove" are images of matter; but if they could have escaped without their armor, they might have escaped from it and left only the empty cover to be battered. Uriel, when he rides on a sunbeam, is material; Satan is material when he is afraid of the prowess of Adam.

The confusion of spirit and matter which pervades the whole narration of the war of heaven fills it with incongruity;

and the book in which it is related is, I believe, the favorite of children, and gradually neglected as knowledge is increased.

After the operation of immaterial agents which cannot be explained may be considered that of allegorical persons, which have no real existence. To exalt causes into agents, to invest abstract ideas with form and animate them with activity has always been the right of poetry. But such airy beings are for the most part suffered only to do their natural office, and retire. Thus Fame tells a tale, and Victory hovers over a general or perches on a standard; but Fame and Victory can do no more. To give them any real employment or ascribe to them any material agency is to make them allegorical no longer, but to shock the mind by ascribing effects to nonentity. In the *Prometheus* of Aeschylus we see Violence and Strength, and in the *Alcestis* of Euripides we see Death, brought upon the stage, all as active persons of the drama; but no precedents can justify absurdity.

Milton's allegory of Sin and Death is undoubtedly faulty. Sin is indeed the mother of Death, and may be allowed to be the portress of hell; but when they stop the journey of Satan, a journey described as real, and when Death offers him battle, the allegory is broken. That Sin and Death should have shown the way to hell might have been allowed; but they cannot facilitate the passage by building a bridge, because the difficulty of Satan's passage is described as real and sensible,[85] and the bridge ought to be only figurative. The hell assigned to the rebellious spirits is described as not less local than the residence of man. It is placed in some distant part of space, separated from the regions of harmony and order by a chaotic waste and an unoccupied vacuity; but Sin and Death worked up a "mole of aggravated[86] soil," cemented with "asphaltus"; a work too bulky for ideal[87] architects.

This unskillful allegory appears to me one of the greatest faults of the poem; and to this there was no temptation, but the author's opinion of its beauty.

To the conduct of the narrative some objections may be made. Satan is with great expectation brought before Gabriel in Paradise, and is suffered to go away unmolested. The crea-

---

[85] *sensible:* perceptible to the senses.
[86] Milton wrote "aggregated" (X, 293).
[87] *ideal:* imaginary, existing only in the mind.

tion of man is represented as the consequence of the vacuity left in heaven by the expulsion of the rebels, yet Satan mentions it as a report "rife in heaven" before his departure.

To find sentiments for the state of innocence was very difficult; and something of anticipation perhaps is now and then discovered. Adam's discourse of dreams seems not to be the speculation of a new-created being. I know not whether his answer to the angel's reproof for curiosity does not want something of propriety: it is the speech of a man acquainted with many other men. Some philosophical notions, especially when the philosophy is false, might have been better omitted. The angel, in a comparison, speaks of "timorous deer," before deer were yet timorous, and before Adam could understand the comparison.

Dryden remarks, that Milton has some flats among his elevations. This is only to say that all the parts are not equal. In every work one part must be for the sake of others; a palace must have passages, a poem must have transitions. It is no more to be required that wit should always be blazing than that the sun should always stand at noon. In a great work there is a vicissitude of luminous and opaque parts, as there is in the world a succession of day and night. Milton, when he has expatiated in the sky, may be allowed sometimes to revisit earth; for what other author ever soared so high or sustained his flight so long?

Milton, being well versed in the Italian poets, appears to have borrowed often from them; and, as every man catches something from his companions, his desire of imitating Ariosto's levity has disgraced his work with the "Paradise of Fools"; a fiction not in itself ill-imagined, but too ludicrous for its place.

His play on words, in which he delights too often; his equivocations, which Bentley endeavors to defend by the example of the ancients; his unnecessary and ungraceful use of terms of art,[88] it is not necessary to mention, because they are easily remarked and generally censured, and at last bear so little proportion to the whole that they scarcely deserve the attention of a critic.

Such are the faults of that wonderful performance, *Paradise Lost*; which he who can put in balance with its beauties must

---

[88] *terms of art:* technical terms.

be considered not as nice but as dull, as less to be censured for want of candor[89] than pitied for want of sensibility.

Of *Paradise Regained* the general judgment seems now to be right, that it is in many parts elegant, and everywhere instructive. It was not to be supposed that the writer of *Paradise Lost* could ever write without great effusions of fancy and exalted precepts of wisdom. The basis of *Paradise Regained* is narrow; a dialogue without action can never please like an union of the narrative and dramatic powers. Had this poem been written, not by Milton but by some imitator, it would have claimed and received universal praise.

If *Paradise Regained* has been too much depreciated, *Samson Agonistes* has in requital been too much admired. It could only be by long prejudice and the bigotry of learning that Milton could prefer the ancient tragedies with their encumbrance of a chorus to the exhibitions of the French and English stages; and it is only by a blind confidence in the reputation of Milton that a drama can be praised in which the intermediate parts have neither cause nor consequence, neither hasten nor retard the catastrophe.

In this tragedy are however many particular beauties, many just sentiments and striking lines; but it wants that power of attracting the attention which a well-connected plan produces.

Milton would not have excelled in dramatic writing; he knew human nature only in the gross, and had never studied the shades of character, nor the combinations of concurring or the perplexity of contending passions. He had read much and knew what books could teach; but had mingled little in the world, and was deficient in the knowledge which experience must confer.

Through all his greater works there prevails an uniform peculiarity of *diction*, a mode and cast of expression which bears little resemblance to that of any former writer, and which is so far removed from common use that an unlearned reader, when he first opens his book, finds himself surprised by a new language.

This novelty has been, by those who can find nothing wrong in Milton, imputed to his laborious endeavors after words suitable to the grandeur of his ideas. "Our language," says Addison, "sunk under him." But the truth is that, both in

[89] *candor:* fairness.

prose and verse, he had formed his style by a perverse and pedantic principle. He was desirous to use English words with a foreign idiom. This in all his prose is discovered and condemned, for there judgment operates freely, neither softened by the beauty nor awed by the dignity of his thoughts; but such is the power of his poetry that his call is obeyed without resistance, the reader feels himself in captivity to a higher and a nobler mind, and criticism sinks in admiration.

Milton's style was not modified by his subject: what is shown with greater extent in *Paradise Lost* may be found in *Comus*. One source of his peculiarity was his familiarity with the Tuscan poets: the disposition of his words is, I think, frequently Italian; perhaps sometimes combined with other tongues. Of him, at last, may be said what Jonson says of Spenser, that "he wrote no language," but has formed what Butler calls a "Babylonish dialect," in itself harsh and barbarous, but made by exalted genius and extensive learning the vehicle of so much instruction and so much pleasure that, like other lovers, we find grace in its deformity.

Whatever be the faults of his diction he cannot want the praise of copiousness and variety; he was master of his language in its full extent, and has selected the melodious words with such diligence that from his book alone the art of English poetry might be learned.

After his diction, something must be said of his versification. "The measure," he says, "is the English heroic verse without rhyme." Of this mode he had many examples among the Italians, and some in his own country. The Earl of Surrey is said to have translated one of Virgil's books without rhyme, and besides our tragedies a few short poems had appeared in blank verse; particularly one tending to reconcile the nation to Ralegh's wild attempt upon Guiana, and probably written by Ralegh himself. These petty performances cannot be supposed to have much influenced Milton, who more probably took his hint from Trissino's *Italia Liberata* and, finding blank verse easier than rhyme, was desirous of persuading himself that it is better.

"Rhyme," he says, and says truly, "is no necessary adjunct of true poetry." But perhaps of poetry as a mental operation meter or music is no necessary adjunct: it is however by the music of meter that poetry has been discriminated in all languages, and in languages melodiously constructed with a due proportion of long and short syllables, meter is sufficient. But one language cannot communicate its rules to another; where meter is scanty and imperfect some help is necessary. The music of the English heroic line strikes the ear so faintly that it is easily lost, unless all the syllables of every line cooperate together; this cooperation can be only obtained by the preservation of every verse unmingled with another as a distinct system of sounds, and this distinctness is obtained and preserved by the artifice of rhyme. The variety of pauses, so much boasted by the lovers of blank verse, changes the measures of an English poet to the periods of a declaimer; and there are only a few skillful and happy readers of Milton who enable their audience to perceive where the lines end or begin. "Blank verse," said an ingenious critic, "seems to be verse only to the eye."

Poetry may subsist without rhyme, but English poetry will not often please; nor can rhyme ever be safely spared but where the subject is able to support itself. Blank verse makes some approach to that which is called the "lapidary style," has neither the easiness of prose nor the melody of numbers, and therefore tires by long continuance. Of the Italian writers without rhyme, whom Milton alleges as precedents, not one is popular; what reason could urge in its defense has been confuted by the ear.

But, whatever be the advantage of rhyme I cannot prevail on myself to wish that Milton had been a rhymer, for I cannot wish his work to be other than it is; yet like other heroes he is to be admired rather than imitated. He that thinks himself capable of astonishing may write blank verse, but those that hope only to please must condescend to rhyme.

The highest praise of genius is original invention. Milton cannot be said to have contrived the structure of an epic poem, and therefore owes reverence to that vigor and amplitude of mind to which all generations must be indebted for the art of poetical narration, for the texture of the fable, the variation of incidents, the interposition of dialogue, and all the stratagems that surprise and enchain attention. But of all the borrowers from Homer Milton is perhaps the least indebted. He was naturally a thinker for himself, confident of his own abilities and disdainful of help or hindrance; he did not refuse admission to the thought or images of his predecessors, but he did not seek them. From his contemporaries he neither courted nor received support; there is in his writings nothing by which the pride of other authors might be gratified or favor gained; no exchange of praise, nor solicitation of support. His great works were performed under discountenance and in blindness, but difficulties vanished at his touch; he was born for whatever is arduous; and his work is not the greatest of heroic poems, only because it is not the first.

Alexander Pope
1688-1744

Alexander Pope was born in London, May 22, 1688, of parents whose rank or station was never ascertained: we are informed that they were of "gentle blood"; that his father was of a family of which the Earl of Downe was the head, and that his mother was the daughter of William Turner, Esquire, of York, who had likewise three sons, one of whom had the honor of being killed, and the other of dying, in the service of Charles the First; the third was made a general officer in Spain, from whom the sister inherited what sequestrations and forfeitures had left in the family.

This and this only is told by Pope; who is more willing, as I have heard observed, to show what his father was not, than what he was. It is allowed that he grew rich by trade; but whether in a shop or on the Exchange was never discovered, till Mr. Tyers told, on the authority of Mrs. Rackett, that he was a linen-draper in the Strand. Both parents were Papists.

Pope was from his birth of a constitution tender and delicate; but is said to have shown remarkable gentleness and sweetness of disposition. The weakness of his body continued through his life, but the mildness of his mind perhaps ended with his childhood. His voice, when he was young, was so pleasing that he was called in fondness the "little nightingale."

Being not sent early to school he was taught to read by an aunt; and when he was seven or eight years old became a lover of books. He first learned to write by imitating printed books; a species of penmanship in which he retained great excellence through his whole life, though his ordinary hand was not elegant.

When he was about eight he was placed in Hampshire under Taverner, a Romish priest, who, by a method very rarely practiced, taught him the Greek and Latin rudiments together. He was now first regularly initiated in poetry by the perusal of Ogilby's Homer, and Sandys's Ovid; Ogilby's assistance he never repaid with any praise; but of Sandys he declared, in his notes to the *Iliad*, that English poetry owed much of its present beauty to his translations. Sandys very rarely attempted original composition.

From the care of Taverner, under whom his proficiency was considerable, he was removed to a school at Twyford near Winchester, and again to another school about Hyde Park Corner; from which he used sometimes to stroll to the playhouse, and was so delighted with theatrical exhibitions that he formed a kind of play from Ogilby's *Iliad*, with some verses of his own intermixed, which he persuaded his schoolfellows to act, with the addition of his master's gardener, who personated Ajax.

At the two last schools he used to represent himself as having lost part of what Taverner had taught him, and on his master at Twyford he had already exercised his poetry in a lampoon. Yet under those masters he translated more than a fourth part of the *Metamorphoses*. If he kept the same proportion in his other exercises it cannot be thought that his loss was great.

He tells of himself in his poems that "he lisped in numbers," and used to say that he could not remember the time when he began to make verses. In the style of fiction it might have been said of him as of Pindar, that when he lay in his cradle, "the bees swarmed about his mouth."

About the time of the Revolution his father, who was undoubtedly disappointed by the sudden blast of popish prosperity, quitted his trade, and retired to Binfield in Windsor Forest, with about twenty thousand pounds, for which, being conscientiously determined not to entrust it to the government, he found no better use than that of locking it up in a chest and taking from it what his expenses required; and his life was long enough to consume a great part of it before his son came to the inheritance.

To Binfield Pope was called by his father when he was about twelve years old; and there he had for a few months the assistance of one Deane, another priest, of whom he learned only to construe a little of Tully's *Offices*.[1] How Mr. Deane could spend with a boy who had translated so much of Ovid, some months over a small part of Tully's *Offices*, it is now vain to inquire.

---

[1] Marcus Tullius Cicero's *De Officiis*.

Of a youth so successfully employed, and so conspicuously improved, a minute account must be naturally desired; but curiosity must be contented with confused, imperfect, and sometimes improbable intelligence. Pope, finding little advantage from external help, resolved thenceforward to direct himself, and at twelve formed a plan of study which he completed with little other incitement than the desire of excellence.

His primary and principal purpose was to be a poet, with which his father accidentally concurred, by proposing subjects and obliging him to correct his performances by many revisals; after which the old gentleman, when he was satisfied, would say, "these are good rhymes."

In his perusal of the English poets he soon distinguished the versification of Dryden, which he considered as the model to be studied, and was impressed with such veneration for his instructer that he persuaded some friends to take him to the coffee-house which Dryden frequented, and pleased himself with having seen him.

Dryden died May 1, 1701, some days before Pope was twelve: so early must he therefore have felt the power of harmony and the zeal of genius. Who does not wish that Dryden could have known the value of the homage that was paid him, and foreseen the greatness of his young admirer?

The earliest of Pope's productions is his "Ode on Solitude," written before he was twelve, in which there is nothing more than other forward boys have attained, and which is not equal to Cowley's performances at the same age.

His time was now spent wholly in reading and writing. As he read the classics he amused himself with translating them; and at fourteen made a version of the first book of the *Thebais*, which, with some revision, he afterwards published. He must have been at this time, if he had no help, a considerable proficient in the Latin tongue.

By Dryden's *Fables*, which had been not long published, and were much in the hands of poetical readers, he was tempted to try his own skill in giving Chaucer a more fashionable appearance, and put *January and May*, and the *Prologue of the Wife of Bath*, into modern English. He translated likewise the *Epistle of Sappho to Phaon* from Ovid, to complete the version[2] which was before imperfect, and wrote some other small pieces, which he afterwards printed.

---

[2] *version:* translation.

He sometimes imitated the English poets, and professed to have written at fourteen his poem upon "Silence," after Rochester's "Nothing." He had now formed his versification and in the smoothness of his numbers surpassed his original; but this is a small part of his praise: he discovers such acquaintance both with human life and public affairs as is not easily conceived to have been attainable by a boy of fourteen in Windsor Forest.

Next year he was desirous of opening to himself new sources of knowledge, by making himself acquainted with modern languages, and removed for a time to London that he might study French and Italian, which, as he desired nothing more than to read them, were by diligent application soon despatched. Of Italian learning he does not appear to have ever made much use in his subsequent studies.

He then returned to Binfield, and delighted himself with his own poetry. He tried all styles, and many subjects. He wrote a comedy, a tragedy, an epic poem, with panegyrics on all the princes of Europe; and, as he confesses, "thought himself the greatest genius that ever was." Self-confidence is the first requisite to great undertakings; he, indeed, who forms his opinion of himself in solitude, without knowing the powers of other men, is very liable to error; but it was the felicity of Pope to rate himself at his real value.

Most of his puerile productions were by his maturer judgment afterwards destroyed; "Alcander," the epic poem, was burnt by the persuasion of Atterbury. The tragedy was founded on the legend of St. Geneviève. Of the comedy there is no account.

Concerning his studies it is related that he translated Tully *On Old Age*; and that, besides his books of poetry and criticism, he read Temple's *Essays* and Locke *On Human Understanding*. His reading, though his favorite authors are not known, appears to have been sufficiently extensive and multifarious; for his early pieces show, with sufficient evidence, his knowledge of books.

He that is pleased with himself easily imagines that he shall please others. Sir William Trumbull, who had been Ambassador at Constantinople, and Secretary of State, when he retired from business fixed his residence in the neighborhood of Binfield. Pope, not yet sixteen, was introduced to the statesman of sixty, and so distinguished himself that their interviews ended in friendship and correspondence. Pope was through his whole life ambitious of splendid acquaintance, and he seems to have wanted neither diligence nor success in attracting the notice of the great; for from his first entrance into the world, and his entrance was very early, he was admitted to familiarity with those whose rank or station made them most conspicuous.

From the age of sixteen the life of Pope as an author may be properly computed. He now wrote his *Pastorals*, which were shown to the poets and critics of that time; as they well deserved they were read with admiration, and many praises were bestowed upon them and upon the Preface, which is both elegant and learned in a high degree: they were, however, not published till five years afterwards.

Cowley, Milton, and Pope are distinguished among the English poets by the early exertion of their powers; but the works of Cowley alone were published in his childhood, and therefore of him only can it be certain that his puerile performances received no improvement from his maturer studies.

At this time began his acquaintance with Wycherley, a man who seems to have had among his contemporaries his full share of reputation, to have been esteemed without virtue, and caressed without good-humor. Pope was proud of his notice, Wycherley wrote verses in his praise, which he was charged by Dennis with writing to himself, and they agreed for a while to flatter one another. It is pleasant to remark how soon Pope learned the cant of an author, and began to treat critics with contempt, though he had yet suffered nothing from them.

But the fondness of Wycherley was too violent to last. His esteem of Pope was such that he submitted some poems to his revision; and when Pope, perhaps proud of such confidence, was sufficiently bold in his criticisms and liberal in his alterations, the old scribbler was angry to see his pages defaced, and felt more pain from the detection than content from the amendment of his faults. They parted; but Pope always considered him with kindness, and visited him a little time before he died.

Another of his early correspondents was Mr. Cromwell, of whom I have learned nothing particular but that he used to ride a-hunting in a tie-wig. He was fond, and perhaps vain, of amusing himself with poetry and criticism, and sometimes sent his performances to Pope, who did not forbear such remarks as were now and then unwelcome. Pope, in his turn, put the juvenile version of Statius into his hands for correction.

Their correspondence afforded the public its first knowledge of Pope's epistolary powers; for his letters were given by Cromwell to one Mrs. Thomas, and she many years afterwards sold them to Curll, who inserted them in a volume of his *Miscellanies*.

Walsh, a name yet preserved among the minor poets, was one of his first encouragers. His regard was gained by the *Pastorals*, and from him Pope received the counsel by which he seems to have regulated his studies. Walsh advised him to correctness, which, as he told him, the English poets had hitherto neglected, and which therefore was left to him as a basis of fame; and, being delighted with rural poems, recommended to him to write a pastoral comedy, like those which are read so eagerly in Italy; a design which Pope probably did not approve, as he did not follow it.

Pope had now declared himself a poet; and, thinking himself entitled to poetical conversation, began at seventeen to frequent Will's, a coffee-house on the north side of Russell Street in Covent Garden, where the wits of that time used to assemble, and where Dryden had, when he lived, been accustomed to preside.

During this period of his life he was indefatigably diligent, and insatiably curious; wanting health for violent, and money for expensive pleasures, and having certainly excited in himself very strong desires of intellectual eminence, he spent much of his time over his books: but he read only to store his mind with facts and images, seizing all that his authors presented with undistinguishing voracity, and with an appetite for knowledge too eager to be nice. In a mind like his, however, all the faculties were at once involuntarily improving. Judgment is forced upon us by experience. He that reads many books must compare one opinion or one style with another; and when he compares, must necessarily distinguish, reject, and prefer. But the account given by himself of his studies was that from fourteen to twenty he read only for amusement, from twenty to twenty-seven for improvement and instruction; that in the first part of this time he desired only to know, and in the second he endeavored to judge.

The *Pastorals*, which had been for some time handed about among poets and critics, were at last printed (1709) in Tonson's *Miscellany*, in a volume which began with the *Pastorals* of Philips, and ended with those of Pope.

The same year was written the *Essay on Criticism*, a work which displays such extent of comprehension, such nicety of distinction, such acquaintance with mankind, and such knowledge both of ancient and modern learning as are not often attained by the maturest age and longest experience. It was published about two years afterwards, and being praised by Addison in *The Spectator* with sufficient liberality, met with so much favor as enraged Dennis, "who," he says,

> found himself attacked, without any manner of provocation on his side, and attacked in his person, instead of his writings, by one who was wholly a stranger to him, at a time when all the world knew he was persecuted by fortune; and not only saw that this was attempted in a clandestine manner, with the utmost falsehood and calumny, but found that all this was done by a little affected hypocrite, who had nothing in his mouth at the same time but truth, candor, friendship, good nature, humanity, and magnanimity.

How the attack was clandestine is not easily perceived, nor how his person is depreciated;[3] but he seems to have known something of Pope's character, in whom may be discovered an appetite to talk too frequently of his own virtues.

The pamphlet is such as rage might be expected to dictate. He supposes himself to be asked two questions: whether the *Essay* will succeed, and who or what is the author.

Its success he admits to be secured by the false opinions then prevalent; the author he concludes to be "young and raw."

> First, because he discovers a sufficiency beyond his little ability, and hath rashly undertaken a task infinitely above his force. Secondly, while this little author struts, and affects the dictatorian air, he plainly shows that at the same time he is under the rod; and while he pretends to give law to others, is a pedantic slave to authority and opinion. Thirdly, he hath, like schoolboys, borrowed both from living and dead. Fourthly, he knows not his own mind, and frequently contradicts himself. Fifthly, he is almost perpetually in the wrong.

[3] Pope ridiculed Dennis as Appius, who becomes enraged by a word of criticism ("Essay on Criticism," lines 585–87).

All these positions he attempts to prove by quotations and remarks; but his desire to do mischief is greater than his power. He has, however, justly criticized some passages: in these lines,

> There are whom heaven has blessed with store of wit,
> Yet want as much again to manage it;
> For wit and judgment ever are at strife:

it is apparent that "wit" has two meanings, and that what is wanted, though called "wit," is truly judgment. So far Dennis is undoubtedly right; but, not content with argument, he will have a little mirth, and triumphs over the first couplet in terms too elegant to be forgotten. "By the way, what rare numbers are here! Would not one swear that this youngster had espoused some antiquated Muse, who had sued out a divorce on account of impotence from some superannuated sinner, and, having been poxed by her former spouse, has got the gout in her decrepit age, which makes her hobble so damnably." This was the man who would reform a nation sinking into barbarity.

In another place Pope himself allowed that Dennis had detected one of those blunders which are called "bulls." The first edition had this line:

> What is this wit . . . ?
> Where wanted,[4] scorned; and envied where acquired?

"How," says the critic, "can wit be *scorned* where it is not? Is not this a figure frequently employed in Hibernian land? The person that wants this wit may indeed be scorned, but the scorn shows the honor which the contemner has for wit." Of this remark Pope made the proper use, by correcting the passage.

I have preserved, I think, all that is reasonable in Dennis's criticism; it remains that justice be done to his delicacy.

> For his acquaintance (says Dennis) he names Mr. Walsh, who had by no means the qualification which this author reckons absolutely necessary to a critic, it being very certain that he was, like this essayer, a very indifferent poet; he loved to be well dressed; and I remember a little young

---

[4] *wanted:* lacked.

gentleman whom Mr. Walsh used to take into his company, as a double foil to his person and capacity. . . . Inquire between Sunninghill and Oakingham for a young, short, squab gentleman, the very bow of the God of Love, and tell me whether he be a proper author to make personal reflections? . . . He may extol the ancients, but he has reason to thank the gods that he was born a modern; for had he been born of Grecian parents, and his father consequently had by law had the absolute disposal of him, his life had been no longer than that of one of his poems, the life of half a day. . . . Let the person of a gentleman of his parts be never so contemptible, his inward man is ten times more ridiculous; it being impossible that his outward form, though it be that of downright monkey, should differ so much from human shape, as his unthinking immaterial part does from human understanding.

Thus began the hostility between Pope and Dennis, which, though it was suspended for a short time, never was appeased. Pope seems, at first, to have attacked him wantonly; but though he always professed to despise him, he discovers, by mentioning him very often, that he felt his force or his venom.

Of this *Essay* Pope declared that he did not expect the sale to be quick, because "not one gentleman in sixty, even of liberal education, could understand it." The gentlemen, and the education of that time, seem to have been of a lower character than they are of this. He mentioned a thousand copies as a numerous impression.

Dennis was not his only censurer; the zealous Papists thought the monks treated with too much contempt, and Erasmus too studiously praised; but to these objections he had not much regard.

The *Essay* has been translated into French by Hamilton, author of the *Comte de Grammont*, whose version was never printed, by Robethon, secretary of the King for Hanover, and by Resnel; and commented by Dr. Warburton, who has discovered in it such order and connection as was not perceived by Addison, nor, as is said, intended by the author.

Almost every poem consisting of precepts is so far arbitrary and immethodical that many of the paragraphs may change places with no apparent inconvenience; for of two or more positions, depending upon some remote and general principle, there is seldom any cogent reason why one should precede the other. But for the order in which they stand, whatever it be, a little ingenuity may easily give a reason. "It is possible," says Hooker, "that by long circumduction, from any one truth all truth may be inferred." Of all homogeneous truths at least, of all truths respecting the same general end, in whatever series they may be produced, a concatenation by intermediate ideas may be formed, such as, when it is once shown, shall appear natural; but if this order be reversed, another mode of connection equally specious may be found or made. Aristotle is praised for naming fortitude first of the cardinal virtues, as that without which no other virtue can steadily be practiced; but he might, with equal propriety, have placed prudence and justice before it, since without prudence, fortitude is mad; without justice, it is mischievous.

As the end of method is perspicuity, that series is sufficiently regular that avoids obscurity; and where there is no obscurity it will not be difficult to discover method.

In *The Spectator* was published the "Messiah," which he first submitted to the perusal of Steele, and corrected in compliance with his criticisms.

It is reasonable to infer, from his letters, that the verses on "The Unfortunate Lady" were written about the time when his *Essay* was published. The lady's name and adventures I have sought with fruitless inquiry.

I can therefore tell no more than I have learned from Mr. Ruffhead, who writes with the confidence of one who could trust his information.[5] She was a woman of eminent rank and large fortune, the ward of an uncle who, having given her a proper education, expected like other guardians that she should make at least an equal match; and such he proposed to her, but found it rejected in favor of a young gentleman of inferior condition.

Having discovered the correspondence between the two lovers, and finding the young lady determined to abide by her own choice, he supposed that separation might do what can rarely be done by arguments, and sent her into a foreign country, where she was obliged to converse only with those from whom her uncle had nothing to fear.

Her lover took care to repeat his vows; but his letters were

[5] Owen Ruffhead's *Life of Pope* (1769), based on materials supplied by William Warburton, Pope's literary executor, was one of Johnson's principal sources.

intercepted and carried to her guardian, who directed her to be watched with still greater vigilance; till of this restraint she grew so impatient that she bribed a woman-servant to procure her a sword, which she directed to her heart.

From this account, given with evident intention to raise the lady's character, it does not appear that she had any claim to praise, nor much to compassion. She seems to have been impatient, violent, and ungovernable. Her uncle's power could not have lasted long; the hour of liberty and choice would have come in time. But her desires were too hot for delay, and she liked self-murder better than suspense.

Nor is it discovered that the uncle, whoever he was, is with much justice delivered to posterity as a "false guardian"; he seems to have done only that for which a guardian is appointed: he endeavored to direct his niece till she should be able to direct herself. Poetry has not often been worse employed than in dignifying the amorous fury of a raving girl.

Not long after, he wrote *The Rape of the Lock*, the most airy, the most ingenious, and the most delightful of all his compositions, occasioned by a frolic of gallantry, rather too familiar, in which Lord Petre cut off a lock of Mrs. Arabella Fermor's hair. This, whether stealth or violence, was so much resented that the commerce of the two families, before very friendly, was interrupted. Mr. Caryll, a gentleman who, being secretary to King James's Queen, had followed his mistress into France, and who being the author of *Sir Salomon Single*, a comedy, and some translations, was entitled to the notice of a wit, solicited Pope to endeavor a reconciliation by a ludicrous poem, which might bring both the parties to a better temper. In compliance with Caryll's request, though his name was for a long time marked only by the first and last letter, C—l, a poem of two cantos was written (1711), as is said, in a fortnight, and sent to the offended lady, who liked it well enough to show it; and with the usual process of literary transactions, the author, dreading a surreptitious edition, was forced to publish it.

The event is said to have been such as was desired; the pacification and diversion of all to whom it related, except Sir George Browne, who complained with some bitterness that, in the character of Sir Plume, he was made to talk nonsense. Whether all this be true, I have some doubt; for at Paris, a few years ago, a niece of Mrs. Fermor, who presided in an English convent, mentioned Pope's work with very little gratitude, rather as an insult than an honor; and she may be supposed to have inherited the opinion of her family.

At its first appearance it was termed by Addison *merum sal* [pure wit]. Pope, however, saw that it was capable of improvement; and, having luckily contrived to borrow his machinery from the Rosicrucians, imparted the scheme with which his head was teeming to Addison, who told him that his work, as it stood, was "a delicious little thing," and gave him no encouragement to retouch it.

This has been too hastily considered as an instance of Addison's jealousy; for as he could not guess the conduct of the new design, or the possibilities of pleasure comprised in a fiction of which there had been no examples, he might very reasonably and kindly persuade the author to acquiesce in his own prosperity, and forbear an attempt which he considered as an unnecessary hazard.

Addison's counsel was happily rejected. Pope foresaw the future efflorescence of imagery then budding in his mind and resolved to spare no art or industry of cultivation. The soft luxuriance of his fancy was already shooting, and all the gay varieties of diction were ready at his hand to color and embellish it.

His attempt was justified by its success. *The Rape of the Lock* stands forward, in the classes of literature, as the most exquisite example of ludicrous poetry. Berkeley congratulated him upon the display of powers more truly poetical than he had shown before; with elegance of description and justness of precepts, he had now exhibited boundless fertility of invention.

He always considered the intermixture of the machinery[6] with the action as his most successful exertion of poetical art. He indeed could never afterwards produce anything of such unexampled excellence. Those performances which strike with wonder are combinations of skillful genius with happy casualty;[7] and it is not likely that any felicity, like the discovery of a new race of preternatural agents, should happen twice to the same man.

Of this poem the author was, I think, allowed to enjoy the praise for a long time without disturbance. Many years afterwards Dennis published some *Remarks* upon it, with very little force, and with no effect; for the opinion of the public

---

[6] *machinery:* supernatural agents, the sylphs and gnomes.
[7] Accident.

was already settled, and it was no longer at the mercy of criticism.

About this time he published *The Temple of Fame*, which, as he tells Steele in their correspondence, he had written two years before; that is, when he was only twenty-two years old, an early time of life for so much learning and so much observation as that work exhibits.

On this poem Dennis afterwards published some remarks of which the most reasonable is that some of the lines represent "motion" as exhibited by "sculpture."

Of the *Epistle from Eloisa to Abelard,* I do not know the date. His first inclination to attempt a composition of that tender kind arose, as Mr. Savage told me,[8] from his perusal of Prior's *Nut-Brown Maid.*[9] How much he has surpassed Prior's work it is not necessary to mention, when perhaps it may be said with justice that he has excelled every composition of the same kind. The mixture of religious hope and resignation gives an elevation and dignity to disappointed love, which images merely natural cannot bestow. The gloom of a convent strikes the imagination with far greater force than the solitude of a grove.

This piece was, however, not much his favorite in his latter years, though I never heard upon what principle he slighted it.

In the next year (1713) he published *Windsor Forest*; of which part was, as he relates, written at sixteen, about the same time as his *Pastorals,* and the latter part was added afterwards: where the addition begins, we are not told. The lines relating to the Peace confess their own date.[10] It is dedicated to Lord Lansdowne, who was then high in reputation and influence among the Tories; and it is said that the conclusion of the poem gave great pain to Addison, both as a poet and a politician. Reports like this are often spread with boldness very disproportionate to their evidence. Why should Addison receive disturbance from the last lines of *Windsor Forest?* If contrariety of opinion could poison a politician, he would not live a day; and as a poet, he must have felt Pope's force of genius much more from many other parts of his works.

[8] Richard Savage, a protégé of Pope's, was a dear friend of Johnson's, who wrote his *Life* (1744).
[9] Prior's "Henry and Emma," an imitation of the ballad of the "Nut-Brown Maid," is highly romantic.
[10] The poem ends with a celebration of the Peace of Utrecht (1713).

The pain that Addison might feel it is not likely that he would confess; and it is certain that he so well suppressed his discontent that Pope now thought himself his favorite; for having been consulted in the revisal of *Cato*, he introduced it by a Prologue; and, when Dennis published his *Remarks*, undertook not indeed to vindicate but to revenge his friend, by *A Narrative of the Frenzy of John Dennis*.

There is reason to believe that Addison gave no encouragement to this disingenuous hostility; for, says Pope, in a letter to him, "indeed your opinion, that 'tis entirely to be neglected would be my own in my own case; but I felt more warmth here than I did when I first saw his book against myself (though indeed in two minutes it made me heartily merry)." Addison was not a man on whom such cant of sensibility could make much impression. He left the pamphlet to itself, having disowned it to Dennis, and perhaps did not think Pope to have deserved much by his officiousness.

This year was printed in *The Guardian* the ironical comparison between the *Pastorals* of Philips and Pope: a composition of artifice, criticism, and literature, to which nothing equal will easily be found. The superiority of Pope is so ingeniously dissembled, and the feeble lines of Philips so skillfully preferred, that Steele, being deceived, was unwilling to print the paper lest Pope should be offended. Addison immediately saw the writer's design, and, as it seems, had malice enough to conceal his discovery, and to permit a publication which, by making his friend Philips ridiculous, made him forever an enemy to Pope.[11]

It appears that about this time Pope had a strong inclination to unite the art of painting with that of poetry, and put himself under the tuition of Jervas. He was nearsighted, and therefore not formed by nature for a painter: he tried, however, how far he could advance, and sometimes persuaded his friends to sit. A picture of Betterton supposed to be drawn by him was in the possession of Lord Mansfield: if this was taken from the life, he must have begun to paint earlier, for Betterton was now dead. Pope's ambition of this new art produced some encomiastic verses to Jervas, which certainly show his

---

[11] Pope wrote an ironical essay (*Guardian* No. 40) pretending to prefer Ambrose Philips' Pastorals to his own, which Steele, editor of *The Guardian*, carelessly accepted without recognizing the irony.

power as a poet, but I have been told that they betray his ignorance of painting.

He appears to have regarded Betterton with kindness and esteem; and after his death published, under his name, a version into modern English of Chaucer's *Prologues*, and one of his *Tales*, which, as was related by Mr. Harte, were believed to have been the performance of Pope himself by Fenton, who made him a gay offer of five pounds, if he would show them in the hand of Betterton.[12]

The next year (1713) produced a bolder attempt, by which profit was sought as well as praise. The poems which he had hitherto written, however they might have diffused his name, had made very little addition to his fortune. The allowance which his father made him, though, proportioned to what he had, it might be liberal, could not be large; his religion hindered him from the occupation of any civil employment,[13] and he complained that he wanted even money to buy books.

He therefore resolved to try how far the favor of the public extended, by soliciting a subscription to a version of the *Iliad*, with large notes.

To print by subscription was, for some time, a practice peculiar to the English. The first considerable work for which this expedient was employed is said to have been Dryden's *Virgil*, and it had been tried again with great success when *The Tatlers* were collected into volumes.

There was reason to believe that Pope's attempt would be successful. He was in the full bloom of reputation, and was personally known to almost all whom dignity of employment or splendor of reputation had made eminent; he conversed indifferently with both parties, and never disturbed the public with his political opinions; and it might be naturally expected, as each faction then boasted its literary zeal, that the great men, who on other occasions practiced all the violence of opposition, would emulate each other in their encouragement of a poet who had delighted all, and by whom none had been offended.

With those hopes, he offered an English *Iliad* to subscribers, in six volumes in quarto, for six guineas; a sum, according to

---

[12] Probably Pope only revised Betterton's work.
[13] Roman Catholics were debarred from public office and the learned professions.

the value of money at that time, by no means inconsiderable, and greater than I believe to have been ever asked before. His proposal, however, was very favorably received, and the patrons of literature were busy to recommend his undertaking, and promote his interest. Lord Oxford,[14] indeed, lamented that such a genius should be wasted upon a work not original; but proposed no means by which he might live without it: Addison recommended caution and moderation, and advised him not to be content with the praise of half the nation, when he might be universally favored.

The greatness of the design, the popularity of the author, and the attention of the literary world, naturally raised such expectations of the future sale, that the booksellers made their offers with great eagerness; but the highest bidder was Bernard Lintot, who became proprietor on condition of supplying, at his own expense, all the copies which were to be delivered to subscribers, or presented to friends, and paying two hundred pounds for every volume.

Of the quartos it was, I believe, stipulated that none should be printed but for the author, that the subscription might not be depreciated; but Lintot impressed the same pages upon a small folio, and paper perhaps a little thinner; and sold exactly at half the price, for half a guinea each volume, books so little inferior to the quartos, that, by a fraud of trade, those folios, being afterwards shortened by cutting away the top and bottom, were sold as copies printed for the subscribers.

Lintot printed two hundred and fifty on royal paper in folio for two guineas a volume; of the small folio, having printed seventeen hundred and fifty copies of the first volume, he reduced the number in the other volumes to a thousand.

It is unpleasant to relate that the bookseller, after all his hopes and all his liberality, was, by a very unjust and illegal action, defrauded of his profit. An edition of the English *Iliad* was printed in Holland in duodecimo, and imported clandestinely for the gratification of those who were impatient to read what they could not yet afford to buy. This fraud could only be counteracted by an edition equally cheap and more commodious, and Lintot was compelled to contract his folio at once into a duodecimo, and lose the advantage of an inter-

---

[14] Robert Harley, Earl of Oxford, was the leader of the Tory Ministry and a personal friend of Pope's.

mediate gradation.[15] The notes, which in the Dutch copies were placed at the end of each book, as they had been in the large volumes, were now subjoined to the text in the same page, and are therefore more easily consulted. Of this edition two thousand five hundred were first printed, and five thousand a few weeks afterwards; but indeed great numbers were necessary to produce considerable profit.

Pope, having now emitted his proposals, and engaged not only his own reputation, but in some degree that of his friends who patronized his subscription, began to be frighted at his own undertaking; and finding himself at first embarrassed with difficulties, which retarded and oppressed him, he was for a time timorous and uneasy; had his nights disturbed by dreams of long journeys through unknown ways, and wished, as he said, "that somebody would hang him."

This misery, however, was not of long continuance; he grew by degrees more acquainted with Homer's images and expressions, and practice increased his facility of versification. In a short time he represents himself as despatching regularly fifty verses a day, which would show him by an easy computation the termination of his labor.

His own diffidence was not his only vexation. He that asks a subscription soon finds that he has enemies. All who do not encourage him defame him. He that wants money will rather be thought angry than poor, and he that wishes to save his money conceals his avarice by his malice. Addison had hinted his suspicion that Pope was too much a Tory; and some of the Tories suspected his principles because he had contributed to *The Guardian*, which was carried on by Steele.

To those who censured his politics were added enemies yet more dangerous, who called in question his knowledge of Greek, and his qualifications for a translator of Homer. To these he made no public opposition, but in one of his letters escapes from them as well as he can. At an age like his, for he was not more than twenty-five, with an irregular education, and a course of life of which much seems to have passed in conversation, it is not very likely that he overflowed with Greek. But when he felt himself deficient he sought assistance; and what man of learning would refuse to help him? Minute

---

[15] Lintot had to issue the work in small convenient duodecimo size, rather than in medium size such as octavo.

inquiries into the force of words are less necessary in translating Homer than other poets, because his positions[16] are general, and his representations natural, with very little dependence on local or temporary customs, on those changeable scenes of artificial life, which, by mingling original with accidental notions, and crowding the mind with images which time effaces, produce ambiguity in diction, and obscurity in books. To this open display of unadulterated nature it must be ascribed that Homer has fewer passages of doubtful meaning than any other poet either in the learned or in modern languages. I have read of a man who being, by his ignorance of Greek, compelled to gratify his curiosity with the Latin printed on the opposite page, declared that from the rude simplicity of the lines literally rendered, he formed nobler ideas of the Homeric majesty than from the labored elegance of polished versions.

Those literal translations were always at hand, and from them he could easily obtain his author's sense with sufficient certainty; and among the readers of Homer the number is very small of those who find much in the Greek more than in the Latin, except the music of the numbers.

If more help was wanting, he had the poetical translation of Eobanus Hessus, an unwearied writer of Latin verses; he had the French Homers of La Valterie and Dacier, and the English of Chapman, Hobbes, and Ogilby. With Chapman, whose work, though now totally neglected, seems to have been popular almost to the end of the last century, he had very frequent consultations, and perhaps never translated any passage till he had read his version, which indeed he has been sometimes suspected of using instead of the original.

Notes were likewise to be provided; for the six volumes would have been very little more than six pamphlets without them. What the mere perusal of the text could suggest, Pope wanted no assistance to collect or methodize; but more was necessary; many pages were to be filled, and learning must supply materials to wit and judgment. Something might be gathered from Dacier; but no man loves to be indebted to his contemporaries, and Dacier was accessible to common readers. Eustathius[17] was therefore necessarily consulted. To read

---

[16] *positions:* attitudes.
[17] A twelfth-century Byzantine commentator on Homer.

Eustathius, of whose work there was then no Latin version, I suspect Pope, if he had been willing, not to have been able; some other was therefore to be found, who had leisure as well as abilities, and he was doubtless most readily employed who would do much work for little money.

The history of the notes has never been traced. Broome, in his preface to his poems, declares himself the commentator "in part upon the *Iliad*"; and it appears from Fenton's letter, preserved in the Museum, that Broome was at first engaged in consulting Eustathius; but that after a time, whatever was the reason, he desisted: another man of Cambridge was then employed, who soon grew weary of the work; and a third, that was recommended by Thirlby, is now discovered to have been Jortin, a man since well known to the learned world, who complained that Pope, having accepted and approved his performance, never testified any curiosity to see him, and who professed to have forgotten the terms on which he worked. The terms which Fenton uses are very mercantile: "I think at first sight that his performance is very commendable, and have sent word for him to finish the 17th book, and to send it with his demands for his trouble. I have here enclosed the specimen; if the rest come before the return, I will keep them till I receive your order."

Broome then offered his service a second time, which was probably accepted, as they had afterwards a closer correspondence. Parnell contributed the "Life of Homer," which Pope found so harsh that he took great pains in correcting it; and by his own diligence, with such help as kindness or money could procure him, in somewhat more than five years he completed his version of the *Iliad*, with the notes. He began it in 1712, his twenty-fifth year, and concluded it in 1718, his thirtieth year.

When we find him translating fifty lines a day, it is natural to suppose that he would have brought his work to a more speedy conclusion. The *Iliad*, containing less than sixteen thousand verses, might have been despatched in less than three hundred and twenty days by fifty verses in a day. The notes, compiled with the assistance of his mercenaries, could not be supposed to require more time than the text. According to this calculation, the progress of Pope may seem to have been slow; but the distance is commonly very great between actual performances and speculative possibility. It is natural to suppose that as much as has been done today may be done tomorrow; but on the morrow some difficulty emerges, or some external impediment obstructs. Indolence, interruption, business, and pleasure, all take their turns of retardation; and every long work is lengthened by a thousand causes that can, and ten thousand that cannot, be recounted. Perhaps no existence and multifarious performance was ever effected within the term originally fixed in the undertaker's mind. He that runs against time has an antagonist not subject to casualties.

The encouragement given to this translation, though report seems to have overrated it, was such as the world has not often seen. The subscribers were five hundred and seventy-five. The copies for which subscriptions were given were six hundred and fifty-four; and only six hundred and sixty were printed. For those copies Pope had nothing to pay; he therefore received, including the two hundred pounds a volume, five thousand three hundred and twenty pounds four shillings, without deduction, as the books were supplied by Lintot.

By the success of his subscription Pope was relieved from those pecuniary distresses with which, notwithstanding his popularity, he had hitherto struggled. Lord Oxford had often lamented his disqualification for public employment, but never proposed a pension. While the translation of Homer was in its progress, Mr. Craggs, then secretary of state, offered to procure him a pension which, at least during his ministry, might be enjoyed with secrecy. This was not accepted by Pope, who told him, however, that if he should be pressed with want of money, he would send to him for occasional supplies. Craggs was not long in power, and was never solicited for money by Pope, who disdained to beg what he did not want.

With the product of this subscription, which he had too much discretion to squander, he secured his future life from want, by considerable annuities. The estate of the Duke of Buckingham was found to have been charged with five hundred pounds a year, payable to Pope, which doubtless his translation enabled him to purchase.

It cannot be unwelcome to literary curiosity that I deduce thus minutely the history of the English *Iliad*. It is certainly the noblest version of poetry which the world has ever seen; and its publication must therefore be considered as one of the great events in the annals of learning.

To those who have skill to estimate the excellence and difficulty of this great work, it must be very desirable to know how it was performed, and by what gradations it advanced to correctness. Of such an intellectual process the knowledge has very rarely been attainable; but happily there remains the original copy of the *Iliad*, which, being obtained by Boling-broke as a curiosity, descended from him to Mallet, and is now by the solicitation of the late Dr. Maty reposited in the Museum. . . .

[Johnson here gives passages from Pope's original copy, together with his final versions.]

The *Iliad* was published volume by volume, as the transla-tion proceeded; the four first books appeared in 1715. The expectation of this work was undoubtedly high, and every man who had connected his name with criticism, or poetry, was desirous of such intelligence as might enable him to talk upon the popular topic. Halifax,[18] who, by having been first a poet, and then a patron of poetry, had acquired the right of being a judge, was willing to hear some books while they were yet unpublished. Of this rehearsal Pope afterwards gave the following account:

The famous Lord Halifax was rather a pretender to taste than really possessed of it. When I had finished the two or three first books of my translation of the *Iliad*, that Lord desired to have the pleasure of hearing them read at his house. Addison, Congreve, and Garth, were there at the reading. In four or five places Lord Halifax stopped me very civilly, and with a speech each time, much of the same kind, "I beg your pardon, Mr. Pope; but there is something in that passage that does not quite please me. Be so good as to mark the place, and consider it a little at your leisure. I'm sure you can give it a little turn." I returned from Lord Halifax's with Dr. Garth, in his chariot; and, as we were going along, was saying to the Doctor that my Lord had laid me under a good deal of difficulty by such loose and general observations; that I had been thinking over the passages almost ever since, and could not guess at what it was that offended his Lordship in either of them. Garth laughed heartily at my embar-rassment; said, I had not been long enough acquainted

<hr>

[18] Charles Montagu, Earl of Halifax.

with Lord Halifax to know his way yet; that I need not puzzle myself about looking those places over and over, when I got home. "All you need to do (says he) is to leave them just as they are; call on Lord Halifax two or three months hence, thank him for his kind observations on those passages, and then read them to him as altered. I have known him much longer than you have, and will be answerable for the event." I followed his advice; waited on Lord Halifax some time after; said, I hoped he would find his objections to those passages removed; read them to him exactly as they were at first; and his Lordship was extremely pleased with them, and cried out, "Ay, now they are perfectly right: nothing can be better."

It is seldom that the great or the wise suspect that they are despised or cheated. Halifax, thinking this a lucky opportunity of securing immortality, made some advances of favor and some overtures of advantage to Pope, which he seems to have received with sullen coldness. All our knowledge of this transaction is derived from a single letter (December 1, 1714), in which Pope says,

I am obliged to you, both for the favors you have done me, and those you intend me. I distrust neither your will nor your memory, when it is to do good; and if I ever become troublesome or solicitous, it must not be out of expectation, but out of gratitude. Your Lordship may cause me to live agreeably in the town, or contentedly in the country, which is really all the difference I set between an easy fortune and a small one. It is indeed a high strain of generosity in you to think of making me easy all my life, only because I have been so happy as to divert you some few hours; but, if I may have leave to add it is because you think me no enemy to my native country, there will appear a better reason; for I must of consequence be very much (as I sincerely am) yours, etc.

These voluntary offers, and this faint acceptance, ended without effect. The patron was not accustomed to such frigid gratitude, and the poet fed his own pride with the dignity of independence. They probably were suspicious of each other. Pope would not dedicate till he saw at what rate his praise was valued; he would be "troublesome out of gratitude, not expectation." Halifax thought himself entitled to confidence; and would give nothing, unless he knew what he should receive. Their commerce had its beginning in hope of praise on one side, and of money on the other, and ended because Pope was less eager of money than Halifax of praise. It is not likely that Halifax had any personal benevolence to Pope; it is evident that Pope looked on Halifax with scorn and hatred.

The reputation of this great work failed of gaining him a patron; but it deprived him of a friend. Addison and he were now at the head of poetry and criticism; and both in such a state of elevation, that, like the two rivals in the Roman state, one could no longer bear an equal, nor the other a superior. Of the gradual abatement of kindness between friends, the beginning is often scarcely discernible by themselves, and the process is continued by petty provocations, and incivilities sometimes peevishly returned, and sometimes contemptuously neglected, which would escape all attention but that of pride, and drop from any memory but that of resentment. That the quarrel of those two wits should be minutely deduced, is not to be expected from a writer to whom, as Homer says, "nothing but rumor has reached, and who has no personal knowledge."

Pope doubtless approached Addison, when the reputation of their wit first brought them together, with the respect due to a man whose abilities were acknowledged, and who, having attained that eminence to which he was himself aspiring, had in his hands the distribution of literary fame. He paid court with sufficient diligence by his Prologue to *Cato*, by his abuse of Dennis, and, with praise yet more direct, by his poem on the "Dialogues on Medals," of which the immediate publication was then intended. In all this there was no hypocrisy; for he confessed that he found in Addison something more pleasing than in any other man.

It may be supposed that as Pope saw himself favored by the world, and more frequently compared his own powers with those of others, his confidence increased, and his submission lessened; and that Addison felt no delight from the advances of a young wit, who might soon contend with him for the highest place. Every great man, of whatever kind be his greatness, has among his friends those who officiously, or insidiously, quicken his attention to offences, heighten his disgust, and stimulate his resentment. Of such adherents Addison doubtless had many, and Pope was now too high to be without them.

From the emission and reception of the Proposals for the *Iliad*, the kindness of Addison seems to have abated. Jervas the painter once pleased himself (August 20, 1714) with imagining that he had reestablished their friendship; and wrote to Pope that Addison once suspected him of too close a confederacy with Swift, but was now satisfied with his conduct. To this Pope answered, a week after, that his engagements to Swift were such as his services in regard to the subscription demanded, and that the Tories never put him under the necessity of asking leave to be grateful. "But," says he, "as Mr. Addison must be *the judge* in what regards himself, and seems to be no very just one in regard to me, so I must own to you I expect nothing but civility from him." In the same letter he mentions Philips as having been busy to kindle animosity between them; but, in a letter to Addison, he expresses some consciousness of behavior inattentively deficient in respect.

Of Swift's industry in promoting the subscription there remains the testimony of Kennett, no friend to either him or Pope.

Nov. 2, 1713, Dr. Swift came into the coffee-house, and had a bow from everybody but me, who, I confess, could not but despise him. When I came to the ante-chamber to wait, before prayers, Dr. Swift was the principal man of talk and business, and acted as master of requests. Then he instructed a young nobleman that the best poet in England was Mr. Pope (a Papist), who had begun a translation of Homer into English verse, for which he must have them all subscribe; "for," says he, "the author shall not begin to print till I have a thousand guineas for him."

About this time it is likely that Steele, who was, with all his political fury, good natured and officious, procured an interview between these angry rivals, which ended in aggravated malevolence. On this occasion, if the reports be true, Pope made his complaint with frankness and spirit, as a man undeservedly neglected or opposed; and Addison affected a contemptuous unconcern, and, in a calm even voice, reproached Pope with his vanity, and, telling him of the improvements which his early works had received from his own remarks and those of Steele, said that he, being now engaged in public business, had no longer any care for his poetical reputation; nor had any other desire with regard to Pope than that [he] should not, by too much arrogance, alienate the public.

To this Pope is said to have replied with great keenness and severity, upbraiding Addison with perpetual dependence, and with the abuse of those qualifications which he had obtained at the public cost,[19] and charging him with mean endeavors to obstruct the progress of rising merit. The contest rose so high that they parted at last without any interchange of civility.

The first volume of Homer was (1715) in time published; and a rival version of the first *Iliad*, for rivals the time of their appearance inevitably made them, was immediately printed, with the name of Tickell. It was soon perceived that among the followers of Addison, Tickell had the preference, and the critics and poets divided into factions. "I," says Pope, "have the town, that is, the mob, on my side; but it is not uncommon for the smaller party to supply by industry what it wants in numbers.—I appeal to the people as my rightful judges, and, while they are not inclined to condemn me, shall not fear the highfliers at Button's."[20] This opposition he immediately imputed to Addison, and complained of it in terms sufficiently resentful to Craggs, their common friend.

When Addison's opinion was asked he declared the versions to be both good, but Tickell's the best that had ever been written; and sometimes said that they were both good, but that Tickell had more of Homer.

Pope was now sufficiently irritated; his reputation and his interest were at hazard. He once intended to print together the four versions of Dryden, Maynwaring, Pope, and Tickell, that they might be readily compared, and fairly estimated. This design seems to have been defeated by the refusal of Tonson, who was the proprietor of the other three versions.

Pope intended at another time a rigorous criticism of

---

[19] He upbraided Addison for subjection to his political leaders and abuse of his public positions.
[20] Thomas Tickell was a protégé of Addison's, and his whole group met at Button's Coffee House.

Tickell's translation, and had marked a copy, which I have seen, in all places that appeared defective. But while he was meditating defense or revenge his adversary sunk before him without a blow; the voice of the public was not long divided, and the preference was universally given to Pope's performance.

He was convinced, by adding one circumstance to another, that the other translation was the work of Addison himself; but if he knew it in Addison's lifetime it does not appear that he told it. He left his illustrious antagonist to be punished by what has been considered as the most painful of all reflections, the remembrance of a crime perpetrated in vain.

The other circumstances of their quarrel were thus related by Pope:

Philips seemed to have been encouraged to abuse me in coffee-houses and conversations, and Gildon wrote a thing about Wycherley, in which he had abused both me and my relations very grossly. Lord Warwick[21] himself told me one day that it was in vain for me to endeavor to be well with Mr. Addison; that his jealous temper would never admit of a settled friendship between us; and, to convince me of what he had said, assured me that Addison had encouraged Gildon to publish those scandals, and had given him ten guineas after they were published. The next day, while I was heated with what I had heard, I wrote a letter to Mr. Addison, to let him know that I was not unacquainted with this behavior of his; that if I was to speak severely to him, in return for it, it should [not] be in such a dirty way; that I should rather tell him himself fairly of his faults, and allow his good qualities; and that it should be something in the following manner. I then adjoined the first sketch of what has since been called my satire on Addison.[22] Mr. Addison used me very civilly ever after.

The verses on Addison, when they were sent to Atterbury, were considered by him as the most excellent of Pope's per-

---

[21] Addison's stepson.
[22] This satiric portrait subsequently appeared as the character of Atticus in the "Epistle to Dr. Arbuthnot" (1735).

formances; and the writer was advised, since he knew where his strength lay, not to suffer it to remain unemployed.

This year (1715) being by the subscription enabled to live more by choice, having persuaded his father to sell their estate at Binfield, he purchased, I think only for his life, that house at Twickenham to which his residence afterwards procured so much celebration, and removed thither with his father and mother.

Here he planted the vines and the quincunx which his verses mention, and being under the necessity of making a subterraneous passage to a garden on the other side of the road he adorned it with fossil bodies, and dignified it with the title of a grotto: a place of silence and retreat, from which he endeavored to persuade his friends and himself that cares and passions could be excluded.

A grotto is not often the wish or pleasure of an Englishman, who has more frequent need to solicit than exclude the sun; but Pope's excavation was requisite as an entrance to his garden, and, as some men try to be proud of their defects, he extracted an ornament from an inconvenience, and vanity produced a grotto where necessity enforced a passage. It may be frequently remarked of the studious and speculative that they are proud of trifles, and that their amusements seem frivolous and childish; whether it be that men conscious of great reputation think themselves above the reach of censure, and safe in the admission of negligent indulgences, or that mankind expect from elevated genius an uniformity of greatness, and watch its degradation with malicious wonder; like him who having followed with his eye an eagle into the clouds should lament that she ever descended to a perch.

While the volumes of his Homer were annually published he collected his former works (1717) into one quarto volume, to which he prefixed a Preface, written with great sprightliness and elegance, which was afterwards reprinted, with some passages subjoined that he at first omitted; other marginal additions of the same kind he made in the later editions of his poems. Waller remarks that poets lose half their praise, because the reader knows not what they have blotted. Pope's voracity of fame taught him the art of obtaining the accumulated honor both of what he had published, and of what he had suppressed.

In this year his father died suddenly, in his seventy-fifth

year, having passed twenty-nine years in privacy. He is not known but by the character which his son has given him. If the money with which he retired was all gotten by himself, he had traded very successfully in times when sudden riches were rarely attainable.

The publication of the *Iliad* was at last completed in 1720. The splendor and success of this work raised Pope many enemies, that endeavored to depreciate his abilities. Burnet, who was afterwards a judge of no mean reputation, censured him in a piece called *Homerides* before it was published; Duckett likewise endeavored to make him ridiculous. Dennis was the perpetual persecutor of all his studies. But, whoever his critics were, their writings are lost, and the names which are preserved are preserved in *The Dunciad*.

In this disastrous year (1720) of national infatuation, when more riches than Peru can boast were expected from the South Sea, when the contagion of avarice tainted every mind, and even poets panted after wealth, Pope was seized with the universal passion, and ventured some of his money. The stock rose in its price, and he for a while thought himself "the lord of thousands."[23] But this dream of happiness did not last long, and he seems to have waked soon enough to get clear with the loss only of what he once thought himself to have won, and perhaps not wholly of that.

Next year he published some select poems of his friend Dr. Parnell, with a very elegant Dedication to the Earl of Oxford, who, after all his struggles and dangers, then lived in retirement, still under the frown of a victorious faction, who could take no pleasure in hearing his praise.

He gave the same year (1721) an edition of Shakespeare. His name was now of so much authority that Tonson thought himself entitled, by annexing it, to demand a subscription of six guineas for Shakespeare's plays in six quarto volumes; nor did his expectation much deceive him; for of seven hundred and fifty which he printed, he dispersed a great number at the price proposed. The reputation of that edition indeed sunk afterwards so low, that one hundred and forty copies were sold at sixteen shillings each.

On this undertaking, to which Pope was induced by a

[23] "Imitation of the Second Satire of the Second Book of Horace," line 134. Speculation in South Sea Company stock occasioned a spectacular boom and crash.

reward of two hundred and seventeen pounds, twelve shillings, he seems never to have reflected afterwards without vexation; for Theobald, a man of heavy diligence, with very slender powers, first in a book called *Shakespeare Restored*, and then in a formal edition, detected his deficiencies with all the insolence of victory; and, as he was now high enough to be feared and hated, Theobald had from others all the help that could be supplied, by the desire of humbling a haughty character.

From this time Pope became an enemy to editors, collators, commentators, and verbal critics, and hoped to persuade the world that he miscarried in this undertaking only by having a mind too great for such minute employment.

Pope in his edition undoubtedly did many things wrong, and left many things undone; but let him not be defrauded of his due praise: he was the first that knew, at least the first that told, by what helps the text might be improved. If he inspected the early editions negligently, he taught others to be more accurate. In his Preface he expanded with great skill and elegance the character which had been given of Shakespeare by Dryden; and he drew the public attention upon his works, which, though often mentioned, had been little read.

Soon after the appearance of the *Iliad*, resolving not to let the general kindness cool, he published proposals for a translation of the *Odyssey*, in five volumes, for five guineas. He was willing, however, now to have associates in his labor, being either weary with toiling upon another's thoughts, or having heard, as Ruffhead relates, that Fenton and Broome had already begun the work, and liking better to have them confederates than rivals.

In the patent,[24] instead of saying that he had "translated" the *Odyssey*, as he had said of the *Iliad*, he says that he had "undertaken" a translation; and in the proposals the subscription is said to be "not solely for his own use but for that of two of his friends who have assisted him in this work."

In 1723, while he was engaged in this new version, he appeared before the Lords at the memorable trial of Bishop Atterbury,[25] with whom he had lived in great familiarity and frequent correspondence. Atterbury had honestly recom-

---

[24] *patent:* copyright.
[25] The Tory Bishop Francis Atterbury was tried for treason by the triumphant Whigs.

mended to him the study of the Popish controversy, in hope of his conversion; to which Pope answered in a manner that cannot much recommend his principles or his judgment. In questions and projects of learning, they agreed better. He was called at the trial to give an account of Atterbury's domestic life and private employment, that it might appear how little time he had left for plots. Pope had but few words to utter, and in those few he made several blunders.

His letters to Atterbury express the utmost esteem, tenderness, and gratitude: "perhaps," says he, "it is not only in this world that I may have cause to remember the Bishop of Rochester." At their last interview in the Tower, Atterbury presented him with a Bible.

Of the *Odyssey* Pope translated only twelve books; the rest were the work of Broome and Fenton: the notes were written wholly by Broome, who was not over-liberally rewarded. The public was carefully kept ignorant of the several shares, and an account was subjoined at the conclusion, which is now known not to be true.

The first copy of Pope's books, with those of Fenton, are to be seen in the Museum. The parts of Pope are less interlined than the *Iliad*, and the latter books of the *Iliad* less than the former. He grew dexterous by practice, and every sheet enabled him to write the next with more facility. The books of Fenton have very few alterations by the hand of Pope. Those of Broome have not been found; but Pope complained, as it is reported, that he had much trouble in correcting them.

His contract with Lintot was the same as for the *Iliad*, except that only one hundred pounds were to be paid him for each volume. The number of subscribers was five hundred and seventy-four, and of copies eight hundred and nineteen; so that his profit, when he had paid his assistants, was still very considerable. The work was finished in 1725, and from that time he resolved to make no more translations.

The sale did not answer Lintot's expectation, and he then pretended to discover something of fraud in Pope, and commenced, or threatened, a suit in Chancery.

On the English *Odyssey* a criticism was published by Spence, at that time Prelector of Poetry at Oxford; a man whose learning was not very great, and whose mind was not very powerful. His criticism, however, was commonly just; what he thought, he thought rightly, and his remarks were recommended by his coolness and candor. In him Pope had the first experience of a critic without malevolence, who thought it as much his duty to display beauties as expose faults; who censured with respect, and praised with alacrity.

With this criticism Pope was so little offended that he sought the acquaintance of the writer, who lived with him from that time in great familiarity, attended him in his last hours, and compiled memorials of his conversation. The regard of Pope recommended him to the great and powerful, and he obtained very valuable preferments in the Church.

Not long after, Pope was returning home from a visit in a friend's coach which, in passing a bridge, was overturned into the water; the windows were closed, and being unable to force them open, he was in danger of immediate death, when the postilion snatched him out by breaking the glass, of which fragments cut two of his fingers in such a manner that he lost their use.

Voltaire, who was then in England, sent him a letter of consolation. He had been entertained by Pope at his table, where he talked with so much grossness that Mrs. Pope was driven from the room. Pope discovered, by a trick, that he was a spy for the Court, and never considered him as a man worthy of confidence.

He soon afterwards (1727) joined with Swift, who was then in England, to publish three volumes of *Miscellanies,* in which amongst other things, he inserted the "Memoirs of a Parish Clerk," in ridicule of Burnet's importance in his own *History*, and a "Debate upon Black and White Horses," written in all the formalities of a legal process by the assistance, as is said, of Mr. Fortescue, afterwards Master of the Rolls. Before these *Miscellanies* is a preface signed by Swift and Pope, but apparently written by Pope, in which he makes a ridiculous and romantic[26] complaint of the robberies committed upon authors by the clandestine seizure and sale of their papers. He tells, in tragic strains, how "the cabinets of the sick and the closets of the dead have been broke open and ransacked"; as if those violences were often committed for papers of uncertain and accidental value, which are rarely provoked by real treasures, as if epigrams and essays were in danger where gold and diamonds are safe. A cat hunted for his musk is, according to Pope's account, but the emblem of a wit winded by booksellers.

[26] *romantic:* extravagant.

His complaint, however, received some attestation, for the same year the letters written by him to Mr. Cromwell in his youth were sold by Mrs. Thomas to Curll, who printed them.

In these *Miscellanies* was first published *The Art of Sinking in Poetry,* which, by such a train of consequences as usually passes in literary quarrels, gave in a short time, according to Pope's account, occasion to *The Dunciad.*

In the following year (1728) he began to put Atterbury's advice in practice, and showed his satirical powers by publishing *The Dunciad,* one of his greatest and most elaborate performances, in which he endeavored to sink into contempt all the writers by whom he had been attacked, and some others whom he thought unable to defend themselves.

At the head of the Dunces he placed poor Theobald, whom he accused of ingratitude, but whose real crime was supposed to be that of having revised[27] Shakespeare more happily than himself. This satire had the effect which he intended, by blasting the characters which it touched. Ralph, who, unnecessarily interposing in the quarrel, got a place in a subsequent edition, complained that for a time he was in danger of starving, as the booksellers had no longer any confidence in his capacity.

The prevalence of this poem was gradual and slow: the plan, if not wholly new, was little understood by common readers. Many of the allusions required illustration; the names were often expressed only by the initial and final letters, and, if they had been printed at length, were such as few had known or recollected. The subject itself had nothing generally interesting; for whom did it concern to know that one or another scribbler was a dunce? If therefore it had been possible for those who were attacked to conceal their pain and their resentment, *The Dunciad* might have made its way very slowly in the world.

This, however, was not to be expected: every man is of importance to himself, and therefore, in his own opinion, to others, and, supposing the world already acquainted with all his pleasures and his pains, is perhaps the first to publish injuries or misfortunes which had never been known unless related by himself, and at which those that hear them will only laugh; for no man sympathizes with the sorrows of vanity.

---

[27] *revised:* edited.

The history of *The Dunciad* is very minutely related by Pope himself, in a Dedication which he wrote to Lord Middlesex in the name of Savage.

I will relate the . . . war of the "dunces" (for so it has been commonly called), which began in the year 1727, and ended in 1730.

When Dr. Swift and Mr. Pope thought it proper, for reasons specified in the Preface to their *Miscellanies*, to publish such little pieces of theirs as had casually got abroad, there was added to them *The Treatise of the Bathos, or The Art of Sinking in Poetry*. It happened that in one chapter of this piece the several species of bad poets were ranged in classes, to which were prefixed almost all the letters of the alphabet (the greatest part of them at random); but such was the number of poets eminent in that art that some one or other took every letter to himself: all fell into so violent a fury that, for half a year or more, the common newspapers (in most of which they had some property, as being hired writers) were filled with the most abusive falsehoods and scurrilities they could possibly devise. A liberty no way to be wondered at in those people and in those papers that for many years during the uncontrolled license of the press had aspersed almost all the great characters of the age; and this with impunity, their own persons and names being utterly secret and obscure.

This gave Mr. Pope the thought that he had now some opportunity of doing good, by detecting and dragging into light these common enemies of mankind; since to invalidate this universal slander it sufficed to show what contemptible men were the authors of it. He was not without hopes that, by manifesting the dullness of those who had only malice to recommend them, either the booksellers would not find their account in employing them, or the men themselves, when discovered, want courage to proceed in so unlawful an occupation. This it was that gave birth to *The Dunciad*; and he thought it an happiness that, by the late flood of slander on himself, he had acquired such a peculiar right over their names as was necessary to this design.

On the 12th of March, 1729, at St. James's, that poem was presented to the King and Queen (who had before been pleased to read it) by the Right Honorable Sir Robert Walpole; and some days after the whole impression was taken and dispersed by several noblemen and persons of the first distinction.

It is certainly a true observation that no people are so impatient of censure as those who are the greatest slanderers, which was wonderfully exemplified on this occasion. On the day the book was first vended a crowd of authors besieged the shop; entreaties, advices, threats of law and battery, nay cries of treason, were all employed to hinder the coming out of *The Dunciad*: on the other side, the booksellers and hawkers made as great efforts to procure it. What could a few poor authors do against so great a majority as the public? There was no stopping a torrent with a finger, so out it came.

Many ludicrous circumstances attended it. The "dunces" (for by this name they were called) held weekly clubs to consult of hostilities against the author: one wrote a letter to a great minister, assuring him Mr. Pope was the greatest enemy the government had; and another bought his image in clay to execute him in effigy, with which sad sort of satisfaction the gentlemen were a little comforted.

Some false editions of the book having an owl in their frontispiece, the true one, to distinguish it, fixed in its stead an ass laden with authors. Then another surreptitious one being printed with the same ass, the new edition in octavo returned for distinction to the owl again. Hence arose a great contest of booksellers against booksellers and advertisements against advertisements; some recommending the edition of the owl, and others the edition of the ass; by which names they came to be distinguished, to the great honor also of the gentlemen of *The Dunciad*.

Pope appears by this narrative to have contemplated his victory over the Dunces with great exultation; and such was his delight in the tumult which he had raised, that for a while his natural sensibility was suspended, and he read reproaches and invectives without emotion, considering them only as the necessary effects of that pain which he rejoiced in having given.

It cannot, however, be concealed that, by his own confession, he was the aggressor, for nobody believes that the letters in *The Bathos* were placed at random; and it may be discovered that, when he thinks himself concealed, he indulges the common vanity of common men, and triumphs in those distinctions which he had affected to despise. He is proud that his book was presented to the King and Queen by the Right Honorable Sir Robert Walpole; he is proud that they had read it before; he is proud that the edition was taken off by the nobility and persons of the first distinction.

The edition of which he speaks was, I believe, that, which by telling in the text the names and in the notes the characters of those whom he had satirized, was made intelligible and diverting. The critics had now declared their approbation of the plan, and the common reader began to like it without fear; those who were strangers to petty literature, and therefore unable to decipher initials and blanks, had now names and persons brought within their view, and delighted in the visible effect of those shafts of malice, which they had hitherto contemplated as shot into the air.

Dennis, upon the fresh provocation now given him, renewed the enmity which had for a time been appeased by mutual civilities, and published remarks, which he had till then suppressed, upon *The Rape of the Lock.* Many more grumbled in secret, or vented their resentment in the newspapers by epigrams or invectives.

Duckett, indeed, being mentioned as loving Burnet with "pious passion," pretended that his moral character was injured, and for some time declared his resolution to take vengeance with a cudgel. But Pope appeased him, by changing "pious passion" to "cordial friendship," and by a note, in which he vehemently disclaims the malignity of meaning imputed to the first expression.

Aaron Hill, who was represented as diving for the prize, expostulated with Pope in a manner so much superior to all mean solicitation, that Pope was reduced to sneak and shuffle, sometimes to deny and sometimes to apologize: he first endeavors to wound, and is then afraid to own that he meant a blow.

The Dunciad, in the complete edition, is addressed to Dr. Swift: of the notes, part was written by Dr. Arbuthnot, and an apologetical[28] letter was prefixed, signed by Cleland, but supposed to have been written by Pope.

After this general war upon dullness he seems to have in-

---

[28] *apologetical:* justificatory.

dulged himself a while in tranquillity; but his subsequent
productions prove that he was not idle. He published (1731)
a poem *On Taste*, in which he very particularly and severely
criticizes the house, furniture, the gardens, and the entertain-
ments of Timon, a man of great wealth and little taste. By
Timon he was universally supposed, and by the Earl of Burlington, to whom the poem is addressed, was privately said,
to mean the Duke of Chandos; a man perhaps too much delighted with pomp and show, but of a temper kind and
beneficent, and who had consequently the voice of the public
in his favor.

A violent outcry was therefore raised against the ingratitude
and treachery of Pope, who was said to have been indebted
to the patronage of Chandos for a present of a thousand
pounds, and who gained the opportunity of insulting him by
the kindness of his invitation.

The receipt of the thousand pounds Pope publicly denied;
but from the reproach which the attack on a character so
amiable brought upon him, he tried all means of escaping.
The name of Cleland was again employed in an apology, by
which no man was satisfied; and he was at last reduced to
shelter his temerity behind dissimulation, and endeavor to
make that disbelieved which he never had confidence openly
to deny. He wrote an exculpatory letter to the Duke, which
was answered with great magnanimity, as by a man who accepted his excuse without believing his professions. He said
that to have ridiculed his taste or his buildings had been an
indifferent action in another man, but that in Pope, after the
reciprocal kindness that had been exchanged between them,
it had been less easily excused.

Pope, in one of his letters, complaining of the treatment
which his poem had found, "owns that such critics can intimidate him, nay almost persuade him to write no more, which is
a compliment this age deserves." The man who threatens the
world is always ridiculous; for the world can easily go on
without him, and in a short time will cease to miss him. I
have heard of an idiot who used to revenge his vexations
by lying all night upon the bridge. "There is nothing," says
Juvenal, "that a man will not believe in his own favor." Pope
had been flattered till he thought himself one of the moving
powers in the system of life. When he talked of laying down
his pen, those who sat round him entreated and implored,

and self-love did not suffer him to suspect that they went away and laughed.

The following year deprived him of Gay, a man whom he had known early, and whom he seemed to love with more tenderness than any other of his literary friends. Pope was now forty-four years old; an age at which the mind begins less easily to admit new confidence and the will to grow less flexible, and when therefore the departure of an old friend is very acutely felt.

In the next year he lost his mother, not by an unexpected death, for she had lasted to the age of ninety-three; but she did not die unlamented. The filial piety of Pope was in the highest degree amiable and exemplary; his parents had the happiness of living till he was at the summit of poetical reputation, till he was at ease in his fortune, and without a rival in his fame, and found no diminution of his respect or tenderness. Whatever was his pride, to them he was obedient; and whatever was his irritability, to them he was gentle. Life has, among its soothing and quiet comforts, few things better to give than such a son.

One of the passages of Pope's life, which seems to deserve some inquiry, was a publication of letters between him and many of his friends, which falling into the hands of Curll, a rapacious bookseller of no good fame, were by him printed and sold. This volume containing some letters from noblemen, Pope incited a prosecution against him in the House of Lords for breach of privilege, and attended himself to stimulate the resentment of his friends. Curll appeared at the bar, and, knowing himself in no great danger, spoke of Pope with very little reverence. "He has," said Curll, "a knack at versifying, but in prose I think myself a match for him." When the orders of the House were examined, none of them appeared to have been infringed; Curll went away triumphant, and Pope was left to seek some other remedy.

Curll's account was, that one evening a man in a clergy-man's gown, but with a lawyer's band,[29] brought and offered to sale a number of printed volumes, which he found to be Pope's epistolary correspondence; that he asked no name, and was told none, but gave the price demanded, and thought himself authorized to use his purchase to his own advantage.

[29] *lawyer's band:* neckband.

That Curll gave a true account of the transaction, it is reasonable to believe, because no falsehood was ever detected; and when some years afterwards I mentioned it to Lintot, the son of Bernard, he declared his opinion to be that Pope knew better than anybody else how Curll obtained the copies, because another parcel was at the same time sent to himself, for which no price had ever been demanded, as he made known his resolution not to pay a porter, and consequently not to deal with a nameless agent.

Such care had been taken to make them public that they were sent at once to two booksellers: to Curll, who was likely to seize them as a prey, and to Lintot, who might be expected to give Pope information of the seeming injury. Lintot, I believe, did nothing; and Curll did what was expected. That to make them public was the only purpose may be reasonably supposed, because the numbers offered to sale by the private messengers showed that hope of gain could not have been the motive of the impression.

It seems that Pope, being desirous of printing his letters, and not knowing how to do, without imputation of vanity, what has in this country been done very rarely, contrived an appearance of compulsion: that when he could complain that his letters were surreptitiously published, he might decently and defensively publish them himself.

Pope's private correspondence thus promulgated filled the nation with praises of his candor, tenderness, and benevolence, the purity of his purposes, and the fidelity of his friendship. There were some letters which a very wise man would wish suppressed; but, as they had been already exposed, it was impracticable now to retract them.

From the perusal of those letters, Mr. Allen[30] first conceived the desire of knowing him, and with so much zeal did he cultivate the friendship which he had newly formed, that when Pope told his purpose of vindicating[31] his own property by a genuine edition, he offered to pay the cost.

This, however, Pope did not accept; but in time solicited a subscription for a quarto volume, which appeared (1737), I believe, with sufficient profit. In the Preface he tells that his letters were reposited in a friend's library, said to be the

---

[30] Ralph Allen, a self-made man, used his fortune to help many authors, including Pope and Henry Fielding.
[31] vindicating: establishing possession of.

Earl of Oxford's, and that the copy thence stolen was sent to the press. The story was doubtless received with different degrees of credit. It may be suspected that the Preface to the *Miscellanies* was written to prepare the public for such an incident; and to strengthen this opinion, James Worsdale, a painter, who was employed in clandestine negotiations, but whose veracity was very doubtful, declared that he was the messenger who carried by Pope's direction the books to Curll.

When they were thus published and avowed, as they had relation to recent facts, and persons either then living or not yet forgotten, they may be supposed to have found readers; but as the facts were minute, and the characters being either private or literary were little known or little regarded, they awakened no popular kindness or resentment: the book never became much the subject of conversation; some read it as contemporary history, and some perhaps as a model of epistolary language; but those who read it did not talk of it. Not much therefore was added by it to fame or envy; nor do I remember that it produced either public praise or public censure.

It had, however, in some degree the recommendation of novelty. Our language has few letters, except those of statesmen. Howell indeed, about a century ago, published his letters, which are commended by Morhoff, and which alone of his hundred volumes continue his memory. Loveday's *Letters* were printed only once; those of Herbert and Suckling are hardly known. Mrs. Philips' (Orinda's) are equally neglected, and those of Walsh seem written as exercises, and were never sent to any living mistress or friend. Pope's epistolary excellence had an open field; he had no English rival, living or dead.

Pope is seen in this collection as connected with the other contemporary wits, and certainly suffers no disgrace in the comparison; but it must be remembered that he had the power of favoring himself: he might have originally had publication in his mind, and have written with care, or have afterwards selected those which he had most happily conceived, or most diligently labored; and I know not whether there does not appear something more studied and artificial in his productions than the rest, except one long letter by Bolingbroke, composed with all the skill and industry of a professed author. It is indeed not easy to distinguish affectation from habit;

he that has once studiously formed a style rarely writes afterwards with complete ease. Pope may be said to write always with his reputation in his head; Swift perhaps like a man who remembered that he was writing to Pope; but Arbuthnot like one who lets thoughts drop from his pen as they rise into his mind.

Before these *Letters* appeared he published the first part of what he persuaded himself to think a system of ethics, under the title of an *Essay on Man*, which, if his letter to Swift (of Sept. 14, 1725) be rightly explained by the commentator, had been eight years under his consideration, and of which he seems to have desired the success with great solicitude. He had now many open and doubtless many secret enemies. The Dunces were yet smarting with the war, and the superiority which he publicly arrogated disposed the world to wish his humiliation.

All this he knew, and against all this he provided. His own name, and that of his friend to whom the work is inscribed, were in the first editions carefully suppressed; and the poem, being of a new kind, was ascribed to one or another as favor determined or conjecture wandered: it was given, says War-burton, to every man except him only who could write it. Those who like only when they like the author, and who are under the dominion of a name, condemned it; and those admired it who are willing to scatter praise at random, which while it is unappropriated excites no envy. Those friends of Pope that were trusted with the secret went about lavishing honors on the new-born poet, and hinting that Pope was never so much in danger from any former rival.

To those authors whom he had personally offended, and to those whose opinion the world considered as decisive, and whom he suspected of envy or malevolence, he sent his *Essay* as a present before publication that they might defeat their own enmity by praise, which they could not afterwards decently retract.

With these precautions, in 1733 was published the first part of the *Essay on Man*. There had been for some time a report that Pope was busy upon a system of morality, but this design was not discovered in the new poem, which had a form and a title with which its readers were unacquainted. Its reception was not uniform: some thought it a very imperfect piece, though not without good lines. While the author was unknown some, as will always happen, favored him as an adventurer, and some censured him as an intruder, but all thought him above neglect: the sale increased, and editions were multiplied.

The subsequent editions of the first Epistle exhibited two memorable corrections. At first, the poet and his friend

> Expatiate freely o'er this scene of man,
> A mighty maze of *walks without a plan.*

For which he wrote afterwards,

> A mighty maze, *but not without a plan:*

for, if there were no plan, it was in vain to describe or to trace the maze.

The other alteration was of these lines:

> And spite of pride, *and in thy reason's spite,*
> One truth is clear, whatever is, is right;

but having afterwards discovered, or been shown, that the *truth* which subsisted *in spite of reason* could not be *clear,* he substituted

> And spite of pride, *in erring reason's spite.*

To such oversights will the most vigorous mind be liable when it is employed at once upon argument and poetry.

The second and third Epistles were published, and Pope was, I believe, more and more suspected of writing them; at last, in 1734, he avowed the fourth, and claimed the honor of a moral poet.

In the conclusion it is sufficiently acknowledged that the doctrine of the *Essay on Man* was received from Bolingbroke, who is said to have ridiculed Pope, among those who enjoyed his confidence, as having adopted and advanced principles of which he did not perceive the consequence, and as blindly propagating opinions contrary to his own. That those communications had been consolidated into a scheme regularly drawn, and delivered to Pope, from whom it returned only transformed from prose to verse, has been reported, but hardly can be true. The *Essay* plainly appears the fabric of a poet: what Bolingbroke supplied could be only the first principles; the order, illustration, and embellishments must all be Pope's.

These principles it is not my business to clear from obscurity, dogmatism, or falsehood, but they were not immediately examined; philosophy and poetry have not often the same readers, and the *Essay* abounded in splendid amplifications and sparkling sentences,[32] which were read and admired with no great attention to their ultimate purpose: its flowers caught the eye which did not see what the gay foliage concealed, and for a time flourished in the sunshine of universal approbation. So little was any evil discovered that, as innocence is unsuspicious, many read it for a manual of piety.

Its reputation soon invited a translator. It was first turned into French prose, and afterwards by Resnel into verse. Both translations fell into the hands of Crousaz, who first, when he had the version in prose, wrote a general censure, and afterwards reprinted Resnel's version with particular remarks upon every paragraph.

Crousaz was a professor of Switzerland, eminent for his treatise of logic, and his *Examen de Pyrrhonisme*, and, however little known or regarded here, was no mean antagonist. His mind was one of those in which philosophy and piety are happily united. He was accustomed to argument and disquisition, and perhaps was grown too desirous of detecting faults; but his intentions were always right, his opinions were solid, and his religion pure.

His incessant vigilance for the promotion of piety disposed him to look with distrust upon all metaphysical systems of theology, and all schemes of virtue and happiness purely rational, and therefore it was not long before he was persuaded that the positions of Pope, as they terminated for the most part in natural religion,[33] were intended to draw mankind away from revelation, and to represent the whole course of things as a necessary concatenation of indissoluble fatality; and it is undeniable that in many passages a religious eye may easily discover expressions not very favorable to morals or to liberty.

About this time Warburton began to make his appearance in the first ranks of learning. He was a man of vigorous faculties,

---

[32] *sentences:* aphorisms.
[33] *natural religion:* religion, such as Deism, based on study of nature rather than Revelation.

a mind fervid and vehement, supplied by incessant and unlimited inquiry, with wonderful extent and variety of knowledge, which yet had not oppressed his imagination nor clouded his perspicacity. To every work he brought a memory full fraught, together with a fancy fertile of original combinations, and at once exerted the powers of the scholar, the reasoner, and the wit. But his knowledge was too multifarious to be always exact, and his pursuits were too eager to be always cautious. His abilities gave him an haughty confidence which he disdained to conceal or mollify, and his impatience of opposition disposed him to treat his adversaries with such contemptuous superiority as made his readers commonly his enemies, and excited against the advocate the wishes of some who favored the cause. He seems to have adopted the Roman Emperor's determination, *oderint dum metuant* [let them hate me as long as they fear me];[34] he used no allurements of gentle language, but wished to compel rather than persuade.

His style is copious without selection, and forcible without neatness; he took the words that presented themselves: his diction is coarse and impure, and his sentences are unmeasured.

He had, in the early part of his life, pleased himself with the notice of inferior wits and corresponded with the enemies of Pope. A letter was produced, when he had perhaps himself forgotten it, in which he tells Concanen, "Dryden I observe borrows for want of leisure, and Pope for want of genius; Milton out of pride, and Addison out of modesty." And when Theobald published Shakespeare, in opposition to Pope, the best notes were supplied by Warburton.

But the time was now come when Warburton was to change his opinion, and Pope was to find a defender in him who had contributed so much to the exaltation of his rival.

The arrogance of Warburton excited against him every artifice of offense, and therefore it may be supposed that his union with Pope was censured as hypocritical inconstancy; but surely to think differently at different times of poetical merit may be easily allowed. Such opinions are often admitted and dismissed without nice examination. Who is there that has not found reason for changing his mind about questions of greater importance?

Warburton, whatever was his motive, undertook without

---

[34] Attributed to Caligula by Suetonius.

solicitation to rescue Pope from the talons of Crousaz, by freeing him from the imputation of favoring fatality or rejecting revelation, and from month to month continued a vindication of the *Essay on Man* in the literary journal of that time, called *The Republic of Letters*.

Pope, who probably began to doubt the tendency of his own work, was glad that the positions of which he perceived himself not to know the full meaning, could by any mode of interpretation be made to mean well. How much he was pleased with his gratuitous defender the following letter evidently shows:—

Sir,

March 24, 1743

I have just received from Mr. R. two more of your "Letters." It is in the greatest hurry imaginable that I write this, but I cannot help thanking you in particular for your "Third Letter," which is so extremely clear, short, and full, that I think Mr. Crousaz ought never to have another answer, and deserved not so good an one. I can only say you do him too much honor and me too much right, so odd as the expression seems; for you have made my system as clear as I ought to have done, and could not. It is indeed the same system as mine, but illustrated with a ray of your own, as they say our natural body is the same still when it is glorified. I am sure I like it better than I did before, and so will every man else. I know I meant just what you explain, but I did not explain my own meaning so well as you. You understand me as well as I do myself, but you express me better than I could express myself. Pray accept the sincerest acknowledgments. I cannot but wish these letters were put together in one book, and intend (with your leave) to procure a translation of part at least of all of them into French, but I shall not proceed a step without your consent and opinion, etc.

By this fond and eager acceptance of an exculpatory comment Pope testified that, whatever might be the seeming or real import of the principles which he had received from Bolingbroke, he had not intentionally attacked religion; and Bolingbroke, if he meant to make him without his own consent an instrument of mischief, found him now engaged with his eyes open on the side of truth.

It is known that Bolingbroke concealed from Pope his real opinions. He once discovered them to Mr. Hooke, who related them again to Pope, and was told by him that he must have mistaken the meaning of what he heard; and Bolingbroke, when Pope's uneasiness incited him to desire an explanation, declared that Hooke had misunderstood him.

Bolingbroke hated Warburton, who had drawn his pupil from him; and a little before Pope's death they had a dispute, from which they parted with mutual aversion.

From this time Pope lived in the closest intimacy with his commentator, and amply rewarded his kindness and his zeal; for he introduced him to Mr. Murray, by whose interest he became preacher at Lincoln's Inn, and to Mr. Allen, who gave him his niece and his estate, and by consequence a bishopric. When he died he left him the property of his works, a legacy which may be reasonably estimated at four thousand pounds.

Pope's fondness for the *Essay on Man* appeared by his desire of its propagation. Dobson, who had gained reputation by his version of Prior's *Solomon*, was employed by him to translate it into Latin verse, and was for that purpose some time at Twickenham; but he left his work, whatever was the reason, unfinished, and, by Benson's invitation, undertook the longer task of *Paradise Lost*. Pope then desired his friend to find a scholar who should turn his *Essay* into Latin prose; but no such performance has ever appeared.

Pope lived at this time "among the great,"[85] with that reception and respect to which his works entitled him, and which he had not impaired by any private misconduct or factious partiality. Though Bolingbroke was his friend, Walpole was not his enemy, but treated him with so much consideration as, at his request, to solicit and obtain from the French Minister an abbey for Mr. Southcote, whom he considered himself as obliged to reward, by this exertion of his interest, for the benefit which he had received from his attendance in a long illness.

It was said that, when the Court was at Richmond, Queen Caroline had declared her intention to visit him. This may have been only a careless effusion, thought on no more: the report of such notice, however, was soon in many mouths;

[85] "Imitation of the First Satire of the Second Book of Horace," line 133.

and, if I do not forget or misapprehend Savage's account, Pope, pretending to decline what was not yet offered, left his house for a time, not, I suppose, for any other reason than lest he should be thought to stay at home in expectation of an honor which would not be conferred. He was, therefore, angry at Swift, who represents him as "refusing the visits of a Queen," because he knew that what had never been offered had never been refused.

Beside the general system of morality supposed to be contained in the *Essay on Man*, it was his intention to write distinct poems upon the different duties or conditions of life; one of which is the *Epistle to Lord Bathurst* (1733) *on the Use of Riches*, a piece on which he declared great labor to have been bestowed.

Into this poem some incidents are historically thrown, and some known characters are introduced, with others of which it is difficult to say how far they are real or fictitious; but the praise of Kyrle, "the Man of Ross," deserves particular examination, who, after a long and pompous enumeration of his public works and private charities, is said to have diffused all those blessings from "five hundred a year." Wonders are willingly told and willingly heard. The truth is that Kyrle was a man of known integrity and active benevolence, by whose solicitation the wealthy were persuaded to pay contributions to his charitable schemes: this influence he obtained by an example of liberality exerted to the utmost extent of his power, and was thus enabled to give more than he had. This account Mr. Victor received from the minister of the place, and I have preserved it that the praise of a good man, being made more credible, may be more solid. Narrations of romantic and impracticable virtue will be read with wonder, but that which is unattainable is recommended in vain: that good may be endeavored it must be shown to be possible.

This is the only piece in which the author has given a hint of his religion by ridiculing the ceremony of burning the Pope, and by mentioning with some indignation the inscription on the Monument.[36]

When this poem was first published, the dialogue, having no letters of direction, was perplexed and obscure. Pope seems

[36] The Pope was burned in effigy every November 17; until 1831, an inscription on the column commemorating the Great Fire of London stated that it was started by Catholics.

to have written with no very distinct idea, for he calls that an *Epistle to Bathurst* in which Bathurst is introduced as speaking.

He afterwards (1734) inscribed to Lord Cobham his *Characters of Men*, written with close attention to the operations of the mind and modifications of life. In this poem he has endeavored to establish and exemplify his favorite theory of the "ruling passion," by which he means an original direction of desire to some particular object, an innate affection which gives all action a determinate and invariable tendency, and operates upon the whole system of life either openly or more secretly by the intervention of some accidental or subordinate propension.

Of any passion thus innate and irresistible the existence may reasonably be doubted. Human characters are by no means constant; men change by change of place, of fortune, of acquaintance; he who is at one time a lover of pleasure is at another a lover of money. Those indeed who attain any excellence commonly spend life in one pursuit, for excellence is not often gained upon easier terms. But to the particular species of excellence, men are directed not by an ascendant planet or predominating humor, but by the first book which they read, some early conversation which they heard, or some accident which excited ardor and emulation.

It must be at least allowed that this "ruling passion," antecedent to reason and observation, must have an object independent on human contrivance, for there can be no natural desire of artificial good. No man therefore can be born, in the strict acceptance, a lover of money, for he may be born where money does not exist; nor can he be born, in a moral sense, a lover of his country, for society, politically regulated, is a state contradistinguished from a state of nature, and any attention to that coalition of interests which makes the happiness of a country is possible only to those whom inquiry and reflection have enabled to comprehend it.

This doctrine is in itself pernicious as well as false; its tendency is to produce the belief of a kind of moral predestination or overruling principle which cannot be resisted: he that admits it is prepared to comply with every desire that caprice or opportunity shall excite, and to flatter himself that he submits only to the lawful dominion of nature in obeying the resistless authority of his "ruling passion."

Pope has formed his theory with so little skill that, in the examples by which he illustrates and confirms it, he has con-founded passions, appetites, and habits.

To the *Characters of Men* he added soon after, in an Epistle supposed to have been addressed to Martha Blount, but which the last edition has taken from her, the *Characters of Women*.[37] This poem, which was labored with great diligence, and, in the author's opinion, with great success, was neglected at its first publication, as the commentator supposes, because the public was informed by an advertisement that it contained "no character drawn from the life"; an assertion which Pope probably did not expect or wish to have been believed, and which he soon gave his readers sufficient reason to distrust, by telling them in a note that the work was imperfect, because part of his subject was "vice too high" to be exposed.

The time, however, soon came in which it was safe to dis-play the Duchess of Marlborough under the name of Atossa, and her character was inserted with no great honor to the writer's gratitude.[38]

He published from time to time (between 1730 and 1740) imitations of different poems of Horace, generally with his name, and once, as was suspected, without it.[39] What he was upon moral principles ashamed to own, he ought to have suppressed. Of these pieces it is useless to settle the dates, as they had seldom much relation to the times, and perhaps had been long in his hands.

This mode of imitation, in which the ancients are familiar-ized by adapting their sentiments to modern topics, by making Horace say of Shakespeare what he originally said of Ennius, and accommodating his satires on Pantolabus and Nomen-tanus to the flatterers and prodigals of our own time, was first practiced in the reign of Charles the Second by Oldham and Rochester; at least I remember no instances more ancient. It is a kind of middle composition between translation and original design, which pleases when the thoughts are unex-pectedly applicable and the parallels lucky. It seems to have

[37] Warburton, who disliked Blount, stated in a note to his edition of 1751 that the lady addressed in the poem was imaginary.
[38] The Duchess of Marlborough was a friend and perhaps a patron of Pope's.
[39] "Sober Advice from Horace" (1734) was published anonymously, and Pope ambiguously disclaimed it. An imitation of Horace's second satire of the first book, it coarsely recommends whoring over adultery.

been Pope's favorite amusement, for he has carried it further than any former poet.

He published likewise a revival in smoother numbers of Dr. Donne's *Satires*, which was recommended to him by the Duke of Shrewsbury and the Earl of Oxford. They made no great impression on the public. Pope seems to have known their imbecility,[40] and therefore suppressed them while he was yet contending to rise in reputation, but ventured them when he thought their deficiencies more likely to be imputed to Donne than to himself.

The *Epistle to Dr. Arbuthnot*, which seems to be derived in its first design from Boileau's address, *A Son Esprit*, was published in January, 1735, about a month before the death of him to whom it is inscribed. It is to be regretted that either honor or pleasure should have been missed by Arbuthnot, a man estimable for his learning, amiable for his life, and venerable for his piety.

Arbuthnot was a man of great comprehension, skillful in his profession, versed in the sciences, acquainted with ancient literature, and able to animate his mass of knowledge by a bright and active imagination; a scholar with great brilliancy of wit; a wit, who, in the crowd of life, retained and discovered a noble ardor of religious zeal.

In the poem Pope seems to reckon with the public. He vindicates himself from censures; and with dignity, rather than arrogance, enforces his own claims to kindness and respect.

Into this poem are interwoven several paragraphs which had been before printed as a fragment, and among them the satirical lines upon Addison, of which the last couplet has been twice corrected. It was at first,

> Who would not smile if such a man there be?
> Who would not laugh if Addison were he?

Then,

> Who would not grieve if such a man there be?
> Who would not laugh if Addison were he?

---

[40] *imbecility:* weakness.

At last it is,

> Who but must laugh if such a man there be?
> Who would not weep if Addison were he?

He was at this time at open war with Lord Hervey, who had distinguished himself as a steady adherent to the Ministry; and, being offended with a contemptuous answer to one of his pamphlets, had summoned Pulteney to a duel. Whether he or Pope made the first attack perhaps cannot now be easily known: he had written an invective against Pope, whom he calls, "Hard as thy heart, and as thy birth obscure," and hints that his father was a "hatter." To this Pope wrote a reply in verse and prose; the verses are in this poem,[41] and the prose, though it was never sent, is printed among his Letters, but to a cool reader of the present time exhibits nothing but tedious malignity.

His last satires of the general kind were two *Dialogues*, named from the year in which they were published, *Seventeen Hundred and Thirty-eight*. In these poems many are praised, and many are reproached. Pope was then entangled in the Opposition; a follower of the Prince of Wales, who dined at his house, and the friend of many who obstructed and censured the conduct of the Ministers. His political partiality was too plainly shown; he forgot the prudence with which he passed, in his earlier years, uninjured and unoffending through much more violent conflicts of faction.

In the first *Dialogue*, having an opportunity of praising Allen of Bath, he asked his leave to mention him as a man not illustrious by any merit of his ancestors, and called him in his verses "low-born Allen." Men are seldom satisfied with praise introduced or followed by any mention of defect. Allen seems not to have taken any pleasure in his epithet, which was afterwards softened into "humble Allen."

In the second *Dialogue* he took some liberty with one of the Foxes, among others; which Fox, in a reply to Lyttleton, took an opportunity of repaying, by reproaching him with the friendship of a lampooner, who scattered his ink without fear or decency, and against whom he hoped the resentment of the legislature would quickly be discharged.

---

[41] The character of Sporus represents Hervey.

About this time Paul Whitehead, a small poet, was summoned before the Lords for a poem called *Manners*, together with Dodsley, his publisher. Whitehead, who hung loose upon society, skulked and escaped; but Dodsley's shop and family made his appearance necessary. He was, however, soon dismissed; and the whole process was probably intended rather to intimidate Pope than to punish Whitehead.

Pope never afterwards attempted to join the patriot with the poet, nor drew his pen upon statesmen. That he desisted from his attempts of reformation is imputed, by his commentator,[42] to his despair of prevailing over the corruption of the time. He was not likely to have been ever of opinion that the dread of his satire would countervail the love of power or of money: he pleased himself with being important and formidable, and gratified sometimes his pride, and sometimes his resentment; till at last he began to think he should be more safe if he were less busy.

The *Memoirs of Scriblerus*, published about this time, extend only to the first book of a work, projected in concert by Pope, Swift, and Arbuthnot, who used to meet in the time of Queen Anne, and denominated themselves the "Scriblerus Club." Their purpose was to censure the abuses of learning by a fictitious life of an infatuated scholar. They were dispersed; the design was never completed; and Warburton laments its miscarriage as an event very disastrous to polite letters.

If the whole may be estimated by this specimen, which seems to be the production of Arbuthnot, with a few touches perhaps by Pope, the want of more will not be much lamented, for the follies which the writer ridicules are so little practiced that they are not known; nor can the satire be understood but by the learned: he raises phantoms of absurdity, and then drives them away. He cures diseases that were never felt.

For this reason this joint production of three great writers has never obtained any notice from mankind; it has been little read, or when read has been forgotten, as no man could be wiser, better, or merrier, by remembering it.

The design cannot boast of much originality; for, besides its general resemblance to *Don Quixote*, there will be found in it particular imitations of the *History of Mr. Oufle*.

[42] Warburton.

Swift carried so much of it into Ireland as supplied him with hints for his *Travels*;[43] and with those the world might have been contented, though the rest had been suppressed.

Pope had sought for images and sentiments in a region not known to have been explored by many other of the English writers; he had consulted the modern writers of Latin poetry, a class of authors whom Boileau endeavored to bring into contempt, and who are too generally neglected. Pope, however, was not ashamed of their acquaintance, nor ungrateful for the advantages which he might have derived from it. A small selection from the Italians who wrote in Latin had been published at London, about the latter end of the last century, by a man who concealed his name, but whom his Preface shows to have been well qualified for his undertaking. This collection Pope amplified by more than half, and (1740) published it in two volumes, but injuriously omitted his predecessor's Preface. To these books, which had nothing but the mere text, no regard was paid; the authors were still neglected, and the editor was neither praised nor censured.

He did not sink into idleness; he had planned a work which he considered as subsequent to his *Essay on Man*, of which he has given this account to Dr. Swift.

March 25, 1736.

If ever I write any more Epistles in verse one of them shall be addressed to you. I have long concerted it, and begun it; but I would make what bears your name as finished as my last work ought to be, that is to say, more finished than any of the rest. The subject is large, and will divide into four Epistles, which naturally follow the *Essay on Man*, viz. 1. Of the extent and limits of human reason and science. 2. A view of the useful and therefore attainable, and of the unuseful and therefore unattainable arts. 3. Of the nature, ends, application, and use of different capacities. 4. Of the use of learning, of the science of the world, and of wit. It will conclude with a satire against the misapplication of all these, exemplified by pictures, characters, and examples.

This work in its full extent, being now afflicted with an asthma, and finding the powers of life gradually declining, he

[43] *Gulliver's Travels*, particularly Book III.

had no longer courage to undertake; but, from the materials which he had provided, he added, at Warburton's request, another book to *The Dunciad*, of which the design is to ridicule such studies as are either hopeless or useless, as either pursue what is unattainable, or what, if it be attained, is of no use.

When this book was printed (1742) the laurel had been for some time upon the head of Cibber; a man whom it cannot be supposed that Pope could regard with much kindness or esteem, though in one of the *Imitations of Horace* he has liberally enough praised *The Careless Husband*.[44] In *The Dunciad*, among other worthless scribblers, he had mentioned Cibber, who, in his *Apology*, complains of the great poet's unkindness as more injurious, "because," says he, "I never have offended him."

It might have been expected that Pope should have been, in some degree, mollified by this submissive gentleness; but no such consequence appeared. Though he condescended to commend Cibber once, he mentioned him afterwards contemptuously in one of his *Satires*, and again in his *Epistle to Arbuthnot*, and in the fourth book of *The Dunciad* attacked him with acrimony, to which the provocation is not easily discoverable. Perhaps he imagined that, in ridiculing the Laureate, he satirized those by whom the laurel had been given, and gratified that ambitious petulance with which he affected to insult the great.

The severity of this satire left Cibber no longer any patience. He had confidence enough in his own powers to believe that he could disturb the quiet of his adversary, and doubtless did not want instigators, who, without any care about the victory, desired to amuse themselves by looking on the contest. He therefore gave the town a pamphlet, in which he declares his resolution from that time never to bear another blow without returning it, and to tire out his adversary by perseverance, if he cannot conquer him by strength.

The incessant and unappeasable malignity of Pope he imputes to a very distant cause. After the *Three Hours after*

---

[44] Colley Cibber, an actor, theater manager, and author, wrote worthless poetry, sentimental comedies, of which *The Careless Husband* (1705) was the most famous, and an autobiography, *An Apology for the Life of Mr. Colley Cibber* (1740). Pope praised *The Careless Husband* in his "Imitation of the First Epistle of the Second Book of Horace," lines 91–92.

Marriage had been driven off the stage, by the offense which the mummy and crocodile gave the audience, while the exploded scene was yet fresh in memory, it happened that Cibber played Bayes in *The Rehearsal*; and, as it had been usual to enliven the part by the mention of any recent theatrical transactions, he said that he once thought to have introduced his lovers disguised in a mummy and a crocodile.[45] "This," says he, "was received with loud claps, which indicated contempt of the play." Pope, who was behind the scenes, meeting him as he left the stage, attacked him, as he says, with all the virulence of a "wit out of his senses"; to which he replied "that he would take no other notice of what was said by so particular a man than to declare that, as often as he played that part, he would repeat the same provocation."

He shows his opinion to be that Pope was one of the authors of the play which he so zealously defended, and adds an idle story of Pope's behavior at a tavern.

The pamphlet was written with little power of thought or language, and, if suffered to remain without notice, would have been very soon forgotten. Pope had now been enough acquainted with human life to know, if his passion had not been too powerful for his understanding, that from a contention like his with Cibber the world seeks nothing but diversion, which is given at the expense of the higher character. When Cibber lampooned Pope, curiosity was excited; what Pope would say of Cibber nobody inquired, but in hope that Pope's asperity might betray his pain and lessen his dignity.

He should, therefore, have suffered the pamphlet to flutter and die, without confessing that it stung him. The dishonor of being shown as Cibber's antagonist could never be compensated by the victory. Cibber had nothing to lose; when Pope had exhausted all his malignity upon him, he would rise in the esteem both of his friends and his enemies. Silence only could have made him despicable: the blow which did not appear to be felt would have been struck in vain.

But Pope's irascibility prevailed, and he resolved to tell the whole English world that he was at war with Cibber; and to

---

[45] *Three Hours after Marriage* (1717), a collaborative effort of Pope, John Gay, and John Arbuthnot, failed; in particular, its scene involving a mummy and a crocodile was hooted off the stage. Cibber provokingly alluded to this when he played Bayes, the author lampooned in *The Rehearsal* (a satire on contemporary drama originally produced in 1671, but constantly updated with current topical allusions).

show that he thought him no common adversary he prepared no common vengeance: he published a new edition of *The Dunciad*, in which he degraded Theobald from his painful pre-eminence, and enthroned Cibber in his stead. Unhappily the two heroes were of opposite characters, and Pope was unwilling to lose what he had already written; he has therefore depraved his poem by giving to Cibber the old books, the cold pedantry, and sluggish pertinacity of Theobald.

Pope was ignorant enough of his own interest to make another change, and introduced Osborne contending for the prize among the booksellers.[46] Osborne was a man entirely destitute of shame, without sense of any disgrace but that of poverty. He told me, when he was doing that which raised Pope's resentment, that he should be put into *The Dunciad*, but he had the fate of Cassandra. I gave no credit to his prediction till in time I saw it accomplished. The shafts of satire were directed equally in vain against Cibber and Osborne; being repelled by the impenetrable impudence of one, and deadened by the impassive dullness of the other. Pope confessed his own pain by his anger; but he gave no pain to those who had provoked him. He was able to hurt none but himself: by transferring the same ridicule from one to another he destroyed its efficacy; for, by showing that what he had said of one he was ready to say of another, he reduced himself to the insignificance of his own magpie, who from his cage calls cuckold at a venture.[47]

Cibber, according to his engagement, repaid *The Dunciad* with another pamphlet, which, Pope said, "would be as good as a dose of hartshorn to him"; but his tongue and his heart were at variance. I have heard Mr. Richardson relate that he attended his father the painter on a visit, when one of Cibber's pamphlets came into the hands of Pope, who said, "These things are my diversion." They sat by him while he perused it, and saw his features writhen with anguish; and young Richardson said to his father, when they returned, that he hoped to be preserved from such diversion as had been that day the lot of Pope.

From this time, finding his diseases more oppressive, and

---

[46] In *The Dunciad*, II, 167–90, Thomas Osborne competes with the equally disreputable publisher Edmund Curll to see who can urinate higher.

[47] *at a venture:* at random. In "Of the Characters of Men," lines 5–8.

his vital powers gradually declining, he no longer strained his faculties with any original composition, nor proposed any other employment for his remaining life than the revisal and correction of his former works, in which he received advice and assistance from Warburton, whom he appears to have trusted and honored in the highest degree.

He laid aside his epic poem, perhaps without much loss to mankind; for his hero was Brutus the Trojan, who, according to a ridiculous fiction, established a colony in Britain. The subject, therefore, was of the fabulous age; the actors were a race upon whom imagination has been exhausted and attention wearied, and to whom the mind will not easily be recalled when it is invited in blank verse, which Pope had adopted with great imprudence, and, I think, without due consideration of the nature of our language. The sketch is, at least in part, preserved by Ruffhead; by which it appears that Pope was thoughtless enough to model the names of his heroes with terminations not consistent with the time or country in which he places them.

He lingered through the next year; but perceived himself, as he expresses it, "going down the hill." He had for at least five years been afflicted with an asthma and other disorders, which his physicians were unable to relieve. Towards the end of his life he consulted Dr. Thomson, a man who had, by large promises and free censures of the common practice of physic, forced himself up into sudden reputation. Thomson declared his distemper to be a dropsy, and evacuated part of the water by tincture of jalap, but confessed that his belly did not subside. Thomson had many enemies, and Pope was persuaded to dismiss him.

While he was yet capable of amusement and conversation, as he was one day sitting in the air with Lord Bolingbroke and Lord Marchmont, he saw his favorite Martha Blount at the bottom of the terrace, and asked Lord Bolingbroke to go and hand her up. Bolingbroke, not liking his errand, crossed his legs and sat still; but Lord Marchmont, who was younger and less captious, waited on the lady, who, when he came to her, asked, "What, is he not dead yet?" She is said to have neglected him with shameful unkindness in the latter time of his decay; yet, of the little which he had to leave, she had a very great part. Their acquaintance began early: the life of each was pictured on the other's mind; their conversation, therefore, was endearing, for when they met there was an immediate coalition of congenial notions. Perhaps he considered her unwillingness to approach the chamber of sickness as female weakness or human frailty; perhaps he was conscious to himself of peevishness and impatience, or, though he was offended by her inattention, might yet consider her merit as overbalancing her fault; and, if he had suffered his heart to be alienated from her, he could have found nothing that might fill her place: he could have only shrunk within himself; it was too late to transfer his confidence or fondness.

In May, 1744, his death was approaching; on the sixth he was all day delirious, which he mentioned four days afterwards as a sufficient humiliation of the vanity of man; he afterwards complained of seeing things as through a curtain and in false colors, and one day, in the presence of Dodsley, asked what arm it was that came out from the wall. He said that his greatest inconvenience was inability to think.

Bolingbroke sometimes wept over him in this state of helpless decay, and being told by Spence that Pope, at the intermission of his deliriousness, was always saying something kind either of his present or absent friends, and that his humanity seemed to have survived his understanding, answered, "It has so." And added, "I never in my life knew a man that had so tender a heart for his particular friends, or a more general friendship for mankind." At another time he said, "I have known Pope these thirty years, and value myself more in his friendship than—" his grief then suppressed his voice.

Pope expressed undoubting confidence of a future state. Being asked by his friend Mr. Hooke, a Papist, whether he would not die like his father and mother, and whether a priest should not be called, he answered, "I do not think it essential, but it will be very right; and I thank you for putting me in mind of it."

In the morning, after the priest had given him the last sacraments, he said, "There is nothing that is meritorious but virtue and friendship, and indeed friendship itself is only a part of virtue."

He died in the evening of the thirtieth day of May, 1744, so placidly that the attendants did not discern the exact time of his expiration. He was buried at Twickenham, near his father and mother, where a monument has been erected to him by his commentator, the Bishop of Gloucester.[48]

---

[48] Warburton became Bishop of Gloucester in 1759.

He left the care of his papers to his executors, first to Lord Bolingbroke, and if he should not be living to the Earl of Marchmont, undoubtedly expecting them to be proud of the trust and eager to extend his fame. But let no man dream of influence beyond his life. After a decent time Dodsley the bookseller went to solicit preference as the publisher, and was told that the parcel had not been yet inspected; and whatever was the reason the world has been disappointed of what was "reserved for the next age."[49]

He lost, indeed, the favor of Bolingbroke by a kind of posthumous offense. The political pamphlet called *The Patriot King* had been put into his hands that he might procure the impression of the very few copies to be distributed according to the author's direction among his friends, and Pope assured him that no more had been printed than were allowed; but soon after his death the printer brought and resigned a complete edition of fifteen hundred copies which Pope had ordered him to print and to retain in secret. He kept, as was observed, his engagement to Pope better than Pope had kept it to his friend; and nothing was known of the transaction till, upon the death of his employer, he thought himself obliged to deliver the books to the right owner, who, with great indignation, made a fire in his yard and delivered the whole impression to the flames.

Hitherto nothing had been done which was not naturally dictated by resentment of violated faith: resentment more acrimonious as the violator had been more loved or more trusted. But here the anger might have stopped; the injury was private, and there was little danger from the example.

Bolingbroke, however, was not yet satisfied; his thirst of vengeance excited him to blast the memory of the man over whom he had wept in his last struggles, and he employed Mallet, another friend of Pope, to tell the tale to the public with all its aggravations. Warburton, whose heart was warm with his legacy and tender by the recent separation, thought it proper for him to interpose, and undertook, not indeed to vindicate the action, for breach of trust has always something criminal, but to extenuate it by an apology. Having advanced, what cannot be denied, that moral obliquity is made more or less excusable by the motives that produce it, he inquires what

[49] See "Imitation of the First Satire of the Second Book of Horace," lines 59–60.

evil purpose could have induced Pope to break his promise. He could not delight his vanity by usurping the work, which, though not sold in shops, had been shown to a number more than sufficient to preserve the author's claim; he could not gratify his avarice, for he could not sell his plunder till Bolingbroke was dead; and even then, if the copy was left to another, his fraud would be defeated, and if left to himself would be useless.

Warburton therefore supposes, with great appearance of reason, that the irregularity of his conduct proceeded wholly from his zeal for Bolingbroke, who might perhaps have destroyed the pamphlet, which Pope thought it his duty to preserve, even without its author's approbation. To his apology an answer was written in a *Letter to the Most Impudent Man Living.*

He brought some reproach upon his own memory by the petulant and contemptuous mention made in his will of Mr. Allen, and an affected repayment of his benefactions. Mrs. Blount, as the known friend and favorite of Pope, had been invited to the house of Allen, where she comported herself with such indecent arrogance that she parted from Mrs. Allen in a state of irreconcilable dislike, and the door was forever barred against her. This exclusion she resented with so much bitterness as to refuse any legacy from Pope, unless he left the world with a disavowal of obligation to Allen. Having been long under her dominion, now tottering in the decline of life and unable to resist the violence of her temper, or, perhaps with the prejudice of a lover, persuaded that she had suffered improper treatment, he complied with her demand and polluted his will with female resentment. Allen accepted the legacy, which he gave to the Hospital at Bath, observing that Pope was always a bad accomptant, and that if to 150£ he had put a cipher more he had come nearer to the truth.

The person of Pope is well known not to have been formed by the nicest model. He has, in his account of the "Little Club,"[50] compared himself to a spider, and by another is described as protuberant behind and before. He is said to have been beautiful in his infancy; but he was of a constitution originally feeble and weak, and as bodies of a tender frame are easily distorted his deformity was probably in part the effect of his application. His stature was so low that, to bring him to a level with common tables, it was necessary to raise his seat. But his face was not displeasing, and his eyes were animated and vivid.

By natural deformity or accidental distortion his vital functions were so much disordered that his life was a "long disease."[51] His most frequent assailant was the headache, which he used to relieve by inhaling the steam of coffee, which he very frequently required.

Most of what can be told concerning his petty peculiarities was communicated by a female domestic of the Earl of Oxford, who knew him perhaps after the middle of his life. He was then so weak as to stand in perpetual need of female attendance; extremely sensible of cold, so that he wore a kind of fur doublet under a shirt of very coarse warm linen with fine sleeves. When he rose he was invested in the bodice made of stiff canvas, being scarce able to hold himself erect till they were laced, and he then put on a flannel waistcoat. One side was contracted. His legs were so slender that he enlarged their bulk with three pair of stockings, which were drawn on and off by the maid; for he was not able to dress or undress himself, and neither went to bed nor rose without help. His weakness made it very difficult for him to be clean.

His hair had fallen almost all away, and he used to dine some times with Lord Oxford, privately, in a velvet cap. His dress of ceremony was black, with a tie-wig and a little sword.

The indulgence and accommodation which his sickness required had taught him all the unpleasing and unsocial qualities of a valetudinary man. He expected that everything should give way to his ease or humor, as a child whose parents will not hear her cry has an unresisted dominion in the nursery.

> C'est que l'enfant toujours est homme,
> C'est que l'homme est toujours enfant.
> [The child is always a man,
> The man is always a child.]

When he wanted to sleep he "nodded in company"; and once slumbered at his own table while the Prince of Wales was talking of poetry.

[51] "Epistle to Dr. Arbuthnot," line 132.

The reputation which his friendship gave procured him many invitations; but he was a very troublesome inmate. He brought no servant, and had so many wants that a numerous attendance was scarcely able to supply them. Wherever he was he left no room for another, because he exacted the attention and employed the activity of the whole family.[52] His errands were so frequent and frivolous that the footmen in time avoided and neglected him, and the Earl of Oxford discharged some of the servants for their resolute refusal of his messages. The maids, when they had neglected their business, alleged that they had been employed by Mr. Pope. One of his constant demands was of coffee in the night, and to the woman that waited on him in his chamber he was very burdensome; but he was careful to recompense her want of sleep, and Lord Oxford's servant declared that in a house where her business was to answer his call she would not ask for wages.

He had another fault, easily incident to those who suffering much pain think themselves entitled to whatever pleasures they can snatch. He was too indulgent to his appetite: he loved meat highly seasoned and of strong taste, and, at the intervals of the table, amused himself with biscuits and dry conserves. If he sat down to a variety of dishes he would oppress his stomach with repletion, and though he seemed angry when a dram was offered him, did not forbear to drink it. His friends, who knew the avenues to his heart, pampered him with presents of luxury, which he did not suffer to stand neglected. The death of great men is not always proportioned to the luster of their lives. Hannibal, says Juvenal, did not perish by a javelin or a sword; the slaughters of Cannae were revenged by a ring.[53] The death of Pope was imputed by some of his friends to a silver saucepan, in which it was his delight to heat potted lampreys.

That he loved too well to eat is certain; but that his sensuality shortened his life will not be hastily concluded when it is remembered that a conformation so irregular lasted six and fifty years, notwithstanding such pertinacious diligence of study and meditation.

In all his intercourse with mankind he had great delight in artifice, and endeavored to attain all his purposes by indirect

[52] *family:* household, including servants.
[53] According to Juvenal (Satire X), the great general Hannibal died by taking poison which he kept in a ring.

and unsuspected methods. "He hardly drank tea without a stratagem." If at the house of his friends he wanted any accommodation he was not willing to ask for it in plain terms, but would mention it remotely as something convenient; though, when it was procured, he soon made it appear for whose sake it had been recommended. Thus he teased Lord Orrery till he obtained a screen. He practiced his arts on such small occasions that Lady Bolingbroke used to say, in a French phrase, that "he played the politician about cabbages and turnips." His unjustifiable impression of *The Patriot King*, as it can be imputed to no particular motive, must have proceeded from his general habit of secrecy and cunning: he caught an opportunity of a sly trick, and pleased himself with the thought of outwitting Bolingbroke.

In familiar or convivial conversation it does not appear that he excelled. He may be said to have resembled Dryden, as being not one that was distinguished by vivacity in company. It is remarkable that, so near his time, so much should be known of what he has written, and so little of what he said: traditional memory retains no sallies of raillery nor sentences of observation; nothing either pointed or solid, either wise or merry. One apophthegm only stands upon record. When an objection raised against his inscription for Shakespeare was defended by the authority of Patrick, he replied,—*horresco referens*—that "he would allow the publisher of a dictionary to know the meaning of a single word, but not of two words put together."[54]

He was fretful and easily displeased, and allowed himself to be capriciously resentful. He would sometimes leave Lord Oxford silently, no one could tell why, and was to be courted back by more letters and messages than the footmen were willing to carry. The table was indeed infested by Lady Mary Wortley,[55] who was the friend of Lady Oxford, and who, knowing his peevishness, could by no entreaties be restrained from contradicting him, till their disputes were sharpened to such asperity that one or the other quitted the house.

He sometimes condescended to be jocular with servants or

---

[54] Samuel Patrick, a classical scholar and lexicographer. Johnson pretends to shudder at speaking of this (*Aeneid*, II, 204) because he was himself a lexicographer.
[55] Lady Mary Wortley Montagu, a noted woman wit; Johnson probably disapproved of her because she wrote risqué verses and was separated from her husband.

inferiors; but by no merriment, either of others or his own, was he ever seen excited to laughter.

Of his domestic character frugality was a part eminently remarkable. Having determined not to be dependent he determined not to be in want, and therefore wisely and magnanimously rejected all temptations to expense unsuitable to his fortune. This general care must be universally approved; but it sometimes appeared in petty artifices of parsimony, such as the practice of writing his compositions on the back of letters, as may be seen in the remaining copy of the *Iliad*, by which perhaps in five years five shillings were saved; or in a niggardly reception of his friends and scantiness of entertainment, as when he had two guests in his house he would set at supper a single pint upon the table, and having himself taken two small glasses would retire and say, "Gentlemen, I leave you to your wine." Yet he tells his friends that "he has a heart for all, a house for all, and, whatever they may think, a fortune for all."

He sometimes, however, made a splendid dinner, and is said to have wanted no part of the skill or elegance which such performances require. That this magnificence should be often displayed, that obstinate prudence with which he conducted his affairs would not permit; for his revenue, certain and casual, amounted only to about eight hundred pounds a year, of which, however, he declares himself able to assign one hundred to charity.

Of this fortune, which as it arose from public approbation was very honorably obtained, his imagination seems to have been too full: it would be hard to find a man, so well entitled to notice by his wit that ever delighted so much in talking of his money. In his letters and in his poems, his garden and his grotto, his quincunx and his vines, or some hints of his opulence, are always to be found. The great topic of his ridicule is poverty: the crimes with which he reproaches his antagonists are their debts, their habitation in the Mint,[56] and their want of a dinner. He seems to be of an opinion, not very uncommon in the world, that to want money is to want everything.

Next to the pleasure of contemplating his possessions seems to be that of enumerating the men of high rank with whom he was acquainted, and whose notice he loudly proclaims not to

[56] A district in London where debtors could not be arrested.

have been obtained by any practices of meanness or servility; a boast which was never denied to be true, and to which very few poets have ever aspired. Pope never set genius to sale: he never flattered those whom he did not love, or praised those whom he did not esteem. Savage, however, remarked that he began a little to relax his dignity when he wrote a distich for "his Highness's dog."

His admiration of the great seems to have increased in the advance of life. He passed over peers and statesmen to inscribe his *Iliad* to Congreve, with a magnanimity of which the praise had been complete, had his friend's virtue been equal to his wit. Why he was chosen for so great an honor it is not now possible to know; there is no trace in literary history of any particular intimacy between them. The name of Congreve appears in the letters among those of his other friends, but without any observable distinction or consequence.

To his latter works, however, he took care to annex names dignified with titles, but was not very happy in his choice; for, except Lord Bathurst, none of his noble friends were such as that a good man would wish to have his intimacy with them known to posterity: he can derive little honor from the notice of Cobham, Burlington, or Bolingbroke.

Of his social qualities, if an estimate be made from his letters, an opinion too favorable cannot easily be formed; they exhibit a perpetual and unclouded effulgence of general benevolence and particular fondness. There is nothing but liberality, gratitude, constancy, and tenderness. It has been so long said as to be commonly believed that the true characters of men may be found in their letters, and that he who writes to his friend lays his heart open before him. But the truth is that such were the simple friendships of the Golden Age, and are now the friendships only of children. Very few can boast of hearts which they dare lay open to themselves, and of which, by whatever accident exposed, they do not shun a distinct and continued view; and certainly what we hide from ourselves we do not show to our friends. There is, indeed, no transaction which offers stronger temptations to fallacy and sophistication than epistolary intercourse. In the eagerness of conversation the first emotions of the mind often burst out before they have considered; in the tumult of business interest and passion have their genuine effect; but a friendly letter is a calm and deliberate performance in the cool of leisure, in the stillness of solitude, and surely no man sits down to depreciate by design his own character.

Friendship has no tendency to secure veracity, for by whom can a man so much wish to be thought better than he is as by him whose kindness he desires to gain or keep? Even in writing to the world there is less constraint: the author is not confronted with his reader, and takes his chance of approbation among the different dispositions of mankind; but a letter is addressed to a single mind of which the prejudices and partialities are known, and must therefore please, if not by favoring them, by forbearing to oppose them.

To charge those favorable representations, which men give of their own minds, with the guilt of hypocritical falsehood, would show more severity than knowledge. The writer commonly believes himself. Almost every man's thoughts, while they are general, are right; and most hearts are pure while temptation is away. It is easy to awaken generous sentiments in privacy; to despise death when there is no danger; to glow with benevolence when there is nothing to be given. While such ideas are formed they are felt, and self-love does not suspect the gleam of virtue to be the meteor of fancy.

If the letters of Pope are considered merely as compositions, they seem to be premeditated and artificial. It is one thing to write because there is something which the mind wishes to discharge, and another to solicit the imagination because ceremony or vanity requires something to be written. Pope confesses his early letters to be vitiated with "affectation and ambition"; to know whether he disentangled himself from these perverters of epistolary integrity his book and his life must be set in comparison.

One of his favorite topics is contempt of his own poetry. For this, if it had been real, he would deserve no commendation, and in this he was certainly not sincere; for his high value of himself was sufficiently observed, and of what could he be proud but of his poetry? He writes, he says, when "he has just nothing else to do"; yet Swift complains that he was never at leisure for conversation because he "had always some poetical scheme in his head." It was punctually required that his writing box should be set upon his bed before he rose; and Lord Oxford's domestic related that, in the dreadful winter of '40, she was called from her bed by him four times in one night to supply him with paper, lest he should lose a thought.

He pretends insensibility to censure and criticism, though it was observed by all who knew him that every pamphlet disturbed his quiet, and that his extreme irritability laid him open to perpetual vexation; but he wished to despise his critics, and therefore hoped that he did despise them.

As he happened to live in two reigns when the Court paid little attention to poetry he nursed in his mind a foolish disesteem of kings, and proclaims that "he never sees courts." Yet a little regard shown him by the Prince of Wales melted his obduracy, and he had not much to say when he was asked by his Royal Highness "how he could love a Prince while he disliked Kings?"

He very frequently professes contempt of the world, and represents himself as looking on mankind, sometimes with gay indifference, as on emmets of a hillock below his serious attention, and sometimes with gloomy indignation, as on monsters more worthy of hatred than of pity. These were dispositions apparently counterfeited. How could he despise those whom he lived by pleasing, and on whose approbation his esteem of himself was superstructed? Why should he hate those to whose favor he owed his honor and his ease? Of things that terminate in human life the world is the proper judge: to despise its sentence, if it were possible, is not just; and if it were just is not possible. Pope was far enough from this unreasonable temper; he was sufficiently "a fool to fame,"[57] and his fault was that he pretended to neglect it. His levity and his sullenness were only in his letters; he passed through common life, sometimes vexed and sometimes pleased, with the natural emotions of common men.

His scorn of the great is repeated too often to be real: no man thinks much of that which he despises; and as falsehood is always in danger of inconsistency he makes it his boast at another time that he lives among them.

It is evident that his own importance swells often in his mind. He is afraid of writing lest the clerks of the post office should know his secrets; he has many enemies; he considers himself as surrounded by universal jealousy; "after many deaths, and many dispersions, two or three of us," says he, "may still be brought together, not to plot, but to divert ourselves, and the world too, if it pleases"; and they can live together, and "show what friends wits may be, in spite of all

[57] "Epistle to Dr. Arbuthnot," line 127.

the fools in the world." All this while it was likely that the clerks did not know his hand: he certainly had no more enemies than a public character like his inevitably excites, and with what degree of friendship the wits might live very few were so much fools as ever to inquire.

Some part of this pretended discontent he learned from Swift, and expresses it, I think, most frequently in his correspondence with him. Swift's resentment was unreasonable, but it was sincere; Pope's was the mere mimicry of his friend, a fictitious part which he began to play before it became him. When he was only twenty-five years old he related that "a glut of study and retirement had thrown him on the world," and that there was danger lest "a glut of the world should throw him back upon study and retirement." To this Swift answered with great propriety that Pope had not yet either acted or suffered enough in the world to have become weary of it. And, indeed, it must be some very powerful reason that can drive back to solitude him who has once enjoyed the pleasures of society.

In the letters both of Swift and Pope there appears such narrowness of mind as makes them insensible of any excellence that has not some affinity with their own, and confines their esteem and approbation to so small a number, that whoever should form his opinion of the age from their representation, would suppose them to have lived amidst ignorance and barbarity, unable to find among their contemporaries either virtue or intelligence, and persecuted by those that could not understand them.

When Pope murmurs at the world, when he professes contempt of fame, when he speaks of riches and poverty, of success and disappointment, with negligent indifference, he certainly does not express his habitual and settled sentiments, but either willfully disguises his own character, or, what is more likely, invests himself with temporary qualities, and sallies out in the colors of the present moment. His hopes and fears, his joys and sorrows, acted strongly upon his mind, and if he differed from others it was not by carelessness. He was irritable and resentful: his malignity to Philips, whom he had first made ridiculous, and then hated for being angry, continued too long. Of his vain desire to make Bentley contemptible, I never heard any adequate reason. He was sometimes wanton in his attacks, and before Chandos, Lady [Mary] Wortley, and Hill, was mean in his retreat.

The virtues which seem to have had most of his affection were liberality and fidelity of friendship, in which it does not appear that he was other than he describes himself. His fortune did not suffer his charity to be splendid and conspicuous, but he assisted Dodsley with a hundred pounds that he might open a shop; and of the subscription of forty pounds a year that he raised for Savage twenty were paid by himself. He was accused of loving money, but his love was eagerness to gain, not solicitude to keep it.

In the duties of friendship he was zealous and constant: his early maturity of mind commonly united him with men older than himself, and therefore, without attaining any considerable length of life, he saw many companions of his youth sink into the grave; but it does not appear that he lost a single friend by coldness or by injury: those who loved him once continued their kindness. His ungrateful mention of Allen in his will was the effect of his adherence to one whom he had known much longer, and whom he naturally loved with greater fondness. His violation of the trust reposed in him by Bolingbroke could have no motive inconsistent with the warmest affection; he either thought the action so near to indifferent that he forgot it, or so laudable that he expected his friend to approve it.

It was reported, with such confidence as almost to enforce belief, that in the papers entrusted to his executors was found a defamatory Life of Swift, which he had prepared as an instrument of vengeance to be used, if any provocation should be ever given. About this I inquired of the Earl of Marchmont, who assured me that no such piece was among his remains.

The religion in which he lived and died was that of the Church of Rome, to which in his correspondence with Racine he professes himself a sincere adherent. That he was not scrupulously pious in some part of his life is known by many idle and indecent applications of sentences taken from the Scriptures; a mode of merriment which a good man dreads for its profaneness, and a witty man disdains for its easiness and vulgarity. But to whatever levities he has been betrayed, it does not appear that his principles were ever corrupted, or that he ever lost his belief of revelation. The positions which he transmitted from Bolingbroke he seems not to have understood, and was pleased with an interpretation that made them orthodox.

A man of such exalted superiority and so little moderation

would naturally have all his delinquencies observed and aggravated: those who could not deny that he was excellent would rejoice to find that he was not perfect.

Perhaps it may be imputed to the unwillingness with which the same man is allowed to possess many advantages that his learning has been depreciated. He certainly was in his early life a man of great literary curiosity, and when he wrote his *Essay on Criticism* had for his age a very wide acquaintance with books. When he entered into the living world it seems to have happened to him as to many others that he was less attentive to dead masters: he studied in the academy of Paracelsus, and made the universe his favorite volume. He gathered his notions fresh from reality, not from the copies of authors, but the originals of nature. Yet there is no reason to believe that literature ever lost his esteem; he always professed to love reading, and Dobson, who spent some time at his house translating his *Essay on Man*, when I asked him what learning he found him to possess, answered, "More than I expected." His frequent references to history, his allusions to various kinds of knowledge, and his images selected from art and nature, with his observations on the operations of the mind and the modes of life, show an intelligence perpetually on the wing, excursive, vigorous, and diligent, eager to pursue knowledge, and attentive to retain it.

From this curiosity arose the desire of traveling, to which he alludes in his verses to Jervas, and which, though he never found an opportunity to gratify it, did not leave him till his life declined.

Of his intellectual character the constituent and fundamental principle was good sense, a prompt and intuitive perception of consonance and propriety. He saw immediately, of his own conceptions, what was to be chosen, and what to be rejected; and, in the works of others, what was to be shunned, and what was to be copied.

But good sense alone is a sedate and quiescent quality, which manages its possessions well, but does not increase them; it collects few materials for its own operations, and preserves safety, but never gains supremacy. Pope had likewise genius; a mind active, ambitious, and adventurous, always investigating, always aspiring; in its widest searches still longing to go forward, in its highest flights still wishing to be higher; always imagining something greater than it knows, always endeavoring more than it can do.

To assist these powers he is said to have had great strength and exactness of memory. That which he had heard or read was not easily lost; and he had before him not only what his own meditation suggested, but what he had found in other writers that might be accommodated to his present purpose.

These benefits of nature he improved by incessant and unwearied diligence; he had recourse to every source of intelligence, and lost no opportunity of information; he consulted the living as well as the dead; he read his compositions to his friends, and was never content with mediocrity when excellence could be attained. He considered poetry as the business of his life, and, however he might seem to lament his occupation, he followed it with constancy: to make verses was his first labor, and to mend them was his last.

From his attention to poetry he was never diverted. If conversation offered anything that could be improved he committed it to paper; if a thought, or perhaps an expression more happy than was common, rose to his mind, he was careful to write it; an independent distich was preserved for an opportunity of insertion, and some little fragments have been found containing lines, or parts of lines, to be wrought upon at some other time.

He was one of those few whose labor is their pleasure; he was never elevated to negligence, nor wearied to impatience; he never passed a fault unamended by indifference, nor quitted it by despair. He labored his works first to gain reputation, and afterwards to keep it.

Of composition there are different methods. Some employ at once memory and invention, and, with little intermediate use of the pen, form and polish large masses by continued meditation, and write their productions only when, in their own opinion, they have completed them. It is related of Virgil that his custom was to pour out a great number of verses in the morning, and pass the day in retrenching exuberances and correcting inaccuracies. The method of Pope, as may be collected from his translation, was to write his first thoughts in his first words, and gradually to amplify, decorate, rectify, and refine them.

With such faculties and such dispositions he excelled every other writer in *poetical prudence*; he wrote in such a manner as might expose him to few hazards. He used almost always the same fabric of verse; and, indeed, by those few essays which he made of any other, he did not enlarge his reputation. Of this uniformity the certain consequence was readiness and dexterity. By perpetual practice language had in his mind a systematical arrangement; having always the same use for words, he had words so selected and combined as to be ready at his call. This increase of facility he confessed himself to have perceived in the progress of his translation.

But what was yet of more importance, his effusions were always voluntary and his subjects chosen by himself. His independence secured him from drudging at a task, and laboring upon a barren topic: he never exchanged praise for money, nor opened a shop of condolence or congratulation. His poems, therefore, were scarce ever temporary.[58] He suffered coronations and royal marriages to pass without a song, and derived no opportunities from recent events, nor any popularity from the accidental disposition of his readers. He was never reduced to the necessity of soliciting the sun to shine upon a birthday, of calling the Graces and Virtues to a wedding, or of saying what multitudes have said before him. When he could produce nothing new, he was at liberty to be silent.

His publications were for the same reason never hasty. He is said to have sent nothing to the press till it had lain two years under his inspection: it is at least certain that he ventured nothing without nice examination. He suffered the tumult of imagination to subside, and the novelties of invention to grow familiar. He knew that the mind is always enamored of its own productions, and did not trust his first fondness. He consulted his friends, and listened with great willingness to criticism; and, what was of more importance, he consulted himself, and let nothing pass against his own judgment.

He professed to have learned his poetry from Dryden, whom, whenever an opportunity was presented, he praised through his whole life with unvaried liberality; and perhaps his character may receive some illustration if he be compared with his master.

Integrity of understanding and nicety of discernment were not allotted in a less proportion to Dryden than to Pope. The rectitude of Dryden's mind was sufficiently shown by the dismission of his poetical prejudices, and the rejection of unnatural thoughts and rugged numbers.[59] But Dryden never desired to apply all the judgment that he had. He wrote, and

---

[58] *temporary:* adapted to some specific occasion; topical.
[59] Dryden's early poems were poor imitations of the metaphysical style.

professed to write, merely for the people; and when he pleased others, he contented himself. He spent no time in struggles to rouse latent powers; he never attempted to make that better which was already good, nor often to mend what he must have known to be faulty. He wrote, as he tells us, with very little consideration; when occasion or necessity called upon him, he poured out what the present moment happened to supply, and, when once it had passed the press, ejected it from his mind; for when he had no pecuniary interest, he had no further solicitude.

Pope was not content to satisfy; he desired to excel, and therefore always endeavored to do his best: he did not court the candor, but dared the judgment of his reader, and, expecting no indulgence from others, he showed none to himself. He examined lines and words with minute and punctilious observation, and retouched every part with indefatigable diligence, till he had left nothing to be forgiven.

For this reason he kept his pieces very long in his hands, while he considered and reconsidered them. The only poems which can be supposed to have been written with such regard to the times as might hasten their publication were the two satires of *Thirty-eight*;[60] of which Dodsley told me that they were brought to him by the author, that they might be fairly copied. "Almost every line," he said, "was then written twice over; I gave him a clean transcript, which he sent some time afterwards to me for the press, with almost every line written twice over a second time."

His declaration that his care for his works ceased at their publication was not strictly true. His parental attention never abandoned them; what he found amiss in the first edition, he silently corrected in those that followed. He appears to have revised the *Iliad*, and freed it from some of its imperfections; and the *Essay on Criticism* received many improvements after its first appearance. It will seldom be found that he altered without adding clearness, elegance, or vigor. Pope had perhaps the judgment of Dryden; but Dryden certainly wanted the diligence of Pope.

In acquired knowledge the superiority must be allowed to Dryden, whose education was more scholastic, and who before he became an author had been allowed more time for

---

[60] "1738," two dialogues now called "Epilogue to the Satires."

study, with better means of information. His mind has a larger range, and he collects his images and illustrations from a more extensive circumference of science. Dryden knew more of man in his general nature, and Pope in his local manners. The notions of Dryden were formed by comprehensive speculation, and those of Pope by minute attention. There is more dignity in the knowledge of Dryden, and more certainty in that of Pope.

Poetry was not the sole praise of either, for both excelled likewise in prose; but Pope did not borrow his prose from his predecessor. The style of Dryden is capricious and varied, that of Pope is cautious and uniform; Dryden obeys the motions of his own mind, Pope constrains his mind to his own rules of composition. Dryden is sometimes vehement and rapid; Pope is always smooth, uniform, and gentle. Dryden's page is a natural field, rising into inequalities, and diversified by the varied exuberance of abundant vegetation; Pope's is a velvet lawn, shaven by the scythe, and leveled by the roller.

Of genius, that power which constitutes a poet; that quality without which judgment is cold and knowledge is inert; that energy which collects, combines, amplifies, and animates— the superiority must, with some hesitation, be allowed to Dryden. It is not to be inferred that of this poetical vigor Pope had only a little, because Dryden had more, for every other writer since Milton must give place to Pope; and even of Dryden it must be said that if he has brighter paragraphs, he has not better poems. Dryden's performances were always hasty, either excited by some external occasion, or extorted by domestic necessity; he composed without consideration, and published without correction. What his mind could supply at call, or gather in one excursion, was all that he sought, and all that he gave. The dilitory caution of Pope enabled him to condense his sentiments, to multiply his images, and to accumulate all that study might produce, or chance might supply. If the flights of Dryden therefore are higher, Pope continues longer on the wing. If of Dryden's fire the blaze is brighter, of Pope's the heat is more regular and constant. Dryden is read with frequent astonishment, and Pope with perpetual delight.

This parallel will, I hope, when it is well considered, be found just; and if the reader should suspect me, as I suspect myself, of some partial fondness for the memory of Dryden, let him not too hastily condemn me; for meditation and inquiry may, perhaps, show him the reasonableness of my determination.

The works of Pope are now to be distinctly examined, not so much with attention to slight faults or petty beauties, as to the general character and effect of each performance.

It seems natural for a young poet to initiate himself by pastorals, which, not professing to imitate real life, require no experience, and, exhibiting only the simple operation of unmingled passions, admit no subtle reasoning or deep inquiry. Pope's *Pastorals* are not however composed but with close thought; they have reference to the times of the day, the seasons of the year, and the periods of human life. The last, that which turns the attention upon age and death, was the author's favorite. To tell of disappointment and misery, to thicken the darkness of futurity, and perplex the labyrinth of uncertainty, has been always a delicious employment of the poets. His preference was probably just. I wish, however, that his fondness had not overlooked a line in which the "zephyrs" are made "to lament in silence."

To charge these *Pastorals* with want of invention is to require what never was intended. The imitations are so ambitiously frequent that the writer evidently means rather to show his literature than his wit. It is surely sufficient for an author of sixteen not only to be able to copy the poems of antiquity with judicious selection, but to have obtained sufficient power of language and skill in meter to exhibit a series of versification which had in English poetry no precedent, nor has since had an imitation.

The design of *Windsor Forest* is evidently derived from *Cooper's Hill*, with some attention to Waller's poem on "The Park"; but Pope cannot be denied to excel his masters in variety and elegance, and the art of interchanging description, narrative, and morality. The objection made by Dennis is the want of plan, of a regular subordination of parts terminating in the principal and original design. There is this want in most descriptive poems, because as the scenes, which they must exhibit successively, are all subsisting at the same time, the order in which they are shown must by necessity be arbitrary, and more is not to be expected from the last part than from the first. The attention, therefore, which cannot be detained by suspense, must be excited by diversity, such as his poem offers to its readers.

But the desire of diversity may be too much indulged: the parts of *Windsor Forest* which deserve least praise are those which were added to enliven the stillness of the scene, the appearance of Father Thames, and the transformation of Lodona.[61] Addison had in his *Campaign* derided the "rivers" that "rise from their oozy beds" to tell stories of heroes, and it is therefore strange that Pope should adopt a fiction not only unnatural but lately censured. The story of Lodona is told with sweetness; but a new metamorphosis is a ready and puerile expedient: nothing is easier than to tell how a flower was once a blooming virgin, or a rock an obdurate tyrant.

The Temple of Fame has, as Steele warmly declared, "a thousand beauties." Every part is splendid; there is great luxuriance of ornaments; the original vision of Chaucer was never denied to be much improved; the allegory is very skillfully continued, the imagery is properly selected and learnedly displayed: yet, with all this comprehension of excellence, as its scene is laid in remote ages, and its sentiments, if the concluding paragraph be excepted, have little relation to general manners or common life, it never obtained much notice, but is turned silently over, and seldom quoted or mentioned with either praise or blame.

That the "Messiah" excels the "Pollio" is no great praise, if it be considered from what original the improvements are derived.[62]

The "Verses on the Unfortunate Lady" have drawn much attention by the illaudable singularity of treating suicide with respect, and they must be allowed to be written in some parts with vigorous animation, and in others with gentle tenderness; nor has Pope produced any poem in which the sense predominates more over the diction. But the tale is not skillfully told: it is not easy to discover the character of either the lady or her guardian. History relates that she was about to disparage herself by a marriage with an inferior; Pope praises her for the dignity of ambition, and yet condemns the uncle to detestation for his pride: the ambitious love of a niece may be opposed by the interest, malice, or envy of an uncle, but

[61] Pope related a conventional tale of a nymph pursued by Pan to account for the origin of the river Loddon.
[62] "The Messiah," imitating Virgil's "Pollio," describes a golden age brought about by a miraculous child; but while Virgil's poem is secular, Pope's is based on the book of Isaiah, at that time supposed to predict the coming of Christ.

never by his pride. On such an occasion a poet may be allowed to be obscure, but inconsistency never can be right.

The "Ode for St. Cecilia's Day" was undertaken at the desire of Steele: in this the author is generally confessed to have miscarried, yet he has miscarried only as compared with Dryden; for he has far outgone other competitors. Dryden's plan is better chosen; history will always take stronger hold of the attention than fable: the passions excited by Dryden are the pleasures and pains of real life, the scene of Pope is laid in imaginary existence. Pope is read with calm acquiescence, Dryden with turbulent delight; Pope hangs upon the ear, and Dryden finds the passes of the mind.[63]

Both the odes want the essential constituent of metrical compositions, the stated recurrence of settled numbers. It may be alleged that Pindar is said by Horace to have written *numeris lege solutis* [in verses not fixed by rule (free verse)], but as no such lax performances have been transmitted to us, the meaning of that expression cannot be fixed; and perhaps the like return might properly be made to a modern Pindarist, as Mr. Cobb received from Bentley, who, when he found his criticisms upon a Greek exercise which Cobb had presented, refuted one after another by Pindar's authority, cried out at last, "Pindar was a bold fellow, but thou are an impudent one."

If Pope's "Ode" be particularly inspected it will be found that the first stanza consists of sounds well chosen indeed, but only sounds.

The second consists of hyperbolical commonplaces, easily to be found, and perhaps without much difficulty to be as well expressed.

In the third, however, there are numbers, images, harmony, and vigor, not unworthy the antagonist[64] of Dryden. Had all been like this—but every part cannot be the best.

The next stanzas place and detain us in the dark and dismal regions of mythology, where neither hope nor fear, neither joy nor sorrow can be found: the poet however faith-

---

[63] A London musical society annually celebrated the feast of St. Cecilia with a concert at which an ode was sung; Dryden contributed "Alexander's Feast" (1697) and Pope an "Ode for Music, On St. Cecilia's Day" (1713). Pope's poem expatiates on the power of music in general, while Dryden's tells a stirring legendary tale of Alexander the Great's burning the city of Persepolis.

[64] *antagonist:* rival.

fully attends us; we have all that can be performed by elegance of diction or sweetness of versification; but what can form avail without better matter?

The last stanza recurs again to commonplaces. The conclusion is too evidently modeled by that of Dryden; and it may be remarked that both end with the same fault, the comparison of each is literal on one side, and metaphorical on the other.

Poets do not always express their own thoughts; Pope, with all this labor in the praise of music, was ignorant of its principles, and insensible of its effects.

One of his greatest though of his earliest works is the *Essay on Criticism*, which if he had written nothing else would have placed him among the first critics and the first poets, as it exhibits every mode of excellence that can embellish or dignify composition: selection of matter, novelty of arrangement, justness of precept, splendor of illustration, and propriety of digression. I know not whether it be pleasing to consider that he produced this piece at twenty, and never afterwards excelled it: he that delights himself with observing that such powers may be so soon attained, cannot but grieve to think that life was ever after at a stand.

To mention the particular beauties of the *Essay* would be unprofitably tedious; but I cannot forbear to observe that the comparison of a student's progress in the sciences with the journey of a traveler in the Alps[65] is perhaps the best that English poetry can show. A simile, to be perfect, must both illustrate and ennoble the subject; must show it to the understanding in a clearer view, and display it to the fancy with greater dignity: but either of these qualities may be sufficient to recommend it. In didactic poetry, of which the great purpose is instruction, a simile may be praised which illustrates, though it does not ennoble; in heroics, that may be admitted which ennobles, though it does not illustrate. That it may be complete it is required to exhibit, independently of its references, a pleasing image; for a simile is said to be a short episode. To this antiquity was so attentive that circumstances were sometimes added, which, having no parallels, served only to fill the imagination, and produced what Perrault ludicrously called "comparisons with a long tail." In their similes the greatest writers have sometimes failed: the ship race, compared with the chariot race, is neither illustrated nor ag-

[65] "Essay on Criticism," lines 219–32.

grandized; land and water make all the difference; when Apollo running after Daphne is likened to a greyhound chasing a hare,[66] there is nothing gained; the ideas of pursuit and flight are too plain to be made plainer, and a god and the daughter of a god are not represented much to their advantage by a hare and dog. The simile of the Alps has no useless parts, yet affords a striking picture by itself: it makes the foregoing position better understood, and enables it to take faster hold on the attention; it assists the apprehension, and elevates the fancy.

Let me likewise dwell a little on the celebrated paragraph in which it is directed that "the sound should seem an echo to the sense";[67] a precept which Pope is allowed to have observed beyond any other English poet.

This notion of representative meter, and the desire of discovering frequent adaptations of the sound to the sense, have produced, in my opinion, many wild conceits[68] and imaginary beauties. All that can furnish this representation are the sounds of the words considered singly, and the time in which they are pronounced. Every language has some words framed to exhibit the noises which they express, as *thump, rattle, growl, hiss*. These, however, are but few, and the poet cannot make them more, nor can they be of any use but when sound is to be mentioned. The time of pronunciation was in the dactylic measures of the learned languages capable of considerable variety;[69] but that variety could be accommodated only to motion or duration, and different degrees of motion were perhaps expected by verses rapid or slow, without much attention of the writer, when the image had full possession of his fancy: but our language having little flexibility our verses can differ very little in their cadence. The fancied resemblances, I fear, arise sometimes merely from the ambiguity of words; there is supposed to be some relation between a *soft* line and a *soft* couch, or between *hard* syllables and *hard* fortune.

Motion, however, may be in some sort exemplified; and

---

[66] The chariot race comes from Vergil (*Aeneid*, V, 144–47), the greyhound and hare from Ovid (*Metamorphoses*, I, 533–39).
[67] "Essay on Criticism," lines 364–83.
[68] *conceits:* fancies.
[69] In Greek and Latin, syllables were long or short, and the basic rhythm of verse was determined by this quantity; English verse is not quantitative, but accentual-syllabic.

yet it may be suspected that even in such resemblances the mind often governs the ear, and the sounds are estimated by their meaning. One of the most successful attempts has been to describe the labor of Sisyphus:

> With many a weary step, and many a groan,
> Up a high hill he heaves a huge round stone;
> The huge round stone, resulting with a bound,
> Thunders impetuous down, and smokes along the ground.[70]

Who does not perceive the stone to move slowly upward, and roll violently back? But set the same numbers to another sense;

> While many a merry tale, and many a song,
> Cheered the rough road, we wished the rough road long.
> The rough road then, returning in a round,
> Mocked our impatient steps, for all was fairy ground.

We have now surely lost much of the delay, and much of the rapidity.

But to show how little the greatest master of numbers can fix the principles of representative harmony, it will be sufficient to remark that the poet, who tells us that

> When Ajax strives some rock's vast weight to throw,
> The line too labors and the words move slow:
> Not so when swift Camilla scours the plain,
> Flies o'er th' unbending corn, and skims along the main;[71]

when he had enjoyed for about thirty years the praise of Camilla's lightness of foot, tried another experiment upon *sound* and *time*, and produced this memorable triplet:

> Waller was smooth; but Dryden taught to join
> The varying verse, the full resounding line,
> The long majestic march, and energy divine.[72]

---

[70] Pope, *Odyssey*, XI, 735–38, describing Sisyphus, who had to spend eternity pushing a great stone up a hill, which then immediately rolled down.

[71] "Essay on Criticism," lines 370–73.

[72] "Imitation of the First Epistle of the Second Book of Horace," lines 267–69.

Here are the swiftness of the rapid race and the march of slow-paced majesty exhibited by the same poet in the same sequence of syllables, except that the exact prosodist will find the line of *swiftness* by one time longer than that of *tardiness*.

Beauties of this kind are commonly fancied; and when real are technical and nugatory, not to be rejected and not to be solicited.

To the praises which have been accumulated on *The Rape of the Lock* by readers of every class, from the critic to the waiting-maid, it is difficult to make any addition. Of that which is universally allowed to be the most attractive of all ludicrous compositions, let it rather be now inquired from what sources the power of pleasing is derived.

Dr. Warburton, who excelled in critical perspicacity, has remarked that the preternatural agents are very happily adapted to the purposes of the poem. The heathen deities can no longer gain attention: we should have turned away from a contest between Venus and Diana. The employment of allegorical persons always excites conviction of its own absurdity: they may produce effects, but cannot conduct actions; when the phantom is put in motion, it dissolves; thus Discord may raise a mutiny, but Discord cannot conduct a march, nor besiege a town. Pope brought into view a new race of beings, with powers and passions proportionate to their operation. The sylphs and gnomes act at the toilet and the tea table what more terrific and more powerful phantoms perform on the stormy ocean or the field of battle; they give their proper help, and do their proper mischief.

Pope is said by an objector not to have been the inventor of this petty nation; a charge which might with more justice have been brought against the author of the *Iliad*, who doubtless adopted the religious system of his country; for what is there but the names of his agents which Pope has not invented? Has he not assigned them characters and operations never heard of before? Has he not, at least, given them their first poetical existence? If this is not sufficient to denominate his work original, nothing original ever can be written.

In this work are exhibited in a very high degree the two most engaging powers of an author: new things are made familiar, and familiar things are made new. A race of aerial people never heard of before is presented to us in a manner so clear and easy that the reader seeks for no further information, but immediately mingles with his new acquaintance, adopts their interests, and attends their pursuits, loves a sylph and detests a gnome.

That familiar things are made new every paragraph will prove. The subject of the poem is an event below the common incidents of common life; nothing real is introduced that is not seen so often as to be no longer regarded, yet the whole detail of a female day is here brought before us invested with so much art of decoration that, though nothing is disguised, every thing is striking, and we feel all the appetite of curiosity for that from which we have a thousand times turned fastidiously away.

The purpose of the poet is, as he tells us, to laugh at "the little unguarded follies of the female sex." It is therefore without justice that Dennis charges *The Rape of the Lock* with the want of a moral, and for that reason sets it below *The Lutrin*, which exposes the pride and discord of the clergy. Perhaps neither Pope nor Boileau has made the world much better than he found it; but if they had both succeeded, it were easy to tell who would have deserved most from public gratitude. The freaks, and humors, and spleen, and vanity of women, as they embroil families in discord and fill houses with disquiet, do more to obstruct the happiness of life in a year than the ambition of the clergy in many centuries. It has been well observed that the misery of man proceeds not from any single crush of overwhelming evil, but from small vexations continually repeated.

It is remarked by Dennis likewise that the machinery is superfluous; that by all the bustle of preternatural operation the main event is neither hastened nor retarded. To this charge an efficacious answer is not easily made. The sylphs cannot be said to help or to oppose, and it must be allowed to simply some want of art that their power has not been sufficiently intermingled with the action. Other parts may likewise be charged with want of connection; the game at ombre might be spared, but if the lady had lost her hair while she was intent upon her cards, it might have been inferred that those who are too fond of play will be in danger of neglecting more important interests. Those perhaps are faults; but what are such faults to so much excellence!

The Epistle of *Eloise to Abelard* is one of the most happy productions of human wit: the subject is so judiciously chosen that it would be difficult, in turning over the annals of the world, to find another which so many circumstances concur to recommend. We regularly interest ourselves most in the fortune of those who most deserve our notice. Abelard and Eloise were conspicuous in their days for eminence of merit. The heart naturally loves truth. The adventures and misfortunes of this illustrious pair are known from undisputed history. Their fate does not leave the mind in hopeless dejection; for they both found quiet and consolation in retirement and piety. So new and so affecting is their story that it supersedes invention, and imagination ranges at full liberty without straggling into scenes of fable.

The story thus skillfully adopted has been diligently improved. Pope has left nothing behind him which seems more the effect of studious perseverance and laborious revisal. Here is particularly observable the *curiosa felicitas* [careful felicity],[73] a fruitful soil, and careful cultivation. Here is no crudeness of sense nor asperity of language.

The sources from which sentiments which have so much vigor and efficacy have been drawn are shown to be the mystic writers by the learned author of the *Essay on the Life and Writings of Pope*;[74] a book which teaches how the brow of criticism may be smoothed, and how she may be enabled, with all her severity, to attract and to delight.

The train of my disquisition has now conducted me to that poetical wonder, the translation of the *Iliad*: a performance which no age or nation can pretend to equal. To the Greeks translation was almost unknown; it was totally unknown to the inhabitants of Greece.[75] They had no recourse to the Barbarians for poetical beauties, but sought for everything in Homer, where, indeed, there is but little which they might not find.

The Italians have been very diligent translators; but I can hear of no version, unless perhaps Anguillara's Ovid may be excepted, which is read with eagerness. The *Iliad* of Salvini every reader may discover to be punctiliously exact; but it seems to be the work of a linguist skillfully pedantic, and his

---

[73] From Petronius, Satyricon.
[74] Joseph Warton, in his *Essay on the Writings and Genius of Pope* (1756); he also made many of the adverse criticisms which Johnson refutes in this section.
[75] As opposed to Greeks who lived in Asia Minor, Sicily, etc.

countrymen, the proper judges of its power to please, reject it with disgust.

Their predecessors, the Romans, have left some specimens of translation behind them, and that employment must have had some credit in which Tully and Germanicus engaged; but unless we suppose what is perhaps true, that the plays of Terence were versions of Menander, nothing translated seems ever to have risen to high reputation. The French, in the meridian hour of their learning, were very laudably industrious to enrich their own language with the wisdom of the ancients; but found themselves reduced, by whatever necessity, to turn the Greek and Roman poetry into prose. Whoever could read an author could translate him. From such rivals little can be feared.

The chief help of Pope in this arduous undertaking was drawn from the versions of Dryden. Virgil had borrowed much of his imagery from Homer, and part of the debt was now paid by his translator. Pope searched the pages of Dryden for happy combinations of heroic diction, but it will not be denied that he added much to what he found. He cultivated our language with so much diligence and art that he has left in his Homer a treasure of poetical elegances to posterity. His version may be said to have tuned the English tongue, for since its appearance no writer, however deficient in other powers, has wanted melody. Such a series of lines so elaborately corrected and so sweetly modulated took possession of the public ear; the vulgar was enamored of the poem, and the learned wondered at the translation.

But in the most general applause discordant voices will always be heard. It has been objected by some, who wish to be numbered among the sons of learning, that Pope's version of Homer is not Homerical; that it exhibits no resemblance of the original and characteristic manner of the father of poetry, as it wants his awful simplicity, his artless grandeur, his un-affected majesty. This cannot be totally denied, but it must be remembered that *necessitas quod cogit defendit*, that may be lawfully done which cannot be forborne. Time and place will always enforce regard. In estimating this translation consideration must be had of the nature of our language, the form of our meter, and, above all, of the change which two thousand years have made in the modes of life and the habits of thought. Virgil wrote in a language of the same general fabric with that of Homer, in verses of the same measure, and in an age nearer to Homer's time by eighteen hundred years; yet he found even then the state of the world so much altered, and the demand for elegance so much increased, that mere nature would be endured no longer; and perhaps, in the multitude of borrowed passages, very few can be shown which he has not embellished.

There is a time when nations emerging from barbarity, and falling into regular subordination, gain leisure to grow wise, and feel the shame of ignorance and the craving pain of unsatisfied curiosity. To this hunger of the mind plain sense is grateful;[76] that which fills the void removes uneasiness, and to be free from pain for a while is pleasure; but repletion generates fastidiousness, a saturated intellect soon becomes luxurious, and knowledge finds no willing reception till it is recommended by artificial diction. Thus it will be found in the progress of learning that in all nations the first writers are simple, and that every age improves in elegance. One refinement always makes way for another, and what was expedient to Virgil was necessary to Pope.

I suppose many readers of the English *Iliad*, when they have been touched with some unexpected beauty of the lighter kind, have tried to enjoy it in the original, where, alas! it was not to be found. Homer doubtless owes to his translator many Ovidian graces not exactly suitable to his character; but to have added can be no great crime if nothing be taken away. Elegance is surely to be desired if it be not gained at the expense of dignity. A hero would wish to be loved as well as to be reverenced.

To a thousand cavils one answer is sufficient; the purpose of a writer is to be read, and the criticism which would destroy the power of pleasing must be blown aside. Pope wrote for his own age and his own nation: he knew that it was necessary to color the images and point the sentiments of his author; he therefore made him graceful, but lost him some of his sublimity.

The copious notes with which the version is accompanied and by which it is recommended to many readers, though they were undoubtedly written to swell the volumes, ought not to pass without praise: commentaries which attract the reader

[76] *grateful:* welcome.

by the pleasure of perusal have not often appeared; the notes of others are read to clear difficulties, those of Pope to vary entertainment.

It has, however, been objected with sufficient reason that there is in the commentary too much of unseasonable levity and affected gaiety; that too many appeals are made to the ladies, and the ease which is so carefully preserved is sometimes the ease of a trifler. Every art has its terms and every kind of instruction its proper style; the gravity of common critics may be tedious, but is less despicable than childish merriment.

Of the *Odyssey* nothing remains to be observed; the same general praise may be given to both translations, and a particular examination of either would require a large volume. The notes were written by Broome, who endeavored not unsuccessfully to imitate his master.

Of *The Dunciad* the hint is confessedly taken from Dryden's *MacFlecknoe*, but the plan is so enlarged and diversified as justly to claim the praise of an original, and affords perhaps the best specimen that has yet appeared of personal satire ludicrously pompous.

That the design was moral, whatever the author might tell either his readers or himself, I am not convinced. The first motive was the desire of revenging the contempt with which Theobald had treated his Shakespeare, and regaining the honor which he had lost, by crushing his opponent. Theobald was not of bulk enough to fill a poem, and therefore it was necessary to find other enemies with other names, at whose expense he might divert the public.

In this design there was petulance and malignity enough; but I cannot think it very criminal. An author places himself uncalled before the tribunal of criticism, and solicits fame at the hazard of disgrace. Dullness or deformity are not culpable in themselves, but may be very justly reproached when they pretend to the honor of wit or the influence of beauty. If bad writers were to pass without reprehension, what should restrain them? *impune diem consumpserit ingens "Telephus"* [Shall an interminable "Telephus" take up an entire day with impunity?][77] and upon bad writers only will censure have much effect. The satire which brought Theobald and Moore

[77] Juvenal, Satire I, lines 4–5.

into contempt, dropped impotent from Bentley, like the javelin of Priam thrown at Neoptolemus.[78]

All truth is valuable, and satirical criticism may be considered as useful when it rectifies error and improves judgment: he that refines the public taste is a public benefactor.

The beauties of this poem are well known; its chief fault is the grossness of its images. Pope and Swift had an unnatural delight in ideas physically impure, such as every other tongue utters with unwillingness, and of which every ear shrinks from the mention.

But even this fault, offensive as it is, may be forgiven for the excellence of other passages; such as the formation and dissolution of Moore, the account of the Traveler, the misfortune of the Florist,[79] and the crowded thoughts and stately numbers which dignify the concluding paragraph.

The alterations which have been made in *The Dunciad*, not always for the better, require that it should be published, as in the last collection, with all its variations.

The *Essay on Man* was a work of great labor and long consideration, but certainly not the happiest of Pope's performances. The subject is perhaps not very proper for poetry, and the poet was not sufficiently master of his subject; metaphysical morality was to him a new study, he was proud of his acquisitions, and, supposing himself master of great secrets, was in haste to teach what he had not learned. Thus he tells us, in the first Epistle, that from the nature of the Supreme Being may be deduced an order of beings such as mankind, because infinite excellence can do only what is best. He finds out that these beings must be "somewhere," and that "all the question is whether man be in a wrong place." Surely if, according to the poet's Leibnitzian reasoning,[80] we may infer that man ought to be only because he is, we may allow that his place is the right place, because he has it. Supreme Wisdom is not less infallible in disposing than in creating. But what is meant by "somewhere" and "place" and "wrong place" it

---

[78] The great classical scholar Richard Bentley was unhurt by Pope's satire of him as Aristarchus (*Dunciad*, IV, 203–74), just as the warrior Neoptolemus was unhurt by a javelin hurled by the aged Priam (*Aeneid*, II, 544–46).

[79] *Dunciad*, II, 35–50, IV, 279–330, 403–18.

[80] Gottfried Wilhelm von Leibnitz (1646–1716), an optimistic philosopher, attempted to demonstrate that this was the best of all possible worlds.

had been vain to ask Pope, who probably had never asked himself.

Having exalted himself into the chair of wisdom he tells us much that every man knows, and much that he does not know himself; that we see but little, and that the order of the universe is beyond our comprehension, an opinion not very uncommon; and that there is a chain of subordinate beings "from infinite to nothing," of which himself and his readers are equally ignorant. But he gives us one comfort which, without his help, he supposes unattainable, in the position "that though we are fools, yet God is wise."

This *Essay* affords an egregious instance of the predominance of genius, the dazzling splendor of imagery, and the seductive powers of eloquence. Never were penury of knowledge and vulgarity of sentiment[81] so happily disguised. The reader feels his mind full, though he learns nothing; and when he meets it in its new array no longer knows the talk of his mother and his nurse. When these wonder-working sounds sink into sense and the doctrine of the *Essay*, disrobed of its ornaments, is left to the powers of its naked excellence, what shall we discover? That we are, in comparison with our Creator, very weak and ignorant; that we do not uphold the chain of existence; and that we could not make one another with more skill than we are made. We may learn yet more: that the arts of human life were copied from the instinctive operations of other animals; that if the world be made for man, it may be said that man was made for geese. To these profound principles of natural knowledge are added some moral instructions equally new: that self-interest well understood will produce social concord; that men are mutual gainers by mutual benefits; that evil is sometimes balanced by good; that human advantages are unstable and fallacious, of uncertain duration and doubtful effect; that our true honor is not to have a great part, but to act it well; that virtue only is our own; and that happiness is always in our power.

Surely a man of no very comprehensive search may venture to say that he has heard all this before, but it was never till now recommended by such a blaze of embellishment or such sweetness of melody. The vigorous contraction of some thoughts, the luxuriant amplification of others, the incidental illustrations, and sometimes the dignity, sometimes the soft-

[81] *vulgarity of sentiment:* ordinary thoughts.

ness of the verses, enchain philosophy, suspend criticism, and oppress judgment by overpowering pleasure.

This is true of many paragraphs; yet if I had undertaken to exemplify Pope's felicity of composition before a rigid critic I should not select the *Essay on Man*, for it contains more lines unsuccessfully labored, more harshness of diction, more thoughts imperfectly expressed, more levity without elegance, and more heaviness without strength, than will easily be found in all his other works.

The *Characters of Men and Women* are the product of diligent speculation upon human life; much labor has been bestowed upon them, and Pope very seldom labored in vain. That his excellence may be properly estimated I recommend a comparison of his *Characters of Women* with Boileau's *Satire*; it will then be seen with how much more perspicacity female nature is investigated and female excellence selected; and he surely is no mean writer to whom Boileau shall be found inferior. The *Characters of Men*, however, are written with more, if not with deeper, thought, and exhibit many passages exquisitely beautiful. "The Gem and the Flower" will not easily be equalled.[82] In the women's part are some defects: the character of Atossa is not so neatly finished as that of Clodio,[83] and some of the female characters may be found, perhaps more frequently among men; what is said of Philomedé was true of Prior.

In the *Epistles to Lord Bathurst* and *Lord Burlington* Dr. Warburton has endeavored to find a train of thought which was never in the writer's head, and, to support his hypothesis, has printed that first which was published last. In one the most valuable passage is perhaps the eulogy on good sense, and the other the end of the Duke of Buckingham.[84]

The *Epistle to Arbuthnot*, now arbitrarily called the *Prologue to the Satires*, is a performance consisting, as it seems, of many fragments wrought into one design, which by this union of scattered beauties contains more striking paragraphs than could probably have been brought together into an occasional work. As there is no stronger motive to exertion than

---

[82] "Of the Characters of Men," lines 141–48.
[83] Atossa, "Of the Characters of Women," lines 115–50; Clodio (later given his real name, Wharton), "Of the Characters of Men," lines 180–207.
[84] "To Burlington," lines 39–46; "To Bathurst," lines 299–314.

self-defense, no part has more elegance, spirit, or dignity than the poet's vindication of his own character. The meanest passage is the satire upon Sporus.

Of the two poems which derived their names from the year, and which are called the *Epilogue to the Satires*, it was very justly remarked by Savage that the second was in the whole more strongly conceived and more equally supported, but that it had no single passages equal to the contention in the first for the dignity of Vice and the celebration of the triumph of Corruption.

The *Imitations of Horace* seem to have been written as relaxations of his genius. This employment became his favorite by its facility; the plan was ready to his hand, and nothing was required but to accommodate as he could the sentiments of an old author to recent facts or familiar images; but what is easy is seldom excellent: such imitations cannot give pleasure to common readers. The man of learning may be sometimes surprised and delighted by an unexpected parallel; but the comparison requires knowledge of the original, which will likewise often detect strained applications. Between Roman images and English manners there will be an irreconcilable dissimilitude, and the work will be generally uncouth and parti-colored; neither original nor translated, neither ancient nor modern.

Pope had, in proportions very nicely adjusted to each other, all the qualities that constitute genius. He had invention, by which new trains of events are formed and new scenes of imagery displayed, as in *The Rape of the Lock*, and by which extrinsic and adventitious embellishments and illustrations are connected with a known subject, as in the *Essay on Criticism*; he had imagination, which strongly impresses on the writer's mind and enables him to convey to the reader the various forms of nature, incidents of life, and energies of passion, as in his *Eloisa, Windsor Forest*, and the *Ethic Epistles*.[85] He had judgment, which selects from life or nature what the present purpose requires, and, by separating the essence of things from its concomitants, often makes the representation more powerful than the reality; and he had colors of language always before him ready to decorate his matter with every grace of elegant expression, as when he accommodates his diction

---

[85] Or *Moral Essays:* "Of the Characters of Men," "Of the Characters of Women," the Epistles to Burlington and Bathurst.

to the wonderful multiplicity of Homer's sentiments and descriptions.

Poetical expression includes sound as well as meaning. "Music," says Dryden, "is inarticulate poetry"; among the excellences of Pope, therefore, must be mentioned the melody of his meter. By perusing the works of Dryden he discovered the most perfect fabric of English verse, and habituated himself to that only which he found the best; in consequence of which restraint his poetry has been censured as too uniformly musical, and as glutting the ear with unvaried sweetness. I suspect this objection to be the cant of those who judge by principles rather than perception; and who would even themselves have less pleasure in his works if he had tried to relieve attention by studied discords, or affected to break his lines and vary his pauses.

But though he was thus careful of his versification he did not oppress his powers with superfluous rigor. He seems to have thought with Boileau that the practice of writing might be refined till the difficulty should overbalance the advantage. The construction of his language is not always strictly grammatical; with those rhymes which prescription had conjoined he contented himself, without regard to Swift's remonstrances,[86] though there was no striking consonance; nor was he very careful to vary his terminations or to refuse admission at a small distance to the same rhymes.

To Swift's edict for the exclusion of alexandrines and triplets he paid little regard; he admitted them, but, in the opinion of Fenton, too rarely: he uses them more liberally in his translation than his poems.

He has a few double rhymes, and always, I think, unsuccessfully, except once in *The Rape of the Lock*.

Expletives he very early ejected from his verses; but he now and then admits an epithet rather commodious than important. Each of the six first lines of the *Iliad* might lose two syllables with very little diminution of the meaning; and sometimes, after all his art and labor, one verse seems to be made for the sake of another. In his latter productions the diction is sometimes vitiated by French idioms, with which Bolingbroke had perhaps infected him.

---

[86] Swift, in a letter to Pope (June 28, 1715), highly praised Pope's Homer but reproved him for "some bad Rhymes and Triplets"; "pray in your next do not let me have so many unjustifiable rhymes to *war* and *gods*."

I have been told that the couplet by which he declared his own ear to be most gratified was this:

> Lo, where Maeotis sleeps, and hardly flows
> The freezing Tanais thro' a waste of snows.[87]

But the reason of this preference I cannot discover.

It is remarked by Watts that there is scarcely a happy combination of words or a phrase poetically elegant in the English language which Pope has not inserted into his version of Homer. How he obtained possession of so many beauties of speech it were desirable to know. That he gleaned from authors, obscure as well as eminent, what he thought brilliant or useful, and preserved it all in a regular collection, is not unlikely. When, in his last years, Hall's *Satires* were shown him he wished that he had seen them sooner.

New sentiments and new images others may produce, but to attempt any further improvement of versification will be dangerous. Art and diligence have now done their best, and what shall be added will be the effort of tedious toil and needless curiosity.

After all this it is surely superfluous to answer the question that has once been asked, whether Pope was a poet?[88] otherwise than by asking in return, if Pope be not a poet, where is poetry to be found? To circumscribe poetry by a definition will only show the narrowness of the definer, though a definition which shall exclude Pope will not easily be made. Let us look round upon the present time, and back upon the past; let us inquire to whom the voice of mankind has decreed the wreath of poetry; let their productions be examined and their claims stated, and the pretensions of Pope will be no more disputed. Had he given the world only his version the name of poet must have been allowed him; if the writer of the *Iliad* were to class his successors he would assign a very high place to his translator, without requiring any other evidence of genius.[89]

---

[87] *Dunciad*, III, 87–88.
[88] Warton's *Essay on Pope* concluded that "the *largest* portion" of Pope's works "is of the *didactic, moral,* and *satiric* kind; and consequently, not of the most *poetic* species of *poetry*."
[89] Johnson added a letter of Pope's and an essay he had published (1756) on Pope's epitaphs.

Thomas Gray

. . . Gray's poetry is now to be considered, and I hope not to be looked on as an enemy to his name if I confess that I contemplate it with less pleasure than his life.

His *Ode on Spring* has something poetical, both in the language and the thought; but the language is too luxuriant, and the thoughts have nothing new. There has of late arisen a practice of giving to adjectives, derived from substantives, the termination of participles, such as the *cultured* plain, the *daisied* bank; but I was sorry to see, in the lines of a scholar like Gray, "the *honied* Spring." The morality is natural, but too stale; the conclusion is pretty.

The poem *On the Cat* was doubtless by its author considered as a trifle, but it is not a happy trifle. In the first stanza "the azure flowers that blow,"[1] show how resolutely a rhyme is sometimes made when it cannot easily be found. Selima, the cat, is called a nymph, with some violence both to language and sense; but there is no good use made of it when it is done; for of the two lines,

> What female heart can gold despise?
> What cat's averse to fish?

the first relates merely to the nymph, and the second only to the cat. The sixth stanza contains a melancholy truth, that "a favourite has no friend," but the last ends in a pointed sentence of no relation to the purpose; if what glistered had been "gold," the cat would not have gone into the water; and, if she had, would not less have been drowned.[2]

The Prospect of Eton College suggests nothing to Gray

---

[1] *blow:* bloom.
[2] The poem ends with the maxim "Nor all that glisters, gold."

which every beholder does not equally think and feel. His supplication to father Thames, to tell him who drives the hoop or tosses the ball, is useless and puerile. Father Thames has no better means of knowing than himself. His epithet "buxom health" is not elegant; he seems not to understand the word. Gray thought his language more poetical as it was more remote from common use: finding in Dryden "honey redolent of Spring," an expression that reaches the utmost limits of our language, Gray drove it a little more beyond common apprehension, by making "gales" to be "redolent of joy and youth."

Of the *Ode on Adversity* the hint was at first taken from "O Diva, gratum quæ regis Antium" [O Goddess, who rulest over Pleasant Antium];[8] but Gray has excelled his original by the variety of his sentiments and by their moral application. Of this piece, at once poetical and rational, I will not by slight objections violate the dignity.

My process has now brought me to the "Wonderful Wonder of Wonders," the two Sister Odes;[4] by which, though either vulgar ignorance or common sense at first universally rejected them, many have been since persuaded to think themselves delighted. I am one of those that are willing to be pleased, and therefore would gladly find the meaning of the first stanza of *The Progress of Poetry*.

Gray seems in his rapture to confound the images of "spreading sound" and "running water." A "stream of music" may be allowed; but where does Music, however "smooth and strong," after having visited the "verdant vales," "roll down the steep amain," so as that "rocks and nodding groves rebellow to the roar"? If this be said of Music, it is nonsense; if it be said of Water, it is nothing to the purpose.

The second stanza, exhibiting Mars's car and Jove's eagle, is unworthy of further notice. Criticism disdains to chase a school-boy to his common-places.

To the third it may likewise be objected that it is drawn from Mythology, though such as may be more easily assimilated to real life. "Idalia's velvet-green" has something of cant. An epithet or metaphor drawn from Nature ennobles Art; an epithet or metaphor drawn from Art degrades Nature. Gray is too fond of words arbitrarily compounded. "Many-

---

[8] Horace, *Odes*, I.35.
[4] "The Progress of Poesy" and "The Bard."

twinkling" was formerly censured as not analogical; we may say *many-spotted*, but scarcely *many-spotting*. The stanza, however, has something pleasing.

Of the second ternary of stanzas the first endeavours to tell something, and would have told it had it not been crossed by Hyperion; the second describes well enough the universal prevalence of poetry, but I am afraid that the conclusion will not rise from the premises. The caverns of the North and the plains of Chile are not the residences of "Glory" and "generous Shame." But that Poetry and Virtue go always together is an opinion so pleasing that I can forgive him who resolves to think it true.

The third stanza sounds big with Delphi, and Aegean, and Ilissus, and Meander, and "hallowed fountain" and "solemn sound"; but in all Gray's odes there is a kind of cumbrous splendour which we wish away. His position is at last false: in the time of Dante and Petrarch, from whom he derives our first school of poetry, Italy was overrun by "tyrant power" and "coward vice"; nor was our state much better when we first borrowed the Italian arts.

Of the third ternary the first gives a mythological birth of Shakespeare. What is said of that mighty genius is true; but it is not said happily: the real effects of this poetical power are put out of sight by the pomp of machinery. Where truth is sufficient to fill the mind, fiction is worse than useless; the counterfeit debases the genuine.

His account of Milton's blindness, if we suppose it caused by study in the formation of his poem, a supposition surely allowable, is poetically true, and happily imagined. But the "car" of Dryden, with his "two coursers," has nothing in it peculiar; it is a car in which any other rider may be placed.

The Bard appears at the first view to be, as Algarotti and others have remarked, an imitation of the prophecy of Nereus.[5] Algarotti thinks it superior to its original, and, if preference depends only on the imagery and animation of the two poems, his judgement is right. There is in *The Bard* more force, more thought, and more variety. But to copy is less than to invent, and the copy has been unhappily produced at a wrong time. The fiction of Horace was to the Romans

[5] Horace (*Odes*, I.15) tells how Nereus, a sea-god, halted the ship in which Paris was abducting Helen to prophesy the defeat of Troy in the Trojan War.

credible; but its revival disgusts us with apparent and unconquerable falsehood. "Incredulus odi" [Not believing, I hate it].[6]

To select a singular event, and swell it to a giant's bulk by fabulous appendages of spectres and predictions, has little difficulty, for he that forsakes the probable may always find the marvellous. And it has little use: we are affected only as we believe; we are improved only as we find something to be imitated or declined. I do not see that *The Bard* promotes any truth, moral or political.

His stanzas are too long, especially his epodes; the ode is finished before the ear has learned its measures, and consequently before it can receive pleasure from their consonance and recurrence.

Of the first stanza the abrupt beginning has been celebrated, but technical beauties can give praise only to the inventor. It is in the power of any man to rush abruptly upon his subject, that has read the ballad of *Johnny Armstrong*,

Is there ever a man in all Scotland—

The initial resemblances, or alliterations, "ruin," "ruthless," "helm or hauberk," are below the grandeur of a poem that endeavours at sublimity.

In the second stanza the Bard is well described; but in the third we have the puerilities of obsolete mythology. When we are told that Cadwallo "hush'd the stormy main," and that Modred "made huge Plinlimmon bow his cloud-top'd head," attention recoils from the repetition of a tale that, even when it was first heard, was heard with scorn.[7]

The "weaving" of the "winding sheet" he borrowed, as he owns, from the northern Bards; but their texture, however, was very properly the work of female powers, as the act of spinning the thread of life in another mythology. Theft is always dangerous; Gray has made weavers of his slaughtered bards by a fiction outrageous and incongruous. They are then called upon to "Weave the warp, and weave the woof," perhaps with no great propriety; for it is by crossing the woof with the warp that men weave the web or piece; and the first

---

[6] Horace, *Art of Poetry*, line 188.
[7] Cadwallo and Modred were legendary Welsh bards; Plinlimmon, a mountain in Wales.

line was dearly bought by the admission of its wretched correspondent, "Give ample room and verge enough." He has, however, no other line as bad.

The third stanza of the second ternary is commended, I think, beyond its merit. The personification is indistinct. Thirst and Hunger are not alike, and their features, to make the imagery perfect, should have been discriminated. We are told, in the same stanza, how "towers" are "fed." But I will no longer look for particular faults; yet let it be observed that the ode might have been concluded with an action of better example: but suicide is always to be had without expense of thought.

These odes are marked by glittering accumulations of ungraceful ornaments: they strike, rather than please; the images are magnified by affectation; the language is laboured into harshness. The mind of the writer seems to work with unnatural violence. "Double, double, toil and trouble."[8] He has a kind of strutting dignity, and is tall by walking on tiptoe. His art and his struggle are too visible, and there is too little appearance of ease and nature.

To say that he has no beauties would be unjust: a man like him, of great learning and great industry, could not but produce something valuable. When he pleases least, it can only be said that a good design was ill directed.

His translations of Northern and Welsh poetry deserve praise: the imagery is preserved, perhaps often improved; but the language is unlike the language of other poets.

In the character of his *Elegy* I rejoice to concur with the common reader; for by the common sense of readers uncorrupted with literary prejudices, after all the refinements of subtilty and the dogmatism of learning, must be finally decided all claim to poetical honours. The *Church-yard* abounds with images which find a mirrour in every mind, and with sentiments to which every bosom returns an echo. The four stanzas beginning "Yet even these bones" are to me original: I have never seen the notions in any other place; yet he that reads them here persuades himself that he has always felt them. Had Gray written often thus it had been vain to blame, and useless to praise him.

[8] *Macbeth*, IV, i, 10.

Selected Bibliography

I. MAJOR WORKS BY JOHNSON

London: A Poem, 1738.
An Account of the Life of Mr. Richard Savage, 1744.
The Vanity of Human Wishes, 1749.
Irene, 1749.
The Rambler, 1750–52.
A Dictionary of the English Language, 1755.
The Idler, 1758–60.
The History of Rasselas, Prince of Abyssinia, 1759.
Edition of *The Plays of William Shakespeare*, 1765.
A Journey to the Western Islands of Scotland, 1775.
Taxation No Tyranny, 1775.
Prefaces, Biographical and Critical, to the Works of the English Poets (*Lives of the Poets*), 1779–81.

II. WORKS ABOUT JOHNSON

A. BIOGRAPHICAL

Boswell, James. *Life of Samuel Johnson, LL. D.* Ed. G. B. Hill, rev. L. F. Powell. Oxford: Clarendon, 1934–64. A good abridgment by Frank Brady is available in Signet Classics.

To supplement Boswell:

Bate, Walter Jackson. *Samuel Johnson.* New York: Harcourt, Brace, Jovanovich, 1975.

Clifford, James L. *Young Sam Johnson.* New York: McGraw-Hill, 1955.

B. CRITICAL

Bate, Walter Jackson. *The Achievement of Samuel Johnson.* New York: Oxford University Press, 1955.

Bronson, Bertrand H. *Johnson Agonistes and Other Essays.* Berkeley: University of California Press, 1965.

Hagstrum, Jean H. *Samuel Johnson's Literary Criticism.*
Minneapolis: University of Minnesota Press, 1952.

Krutch, Joseph Wood. *Samuel Johnson.* New York:
Henry Holt, 1944.

Lipking, Lawrence. *The Ordering of the Arts in
Eighteenth-Century England.* Princeton: Princeton
University Press, 1970.

Raleigh, Walter. *Six Essays on Johnson.* Oxford: Clarendon, 1910.

Wimsatt, W. K. *The Prose Style of Samuel Johnson.*
New Haven: Yale University Press, 1941.

The SIGNET CLASSIC Poetry Series

☐ **THE SELECTED POETRY OF BROWNING edited by George Ridenour.** Includes *Pauline*, selections from *The Ring and the Book*, *St. Martin's Summer*, *Fra Lippo Lippi*, *Childe Roland to the Dark Tower Came*, and longer works often omitted in standard anthologies. Introduction, Chronology, Bibliography. (#CE1391—$2.25)

☐ **THE SELECTED POETRY AND PROSE OF BYRON edited by W. H. Auden.** A comprehensive collection which includes *Beppo*, *Epistle to Augusta*, selections from *Don Juan*, *Childe Harold*, *English Bards* and *Scotch Reviewers*, and extracts from the journals and letters. Introduction, Chronology, Bibliography. (#CJ1151—$1.95)

☐ **THE SELECTED POETRY OF KEATS edited by Paul de Man.** The major long poems, all the "Odes," many sonnets, and several letters. Introduction, Chronology, Bibliography. (#CJ1326—$1.95)

☐ **THE CANTERBURY TALES, A Selection, by Geoffrey Chaucer.** Edited and with an Introduction by Donald R. Howard. A en route to the shrine of Thomas à Becket in Canterbury group of stories told by an oddly assorted band of pilgrims Cathedral. Includes a Glossary of basic Middle English words. (#CE1286—$2.50)

☐ **THE SELECTED POETRY OF WILLIAM BLAKE edited by David V. Erdman.** Included are the great lyrics, the longer political and religious poems, such famous works as *Songs of Innocence* and *Songs of Experience*, as well as the remarkable poetry gleaned from his Notebook and letters. (#CE1373—$2.95)

Recommended MENTOR and
SIGNET CLASSIC Reading

☐ **PARADISE LOST and Other Poems by John Milton.** The greatest epic poem of the English language, together with Milton's tragedy, *Samson Agonistes* and his elegy, *Lycidas*. Newly annotated and with a Biographical Introduction by Edward Le Comte. (#ME1881—$2.25)

☐ **THE INFERNO by Dante.** Translated by John Ciardi. Part I of *The Divine Comedy*, one of the world's great poetic masterpieces in a new verse translation by a celebrated contemporary poet. (#ME1957—$2.50)

☐ **THE PURGATORIO by Dante.** Translated by John Ciardi. Part II of Dante's classic *The Divine Comedy*, rendered in verse by the translator of the Mentor edition of *The Inferno*. (#MJ1793—$1.95)

☐ **THE PARADISO by Dante.** This long-awaited original verse translation by John Ciardi completes the most exciting modern translation of *The Divine Comedy*. With an Introduction by John Freccero. (#ME1893—$2.25)

☐ **LEAVES OF GRASS by Walt Whitman.** Introduction by Gay Wilson Allen, New York University. The text of this edition is that of the "Deathbed," or 9th edition, published in 1892. The content and grouping of the poems were authorized by the poet for the final and complete edition of his masterpiece. (#CJ1395—$1.95)

☐ **IDYLLS OF THE KING AND A SELECTION OF POEMS by Alfred Lord Tennyson.** Foreword by George Barker. The famous Arthurian romance and other poetry by the famous Victorian bard, including selections from *The Princess, In Memoriam A.H.H.,* and *Maud.* (#CJ1382—$1.95)

Buy them at your local

bookstore or use coupon

on next page for ordering.

MENTOR Anthologies of Special Interest